Praise for Kirsten Miller's Kiki Strike series

KiKi SⴂRiKⅇ: Inside the Shadow City

A Teenreads Best Book of the Year
A *Washington Post* Best Book of the Year
A *San Francisco Chronicle* Best Book of the Year
A YALSA Popular Paperback for Young Adults Pick
An Al Roker Book Club Pick

★ "A fascinating, convoluted mystery/adventure." —*Booklist*, starred review

"An absurdly satisfying romp." —*Kirkus Reviews*

"Miller pulls readers in immediately and takes them on a series of twists and turns, culminating in a thrilling climax." —*SLJ*

"Deliciously entertaining." —*Publishers Weekly*

KiKi SⴂRiKⅇ: The Empress's Tomb

A Book Sense Children's Pick
A New York Public Library Book for the Teen Age
An Al Roker Book Club Pick

"Kiki Strike is *GL*'s hero!" —*Girls' Life*

"These characters are sassy, spirited and smart." —*Kirkus Reviews*

"Just as thrilling and as much fun as the first." —*SLJ*

"This book is every bit as delightful as the first in the series. The characters are very colorful, and you feel as if they are your friends." —*VOYA*, teen reviewer

Inside the Shadow City

Kirsten Miller

BLOOMSBURY

NEW YORK   LONDON   NEW DELHI   SYDNEY

Text copyright © 2006 by Kirsten Miller
Frontispiece illustration copyright © 2006 by Eleanor Davis

First published in the United States of America in 2006
by Bloomsbury Children's Books
Paperback edition published in 2007; this edition published in January 2013
www.bloomsbury.com

The Library of Congress has cataloged the hardcover edition as follows:
Miller, Kirsten.
Kiki Strike : inside the shadow city / by Kirsten Miller.—1st U.S. ed.
p.   cm.
Summary: Life becomes more interesting for Ananka Fishbein when, at the age of twelve, she
discovers an underground room in the park across from her New York City apartment and meets a
mysterious girl called Kiki Strike who claims that she, too, wants to explore the subterranean world.
ISBN-13: 978-1-58234-960-2 • ISBN-10: 1-58234-960-6 (hardcover)
[1. Underground areas—Fiction. 2. Crime—Fiction. 3. Identity—Fiction.
4. New York (N.Y.) —Fiction.] I. Title.
PZ7.M6223Kik 2006   [Fic]—dc22   2005030945

ISBN 978-1-59990-920-2 (reissue)

Typeset by Westchester Book Composition
Printed in the U.S.A. by Thomson-Shore, Dexter, Michigan
2 4 6 8 10 9 7 5 3 1

The advice given in this book, including first aid information, is meant as a
literary device and an amusing sidebar. The author and publisher are not
responsible for any accidents or injuries that may occur by following it.
Refer instead to the American Red Cross.

Manufactured by Thomson-Shore, Dexter, MI (USA); RMA586LS789, December, 2012

For the wonderfully irregular Caroline McDonald,
who first discovered the secret of Kiki Strike
but didn't live to share it

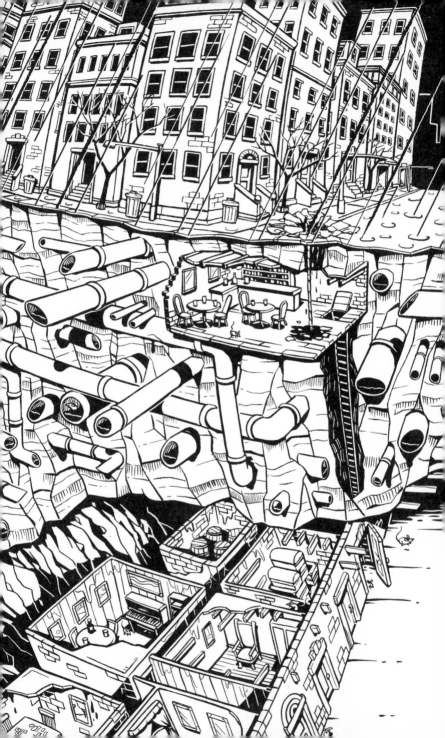

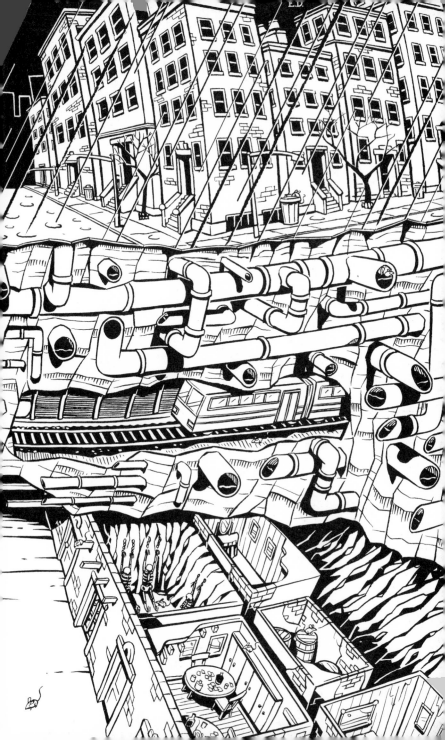

TO WHOM IT MAY CONCERN:

By taking the time to open this book, you've become a member of a very elite group: The Curious. I can't tell you how pleased I am that we've found each other. As you must have noticed, there aren't many of us around.

Contained on these pages is a true account of my first adventure with the legendary Kiki Strike. If you're looking for a thrilling story to keep you entertained on those rainy days when you have nothing better to do, it should serve that purpose quite nicely. But if you're interested in learning a few essential skills along the way, all the better. Of course, I'm not speaking of the kind of skills you're likely to learn in any classroom. Hopefully, I'll be able to provide you with an altogether more useful education.

Happy Reading,

Ananka Fishbein

Chapter 1

The Shadow City

Until the age of twelve, I led what most people would consider an unexceptional life. My activities on an average day could be boiled down to a flavorless mush: I went to school, I came home, I took a bath, and I went to bed. Though I'm certain I didn't realize it at the time, I must have been terribly bored.

Then, early one Saturday morning, I happened to glance out my bedroom window. Across the street from my apartment building, a little park had been sucked into an enormous hole. Roughly ten feet from side to side and seemingly bottomless, the crater had swallowed two Japanese pagoda trees, an old marble birdbath, and a statue of Washington Irving. The park bench where I had sat just the day before teetered on the muddy lip of the hole.

Holes of this sort are rare in New York City, where the earth is sealed beneath a layer of asphalt, and one can go for years without catching sight of actual dirt. Ordinarily, such a spectacle would have drawn a crowd.

But it was a dismal November day, and the streets were deserted. Black clouds hovered above the roofs, and a bone-chilling mist had licked every surface. In the buildings on the opposite side of the park, the windows formed a checkerboard of pulled blinds and drawn curtains. At street level, the hole was hidden from view by an ivy-covered fence that stubbornly circled what was left of the park. A delivery van with a cross-eyed dragon painted on its side sped past without even slowing, headed toward the narrow streets of Chinatown.

Leaning out my third-story window, I noticed a peculiar bulge on the section of fence nearest the hole. An orange rope had been tied to one of the pickets, and I followed its long end with my eyes, through a row of mangled juniper bushes and over the side of the hole. As I watched, the rope began to thrash violently, and then two tiny hands and a head smeared with filth appeared. The creature to which they belonged took little time to pull itself over the edge of the pit. From a distance, it didn't appear human. Its entire body was caked in muck, and its hair was plastered to the sides of its head. When it stood upright, I could see that it was extremely short, and with nothing to guide me but my imagination, I determined it might be a highly intelligent monkey or a troll of some sort.

For a moment, the thing peered back into the hole, apparently hesitant to leave. Then it looked up at me, as if it had known all along that I would be watching at the window. Even now, six years later, I can still see its eyes, which looked colorless and without expression—like those of a statue come to life. It all seemed quite sinister until the creature offered a little wave, its hand cupped

in the singular style of British royalty. It jumped back
into the hole, only to reemerge minutes later. Before it
scampered over the fence and disappeared into the mist,
I could have sworn that I saw it grin.

Looking back, it's hard to imagine what my life might
have become if I hadn't thrown an old coat over my
nightgown, shoved my bare feet into a pair of furry pink
snow boots, and run outside for a closer look. I've found
that such opportunities are few and far between. If you
miss them—or like most people simply fail to recognize
them—there's no guarantee that another chance will ever
come your way.

⚜   ⚜   ⚜

At the edge of the hole, I bent down on my hands
and knees and peered into the abyss. The mist had turned
to an icy rain that seeped into the lining of my boots
and trickled over my toes. Mud oozed between my fingers,
and in one of the hundreds of dark apartments that had
turned a blind eye to the scene below, a dog howled a muffled warning. The orange rope still dangled inside the hole,
its knotted end slowly sinking into the mud at the bottom.

The pit itself was far larger than I had imagined, and
there was little to see where the earth had given way. But
the hole had opened into an underground chamber that
extended off to one side, the ground above it still solidly
in place. In an oddly generous gesture, the creature had
left a flashlight behind. It stood upright on a table and
cast a column of light that illuminated a little room, half
of it destroyed by Washington Irving, the other half still
perfectly intact.

To those of you who are sticklers for safety and approach life with all the caution of amateur beekeepers, I can offer no excuse for what I did then. I'll admit that a more mature human being would never have let her curiosity take control.

Thankfully, I was twelve years old and fully prepared to meet the challenge at hand.

※ ※ ※

Unaccustomed to scaling ropes in nasty weather, I slipped and landed in a puddle next to Washington Irving, who lay facedown in the mud, pinned by a pagoda tree. Wincing with pain, I used his right ear to pull myself up, then turned to face the light.

The room was in many ways remarkably clean. A few passes with a broom, and it would have been ready to receive visitors. Only a couple of clumps of earth and a shrub or two lay scattered across the floor. Four shabby tables stood awkwardly in the center, shielded by mismatched chairs. Gilded mirrors, their paint shedding piles of chips, clung to the ragged brick walls. Across from them was a makeshift bar—no more than a wooden counter backed by three shelves lined with strange bottles. I felt certain that nothing in the room had ever seen the twenty-first century—or even the twentieth, for that matter. I knew I had entered an ancient world.

I picked up the flashlight and followed a trail of tiny muddy footprints behind the bar. On the highest shelf, a lone book stood propped against a bottle. I pulled myself onto the counter and performed an acrobatic stretch to reach it. But the moment my fingers brushed the book's spine, the flashlight slipped from my grasp, shattered a bottle of foul-smelling liquid, and crashed to the floor. I shoved the book into my pocket and jumped off the bar to retrieve the flashlight.

Where the flashlight had rolled to a stop, the room's floor appeared warped, and one of the wooden boards jutted up at its end. I bent down to take a look, and on closer inspection I saw that several of the floorboards were made from a different wood than their neighbors. Near the upturned board, which I now realized was an ingeniously disguised handle, was a message written in mud. "Open me," it demanded in a straightforward fashion, so I did. Grasping the edge of the board, I pulled with all the strength I could muster, and the warped floorboards reluctantly rose to reveal another hole.

Just wide enough to accommodate the girth of a big-bellied man, the second hole had a metal ladder attached to one side that creaked as I climbed down. I descended through fifty feet of tightly packed soil and rock before I reached a door that opened onto the side of a much larger tunnel—one that ran parallel to the city street far above. As I stepped through the doorway, a surge of electricity coursed through my body as if I had hopped on the third rail of a subway track. My spine tingled, my fingers trembled, my mouth dried up, and my hair stood on end. I found myself unsure whether to laugh with delight or break into tears.

What I saw, deep beneath the streets of New York, was the kind of structure—not unlike the Empire State Building, the Egyptian pyramids, or the Great Wall of China— that leaves people speechless, their mouths hanging open.

Roughly twelve feet from top to bottom, with brick walls and a ceiling of sturdy wooden beams, the tunnel stretched in two directions until both ends curved out of sight and disappeared into the darkness. I counted at least a dozen doors lining the walls, each door a different color and style.

Just as I reached for a crystal doorknob, I heard voices echoing in the room above and the thud of heavy work boots on the wooden floor. I suppose an ordinary response might have been to hide, but something told me that the trapdoor I had come through should never be discovered. I scrambled back up the ladder to the first room, closed the trapdoor behind me, and rubbed out the message written in mud.

Peeking over the edge of the bar, I saw two city workers in fluorescent orange safety vests standing awestruck in the center of the room.

"Ever seen anything like this before?" asked the larger of the two men.

"Nope," said the other after a long pause. "Not me, but back when I was a kid and my dad worked for the city, he told me a story I could never get out of my head. He said these guys were putting in pipes to one of the skyscrapers that went up near Chinatown about twenty years back. They were tunneling about fifty feet down when all of the sudden they broke into an open space. Can you believe it? An open space fifty feet underground?"

"Was it a subway tunnel?"

"Nah, they were deeper than the subway. There isn't supposed to be *anything* that far down around Chinatown."

"Well, what was it?"

"It was a room like this one—but bigger, a lot bigger. And it was done up like some kind of fancy Chinese bedroom, with straw mats on the floor and pillows all over the place. My dad said there were these weird silk screens with little dragons painted all over them."

"Was there somebody hiding down there?"

"No. That was the strange part. They could never find an entrance to the place."

"What do you mean they couldn't find an entrance?"

"I mean there was no door, no way for people to get inside. It was just a room, fifty feet underground, with no door."

"Uh," grunted the other, unimpressed. "So what happened to it?"

"Nothing. They had to take the pipes around it. My guess is it's still down there somewhere. When I was a kid, I tried to get my dad to let me dig for it."

"What do you think they're gonna do with this one?"

"Fill it in, I'd bet. It's too dangerous. Some dumb kid'd probably fall in and get himself killed."

"Well, if they're just gonna fill it in, I better take a souvenir," said the fat man.

The other man laughed. "What do you want, a chair?"

"No, I'd settle for one of those bottles," the large man announced, stomping over to the bar, the floorboards groaning beneath his weight.

I crouched in the corner of the bar, knowing I was destined for discovery. So as the fat man rounded the corner and reached for a blue bottle, I stood up and said hello. I don't think I realized just how filthy I was or how unusual my appearance had become, because the last thing I expected was to hear the man squeal like a wounded piglet. He dropped the bottle and ran across the room toward the opening of the hole. His partner stood back in shock as the fat man tried to pull his mammoth body up the rope.

"What do you think you're doing?" the partner asked as it became ridiculously clear that his friend would never make it to the safety of the street.

"I just saw the devil!" the fat man gasped.

"Have you gone nuts?" demanded the thinner man, now thoroughly annoyed.

"Go look if you don't believe me," the other insisted. Again I heard footsteps in my direction, and soon a flashlight was shining into my eyes. A look of terror mangled the thin man's face.

"Would you mind pointing that elsewhere?" I asked politely.

"George, get back here," called the man. "It's not the devil, you dolt. I think it's a girl." He bent down to study my face. "If you *are* a girl, I can tell you one thing for sure. You're in a whole lotta trouble."

Two burly, bad-tempered policemen pulled me out of the pit. Construction workers were already building a tall plywood fence around the park, shielding it from the eyes of the curious. On the surface, I was barraged with questions. Who was I? What did I think I was doing down there? Didn't I know I could have been seriously injured? What kind of girl *was* I? Did I know how mad my parents would be? What was their phone number?

Years of watching crime shows on television had taught me how to handle such situations, and I refused to give them any information. Instead, I played dumb, and eventually one of the policemen gave me a roll of paper towels and told me to clean myself off and wait in the back of his squad car. I was only making things worse for myself, he insisted, but I knew better than that.

I've always found that one of the biggest benefits of being a girl is that most people refuse to take you seriously. While boys must be constantly monitored and are always the first suspects when anything goes wrong, everyone expects girls to do what they're told. It may seem a little insulting at first, but low expectations can be a blessing in disguise. If you're smart, you can use people's foolishness to your own advantage. It's amazing what you can get away with when no one bothers watching.

As soon as I began scraping the mud from my arms and legs, I noticed the policemen's attention beginning to drift. A few minutes later, one walked to the edge of the hole to monitor the progress while the other directed a stream of traffic around a backhoe that was uprooting the park's little fence. When the backhoe pulled into the road, the poor fence gripped in its teeth like a limp and wounded snake, I was temporarily shielded from view. I simply sprinted across the street and up the stairs to my apartment.

★ ★ ★

Saturday mornings, my parents rarely woke before noon. Always an early riser, I would use those precious hours to devise my own entertainment. After a well-balanced breakfast of pudding or pie, I'd settle down to watch R-rated movies on a temperamental television set that had come into the world long before I had. Occasionally, just for laughs, I'd move the furniture and play a quick game of handball against the living room walls.

I had tested the limits and determined that nothing short of fireworks and a marching band would bring my parents shuffling out of their bedroom before midday. So as I opened the door to my apartment, a filthy fugitive from justice, I felt perfectly confident that I was in the clear. I stripped out of my muddy clothing at the door and tiptoed to the bathroom. There, I wrapped the clothes in a pillow-case, intending to take them to the basement laundry room as soon as I had showered. I dropped the bundle into the hamper, where it landed on the bottom with an unusually heavy thump. That's when I remembered the book.

As I thumbed through its pages, I could tell it was no ordinary book. Entitled *Glimpses of Gotham,* it appeared at first to be a guidebook to the city of New York in 1866. But instead of listing historic sites or four-star restaurants, it guided its readers through the "darker side" of the city. The author, a man by the name of Pearcy Leake III, had gone to great pains to visit every slum, saloon, and gambling parlor in lower Manhattan.

He described in thrilling detail huge "bear baiting" pits dug into the basements of waterfront saloons, in which bears and dogs would fight to the bloody end, cheered by scoundrels and outlaws of every conceivable type. He wrote about the opium dens in Chinatown, where men and women lounged for days on dirty mats, lost in their narcotic comas. He even told of an evening he had spent trapped in the second-floor gambling parlor of a run-down mansion after a herd of angry pigs had seized the ground floor of the building.

Sitting on my bathroom floor, I studied *Glimpses of Gotham* for hours. The book's previous owners must have been equally intrigued, for the margins were crammed with the markings of numerous pens and pencils. Even the illustrations—fanciful sketches of river pirates, dance halls, and roving bands of teenage delinquents— had not escaped comment.

But it wasn't until I came across a short passage with the heading "The Shadow City" that my heart began to beat wildly.

Police raids are common in the more colorful parts of town, and gentlemen explorers may be mistaken for common criminals. However, if in the midst of your adventures, you find yourself in a bit of a spot, do not despair. Simply ask the way to the Shadow City. Almost every palace of ill repute on the isle of Manhattan will have an entrance to the city, a network of tunnels that can serve as a handy escape route when things get hairy. And if you are not disturbed by the thought of the countless criminals who make it their home, the Shadow City also offers an excellent means of getting about when the weather aboveground is unpleasant.

Be forewarned. The tunnels of the Shadow City are uncharted territory, and anyone willing to give you directions is likely to lead you astray. Many have wandered for days without finding a suitable exit to the world above. Others have never escaped.

By the time I lifted my eyes from the page, I knew one thing for certain. I had discovered the Shadow City.

And if it were even half as vast as *Glimpses of Gotham* suggested, then I had seen only one small section of the tunnels that lay deep beneath New York. A hidden world of thieves, murderers, and pirates was about to be explored for the first time in a hundred years—not by scientists or engineers, but by *me*.

✦ ✦ ✦

When I woke the next morning, the hole had been filled in, and the little park looked as if it had been rearranged in the middle of the night by an insomniac housekeeper. Washington Irving greeted a different side of the street, new shrubs had been planted, and the pagoda trees were missing. But otherwise, there was little to suggest that the park had been consumed by a sinkhole a mere twenty-four hours earlier. My only entrance to the Shadow City was gone for good.

I purchased copies of every New York newspaper, expecting to find a story about the little room, and perhaps even a brief mention of the mysterious girl who had escaped from police custody.

Mixed in with dreary stock market reports and coverage of city council meetings, I found:

1. A fascinating account of a three-foot-tall monkey man with steel claws who was terrorizing India
2. A tenderhearted story about a Brooklyn family's tearful reunion with a kitten that had fallen down a sewer drain

3. An investigative journalist's report on secret shipments of grade "E" (for edible) horse meat that were routinely delivered to school cafeterias around Queens

But there was no mention of the hole that had swallowed an entire park. And although I was disappointed that I hadn't been immortalized in print, I knew that it meant that the Shadow City was safe. Only the little room had been exposed, and while it might long live in the lore of New York's construction workers, it wasn't enough to interest the *New York Times*. The creature and I were still the only two who knew that the tunnels existed.

I can imagine what you're thinking. What could a twelve-year-old girl do with such information? While I should warn you against underestimating the abilities of twelve-year-old girls, I'll admit that I can't say for sure what might have happened if I hadn't met the person the world would come to know as Kiki Strike.

HOW TO TAKE ADVANTAGE OF BEING A GIRL

In the six years since this story took place, I've had the good fortune to enjoy (and survive) countless adventures. Each time I acquired a new skill, I recorded step-by-step instructions in one of my secret diaries. Until now, those diaries have sat undisturbed on my bedroom shelves, cleverly disguised as Harlequin romances. But the day has finally come to open them up and share what I've learned with a few worthy students.

However, before I can teach you how to perform complex tasks, such as caring for a friend who's been attacked by wild animals, you should first learn to use the powers you already possess. These include:

The Element of Surprise

No one takes you seriously? Let people believe what they want to believe, and the element of surprise will always work in your favor. If they think you're weak, you can surprise them with strength, and if they assume you're stupid, you'll out-think them every time. Remember, low expectations can be a blessing in disguise.

Invisibility

I've always found it amusing that many people will say just about anything in front of a girl—as if she couldn't possibly understand. Before the age of fifteen, you will see things that no one else will see, and hear things that no one else will hear. Keep your ears open at all times, and use the information you gather to your advantage.

The Benefit of the Doubt

Most people are willing to give young girls the benefit of the doubt. Girls are too sweet and innocent, they think, to be up to no good. A clever story—generally one involving a search for a missing kitten—can get you out of trouble in nine out of ten situations. Remember, a tear or two will make any tale more believable.

The Art of Disguise

A girl's biggest advantage is her ability to change her appearance at will. If you're handy with a brush and have more than one change of clothing in your closet, you can easily assume the appearance of at least five different people. Eventually, the prudent use of hair color and makeup can make your disguise repertoire limitless.

Size

So what if you're not tall enough to see above a steering wheel? Being small in stature does come with its benefits. You can hide almost anywhere. Disappear into any crowd. Fit into spaces that no adult could cram herself into and go places adults could never go. Make use of your size before it's too late!

Chapter 2

The Devil in the Details

My first adventure with Kiki Strike is now part of her legend. In fact, you may already be familiar with the story. Over the past six years, I've heard it told time and time again—at parties, on airplanes, even once in the ladies' room at Bergdorf's. Whenever people shake their heads in disbelief and refuse to acknowledge a grain of truth, I have to laugh. Because I was *there*. And even though this particular story has been making the rounds for years, it's remained more fact than fiction. I'm just here to supply you with the details.

The story begins at the Atalanta School for Girls on the Upper East Side of Manhattan, not long after my discovery of the Shadow City. It was ten minutes to three. Ten minutes until winter break and two weeks of freedom. With so little time left on the clock, all hell was breaking loose. What had begun as a few cautious whispers between friends had turned into an ear-shattering free-for-all that was beginning to threaten the peace and quiet of the other classrooms on our hall.

Our teacher Ms. Jessel—who bore a striking resemblance to Snow White and possessed an unfortunate fashion sense to match—had made several attempts to restore order. However, it took the appearance of the principal, a rather stern, wizened old woman whose age we estimated at about 105, to shut our mouths and return us to our seats.

"Girls," said the principal with a disapproving glance at Ms. Jessel. "We haven't much time left. Why don't we try something a little more productive than screeching like a bunch of banshees? For the next ten minutes, I'd like to go around the room and have each of you tell me what you intend to be when you grow up."

If I remember correctly, most of our responses were either incredibly boring or completely ridiculous. Dylan Handworthy wanted to be a socialite. Rebecca Gruber, who had hair growing in unusual places, thought she'd like to be a bear trainer. I informed the class that I intended to be a marine biologist who studied giant squid, and received a nod of approval from the principal.

The last girl to answer sat at the back of the class, hidden behind Lizzie Fitzsimmons, who was well into a growth spurt that wouldn't end until she reached the eighth grade and a full six feet.

"You in the back," said the principal. "Don't think you can hide. Tell me. What would you like to be?"

"Dangerous," said the hidden girl, without a second's hesitation. Everyone in class spun around in their seats. There behind Lizzie was a tiny girl no one could recall having seen before. For a moment, I was certain I had misheard her.

"I'm sorry," said Ms. Jessel with a patronizing smile smeared across her face. "I'm not sure the principal and I understood you."

The girl held her ground. "When I grow up, I'd like to be dangerous."

The principal and Ms. Jessel exchanged a look. "What is your name, my dear?" asked the principal in a tone that indicated she'd be keeping a careful eye on her.

"Kiki Strike," the girl responded matter-of-factly, and as if on cue, the bell rang.

All it took was a single sentence, and Kiki Strike had me hooked. Who was she, I wanted to know, and where had she come from? Why did she want to be dangerous? And—most importantly—how had she managed to attend the Atalanta School without attracting anyone's attention?

The Atalanta School for Girls was the kind of private school where everyone knew everyone else. Not only that, they knew what your parents did for a living, how much money they made, what kind of house you lived in, and whether the shoes you wore were designer or knockoffs. As early as the first grade, each student was handed one of two labels: You were either a girl who had brains or a girl who had everything. The scholarship girls traveled to school on city buses that originated in parts of town you didn't walk through at night. They were silent, studious, and clearly out of their element. The rich girls, on the other hand, had French au pairs, famous last names, and chauffeured cars that waited for them on the corner.

Their tuition fees made it possible for the students on scholarship to receive a first-class education—a fact the rich girls were eager to point out whenever the opportunity arose.

Of all the girls at the Atalanta School, I was the only one who couldn't be labeled. My great-grandfather had invented control-top panty hose—a stroke of evil genius that could have kept my family fat and happy for generations. But having lived the life of the idle rich, he wanted something better for his only son. So he took his vast fortune and placed every cent into a trust fund that would provide each of his descendents with a top-notch education—and nothing else. Thanks to my great-grandfather, I could afford to attend the ritziest school in Manhattan, but I couldn't pay for a decent haircut.

That's because the old man had outsmarted himself. Neither his son nor my mother, his only grandchild, inherited his love of money. They made no attempts to scale corporate ladders. They didn't save their pennies and invest wisely. Instead, they simply took advantage of the trust fund and stayed in school their entire lives, accepting a few odd jobs here and there to cover the cost of food, clothing, and reading material. By the time I was twelve, my mother had three PhD's, and my father was working on his second. As far as I knew, neither of my parents was employed.

Given my unusual background, the other girls at the Atalanta School didn't know what to make of me. To the girls who had everything, I wasn't exactly a "bloodsucker" like the scholarship students, but with my cheap shoes and homemade hairstyle, I certainly wasn't one of *them*. The girls with brains, on the other hand, considered me a dunce. They weren't far off the mark. The fact is, unlike my parents, I thought school was an utter waste of time.

Long before I reached the seventh grade I knew I had better things to think about than grammar or long division. I had spent the first twelve years of my life in a large, dilapidated apartment near New York University, which my mother and father had filled with books on every imaginable subject. Stacks of books lined every room, some seeming to hold up the walls and others balanced so precariously that they threatened to topple and bury us all in an avalanche of accumulated wisdom. Every closet had been converted into a miniature library of sorts, each devoted to a particular topic. In the bathroom, there were books on the history of plumbing, Roman sewers, aquatic reptiles of North America, coprolites, and Freud. The kitchen cabinets stored scholarly tomes covering the use of poison throughout the ages and medical texts devoted to scurvy, gout, and flatulence.

The one subject missing from our library was children's literature. (Neither of my parents found children very interesting.) So instead of building a relationship with Dr. Seuss, I educated myself on subjects I had discovered on my own. At the age of twelve, I was still a little hazy on my multiplication tables, but I considered myself an expert on at least five subjects:

1. giant squid
2. human sacrifice among the Aztec and Maya

3.   carnivorous plants
4.   alien abduction
5.   Greek mythology

Since stumbling upon the Shadow City, I had been hard at work on a new subject, and my studies kept me occupied during the long, lonely winter break that followed Kiki Strike's first appearance.

For days, I pored through *Glimpses of Gotham* and ransacked my parents' library until the floor of my bedroom was covered with listing towers of books, and I was left with only a narrow passage from the door to the bed. Hours upon hours were spent curled up in a chair reading every history of New York I could find until my eyes grew so tired that the words melted into gibberish. Yet no matter how many books I skimmed or scoured, the Shadow City continued to elude me. I discovered hundreds of underground worlds—beneath Paris and Rome, even under tiny villages in Turkey. But historians and scientists alike appeared to agree that New York had always strived to rise high above the ground and had never stooped to tunnel beneath it.

OTHER UNDERGROUND WORLDS

The Catacombs of Paris
A city of the dead, the catacombs are an elaborate network of tunnels that stretch for hundreds of miles beneath the city of Paris and serve as a final resting place for millions of Parisians. Although stretches of the catacombs have been explored and mapped, no one knows their true extent. Over the years, dozens of foolhardy thrill-seekers have entered the tunnels, only to perish in the labyrinth, their bodies never recovered.

The Necropolis of Alexandria, Egypt
Another enormous city of the dead, the Necropolis was utterly forgotten for centuries. A tiny entrance was discovered by a seven-year-old boy who used the miles of tunnels as his personal playground before finally leading archaeologists to the Necropolis in 1998.

The Ancient City of Rome
Modern Rome is built atop the ruins of its ancient predecessor. Often unbeknownst to those who live there, the cellars of many of the city's oldest buildings open directly into the temples, palaces, and streets of the ancient city. During WWII, some Italian Jews were able to evade the Nazis for months or years by hiding in the forgotten city.

Derinkuyu, Turkey
Beneath the small town of Derinkuyu lies the largest of at least 150 underground cities in the Anatolian region of Turkey. For over a millennium, tens of thousands of people spent their lives in this dark subterranean world complete with everything from wineries to stables. The true scale of Derinkuyu is still unknown. Tunnels leading to new rooms and linking Derinkuyu to other underground cities are frequently unearthed. Since Derinkuyu was first discovered in 1963, at least eight stories have been uncovered, and some experts estimate that there may be as many as twenty-seven.

Pendleton, Oregon
During the nineteenth century, thousands of Chinese men came to the U.S. to build the transcontinental railroads. Sadly, when the work was complete, they found themselves unwanted in most towns. Undaunted, they chose to build their own cities—underneath existing towns. Several of these cities, such as the one beneath Pendleton, Oregon, have been discovered. However, there may be other underground Chinese cities across the U.S. that have yet to be found.

Finally, in desperate need of a little fresh air, I left my books behind and set out on foot in search of the Shadow City. At first, I planned to leave my own neighborhood, imagining there would be nothing along the familiar streets that could have escaped my notice. But the moment I stepped through the door of my apartment building, I began to see a different city.

Every block I passed held a clue to New York in the days when the Shadow City flourished. Watching other people on the streets as they went about their business, chattering into their cell phones or hurrying to return unappreciated Christmas gifts, I realized that I could see things they couldn't. High above my head were faded advertisements for defunct carriage companies and snake oil treatments, their paint still faintly legible on the sides of old buildings. A rusted hitching post that hadn't seen a horse in a hundred years solemnly stood guard in front of a small brick house. Even the cobblestones that peeked through the asphalt were evidence of a world that was now invisible to all but a chosen few.

As a young child, I had always felt a bit cheated that I hadn't been born with a superhuman power, such as the ability to stop time or control the weather. I would even have settled for something as simple as ESP. But as I walked through the streets of New York that day, it began to dawn on me that I had finally discovered my special gift. Somehow, in return for my days of reading, I had acquired the ability to see things that no longer existed. By merely squinting my eyes, I could envision the city the way it had appeared 150 years before I was born.

What I saw was a dark and dangerous place that looked nothing like the New York that I knew. There were no skyscrapers or streetlights, just rows upon rows of tiny brick buildings, all sinking into the thick black mud that smothered and splattered the city. Monstrous pigs trotted alongside horse-drawn carriages, stopping here and there to root through the mountains of garbage that lined the streets. Rats and half-fed urchins lurked in every shadow, waiting for a chance to pounce. I could see the filth, hear the calls of the street vendors, and practically smell the outhouses. But to my great disappointment, the one thing that always remained hidden from view was the Shadow City.

For an entire week, I did little more than wander the streets, taking note of everything I had overlooked for twelve years. I peered into windows, climbed fences, and filled three spiral notebooks with observations and sketches. Had I been anything other than an innocent-looking girl, my activities would have certainly attracted suspicion, but few people seemed to notice me at all. Their eyes skipped over me as if I were no more dangerous than a fire hydrant or a garbage can.

One evening, on my way home from a full day of investigations, I passed a lonely store on Second Avenue. The sky was swollen with snow, and the wind raced through the streets, lifting piles of dead leaves and spinning them into frenzied tornadoes. The lights in the store flickered momentarily, just long enough to catch my eye and direct it to a weathered display in the shop's front window, where several old maps rested upon a thick carpet of dust.

Two of the maps were familiar. I had come across copies of them in my parents' library. One, nearly six feet in length, showed the island of Manhattan as it had appeared 200 years earlier, when cattle still grazed on the land where the Empire State Building would one day stand, and an open sewer flowed along what is now Canal Street. The second map featured a tiny sketch of the old Dutch streets that snaked across the southernmost tip of the island, twisting and turning with little rhyme or reason. A third map lay closest to the window but was so blackened with grime that it was impossible to identify. Driven by curiosity, I stepped into the store, hoping to see the map up close.

A child-sized woman sat on a stool behind the shop's counter, her legs crossed daintily, though they dangled two feet above the floor. Her hair, which was the color and texture of an enormous dust bunny, was pushed from her face by a pair of large glasses that sat perched atop her head. When I asked to see the map in the window, she smiled and hopped off her stool. She didn't ask *which* map I wanted to see, nor did she question why a girl of my age should be trusted with what was certainly a rare and expensive item.

I stood dumbfounded by my good luck, watching the top half of the woman's body disappear as she reached into the display to retrieve the map. When she emerged, she primly held the plastic to her lips and blew a cloud of dust toward the window before handing the map to me.

I had never seen anything like it before. Rather than a map of Manhattan, it was the blueprint for what looked to be three rows of little rooms, each row connected by a long hallway.

"Do you know what that is?" asked the woman

in a thick Russian accent. Her dark eyes twinkled mischievously.

"No," I admitted.

"It is the Marble Cemetery."

"Really?" I asked, pretending to be interested. In general, I find graveyards as fascinating as the next person, but I had more pressing matters to consider.

"You have seen it?" she asked. I shook my head, and the woman sighed. "I am not surprised. Most people do not even know it is there. You would like to take a look?"

"I should really get home," I said as politely as possible. My feet ached from walking the city all day, and I was pretty sure that the woman was insane.

"But it will only take a minute," she pleaded. "It is very close by."

"Okay," I mumbled, zipping up my coat and heading for the door.

"Oh no," the woman giggled girlishly. "There is no need to go outside. You will come with me to the storeroom. It is the very best place to see the cemetery."

Most of the time I feel no need to obey adults whose sanity I question. But I was convinced that the tiny woman was peculiar but harmless, so I followed her up a rickety spiral staircase.

The room above the shop was crammed to the ceiling with books and bore a remarkable resemblance to my parents' bedroom. The woman, who had introduced herself as Verushka on our way up the stairs, led me to a window set in the back of the building.

"There it is," she said, pointing out the window. "The Marble Cemetery."

I pushed a box of moldy French dictionaries out of my path and stood in front of the window. Below us lay an empty plot of land the size of a football field. It was carved out of the center of the block and surrounded by a high wall that kept the buildings around it from intruding. I had walked down Second Avenue thousands of times and never suspected that anything quite so remarkable might lie behind its storefronts and apartment buildings.

"Where are the graves?" I asked, searching for tombstones.

"They are underground, of course." Verushka laughed. "The square blocks of marble you see in the grass? These are the entrances to the vaults. There are dozens of tombs beneath the ground. It is a village of the dead."

"How can I get down there?" I asked, thrilled to find a way beneath the streets.

"You cannot. Only the families of the dead are allowed inside the Marble Cemetery—and no one has been buried here for many years. But you can step onto the fire escape if you would like a better look."

I opened the storeroom window and was struck by a blast of icy wind. The fire escape was swinging from side to side. I glanced back at Verushka, who shook her head in disappointment.

"You cannot catch fish if you are afraid of the water," she chided me.

I hit my head on the windowsill as I crawled onto the fire escape, and it took a few moments for the dizziness to pass. Once I could focus on the graveyard below, I found it hard to imagine that so impressive a space could remain hidden in the middle of Manhattan. The grass was a surreal shade of green one sees alongside Scottish castles, the color made more vivid by the dreariness of the surroundings.

As I gaped in amazement, the unmistakable sound of a key scraping against a lock echoed through the cemetery. From the fire escape, I could see everything but the small section that lay beneath my feet. Dropping to my knees, I peered through the iron bars and caught sight of someone opening the gate that hid the graveyard from the bustle of Second Avenue. A relative of the dead, I assumed at first, but there was something about the person's size and the unusual color of her hair that almost knocked me off balance and over the side of the fire escape. The gate swung shut and the person disappeared from view. Though I hadn't seen her face, by the time I crawled back inside the storeroom, I was convinced that the person in question was none other than Kiki Strike.

"There was a girl in the cemetery," I whispered to Verushka.

"How odd," she remarked, showing no sign of surprise.

HOW TO CATCH A LIE

One of the most important skills you can learn is how to recognize a lie when you hear one. Over the years, I've encountered enemies who tried to lead me astray and imposters who wanted to swindle me. In each case, I've been able to see through their deceptions, and I can assure you that the truth did not set them free.

Identifying a lie is not always easy. As you may have noticed, people who make a habit of lying are often quite good at it. But if you suspect you're being hoodwinked, don't say a word. Just pay attention. The following clues should tell you if someone's trying to pull the wool over your eyes.

Listen to Her Voice

A liar is a person with something to hide. And no matter what that something may be, it's probably weighing heavily on her mind. As a result, a liar must make an effort to avoid giving too much away. She'll speak more slowly and pause before answering questions. As she grows more anxious, her voice may start to sound higher. When she does respond, she'll be careful not to offer specific information and may say something vague like, "I couldn't have murdered Hank. I was busy that day."

Study Her Face

Most people are terrible actors. A liar may have her story straight, but if she can't control her face, she'll be as easy to spot as a soap opera star in a Shakespeare play. A person who's telling the truth will laugh, grimace, or cry when appropriate, but a liar may have to think about it first. She may even be concentrating so hard on what to do that she'll blink less and hold her head unnaturally still.

See if She Squirms

When it comes to body language, there are two types of liars—the fidgeters and the control freaks. The fidgeters can't sit still. They shift around in their seats, tap their feet, or play with their jewelry. They also touch their faces more often—rubbing their noses, running their fingers through their hair, or brushing their hands against their mouths. The control freaks, on the other hand, go out of their way to avoid looking nervous. They may move very little and avoid gesturing altogether. Some will even go so far as to cross their arms or sit on their hands.

Hide-and-Go-Seek

it had been more than a week since I had last thought of Kiki Strike, but the instant I saw her at the Marble Cemetery, I was spellbound once more. I suppose some people might have mistaken the encounter for coincidence. But I had long suspected that there are few true coincidences in this world. Something—or someone—was bringing the two of us together.

For the first time in my life, I grew impatient for winter break to end. Hoping one of my classmates could give me the lowdown on the mysterious Kiki Strike, I even arrived early the first day back, only to find that two weeks of presents and parties had erased her from everyone's memories. I was left with no other option but to wait for class to begin, keeping my eye trained on Kiki's desk at the back of the room.

Seconds before the bell rang, I saw her. She was even smaller than I remembered—more like a mythical creature than a human being. She was dressed entirely in black, and though I've heard her hair described as blond, the truth was that it lacked any color at all. Instead it was a shocking, almost translucent white, and her skin was a bloodless hue common to corpses and cave-dwelling creatures. In fact, the only color about her person was in the form of two little rubies—one in either ear. Though my description may sound ghoulish, I assure you that the total package was surprisingly attractive.

I watched, thinking myself unnoticed, as she removed a notebook (black) and a pen (black) from a leather satchel (also black). She spent a moment arranging these tools on her desk, and just as she finished, her eyes snapped up and caught mine. I could feel my face flushing a deep red, for she seemed to be examining every last detail of my appearance. Her pale blue eyes—so light, they were milky—gave nothing away. Her mouth neither smiled nor twitched nor grimaced nor frowned. Finally, she raised one eyebrow, and held it arched high for a moment before she allowed it to fall. I spun around to face the front of the class, my cheeks burning with humiliation. I swore to myself that I would not be caught again.

★ ★ ★

For two months, I did my best to stay out of sight as I stalked Kiki Strike among the library stacks and shadowed her through the forest of gym lockers in the school's basement. But though I tried to be discreet, surveillance was a craft that didn't come naturally to me. I almost blew my cover one afternoon in the library when I tripped over a kindergartner who was cramming a peanut butter sandwich between two copies of *Oliver Twist*. And I was certain I'd heard someone laugh the day I was mysteriously drenched while hiding in a shower stall in the gym's locker room.

Neglecting my homework, I spent my evenings inventing more foolproof methods of spying on Kiki Strike. I even glued a mirror inside one of my textbooks so I could watch her at the back of the classroom. But everything I saw just made her seem stranger. Kiki said nothing during class, and our teachers never called on her. In fact, she was so successful at blending in that everyone seemed to look right through her.

After several weeks of watching her, I began to wonder if Kiki might be watching someone else. She showed no interest in making friends, but on several occasions, I saw her studying a group of ninth graders like a scientist keeping track of a pack of gorillas. Following her lead, I made my own list of observations.

1. Kiki Strike always wore black.
2. She carried her black notebook everywhere, but never took notes during class.
3. She was nowhere to be found during lunch.
4. No one else seemed to know she existed.
5. She possessed a remarkable ability to disappear at will.

This last observation—or lack thereof—was the main reason my list stopped short. Countless times on countless days, I would follow Kiki down one of the corridors only to turn a corner and find myself pursuing the wrong girl.

By March, I grew frustrated. I made up my mind to follow Kiki Strike home, hoping to uncover her secrets once and for all. Were there flowery curtains on her bedroom windows? Did her mother meet her at the door with a big hug? Were there other little Strikes running about? I hoped not. The chance that Kiki might be an ordinary girl filled me with dread.

I wouldn't have admitted it, but Kiki had given me a glimmer of hope. Until she had arrived at the Atalanta School, I had resigned myself to a lonely existence. No one ever passed me notes or invited me to parties. As far as my schoolmates were concerned, I wasn't even there. Kiki was invisible, too, but she appeared to like it that way. She wasn't interested in being popular. For some reason I had yet to discover, she had chosen to be dangerous instead. More than anything, I wanted to learn her secret. And if Kiki Strike turned out to be just another social misfit, I would be crushed. But that was a risk I was willing to take.

I suppose you're thinking that I could have asked her, but if so, you're missing the point. A girl who's announced that she'd like to be dangerous is hardly a reliable source of information. I wasn't interested in what Kiki wanted me to know or was willing to tell me. I wanted the truth, and I needed a way to see it for myself.

☆   ☆   ☆

The day I decided to follow Kiki Strike home, I skipped my last class and prepared to hide outside the school and wait for her to appear. It wasn't until I opened the front door that I realized I had failed to check the weather report. The steps of the school were covered with snow, and I worried that my tracks might give me away. But I was too curious to postpone my plan. I wrapped a beige scarf about my head for camouflage and searched for a hiding place.

I didn't have to look for long. The exterior of the Atalanta School was riddled with countless nooks and crannies just large enough to conceal a girl—though few girls chose to use them. We had all heard the story of the boy who had hidden in one of the crevices back in the days when the looming Gothic structure had been a home for wayward children. Before the boy could make his escape, a daggerlike icicle fell from a window ledge and speared him through the chest. Every winter, at least one hysterical girl would claim to have seen his ghost staggering through the halls, the melting ice leaving a watery trail.

I had always believed the story was nonsense, but when I looked up at the building that afternoon, I could see crops of icicles growing under every window. I kept a safe distance and crouched in the shadow of a boxwood bush near the school's only exit—an iron gate that opened onto the sidewalk.

Shortly after the three o'clock bell, Kiki Strike emerged from the building and walked briskly down the path that led to the gate. Wearing a military-style coat that reached down to her ankles and a Cossack hat of the blackest fur, she looked as dangerous as anyone under five feet could. More importantly, because she was dressed entirely in black, she stood out against the snow. For once, I thought, she had nowhere to hide.

Thanks to the weather, the streets were empty, and for the first few blocks, I was able to follow Kiki at a safe distance. From the school, she walked west on Sixty-eighth Street. There was no car waiting for her on the corner of Lexington Avenue, and she passed both the subway station and the bus stop without even a glance. Just past Madison Avenue, I saw the trees of Central Park stretching above the mansions that lined either side of the block. As we drew closer to the park, the city appeared to come to an end. Two or three cars inched along Fifth Avenue, their wheels leaving icy tracks that disappeared in moments as the snow reclaimed the street. Murky, yellow pools of light lapped at the poles of two streetlamps, and the eyes of a statue peeked out from beneath a thick white blanket.

Kiki stood at the edge of the park, her gloved hand resting on a stone wall. Against the wild white backdrop of the park, she appeared even smaller, and the rocks and trees held back by the wall threatened to swallow her alive. I watched from the other side of the avenue and hoped she didn't plan to make her way through the park. The afternoon light had already begun to dim. By four o'clock, it would be dark, and Central Park is not a place you want to find yourself at night. Even during the day, it can be difficult to navigate. Its wooded paths twist, turn, and circle back on themselves. The park is nothing less than a giant labyrinth—a maze constructed to fool city dwellers into believing they've left civilization behind, when in reality, they're never more than a few hundred yards from a Starbucks.

When the sun is shining and the park is peaceful, getting lost can be enjoyable. At night, however, the maze holds more than its share of monsters. In the weeks before I found myself following Kiki Strike, the local news had been filled with stories of roving bands of teenage boys who began gathering in the park as soon as the sun set. Dressed in dark colors, their identities concealed beneath layers of war paint, they delighted in ambushing people who were foolish enough to wander into their domain. A businessman, cutting through the park on his way home one night, was forced to swim a half dozen laps in the freezing, polluted waters of Central Park Lake. Not long afterward, a woman and her daughter were discovered one morning, marooned in the snow monkey habitat in the park zoo. Given the frigid New York weather, they might have met a less amusing fate if the monkeys hadn't taken pity and huddled with them for warmth during the night.

As you might imagine, I wasn't thrilled by the prospect of coming face-to-face with the resident thugs of Central Park. Yet when Kiki Strike climbed on top of the wall and leaped into the wilderness, I followed without hesitation.

Kiki maneuvered her way through the frozen park like a seasoned Sherpa. I tried to keep out of sight as she wound around bushes, lakes, and rocks, but the snow had slowly begun to collect on her coat, and it no longer stood out as clearly as it once had. I was forced to move closer and closer in order to see her against the trees. When we reached the Great Lawn—a vast stretch of meadow in the middle of the park—my eyes strained to see through the blizzard. With each step, Kiki Strike, now covered head to toe in snow, started to vanish.

Desperate not to lose sight of her, I began to run,

aware that I could face discovery at any moment. My feet, frozen by the snow that had collected in my inappropriate footwear, refused to cooperate. I slipped and fell to my hands and knees, and as I struggled to pull myself upright, I saw a blurry figure slip into the woods. I found myself standing alone in the middle of an empty meadow, shin-deep in snow and wondering if I had been undone by the weather or outwitted by Kiki Strike.

I made a few wrong turns on my way out of the park, and the sun disappeared before I reached the safety of Fifth Avenue. In preparation for my long journey home, I leaned against a tree to catch my breath and shake the snow out of my shoes. Three young men dressed in camouflage emerged from a mansion just east of the avenue. Big, well-fed types with expensive boots and carefully unkempt hair, they shuffled across the street, heading toward the park. Figuring they were up to no good, I pressed myself up against the tree, and prayed I would go unnoticed.

"It's not going to get away tonight," I overheard one boy say. "They've put a bounty on its head."

"Do you really think it'll come back?" asked another nervously.

"I'd bet my life on it."

"You might have to, considering what it did to Julian. Did you see his face? It broke his nose," snickered one of the boys.

"Look, Julian was just caught off guard. It's not going to happen again. You got your phones?"

"Yeah."

"If any of us see it, we're going to call the others.

We're not taking any chances, right? Whatever it is, it's supposed to be pretty small. If we're all together, we should be able to catch it before it hurts anyone else."

Peering cautiously around the tree, I saw the trio stop by the park's stone wall and furtively check the street in either direction. Once a southbound taxi disappeared from sight, they vaulted the wall and vanished between the trees. Had I been less worried about losing my toes to frostbite, I might have followed them. Their conversation had captured my interest. Fear of the mysterious "IT" had made their voices quiver unnaturally, and I wondered what could have inspired such agitation in three full-grown hoodlums.

By the time I reached the lobby of my apartment building, my body was numb, and the humid heat of the stairwell made my skin prickle with pain. Amazingly, I survived with all of my fingers and toes intact, although both of my feet took hours to thaw. Later that night, as I was getting ready for bed, a snippet from the evening news caught my attention.

Two teenage boys from wealthy Manhattan families were released this evening from Beth Israel Hospital and immediately placed under arrest on charges of assault and criminal mischief stemming from a bizarre incident in Central Park. Thomas Vandervoort and Jacob Harcott stand accused of attacking a jogger near the Literary Walk. According to authorities, they viciously beat the man, a retired advertising executive, and then forced him to don a pink tutu. The boys, members of a gang that's been

terrorizing Central Park for months, were preparing
to tie the jogger to a statue of Shakespeare when they
were set upon by what has been described as a large
elf or albino leprechaun.

Neither Vandervoort nor Harcott has offered his
version of events, but the jogger, who admits to feel-
ing quite woozy at the time, insists that his savior
was no more than four feet tall and wearing a
Russian-style fur hat.

By morning, the newspapers were having great sport
with the jogger, who had offered a ten-thousand-dollar
reward for any information regarding the albino elf that
had saved his life. A story in the *New York Post* featured a
blurry mug shot of the Lucky Charms leprechaun along
with a caption that read:

Wanted: The Central Park Vigilante
Reward: A Pot of Gold

The thought of collecting the reward crossed my mind
once or twice. In fact, nothing would have pleased me
more than to tell the world that the mysterious crime-
fighting leprechaun was just a twelve-year-old girl. But
Kiki Strike's secrets were worth far more to me than a pot
of gold. And I wasn't going to give up until I had them all.

☆   ☆   ☆

The next day, I dropped by Verushka's bookstore on Second Avenue, hoping that the Marble Cemetery might

offer a clue to Kiki Strike's identity. When I arrived, I found the store dark and deserted. The window display had been altered to showcase a collection of Grimm's fairy tales. Where the map of the Marble Cemetery had once lain was a thick book with an image of Briar Rose on its cover, her dainty finger poised above a spindle. A faded sign pinned to the door of the shop read: "Closed until further notice." I was about to leave, when I spotted a red envelope tucked in the side of the door. My name was written on the front.

I tore open the envelope and fished out the note inside.

You're not very good at following people, it read in a tight, controlled hand. *If you want to know something, perhaps you should ask.* It was signed Kiki Strike.

HOW TO FOLLOW SOMEONE . . . WITHOUT GETTING CAUGHT

One of the many tricks I've learned from the remarkable Kiki Strike is the fine art of "tailing." You may be tempted to think that following someone is a simple skill to master. Don't fool yourself! Tailing demands patience, concentration, ingenuity, and most of all, preparation. Before you attempt the real thing, try following a teacher, a brother, or parent just for fun. (Who knows what you might find out!) Once you feel like you're starting to get the hang of it, you can rely on these helpful pointers . . .

1. When following someone, never get too close. Stay at a distance or walk on the opposite side of the street. Try to avoid looking directly at the person. Whenever possible, watch her out of the corner of your eye.
2. Everyone has a unique way of walking. Does the person you're following have a limp? Does she swing her behind

from side to side? If you can memorize her walk, you'll be able to keep an eye on her from a distance.

3. If you think the person you're following has spotted you, turn and have a nice chat with a stranger on the street. The stranger may think you're a lunatic, but the person you're tailing will think you're harmless.

4. By walking ahead of your target, you can erase any suspicions she might have. Just take a small mirror from a compact, cup it in the palm of your hand, and use it to keep track of the person behind you. If you don't have a mirror handy, you can use other reflective surfaces, such as store windows.

5. Don't call any attention to yourself. Never wear loud colors or shirts with slogans or logos. In general, try not to look too fabulous.

6. Change your appearance by pulling your hair into a ponytail or trading your glasses for sunglasses.

7. Wear comfortable clothing. Never try to break in a new pair of shoes while following someone. And try to be dressed for the weather.

8. Always carry a few extra dollars. You may have to jump on a bus or catch a cab on a moment's notice.

Chapter 4

School for Scandal

When I first read Kiki Strike's note, I felt like a Peeping Tom who'd been caught peering through her neighbors' windows or rifling through their garbage. Fortunately, it didn't take long to swallow my shame and decide that I might as well take Kiki up on her offer. Our endless game of hide-and-seek had grown tiresome, and I was ready to get some answers the old-fashioned way.

The following Monday, I watched through a window overlooking the school's entrance until I saw Kiki make her way into the building. The second I spotted her black fur hat, my brain began tingling with anticipation. But when the first bell rang, Kiki's desk was still empty and a pop quiz on the many wives of King Henry VIII had been slapped down in front of me.

As I struggled to remember which of Henry's wives had kept their heads, a crime was being committed. By the time I turned in a half-answered test, the hallways were buzzing. I stepped out of my classroom and squeezed past a group of ninth graders who were clustered near the bathroom

"I heard they broke in while she was in swimming class," I heard one girl say.

"Who leaves something like that in her gym locker?" another asked.

"It wasn't just sitting there waiting for somebody to take it, you imbecile," a third girl huffed. "It was inside a locked jewelry box. She had the key around her neck."

"Somebody took Erica Whittaker's tennis bracelet last week," announced another. "They opened her locker like a pro. It's got to be one of the scholarship girls."

"Oh my God!" yelped a girl who was frantically tugging at her earlobes. "My emerald earrings are still in my locker!"

"Nobody's going to steal your crappy jewelry, Courtney," snickered the first girl. "Everyone knows it's all fake."

"I hope they never find it," I heard a nearby scholarship girl whisper to a friend. They shared a smile that froze in panic when they saw I'd overheard them.

"What's going on?" I asked a girl from my algebra class. Under ordinary circumstances, she would have ignored me, but this time the gossip was too good not to share.

"Someone stole Sidonia's ring." She pointed in the direction of a haughty ninth grader with jet-black hair and yellow eyes who was exiting the principal's office at the end of the hall.

"This morning?" I asked, suddenly feeling a bit queasy.

"Yeah," said my classmate with a nasty grin. "There's a dead girl walking the halls today."

As anyone at the Atalanta School could have told you, Sidonia Galatzina wasn't your average crime victim. She was the last princess in the exiled royal family of the former kingdom of Pokrovia, and the ring she had so carefully concealed was no ordinary piece of jewelry. Featuring an enormous diamond in the palest shade of pink, it had graced the fingers of countless queens and was rumored to have been on Sidonia's aunt's right hand when she was murdered the night before her coronation.

It wasn't the theft itself that had the whole school talking. Everyone wanted to know who had dared to mess with Sidonia, the tyrant of the Atalanta School for Girls. Aside from being thoroughly evil, Sidonia—or the Princess, as everyone called her—was beautiful, rich, and unusually charming. Most adults found her entrancing, with her dimpled cheeks, European accent, and impeccable grooming. One heartwarming smile or girlish giggle, and they fell under her spell. Few could see that Sidonia had been born with a heart filled with venom and a natural ability for wreaking mayhem. By my count, she was personally responsible for a dozen nervous breakdowns and at least one case of hives. School legend had it that she had forced five scholarship girls to transfer to other schools in her kindergarten year alone.

The Princess traveled with a pack of four girls who mimicked her in every way. If she arrived at school in a miniature mink coat, the others would appear the next day in identical furs, looking like a ferocious band of well-groomed squirrels. If Sidonia adopted a new hairstyle, they all scrambled to their hairdressers no matter how unflattering the results. But however ridiculous they may have appeared, the Princess's friends were best avoided. Like the other girls who lacked protective layers of designer clothing, I stayed out of their way. For the most part The Five, as they called themselves, left me alone. There was usually far easier prey to be had. They ate a scholarship girl for lunch every day.

I wouldn't have given the Princess's ring much thought had the theft not reeked of Kiki Strike. Only a girl who was new to the school could have made such an idiotic mistake, and Kiki had been cutting class at the time of the crime. I was disturbed to discover her criminal tendencies, but I was curious to see how she had done it. Getting past two locks demanded skills most seventh graders didn't possess. So when the classroom doors closed for second period, I slipped downstairs to the pool's locker room and examined the front of the Princess's locker. I found no evidence of tampering, and the combination lock looked as sturdy as any other.

"Forget something?" snarled a voice behind me. I felt the contents of my stomach begin to bubble as I turned to see one of The Five, a ninth grader named Naomi Throgmorton. Naomi had the honor of being the Princess's very best friend—not to mention her favorite victim. Though she was said to be the prettiest of The Five, Naomi was also the poorest, and the Princess treated her like something she'd found floating in a public toilet.

Thanks to Naomi, watching The Five arrive at school each morning had become something of an Atalanta spectator sport. Nothing could send the Princess into a tantrum like seeing her best friend show up in a particularly flattering outfit. Sidonia would even send Naomi home to change whenever she thought she was in danger of being outshone. A day or two of mean jokes always followed, just in case Naomi hadn't learned her lesson. On those days, it wasn't unusual to come across Naomi sobbing in the girls' room during classes. We learned very quickly to leave her alone. She may have been wounded, but she was still dangerous.

"Hey, Sidonia," Naomi called. "I caught a prowler."

A pair of kitten heels clicked against the tile floor. The Princess turned a corner and sauntered over to where I stood. She smiled sweetly, flashing her trademark dimples before pushing me back against the locker.

"Do I know you?" she sneered in her sinister accent as her yellow eyes looked me up and down.

I shook my head, too scared to speak.

"You're not in the ninth grade, are you?"

"Seventh," I managed to mumble.

"Eww," she said, taking a step back as if I were contaminated. "What's your name?"

"Ananka Fishbein."

"It suits you. An ugly name for an ugly little girl."

Naomi snickered at the Princess's joke.

"Now give me my ring," the Princess demanded.

"I didn't take it, Sidonia."

"Eww. She said my name. Don't do that again, piglet." The Princess jabbed a finger into the ring of baby fat I was still hoping to lose. "If you aren't a thief, why are you breaking into my locker?"

"I'm not. I just wanted to see how she did it." I whimpered.

"How *who* did it?" the Princess growled in frustration.

The door to the locker room swung open, and the voice of the principal echoed through the room.

"What in heaven's name is going on in here? Why aren't you girls in class?"

"We caught the person who stole my ring," said the Princess, transforming back into her sweet little girl disguise. "We were just coming to turn her in."

"Is that so?" said the principal. She was one of the few who were immune to the Princess's charms. Peering down at me, she almost smiled. "You're the girl in Ms. Jessel's class. The one who wants to study giant squid. Ananka, if I'm not mistaken."

I nodded mutely.

"Squid," giggled Naomi.

"That's enough," demanded the principal. "Now, Ananka, is there any truth in what these two vigilantes are saying?"

"No, ma'am. I didn't steal anything."

"She's a filthy little liar," insisted the Princess. "We found her trying to break into my locker again. And look at what she's wearing. She could definitely use the cash."

"Would you please empty your pockets for me, Ananka?" the principal sighed.

I dumped the contents of my pockets—three quarters, one barrette, my retainer, and a wad of lint—onto one of the locker room benches and allowed the principal to give me a quick frisking.

"So far she appears to be telling the truth," the principal announced.

"Maybe she needs to be strip-searched," offered Naomi.

"Why don't you both get back to class and let me do

the detective work?" the principal snapped. "Come along, Ananka. Let's go have a look in your locker."

As the principal guided me toward the stairs, I caught a glimpse of the Princess's face. Her eyes bulged, her nostrils flared, and her mouth stretched into a mean smirk.

"You're dead, squid girl," she mouthed silently.

Against my better judgment, I threw up on the principal's shoes.

⚐   ⚐   ⚐

I could have spared everyone a lot of trouble if I had chosen to rat on Kiki Strike. The Princess's mother was outraged that a common criminal was mingling with the heiresses at the Atalanta School. At her insistence, other lockers and backpacks were ransacked, with those of the scholarship girls particularly scrutinized. A locksmith's daughter was treated to an Inquisition-style grilling, and for days, everyone's eyes were on everyone else's hands. Throughout it all, I kept quiet, telling myself that a snitch is worse than a thief. But deep down inside, I simply hated the Princess too much to help her.

After a thorough search of my belongings failed to uncover the ring, I thought The Five might leave me alone. They didn't, of course. They stalked me for days, waiting patiently for the right moment to attack. No matter where I went, the Princess or one of her friends was always close by. They lingered in the library, whispering "squid girl" from behind outdated copies of *Lucky* magazine. As I navigated the hallways between classes, they followed in full formation, cackling cruelly if I happened to trip or drop a book. Eventually, I could barely pay a visit to the restroom without being escorted by half the ninth grade.

On April 1, Sidonia finally made her move. Aside from the rotten squid I had discovered hanging in my locker that morning, it had been a relatively peaceful school day. When the last bell rang, I slowly gathered my things, giving the other girls plenty of time to clear the building. By the time I closed my locker and started for the exit, the halls were eerily empty.

I stepped outside, into the courtyard, and discovered where everyone had gone. They were all there, waiting for me, and at the head of the crowd stood The Five, dressed to the nines and ready for battle. The Princess stepped forward, her most glorious teacher-dazzling smile displayed in all its splendor.

"Well, *there* you are, squid girl!" she exclaimed in fraudulent friendliness as she linked her arm with mine and leaned in close. Her breath smelled of violets and toothpaste. "We've been looking all over for you!" I tried to break free, but she tightened her grip on my arm and with almost superhuman strength turned me to face the crowd. "We thought you might be busy stealing someone else's jewelry. You know, a little something special to go with that stunning outfit you've got on. Let me guess. Last season's Goodwill? Or did you have to mug a homeless person for it?"

She paused as if expecting an answer, and I desperately wanted to respond. I searched for something witty to say, but with so many eyes trained in my direction, my brain was barren. Instead, I stood there mutely. It wasn't my finest moment.

"Oh well," the Princess continued. "Keep your fashion secrets to yourself. Listen, there's something we want to talk to you about. We've been keeping an eye on you lately, and well, we think you're damaging our school's reputation. I mean, *really,* squid girl, when are you going to go on a diet? Don't you know that fatties like you make the rest of us look bad?"

As Sidonia hurled her best insults at me, I noticed Kiki Strike standing at the edge of the crowd. It was the first time I had seen her in days. Unlike the other girls, who appeared riveted by the spectacle—some watching with amusement, others in sheer horror—Kiki paid no attention as she calmly jotted something down in her little black notebook. She glanced up at me briefly as she ripped the page out and folded it neatly. I saw Kiki hand the note to one of The Five, whisper in her ear, and disappear into the crowd.

The note was quickly passed to Sidonia, her friend practically drooling with excitement.

"Someone just gave this to me. She said it's some juicy information about Squidie here."

Sidonia hastily unfolded the note and held it up for both of us to read. "Let's take a look, shall we?"

Written on the page were three terse sentences.

You're wasting your time. She's not the one you're after.
Have a look in your best friend's handbag.

Sidonia's jaw dropped and her precious dimples fled. Her professionally manicured hand crumpled the note into a tight ball.

"Who wrote this?" she shrieked.

"That girl over there," stammered her frightened friend, pointing to an empty spot in the crowd. The sea of girls parted to avoid the finger. "I mean. She was there. She gave that to me."

"*Who* was there?" demanded Sidonia.

"I don't know."

"What do you mean, you don't know? Are you blind *and* stupid? What did she look like?"

"I didn't get a good look at her, Sidonia, but I think she might have been really short."

"Just shut up. You're completely worthless," snarled the Princess as she pushed the girl aside. "Naomi! Get over here now!"

The Princess snatched Naomi's handbag and dumped everything inside it onto the grass. She spread the contents around with her foot, and then bent down to pick up a coin purse. There, inside, was the pink diamond ring.

"I—I have no idea how it got there, Sidonia," stammered Naomi, a hot red flush spreading across her entire body. "That weird-looking girl must have slipped it into my bag."

The Princess's eyes narrowed, and she spoke in a carefully controlled voice. "What do you mean, 'weird-looking'?"

"She's got white hair, and she's as pale as a ghost. I think I've seen her before. She's really creepy."

"Let's go," Sidonia said, jerking Naomi roughly by the arm. "I'm not done with you yet!" she stopped to shout in my face before forcing her way through the crowd to a silver Bentley that was waiting for her outside the school gates.

After the Princess's departure, the crowd splintered into a dozen little groups as girls turned to their friends to marvel over what had happened. Thankfully, I was no longer the main attraction—everyone was taking guesses at the contents of the note and the identity of its mysterious author. I passed through the chattering mob and made my way to the safety of the street. I walked for blocks before I could think clearly. All I knew was that something miraculous had happened—and that Kiki Strike was responsible.

✾ ✾ ✾

Night fell long before I reached Old St. Patrick's Cathedral, a few blocks north of my home. True darkness is rare in Manhattan, which at night remains in a state of permanent twilight. But set back from the street, away from the lights of passing cars, the cathedral squatted in the shadow of a massive wall that circled both the church and its graveyard. The entire block had the appearance of a medieval fortress, its upper reaches barely visible against the starless sky.

Whenever I passed by on my way home from school, the gates of the cathedral were always locked, allowing only a tantalizing glimpse of a cemetery teeming with moss-covered tombstones and marble monuments to the dead. As usual, I slowed my stride, and tried to peer through the gloom. What looked like a ghostly face peeked out from behind a tall tree just to the left of the entrance. I almost shrieked and started to run, but it only took a few steps before my curiosity conquered my fear of the dark. I turned back toward the church, trying to convince myself that I hadn't seen anything that couldn't be explained by an eighth-grade science book.

The gates opened at my halfhearted touch. As I approached the tree, I was unnerved to see the face reappear, sporting a very unholy grin.

"Hello," it said, and I jumped backward, stumbling over a tiny gravestone. The face laughed, and I realized it was attached to a small girl, her hair tucked beneath the hood of a black jacket. "A little late for church, aren't you?" asked Kiki Strike, stepping out from behind the tree and pulling back her hood.

"What are you doing here?" I asked stupidly.

"Waiting for you."

"Oh," I responded, finding it difficult to concentrate. I couldn't help thinking that she didn't look quite real. Up close, her skin was too pale, and her features too carefully crafted. She was, at the same time, both very pretty and extremely odd-looking. I asked the only question that popped into my head. "Why did you steal the ring?"

Kiki raised an eyebrow. "Didn't you learn anything today? It's not polite to accuse people of crimes they didn't commit."

"So it was true about Naomi?"

"Of course it was. When a story's *that* good it's got to be true."

"But how did you know that the ring was in Naomi's handbag?"

"I know a lot of things," Kiki said matter-of-factly.

"About The Five?"

"Among others," she replied in a slightly taunting tone.

"What are you getting at?" I demanded. "Are you saying you know something about me?"

For a moment she was quiet. Her pale eyes wandered across my face as if she were searching for something she'd seen before.

"Let's see. I know you're short on friends. I also know you're a little strange. And I figure you must be pretty bored, or you wouldn't have spent so much time following me around. But I know a few other things that make me think you might be very interesting."

I couldn't tell whether I should be frightened or flattered. No one had ever found me interesting before.

"Is that good or bad?" I asked.

"That, Miss Fishbein, is entirely up to *you*."

She handed me a slip of paper and then headed for the street, leaving me in front of the empty church, still thinking of all the questions I should have asked.

Halfway to the gates, Kiki turned and waved good-bye, her hand cupped in a familiar fashion. As far as I knew, only a small group of people shared the same style of wave. And since I was fairly sure that Kiki Strike wasn't a member of the British royal family, there was only one conclusion to reach. The shock hit me like a thundering wildebeest. Kiki Strike was the creature that had crawled out of the hole in front of my house. I wasn't the only person who had seen the Shadow City. She had gotten there first. For a moment, it seemed as if everything I had worked for had been stolen from me. Then I looked down at the piece of paper I was holding. *Café des Amis, Saturday, 09:00*, it said. I had been invited to breakfast.

☆   ☆   ☆

Kiki Strike sat at a small outside table with the gossip section of the *New York Post* spread out in front of her. An enormous bowl of café au lait held the paper in place as a cold April breeze tried to blow it into the street. A green felt beret sat atop her head at a cocky tilt, and the starched collar of a khaki uniform peeked over the paper.

"You're late," she snapped as I approached, not bothering to look up. "If you're going to work with me, you'll have to learn to be on time."

"Who said we were going to be working together?" I shot back.

"How else do you expect to find the Shadow City?" she asked nonchalantly, licking her finger to turn a page.

"You've found another entrance, haven't you?"

Kiki looked up, her eyes glistening dangerously, like icebergs at sunset.

"We've got a lot to do today," she said, ignoring the question and standing up. She was wearing a Girl Scout uniform, complete with a sash covered entirely—front and back—with badges.

"You're a Girl Scout?" I scoffed. "Shouldn't you have outgrown that sort of thing by now?"

"Maybe, but the Marines wouldn't take me." She tossed a bag over the table to me. "Guess what," she said. "Today you're a Girl Scout, too. We're going incognito."

"No way. I have to wear one of those?" Two years

earlier, I had left the Girl Scouts in disgrace after sharing an illustrated edition of *A Man's Body* with my fellow troops. I had hoped to never see another Girl Scout uniform as long as I lived.

Kiki glared at me. "You'll wear it if you're coming with me," she said.

Ten minutes later, I emerged from the bathroom of the café wearing a polyester uniform that rubbed uncomfortably in all the wrong places. A waitress smiled down at me.

"Aren't you just the cutest! I was a Girl Scout, too, when I was little."

"I'm not in the Girl Scouts, I'm undercover," I snarled back at her.

"Oh, isn't that just perfect!" She beamed. I resisted the urge to give her a good kick and stomped out to the street, where Kiki was waiting. She looked me over and straightened my collar.

"Not bad." She grinned. "You look good in a uniform, but we're going to have to work on your posture."

Our first stop was a Girl Scout meeting in the basement of a ramshackle church in Morningside Heights, its ancient steeple leaning ominously toward a row of little houses across the street. In the basement, which smelled of mold and mothballs, the meeting had already begun. An unremarkable group of girls sat Indian-style in a circle on the cold, concrete floor. A couple of them shifted to make room for us.

"You're just in time, Kiki," said a plump, pleasant-looking

woman dressed in an ill-fitting Scout leader uniform. "Luz Lopez is just about to share her latest project with us. Let's all give her a hand."

The Girl Scouts clapped obediently, and a sullen girl with long curly hair pulled back tightly from her face rose from their midst. She walked briskly to the front of the room and stopped in front of a table covered with a tattered sheet. With an unexpected flourish, she snapped the sheet from the table, revealing a small electronic device. Speaking quickly but carefully, the girl addressed the crowd.

"The invention you see has been put to the test and has proven highly successful in the field. My mother keeps a small patch of flowers in front of our building. For the last few months, someone has been wrecking her garden. Personally, I couldn't care less about plants, but my mother was very upset. The evidence speaks for itself, I think."

Luz retrieved a handful of Polaroids from the pocket of her uniform and passed them out to the group. Each picture showed a different view of the sad remains of a little garden. Mangled tulips were strewn across the sidewalk, their bulbs squashed into pulp. Dozens of dainty, brightly colored pansies lay dying on the windshields of nearby cars, and a clump of sweet peas dangled from the limb of a tree.

"I always suspected Mrs. Gonzalez, one of our neighbors. She's never liked my mother, and she's always saying rude things to my sisters. But I didn't have any proof, and my mother was too polite to accuse Mrs. Gonzalez. I tried staking out the garden, but the damage appeared to occur in the hours after my curfew, and my mother wouldn't let me stay outside to watch.

"That's when I had my stroke of genius. I found an old baby monitor in the trash outside my building, and with a few adjustments, I was able to convert it into the apparatus you see before you—a short-range bugging device."

Luz picked up the baby monitor and held it up for everyone to see.

"Mrs. Gonzalez likes to talk—*a lot*. From what I had observed, when she wasn't destroying other people's gardens, she was usually sitting on her big butt in her kitchen, gossiping with her friends. I knew that if I could hide my bug inside her kitchen, I'd hear her bragging about what she'd done to my mother's flowers.

"So I started hanging around with Mrs. Gonzalez's daughter, Rosie. Nobody else will talk to her since she always got her fingers in her nose. After a few days, I invited myself over to Rosie's house for some *arroz con leche*. While I was there, I planted my device under her kitchen sink. Then all I had to do was tune my scanner to the right frequency and wait for Mrs. Gonzalez to confess her crimes."

"Luz!" the horrified Scout leader broke in. "You can't bug people's homes! Are you aware that you've committed a felony? The Girl Scouts do not condone illegal activities!"

"The Girl Scouts," replied Luz, filled with righteous indignation, "believe in truth, justice, and the American way. Which part of that did I violate? In my opinion, nothing could be less American than destroying other people's gardens."

Kiki leaned over to me.

"We have our first recruit," she whispered, reaching into her backpack and pulling out a golden envelope with Luz's name inscribed on the front.

"Recruit?" I asked.

HOW TO KNOW IF SOMEONE'S EAVESDROPPING

So you think that the very personal conversation you just had with your friend Petunia will always stay between the two of you? How can you be sure that there wasn't a third person quietly listening in as you spilled your deepest, darkest secrets?

There are countless ways to eavesdrop on other people's conversations, and many don't cost much more than the average taco platter. Fortunately, spying on other people tends to be illegal in most countries. But if your foe is desperate to listen, breaking the law may not be her biggest concern. That doesn't mean you have to make it easy for her. Learn to be wary of the following tools:

Stethoscopes
A devious criminal can use an ordinary stethoscope to listen to conversations through walls and doors. However, unless your enemies happen to be members of the medical community, they may find it difficult to get their hands on one. Unfortunately, a reasonable alternative can be crafted from a funnel (or the top of a plastic soda bottle) and some rubber tubing.

Voice-Activated Recorders
The shelves of your local office supply store are stacked high with cheap versions of this low-tech spying device. Some can be as small as a box of matches and are easy to hide in a pocket, a handbag, or a bra.

Cordless Phones
Always think twice before spilling your secrets over a cordless phone. If it's not digital, anyone with a police scanner can listen in. (In fact, many sick individuals stay up-to-date on the latest gossip by eavesdropping on their neighbors' conversations.)

Baby Monitors

Some of the best "bugging" devices available, these cheerful-looking contraptions can be used for evil purposes. If you're sitting within range, a baby monitor will broadcast whatever you say over the airwaves, where your conversations can be picked up by police scanners or other baby monitors.

Conference Calling

Say someone wants to listen in on a conversation between you and a friend. If they have conference (or three-way) calling, they can place a call to your phone and wait for you to answer. Once you say hello, they can simply speed dial your friend's number. You may both assume that the other person placed the call, and the sneaky third person can sit back and quietly listen to the conversation.

Chapter 5

The Bank Street Irregulars

Some people, I've found, are almost bursting at the seams with the desire to let you get to know them better. Ask one innocent question, and within ten minutes, you'll learn that their beloved pet Chihuahua suffers from halitosis, that their grandfather once wrestled an alligator, and that they secretly dream of being a Las Vegas showgirl. As entertaining as these people may be, experience has taught me that those who say the most are often those who know the least. Quiet people keep their secrets to themselves. That's what makes them interesting—and generally worth the wait.

I suppose it goes without saying that Kiki Strike was not a talker. In fact, on that first day we spent together, she didn't say much at all, and I have to admit I was a little surprised. We shared at least one secret that demanded discussion, and I was anxious to hear what she knew about the Shadow City. But although it was clear that Kiki had a plan, she didn't choose to reveal it. I found myself following silently alongside her as she marched down Amsterdam Avenue, her eyes darting into alleys and doorways as if she were patrolling the street.

That's not to say that I didn't insist on being let in on her plan the minute we left Luz. But Kiki simply arched an eyebrow and broke into a Cheshire Cat–like grin. Have a little patience, she told me, and refused to say another word. In the long silence that followed, I studied my pale companion and realized that I knew nothing about her—apart from the fact that she knew things she had no business knowing. I suspected she was well on her way to becoming truly dangerous, and the only thought that offered any comfort was the thought that I might not be in it alone for long.

After our encounter with Luz Lopez, we made a brief visit to another Girl Scout meeting, this one held in a dark, wood-paneled classroom on the campus of Columbia University. The blinds were pulled, and the flames of a dozen Bunsen burners lit the room. Surrounding each flame were three or four girls wearing black leather aprons and protective goggles, which lent them the appearance of giant, wingless insects.

At the front of the classroom, on a massive table, was a sinister-looking system of glass beakers and tubes. A strange liquid in a toxic shade of purple coursed through the coiled tubes, bubbled ominously in the beakers, and finally dripped into a bowl manned by one of the Girl Scouts. The entire room stank of marshmallows and grape.

A Scout leader advanced toward us with a pair of metal tongs. Pinched between them was a sandwich bulging with melted marshmallows and dripping chocolate.

"Nice to see you back, Kiki. S'more?" she asked, thrusting the tongs under Kiki's nose.

"No thanks," said Kiki, recoiling from the s'more as if it were poisoned.

"Suit yourself," said the woman, turning to supervise a group of girls whose s'mores kept bursting into flame.

"What's the purple stuff in the beakers?" I asked Kiki.

"Punch," she said. "It's snack time."

Summoning my powers of observation, I let my eyes roam the classroom. Aside from the rather unusual methods of food preparation being used, I immediately noticed at least two things that weren't quite right. For starters, the Scout leaders who milled about the room, making sure that safety precautions were followed, were all extremely young. Judging solely by their faces, a couple of them weren't old enough to be in charge. But even the most youthful of the Scout leaders had a helmet of silver hair and walked with the slow, painstaking gait of the elderly. It was as if new faces had been magically attached to ancient bodies.

I also noticed, as I filled a paper cup with punch, that the girl standing by the punch bowl had been involved in an accident. She wore her hair in dreadlocks, and on one side of her head they brushed against her shoulder. On the other side, however, her hair was at least four inches shorter and singed at the bottom, as if it had been set on fire. I returned with my punch to Kiki's side, but kept my eye on the girl with the lopsided hairdo.

"Her name's DeeDee Morlock," said Kiki, hopping onto a stool situated a safe distance from the s'mores. "This is her father's classroom. As I'm sure you've guessed, he's a chemistry professor."

"What happened to her hair?" I asked.

"It caught on fire during an experiment she was conducting. She's lucky, though. The substances she was working with could have destroyed her whole block."

"So she's a chemist, too?"

"She puts her father to shame," said Kiki. "Notice anything unusual about the Scout leaders?"

"Yeah. What's wrong with them? Why do they all have gray hair?"

"Nothing's *wrong* with them. You'll have gray hair, too, when you're their age. Mrs. Lupinski's the youngest, and she turned eighty-five last week. Surprised?" she asked, noting what must have been a look of pure astonishment on my face.

"How's it possible?"

"A couple of weeks ago, our new friend DeeDee succeeded in refining a particularly dangerous strain of botulism. Do you know what that is?"

"It's the deadliest poison on earth," I answered. There was an entire book devoted to the subject tucked between some cans of tuna in my kitchen. I had once skimmed it while waiting for the kettle to boil. "But some women have it injected into their faces. It paralyzes the muscles and makes wrinkles disappear."

"Exactly. Unfortunately, it's too expensive for most Scout leaders, so DeeDee whipped them up a batch. Now they're all wrinkle-free and fabulous."

"That was nice of DeeDee," I said, feeling a little uncomfortable.

"By all accounts, she's a very nice girl," Kiki noted in a scientific fashion, as if she were observing the markings on a rare species of toad.

Once snack time had finished, Kiki hopped off her stool.

"Unless you're desperate to learn how to macramé, we're not staying for arts and crafts," she announced. I reached to gather my things, but Kiki stopped me. "Wait here. There's one more thing I have to do." She left me standing on my own while she marched across the room and pulled DeeDee aside. I witnessed the exchange of another mysterious golden envelope. When she returned, she met me with a devilish wink. "We'll talk later," she said, anticipating my question. "We've got another meeting to go to, and it's important to get there before it starts."

Without any further explanation, we left Columbia University and caught a subway downtown to the East Village. When we emerged at Astor Place, it was late afternoon. I struggled with my polyester uniform, which was sticking to me uncomfortably, and tried to keep up with Kiki as she hurried toward an old Yiddish theater that doubled as a community center. Its walls were plastered with advertisements for anarchist meetings, dating services, and guitar lessons.

The minute we stepped inside, we were immediately set upon by two chipper girls, both dressed in Girl Scout uniforms that somehow seemed vaguely punk. One of them grabbed my arm and spun me around.

"This is the best one yet!" she chirped.

"Definitely," the other agreed. "How d'you get your hair that color? It's so dull and lifeless!"

"And those shoes! You look like you held up a Payless."

"I don't know what you're talking about," I sputtered once I finally regained my balance. Kiki was doubled over with laughter.

"Oh my God, you totally deserve an Oscar," said one of the girls, laughing so hard, she could barely get the words out.

"Yeah, you're my hero, Betty," said the other.

"Who's Betty?" I asked.

"She's not Betty," Kiki added.

"Are you sure?" asked one of the girls incredulously.

"Positive," said Kiki, giving my hair a yank.

The two girls looked at each other, suddenly serious.

"I could have sworn we had her this time."

"I know," said the other. "C'mon, let's go look around some more." They turned and headed toward a large group of girls who were gathering in the center of the room, waiting for the meeting to begin.

"What was *that* about?" I asked Kiki once they were out of earshot.

"You'll see soon enough," she said. "I'd hate to ruin the suspense."

The meeting was called to order, and one of the Scout leaders stepped up to the group of girls.

"Okay," she said, as if performing a tiresome ritual. "Let's get this over with. Which of you is Betty Bent?" No one said a thing. All the girls looked eagerly around the room, examining their neighbors. "We're not getting started until you tell us who you are today, Betty," warned the exasperated woman. After a long pause a hand slowly rose from the crowd. "Please stand up," said the Scout leader.

A girl with long, stringy blond hair, thick glasses, and a slight hump stood up, smiling nervously. The group broke into the kind of worshipful applause that's usually reserved for divas and dictators.

"You're a genius!" shouted one of the girls who had accosted me earlier.

"Well, Betty," said the Scout leader, shaking her head in disapproval. "You've really outdone yourself. But may I suggest that our master of disguise come to the next meeting as the real Betty Bent?"

"Who's the real Betty Bent?" whispered the hump-backed girl, and the Girl Scouts roared with laughter.

"What does she really look like?" I whispered to Kiki.

"Beats me," she replied. "Last week she was Korean."

Once again, when the meeting was under way, Kiki showed no interest in sticking around. We had seen what we had come to see, and it was time to make our exit. On our way out the door, Kiki stealthily slipped a gold envelope to a surprised Betty Bent, who was still trying to blend into the crowd. Betty looked down at the envelope in her hand and opened her mouth as if to speak, but before she could ask the meaning of it all, we were gone.

Back on the street, Kiki and I walked in silence until I took notice of my surroundings and discovered we were on Cleveland Place, only a few yards away from my home. My disappointment grew when I realized that I would have to wait for the secret of the envelopes to be revealed. Before we separated, Kiki asked me to meet her the next morning at seven o'clock on the corner of Mott and Mosco streets in Chinatown.

"There's one more person I'd like you to meet before we talk," she said as she deposited me at my doorstep. "And you won't need the uniform."

☆ ☆ ☆

In all of Manhattan, only Chinatown is bustling at seven o'clock on a Sunday morning. By the time I made my way to Mott Street, the narrow roads were teeming with people, all winding around stands selling unusual merchandise. At one stand, a man sorted though a barrel of freeze-dried octopi, while at another a woman wearing thick gloves arranged a heap of enormous fruit, each covered with hundreds of spikes so sharp they could easily puncture a finger. Shops specializing in counterfeit goods disappeared behind sliding metal grates whenever a police car passed by.

Kiki Strike, dressed in black and looking alarmingly chic, stood in front of a little fish shop that spilled out onto the sidewalk. Thin streams of blood trickled into the street and an overpowering odor of death issued from the shop's open front. Giant silver fish the size of small children lay smothered in ice, their mouths stretched wide as if gasping for one last breath. A large plastic tub was filled to the brim with hundreds of brightly colored crabs, all struggling to make a desperate escape. One scuttled across my foot and disappeared into a sewer drain.

"She's in there," said Kiki, pointing at a tiny temple

across the street from the fish shop. "She'll be out any minute now."

I watched the front door of the temple with great anticipation. As it opened, I caught a quick glimpse of a mammoth golden Buddha that crouched at the end of a dark room and glittered alluringly in the morning sunlight. A stunning girl emerged wearing a silk dress embroidered with emerald chrysanthemums, her hair pulled back in a prim bun. She caught sight of Kiki and made a beeline for her across the street.

"What do you want?" she demanded in a gruff voice that didn't match her doll-like appearance. "You know I got kicked out. Did you come to rub it in?"

"So you got booted out of the Girl Scouts." Kiki shrugged. "Who cares?"

Both of us stared at her. I had come to believe that Kiki took the Girl Scouts rather seriously.

"Then why are you here?" asked the girl.

"I wanted you to meet someone."

"I know who she is," said the girl, giving me a brisk once-over. "I have better things to do than hang around with Atalanta girls."

"Do you?" asked Kiki knowingly, and the girl softened. "Anyway, I wanted you two to meet in person. This is Oona Wong," she said to me.

"Nice to meet you," I said. "How do you know who I am?"

Oona finally cracked a smile and winked at Kiki. "I once made an ID card for someone who needed access to Atalanta. I had to go through the picture files on your school's computer to find a reasonable match. I never forget a face."

"Oona's the best hacker in Manhattan," said Kiki.

"And forger," added Oona proudly.

"That's why she got kicked out," said Kiki.

"Counterfeit Girl Scout badges," Oona explained. "I should have known better than to sell a Model Citizen badge to that girl who was stealing the cookie money."

"To be honest, Oona, I always thought the badge business was beneath you," said Kiki.

"So you came all the way to Chinatown to tell me?" Oona asked, her head cocked and her hands on her hips.

"No, I wanted to give you something." Kiki calmly retrieved a small golden envelope from her bag. "Since you don't have a permanent mailing address, I had to hand deliver it."

"Are you having a party or something?" asked Oona.

"Or something," said Kiki. "I thought you might be looking for new ways to pass the time now that you're no longer welcome in the Girl Scouts." She handed the envelope to Oona. "Come on, Ananka. We should go," she said to me.

We walked away as Oona impatiently tore open the envelope. We were almost to the end of the block when we heard Oona's voice calling out through the crowd.

"I'll be there!" she yelled.

Walking north from Chinatown Kiki and I soon found ourselves on a deserted cobblestone street in SoHo. Unable to stifle my curiosity any longer, I stopped in front of a narrow building that looked as though it had been sawed in half.

"Okay," I demanded. "What's going on?" If I wanted to feel left out, I could always spend more time at school.

Kiki grinned like a cat that had swallowed an entire pet store's worth of canaries.

"Mind if we discuss it over coffee?" she asked, pointing to a café across the street.

"Why not?" I shrugged.

We sat at a table toward the back of the empty café. A pair of waitresses milled about, gossiping noisily in French as they filled saltshakers and wiped down plastic menus with filthy sponges. Kiki scanned the room for potential eavesdroppers, then settled into a chair. She called out in French to one of the waitresses, then turned her attention to me.

"What did you think of the other girls?" she asked.

"They're amazing," I admitted. "But I'm not sure why you're recruiting them."

"You can't see how a mechanical genius, a chemist, a master of disguise, and a forger could come in handy?" Kiki snorted.

"Well, I might if I knew what we were doing."

Kiki looked as if she questioned my sanity. "We're going to explore the Shadow City."

My heart nearly burst through my ribs. "So you *have* found another entrance."

"Of course I have."

A single thought popped into my head. I still don't know how it got there.

"The Marble Cemetery."

"You guessed!" she exclaimed, sounding genuinely impressed.

"How did you find it?"

One of the waitresses placed a steaming bowl of café au lait in front of us. Kiki stirred her coffee and took a quick sip.

"I've known about it all along."

Kiki Strike set down her coffee cup, leaned back in her chair, and looked me in the eye.

"There once was a man named Augustus Quackenbush," she began.

"*Quackenbush?*" I interrupted. "That doesn't sound like a real name."

"Just *listen,* Ananka. Augustus Quackenbush was a very rich man," she continued. "He owned a shop that sold the fanciest clothes in New York. In fact, his business was so successful that in 1852, he was able to pay a fortune for one of the vaults in the Marble Cemetery. I guess in those days, it was *the* place to be buried.

"Then, right after he bought the vault, Quackenbush went broke. He'd spent every last penny on a huge shipment of fabric from Paris. But the ship carrying the cloth was captured by pirates on its way to New York, and none of the booty was ever recovered.

"Augustus Quackenbush didn't like the idea of being poor. So he decided that if he couldn't afford to *buy* the fabric he needed to keep his business going, he'd just have to steal it. But in order to get started, Quackenbush needed the help of an experienced criminal. Lucky for him, he knew just the person for the job—a man he'd met in a gambling parlor. His name was Pearcy Leake III."

"The guy who wrote *Glimpses of Gotham*?" I asked.

"Exactly. Before he started writing books, Pearcy Leake made his living as a con man. His specialty was sweet-talking his way into old ladies' wills, but he wasn't opposed to a little larceny here and there. When Quackenbush offered him the job, he was thrilled. But once he'd thought things through, he realized that the location of Augustus Quackenbush's shop was going to cause problems. It was on Broadway, the busiest street in the city. There was no way to deliver stolen goods to the shop without being seen by half of New York.

"When it was all starting to seem hopeless, Quackenbush happened to mention his vault in the Marble Cemetery and Leake had a stroke of genius. He suggested that they build an underground tunnel that would link the empty vault to the basement of Quackenbush's shop ten blocks away. Once the tunnel was built, they could hire a crew of thieves, disguise them as grave diggers, and smuggle stolen fabric into the shop using the deserted cemetery as a loading dock.

"They spent six months digging the tunnel. Leake insisted they take another two months to connect their tunnel to the Shadow City. He figured that if anything ever went wrong, it would make the perfect escape route. Of course, nothing ever went wrong, and Quackenbush and Leake became two of the richest men in New York.

"Augustus Quackenbush dropped dead in 1867, and a couple of years later, Pearcy Leake mysteriously disappeared. Their tunnel was forgotten. But it's still down there, just waiting for someone to use it."

"Give me a break. How could you possibly know all that?" I demanded.

"Augustus Quackenbush was my great-great-grand-father," Kiki said. "A few years ago, I inherited a house that once belonged to him. When we were renovating, a workman found his diary and a copy of *Glimpses of Gotham* hidden behind a stone in the fireplace. Because I'm a relative of the dead, I was able to get a key to the Marble Cemetery, even though Augustus Quackenbush isn't even buried there."

"He's not?" I asked.

"Well, he couldn't risk anyone finding the tunnel, so he was secretly buried elsewhere."

"Where?"

"In my front yard," said Kiki nonchalantly.

For a moment I was speechless. And although I knew I shouldn't judge people by their relatives, I wondered if Kiki Strike was up to no good. I was beginning to understand how the other girls might play a part in Kiki's plans, but I had no idea why she would need someone like me. If I had any unusual talents, I had yet to discover them.

"Why me?" I asked. "I can't hack computers or make surveillance equipment. What good am I to you?"

Kiki shook her head as if I had missed the point. "Other than me, you're the only person alive who's seen the Shadow City. That morning you watched me climb out of the hole in front of your house, I had a hunch you'd find the trapdoor. I left you my copy of *Glimpses of Gotham* just to make it a little easier. But believe it or not, Ananka, there aren't too many people who'd jump into a hole just to see what's down there. You even followed me into Central Park in the middle of a blizzard. Your tailing skills stink, but you've got guts.

"Besides, you're far more important to this operation than you think. We'll have to do a lot of research before we explore the Shadow City, and I'd rather not have some nosy librarian breathing down my neck. Your library has all the books we could possibly need."

"How do you know about my library?" I asked.

"I didn't know it was a secret," said Kiki vaguely.

"But why didn't you just tell me what was going on? Why did you have to drag me to half the Girl Scout meetings in Manhattan?"

"You spent two months following me around, so I figured you're the sort of person who likes to see things for herself. That's why I let you see me at the Marble Cemetery. And I took you to meet the other girls so you'd know exactly what I was up to."

It was neither the first nor the last time I would be surprised by how well she knew me.

"Okay," I sighed. "When do we get started?"

Kiki reached into her bag and pulled out one of the mysterious golden envelopes.

"This one is for you."

I opened the envelope and pulled out a printed card.

Outgrown the Girl Scouts? it read in large letters. *Join the Irregulars, and begin the greatest adventure of your youth. First meeting to be held at 17:00 on the second Saturday in April at 133½ Bank Street. Absolute secrecy required. No disguises, recording equipment, or toxic substances allowed inside.*

"The Irregulars?" I asked, slightly confused.

"It's the name of our new troop." She paused as if waiting for a laugh. "Well, *I* thought it was funny," she added when it became clear that I didn't get the joke.

"What do we do if one of the girls doesn't want to join?"

Kiki stopped smiling. "We'll have to kill her, won't we?"

I stared at her in horror until she broke into a grin.

"Come on, that's hilarious," she insisted.

⭐ ⭐ ⭐

The Atalanta School for Girls had seen the last of Kiki Strike. Until the second Saturday in April, I was on my own again. Now that Kiki's plans for the Shadow City were under way, she had better things to do, she informed me, than memorize state capitals. I wished I could follow her lead, but I knew my mother and father would never let me blow off the seventh grade. They didn't care what clothes I wore or what I ate for dinner, but missing school was not an option. I was jealous that Kiki's parents seemed to have their priorities in order. While Kiki Strike was preparing for a great adventure, I would have to finish the school year, and that meant dealing with the Princess by myself.

When I arrived at school the following Monday, I found The Five hovering around my locker. I was pleasantly surprised to discover that my stomach remained calm and my heartbeat slow and steady. Even without Kiki around to rescue me, I wasn't afraid. Somehow, the Princess had lost her power over me.

"Step back!" Sidonia snapped at her posse as I approached. The large pink diamond on her right hand glittered under the fluorescent lights. "Give me some space, you morons."

I walked past her to my locker and started to dial the combination.

"I know you didn't steal my ring," said the Princess coldly. I braced for an apology that wasn't going to come. "Naomi saw the girl who passed the note. Is she a friend of yours? What's her name?"

"When did you start taking an interest in seventh graders, Sidonia?" I asked. "Are you having trouble making friends your own age?"

The Princess gritted her teeth and took a deep breath.

"Naomi said the girl didn't look very healthy. A bit on the pale side and awfully small for her age. I hope she's eating well. I would hate for my hero to fall ill."

Whatever Sidonia was after, it couldn't be good. I turned around to look her in the eye.

"You've got your ring back, so why don't you go harass some fourth graders and leave me alone."

The Princess frowned, and for a moment I thought she might slap me. Instead, she bared her teeth in what passed for a smile.

"By the way, where is your friend today? I'd love to thank her in person. Do you think you could arrange a meeting?"

I still didn't buy it. The Princess never thanked anyone for anything. Common courtesy was too common for her. I glanced over at Naomi, who looked as though she'd aged ten years over the weekend. Somehow, she must have convinced the Princess she was innocent.

"I'm not her social secretary," I answered. "If you want to meet my friend so badly, you'll have to find her yourself."

The Princess's cheeks colored with rage. "If you insist, squid girl," she hissed.

"Squid girl?" I laughed. "If that's the best you can come up with, it's a good thing you're rich. You'd suck as a scholarship student."

I spent the rest of the day wishing Kiki Strike had been there to see the Princess stomp off in a huff.

☆   ☆   ☆

The following weekend, I set out for the first meeting of the Irregulars at 133½ Bank Street in Greenwich Village. When I reached what I thought was the right block, I walked up and down the street, searching for the building. After several trips, I came to the conclusion that while there was a 133 and a 134, there was certainly no *133½* Bank Street. I sat down on a stoop to review my options, and was soon joined by DeeDee Morlock. Her dreadlocks had been trimmed to a uniform length, and she was wearing a violet dress sprinkled with acid burns. I watched as she walked up and down the street, occasionally pausing to reread her invitation. Eventually she stopped in front of me, her confusion written on her face.

"Excuse me. Do you know where I can find *133½* Bank Street?" she asked. I didn't blame her for failing to recognize me from the Girl Scout meeting. I knew I wasn't particularly memorable.

"I wish I did. I'm looking for it, too," I said.

"Oh, hi. I'm DeeDee." She smiled, offering a hand,

which I noticed was stained an unusual shade of green. "Are you a member of . . ." She remembered the secret nature of the gathering and caught herself before giving too much away.

"Ananka," I said, shaking her hand. "And yes. I mean I guess we'll both be members. That's if we can find the right address."

"Yeah, it's weird, isn't it? It's like the building just disappeared."

A thought flashed through my mind.

"It's a hidden house," I said.

"What's a hidden house?" DeeDee asked, eyeing me carefully.

"They're all over Greenwich Village," I explained. "But hardly anybody knows they're here. You can't see them from the street. They're hidden behind other buildings. They used to be stables or servants' quarters—things like that."

"Do you think that could be the entrance?" asked DeeDee, pointing to a wooden gate on the side of the building where I sat. It was roughly the same height and width as a large horse.

"It must be," I said, rising to my feet.

We stood nervously in front of the gate. DeeDee reached for a bronze door knocker in the shape of a severed hand.

"Hey, you!" shouted someone from across the street, and we both jumped. It was Oona Wong, dressed in a black, ninja-inspired jumpsuit. "Is that the way in?"

Immediately after we had knocked at the gate, it opened to reveal a tiny woman with unnaturally red hair, wearing a shirtdress that flattered her thin but muscular build. She looked both ways down the street before quickly pulling us inside.

"You are very punctual," she said in a thick Russian accent. "This is a good sign."

"Verushka?" I sputtered. Though the hair and clothing were different, the voice was unmistakable. She smiled at me and placed a hand on my shoulder.

"It is a pleasure to see you again, my dear."

"Are you Kiki's mother?" asked DeeDee.

"No," said Verushka sadly. "Her parents have been dead for many years. I am only the housekeeper. Come, I will take you inside. Then I must return for the other girls. I think they will not find the house."

"I've never seen a housekeeper with muscles like hers," whispered Oona as Verushka turned to lead us through a brick passageway.

"Neither have I," I agreed.

We left the passageway and entered an enchanted world. A wall of ivy, shooting its tendrils in every direction, encircled a patch of meadow. Golden daffodils rose from the ground in random bunches. A breeze pushed its way through the high, unmanicured grass and shook the wild rosebushes that grew among the ivy, stirring a storm of pink petals. In the center of the garden, hidden beneath the limbs of an enormous weeping willow, was an ancient wooden cottage with shuttered windows and two toylike chimneys. It was a house fit for Little Red Riding Hood or Snow White. The only proof that we hadn't been transported to another time and place was the quick, angry blare of a car horn from beyond the walls.

"This is amazing," said DeeDee, spinning around to take it all in.

"It is safe," said Verushka cryptically as she led us up a stone path and left us at the front door of the cottage. I scanned the yard in vain for any signs of August Quackenbush's grave, and then stepped into a living room that was stark and modern.

"This is more my style," said Oona appreciatively, stroking a wooden chair that looked more like a prop from a science fiction movie than a piece of furniture. Television monitors covered one entire wall of the small living room, each screen showing a different view of the house's surroundings. On one, I watched Verushka guiding two more girls through the brick passageway. On another, I saw Kiki exiting a room in another part of the house, a rolled-up map tucked under her arm.

Seconds later, Verushka arrived at the front door with Luz Lopez and a girl I assumed was Betty Bent in tow. This time Betty was a pretty olive-skinned girl with glossy black hair cut into a bob. Kiki stopped her at the door.

"Is this a disguise?" she demanded.

"No," said Betty shyly. "I followed the instructions. But I'm feeling kind of naked."

"You can put your sunglasses on if it will help," said Kiki.

"Thanks," murmured a grateful Betty, quickly hiding her eyes behind the largest sunglasses I'd ever seen.

Kiki turned to the rest of us.

"Welcome, ladies," she said. "Would you like to take a seat?"

We sat side by side on the two large sofas in the small

living room. Kiki unrolled the map and taped it to the fireplace mantel. It was a street map of downtown Manhattan. Next to it, she placed a hand-drawn diagram of the Shadow City. The other girls looked at one another in confusion.

"I'll make the introductions," Kiki announced. "Luz Lopez is one of the finest mechanical engineers in New York. Although her mother doesn't know it, she is secretly designing a small robot that can be programmed to do most of her household chores. DeeDee Morlock is a chemist. In a few short minutes, she can concoct the deadliest poisons and craft the most powerful explosives. We should all be thankful that she's chosen to use her powers for good instead of evil. As for Betty Bent, this is the first time in over four years that anyone has seen her without a disguise. Oona Wong is a master forger and computer hacker. She's been breaking the law since the age of five. And this," she said, turning to me, "is Ananka Fishbein. She will be our urban archaeologist. Not only does she know more about this city than most history professors, she has access to one of the most *useful* libraries in the country."

"Who are you?" asked Luz in a businesslike fashion.

"My name is Kiki Strike."

Betty Bent raised her hand. "What do you do?" she asked timidly.

"Anything I want," said Kiki Strike. "Now allow me to tell you why I've invited you here today. As you've seen, each of you has an unusual gift—a gift that has gone unappreciated by your parents, your teachers, and even the Girl Scouts. You could choose to spend your youth winning grade-school science fairs or, in Oona's case, trying to avoid juvenile hall. Or you could choose to do something truly spectacular. I think it's time to put your skills to real use. If you join the Irregulars, you will embark on one of the greatest adventures of all time."

"Will it be dangerous?" asked DeeDee.

"That's an interesting question coming from a girl who nearly blew up her own house," Kiki responded.

"Good point," noted DeeDee thoughtfully.

"Come on, let's hear it, then," said Oona.

"Okay," said Kiki, "but what I'm about to tell you can never leave this room. If one of you decides to confide in your friends or parents, you'll have the rest of us to deal with. And I'm pretty sure you don't want to be on Oona's bad side."

"That's right," said Oona, glaring at each of us.

"Ananka and I have uncovered evidence of an underground city deep beneath downtown Manhattan." Kiki gestured to the map. "It's called the Shadow City, and it was built about two hundred years ago by criminals looking to smuggle goods and hide from the police. If I'm right, there are huge tunnels about seventy feet underground," she said, pointing at the diagram she'd drawn. "They're connected to the surface by long ladders that lead to hidden rooms underneath buildings throughout the city.

"Right now, we're the only ones who know the Shadow City exists. Even Ananka and I don't know what's down there yet. We've only seen a tiny part of it, and it was never completely explored, even back when it was still in use."

"Do you think there's treasure down there?" asked Luz.

"That's what I'm hoping," said Kiki. "But before we start to search for treasure, the Irregulars are going to map all the entrances to the Shadow City."

"Who wants a map if we could have treasure?" demanded Oona.

Kiki rolled her eyes. "Really, Oona. I thought you of all people would understand. It's very simple. If we have the only map, we control the Shadow City."

"So what?" asked Oona.

"If we don't control the Shadow City, someone else will."

HOW TO PREPARE FOR ADVENTURE

The scouts were onto something when they advised their members to "Be Prepared." They understood that those who prepare will prevail.

If you want to be prepared for adventure of any magnitude, make sure to carry the following tools in your handbag at all times.

1. **A Compass:** Always know where you are—and where you're going. Even the most familiar environments can be confusing under certain conditions, such as rain, snow, or darkness. Getting lost is not only dangerous, it's a waste of time.

2. **A Pocket Flashlight:** You can purchase inexpensive flashlights no larger than a pen at most discount stores. Keep one on your person at all times—even if you're not afraid of the dark.

3. **A Swiss Army Knife (or Equivalent):** A standard SAK comes with a valuable set of tools that can help you out of countless scrapes—such as a screwdriver, scissors, a magnifying glass, and a nail file. Do not attempt to board an airplane with one unless you enjoy a good frisking.

4. **A Credit Card (Expired):** Should you find yourself locked in (or out) of a room, a credit card can be used to open a surprising number of doors. Practice on a bathroom door until you master the technique.

5. **A Notebook and Pen:** Boring? Perhaps. But these are the two most essential tools of any adventurer. Always keep track of what's been said, where you've been, and what you've learned.

6. **Duct Tape:** Take a roll with you wherever you travel. It can be used to immobilize criminals, fix essential equipment, and make a cute skirt if you're in a bind.

7. **Chewing Gum:** Fresh breath should be a priority for everyone. However, gum also comes in handy if you want to jam a car's ignition or stick notes in secret places.

8. **First Aid Supplies:** If you can't understand how these might come in handy, please refer to the end of chapter 8.

Chapter 6

The Best-Laid Plans

Confidence is the force that runs the world. Mixed with a dose of charm, it has the power to produce everything from prom queens to presidents. You see, the sad truth of the matter is, most people are hopelessly gullible. Look us in the eye and spin a good story, and we'll be more than happy to believe you. You could tell the average person that the moon is made of cheese, and if you said it with a pleasant smile and the right amount of conviction, her only question would be "Cheddar or Swiss?" Tell five twelve-year-old girls that they can take control of an underground city and if you say it like there's not a doubt in your mind, they'll never ask how.

Leaning casually against the fireplace, Kiki Strike oozed confidence. With one arched eyebrow, she made it clear that there were no questions that couldn't be answered, no arguments she couldn't defeat. But while we may have had our reservations, Kiki had already won us over. It didn't matter if she were mad, malevolent, or simply mistaken. At that moment, all that mattered was that, of all the thousands of girls in Manhattan, she had chosen only five. She had seen things in us that no one else had ever bothered to look for.

DeeDee was the first to speak up.

"I thought you said we were the only ones who knew about the Shadow City. Has someone else found the tunnels?" she asked.

Kiki pulled a scrap of newspaper from her pocket and handed it to DeeDee.

"It's a story from the *New York Times*," she announced. "Six weeks ago, the police got word that a shipment of counterfeit designer handbags had made its way from Shanghai to Chinatown. But when the cops got to the address on Canal Street, they found an ordinary herb shop. They tore open boxes and dumped out every drawer, but they couldn't uncover anything hotter than chili powder.

"They were about to leave empty-handed, when one of the cops remembered a story he'd heard about secret rooms hidden beneath some of the older buildings in Chinatown. So he went back for another look, and sure enough, he found a trapdoor in the shop's basement. Below it was a hidden room filled with not-so-designer handbags. From the description in the article, the hidden room sounds a lot like the room Ananka and I discovered. If any of the smugglers had bothered to look a little harder, they might have found a second trapdoor." Like a character in a movie, Kiki paused for dramatic effect. "One that led to the Shadow City."

DeeDee passed the article to me. The picture that

accompanied the story showed a young policeman standing in front of a dingy building in Chinatown, dozens of
counterfeit handbags dangling from his arms. Nearby,
two handcuffed men leaned against a van with a cross-
eyed dragon painted on its side. I heard a faint gasp behind me. Oona was reading over my shoulder. Kiki's eyes
darted in our direction.

"Anyone you know?" she asked Oona.

Oona shook her head, but the expression on her face
said otherwise. She looked like she'd been zapped by an
electric cattle prod, and her breathing was fast and shallow. Kiki held Oona's eye for the briefest of moments before she continued with her explanation.

"As I was saying, Chinatown is full of secret rooms
and smugglers. Unless we take action, someday soon,
someone is going to find an entrance to the Shadow City.
My guess is that it won't be the police. And there's
no telling what could happen if smugglers take control of
the tunnels. But if we have a map, we can use it to keep
the Shadow City free of criminal scum. We'll block any
entrance that's in danger of being discovered."

"Just out of curiosity, why shouldn't we tell the police
about the Shadow City?" asked DeeDee.

"We could," said Kiki with a shrug. "But where's the
fun in that? Besides, if there *is* treasure down there, do
you think the police would let *us* keep it?"

That was all that the rest of us needed to hear.

Kiki spent an hour answering everyone's questions,
but as soon as the sun began to set, she called an abrupt
end to the gathering.

"When's the next meeting?" asked Luz.

"Monday evening," said Kiki. "I need to get a few supplies together. Ananka, do you mind if we meet at your house? We'll need to use your library."

"Sure," I muttered, overcome by a tsunami of dread. It may be difficult to believe, but I had never invited anyone to my home.

☆ ☆ ☆

I spent the following day tidying my apartment in time for the second meeting of the Irregulars. For as long as I could remember, the place had never received a proper cleaning. Aside from my father's aunt Beatrice, who had lost both her vision and sense of smell in an unfortunate deep-sea fishing accident, no one ever came to visit. As a result, we had no reason to pick up after ourselves, and our sloppiness had gotten out of control.

I devoted an exhausting hour to removing the splatter from a batch of spaghetti sauce that lent one wall of our kitchen the appearance of a gory crime scene. In the bathroom, I discovered a patch of mold growing on the tiles that had assumed the size, shape, and texture of a small wombat. My parents watched with growing amusement as I traveled from room to room with my bucket, rags, and bottle of hot pink household cleaner.

"I didn't know we could afford a maid, Bernard," I heard my mother say to my father as I passed by.

"You'd be surprised, Lillian, child labor is remarkably affordable these days," my father replied.

"I *knew* there was a reason we wanted a child," said my mother.

"Think of it. If we'd only had three or four more,

we could rent Ananka out to the neighbors," said my father.

"You're hilarious," I huffed, wishing my parents would take me seriously. "You know, I could use a little help. My friends will be here soon, and this place is revolting. Haven't you noticed the smell?"

"If there's a smell in here, it never seemed to bother you before, Ananka. We'd like to help, but your father's giving a lecture tonight, and we have to prepare. Besides, haven't you heard? The Fishbeins don't do windows."

"Or floors or bathtubs or dishes or laundry, I guess."

"Isn't she witty?" said my father. "She must get that from me."

I gritted my teeth and tried to stay calm.

"Well, if you aren't going to help, will you at least stay out of the way when my friends show up? We're working on a very important project."

"Interfere with your schoolwork?" said my mother with the same infuriating smile I'd seen her offer the mentally challenged. "We wouldn't dream of it, dear."

I grabbed my bucket and sponges and stomped off toward the bedrooms.

"Don't forget to iron the sheets," called my father. "I like mine with a smidgeon of starch."

☆   ☆   ☆

When the first of the Irregulars arrived, I was still a nervous wreck. Before I opened the door, I uttered a silent prayer to keep them from noticing the spiderwebs I had been unable to reach or the mouse that lived in the cupboard under the kitchen sink. I shouldn't have worried, however, because the only thing each of the girls did as she stepped through the door was stare at the towers of books that lined the walls.

Kiki and Oona arrived first. They both looked so effort-lessly glamorous that I felt dowdy in their presence. Oona wore a silk dress in a vibrant shade of scarlet and the sort of floppy hat that usually only looks good on movie stars. Kiki, dressed casually in black, almost seemed to glow. I was slightly relieved when DeeDee showed up in a yellow skirt covered with purple blotches, followed by Luz in a rather unflattering gray outfit that showcased a little pot-belly I hadn't noticed before. Betty was the last to knock at the door. Still out of disguise, but hiding behind another pair of enormous sunglasses, she was soon so busy scan-ning the titles of books along the hall that she didn't spot the spider that dangled inches above her head.

Once we were all seated in my decontaminated living room, Kiki retrieved a pile of index cards from her satchel.

"This is even more impressive than I expected," she said, her eyes still skipping across the spines of my parents' books. "Is there some kind of organizational system?"

"Tell me what we're looking for, and I'll tell you where to find it," I replied, feeling suddenly confident. Most people would have found our library hopelessly confus-ing. But having spent twelve lonely years searching for subjects to keep myself entertained, I knew where to find almost any title.

"Okay, then. Here are our assignments. Before we pay our first visit to the Shadow City, we need to do a little research." Kiki handed a card to Luz. "Luz, you're going to learn all you can about underground New York. You won't find any information on the Shadow City, but we need to know where all the subway tunnels, water pipes, and sewers are. I think we'll be too far down to run into any of them, but we should make sure. I don't want any surprises."

Next, Kiki addressed DeeDee.

"You're going to be studying the use of explosives in dangerous situations. We may come across barred doors or parts of the Shadow City that have been walled up. We'll need to find a way to get past any obstacles.

"And no surprises for you, Betty," said Kiki, handing out another card. "You're going to design our uniforms. They should be tough, comfortable, waterproof, and reasonably fashionable.

"Oona," Kiki continued, "we need to know everything we can about picking locks that date from the nineteenth century."

"Picking locks really isn't my thing," Oona complained. "Aren't there any documents that need forging?"

"There will be," Kiki snapped. "But this is what we need to know right now. I was planning to invite a lock-picking prodigy to join the Irregulars, but the girl I had in mind turned out to be extremely untrustworthy."

Oona snatched the card from Kiki's fingers. "Just my luck," she muttered under her breath.

"And here are a few locks to practice with," said Kiki. She pulled out a sack filled with ancient and rusty locks and tossed it to Oona. Then she turned to me and held out the last of the index cards.

"This subject should be self-explanatory," she said.

I looked down at the card and discovered a single word.

Rats, the card read. Instantly, my skin began to crawl.

"There's no doubt they're down there," Kiki said with a touch of sympathy. "We have to be prepared. You guys can go ahead and get started. I've already found what I need." I followed her eyes to a pile of books stacked on the fireplace mantel. For a moment, I thought she was mistaken. The only books in that area were on diamonds and precious stones—subjects that, as far as I knew, had nothing to do with the Shadow City. But rather than say anything, I assumed there was a reason for everything. I left Kiki alone in the living room and guided the other girls to the information they would need. Then I went off in search of the rat-related books, which were housed underneath the kitchen sink, in a rodent-proof box next to the home of our resident mouse.

☆ ☆ ☆

My mother had named the mouse Hubert Jr., in honor of her father, who had claimed to be the world's foremost expert on rodents. A man of great compassion, my grandfather had once planned to devote his talents to ridding the world of rodent-borne diseases. (As a teenager, Hubert Sr. had repeatedly tried to contract the bubonic plague in order to cure himself.) However, when he discovered that his medical training would require the sacrifice of scores of lab rats, he became so disgusted with the human race that he chose to focus on saving the rodents—not their tormentors.

Like most sane people, my parents and I did not share my grandfather's love of all things small and furry.

But out of respect for him, we had never attempted to harm Hubert Jr. He had been allowed to live a long and productive life (for a rodent) and in a way, he had become a part of the family.

Rats, however, are not mice. Hubert Jr. was old and feeble, but he was still somewhat charming. Rats, on the other hand, are filthy, flea-ridden creatures with teeth as sharp as hypodermic needles. In New York, they will always be the subjects of legend. Gangs of hungry rats are said to roam the city's subway tunnels, searching for unlucky transit workers who've become separated from their crews. And you don't have to live long in the city before you hear a story about a giant rat that climbed into a cradle with a sleeping baby and feasted on its fingers and toes.

If, on some future visit to New York, you happen to come across a solitary rat in an alleyway or on a subway platform, odds are it will scamper away. Don't be misled by this behavior. If you remember nothing else, remember this: New York rats aren't afraid of people. They consider us a delicacy.

I had only to skim a couple of the books I found under the kitchen sink before I realized the hopelessness of my task. As I read from a book entitled *The Devil's Army,* I began to doubt whether six girls could ever be a match for the rats of the Shadow City.

Nature's super-villains, the powers of the rat are humbling to behold. The beady-eyed beasts can scamper up the slickest surface, leap three feet in the air, and squeeze through openings the size of

*gumballs. With their sharp teeth and amazing pow-
ers of concentration, they are able to gnaw through
an astounding variety of materials. Entire buildings
have been known to collapse after rats have eaten
through the support beams.*

*Once they have invaded a home, rats are almost
impossible to expel. Traveling in groups called "mis-
chiefs," they outwit all but the most ingenious traps
and employ taste testers to identify poisoned food.
Many a frustrated apartment dweller has resorted to
flinging them out of a window, only to discover that
rats can survive falls from as high as six stories.*

*Mankind is in danger of losing our war against
rats. To avoid defeat, we must stop underestimating
the cunning of our enemy. We should avoid thinking of them as lowly rodents, and realize that they
are more intelligent than we have ever imagined.
Recent university studies, for example, have shown
that rats can count—though they rarely make it past
the number five. What other secret skills might they
be hiding?*

As I shut *The Devil's Army,* I noticed an old spiral
notebook tucked between *The Scourge of Europe* and *Rat
Fancier.* In the corner was my grandfather's name, Hubert Snodgrass. I thumbed through the notebook's brittle,
yellowing pages. The first, rather dull section was devoted
to sketches of rat ears in various shapes and sizes. When
I flipped to the second section, however, I found an intri-
cate drawing of a device that resembled a battery-powered

kazoo. The title, written in a fancy script, read, *Invention #466. The Reverse Pied Piper.*

I knew I had found what I needed. My eyes scanned the smaller print at the bottom of the page. *An effective rodent-removal device that does not cause injury or death.* Reading on, I learned that my grandfather, in the course of his studies, had discovered that rats could be driven to distraction by sounds that the human ear can't even detect. He developed the Reverse Pied Piper, a miniature megaphone of sorts, which could emit a blast of sound that would have no effect on a human being, but would cause a rat to run as far as possible in the opposite direction. They would abandon their nests—even leave their food and helpless offspring behind—just to escape from the noise. Amazingly, laboratory tests had proven that just the memory of the sound could keep rats at a distance.

Apparently, my grandfather had considered even this too cruel, and his notes showed that he had abandoned the project. Fortunately for the Irregulars, I was no rat-lover. Once I had studied my grandfather's drawings, I decided to ask Luz if she could make a Reverse Pied Piper. I said a quiet good-bye to Hubert Jr. and left to join the rest of the Irregulars.

On my way to the living room, I bumped into my mother and father, who were leaving for their lecture.

"We were just chatting with your little blond friend," my mother said, adjusting her hair and beaming down at me. "You're lucky to have such an intelligent study partner. I hope this means your grades will be improving? You're too smart to keep getting C's."

Hope away, I thought. "You promised you wouldn't interfere with my schoolwork," I said.

"I beg your pardon, my dear, but we were passing through the living room when your friend asked your mother a question," my father scolded.

I turned to my mother in surprise. "Kiki asked you a question?"

"Yes, something about the long-term effects of poisoning. I showed her a couple of books that I thought might help. She said you two were writing a paper about that unfortunate foreign politician who was poisoned by his rivals. It sounded very exciting. By the way, where is your friend from? She has such a charming accent."

"Accent?" I asked. "Kiki doesn't have an accent."

"Oh, dear," said my mother. "You should try to be a little more observant, Ananka. And make sure to give your friend something to eat. She looks a little malnourished to me."

✦   ✦   ✦

It had been hours since the meeting had kicked off, and slowly the girls began to trickle back into the living room. Betty was first, carrying a stack of books and an oversized pad of drawing paper. Oona emerged next with the sack of locks and two wire hangers tucked under her arm. She plopped herself down on the sofa, pulled an emery board from her handbag, and proceeded to file her nails, which were broken and jagged. DeeDee and Luz chose to sit in a shadowy alcove at the back of the room. Every few minutes, they would lean toward each other and exchange a barrage of angry whispers.

"Okay, let's see what you've got," said Kiki. "Betty, you're up. Show us your ideas for uniforms."

Betty's hands and forearms were smeared with charcoal. She flipped to a page in her artist's pad and held it up for the group to see.

"Sorry," Betty whispered. "I know it's not very good, but maybe you could use your imaginations."

"How about that? You really *are* as crazy as you look!" cried Oona in mock astonishment as she studied a marvelously lifelike drawing of Kiki wearing a black jumpsuit. "That's amazing. I've never seen anything like it before."

Betty blushed.

"It's probably not what you were expecting. But I did consider the standard catsuit. You know, like the one Cat Woman wears. It's attractive, but it's really not that practical. My design has a looser fit so we can wear our own clothes underneath, and the seams are made of waterproof Velcro, so the suit can be pulled on or taken off in a couple of seconds."

"Good thinking," said Kiki, nodding with approval. Betty managed a nervous smile.

"I got the idea for the fabric from this book on military textiles." She opened the book to an image of a handsome Marine filling a large sack with grenades. "See the duffel bag he's carrying? You can buy them in the Army and Navy store near my house. They're made of a material that repels water, resists flames, and can't be punctured. I once overheard the man in the store saying it's used to make bulletproof vests. But the company that designed the fabric found a way to manufacture it cheaply, so now they make other things out of it, too. I'm pretty sure it's tough enough to protect us from whatever's down there." She raised her eyes and looked cautiously around the room, but she quickly lost her nerve and returned her gaze to the pile of books.

"Umm . . . just a few more things. First, we're all going to need boots. Since we don't know what's down there, I think it's safest to go with knee-high boots, but we'll also want something with good traction. So I thought these might work." She pulled a fly-fishing catalog out of the pile. I couldn't imagine where she might have found it. No one in my family had ever been within a hundred miles of a crisp mountain stream. Betty held up a picture of a pair of tall black boots. "They've got little spikes on the bottom, so you can anchor yourself against the current. And they come in boys' sizes, of course, not girls', but I think we can make do." She turned a page in the drawing pad and held up a very flattering sketch of me wearing the tall black boots.

"They'll be good for defensive purposes as well," noted Luz. "Give somebody a good kick with one of those, and he'll be feeling it for weeks."

"I hadn't thought of that," said Betty. "Do you think we'll be kicking people?" she asked Kiki.

"Don't worry. We'll let Luz do all the kicking," said Kiki. "Anything else?"

Betty struggled to recapture her train of thought. "Oh, right. The hard hats. I think a spin on the classic miner's hat, with a flashlight in front, should work nicely. I'll have to find small ones and adapt them to the size of our heads. It shouldn't be too difficult."

"I also thought it would be a good idea for the Irregulars to have a logo. You know, to give the outfits a little flare." She flipped a page and revealed a drawing of a small golden *i* she had designed to look like a girl in motion.

"Fantastic," said Kiki as the girls broke into a round of applause. "Great job, Betty. Oona?"

Oona stepped forward with the bag of locks and the two hangers, the ends of which had been bent into bizarre shapes.

"These old locks are a cinch," she boasted. "If I had been around a hundred years ago, I could have made a killing as a thief. The only problem was that I tried to pick them with a bobby pin like you always see in the movies, and I ended up breaking all of my nails. Then I found these wire hangers." She picked up a lock and inserted a wire hanger. "You can twist the wires into any shape you need. All you've got to do is listen closely and make sure all the tumblers are compressed." She flicked her wrist, and the lock sprang open.

"Here, Fishbein. You try." She closed the lock and tossed it to me. "I've already shaped the wire to fit that style of lock, so it won't be too hard. Just put your ear as close as you can, and listen for three little clicks." I turned the wire carefully. One by one, three little clicks sounded and the lock opened again.

"According to the books, there were only a few styles

of lock in use back then," said Oona. "I think we should make six small kits that will have wires shaped to fit each kind of lock. That way, any of us can do the honors, and I won't always have to be the one ruining my manicure."

"Great," said Kiki as Oona sat down and resumed filing her nails. "Ananka, are you ready to tell us about rats?"

"There are rats in the Shadow City?" squealed DeeDee.

"Don't wet your pants, DeeDee," said Kiki. "Rats are everywhere in New York. There's probably a nest in this building somewhere."

The other girls squirmed.

"It's okay, I think I've found something that will make us all feel better," I told them. "I was going through some of my grandfather's old papers, and it turns out he invented a device that should get rid of the rats in the Shadow City."

"Your grandfather was an inventor?" asked Luz.

"He was a lot of things, including a little strange. He probably liked rats more than people, but he understood that the rest of us prefer to stick with our own species. So he invented something he called 'The Reverse Pied Piper.'" I explained the way the device worked, repelling rats without doing them any harm.

"That's perfect," said Kiki. "The last thing we need is to end up wading through a bunch of dead rats. Luz, do you think you could make a couple of these things?"

"Sure," replied Luz as she studied a drawing of the Reverse Pied Piper. "I can have a working model in a couple of weeks."

"Excellent. We're making good progress," Kiki said. "DeeDee, what about you?"

I saw Luz look up and catch DeeDee's eye.

"It's complicated," replied DeeDee. "I mean, the explosives part is pretty easy. Just a simple mixture of a few household chemicals would be enough to blow a hole in a wall without taking the whole tunnel down. But there's one little problem."

"It's hardly a *little* problem," said Luz, taking over. "The Shadow City isn't the only thing under New York. It's a big mess down there. There are all sorts of wires—telephone, cable, you name it. I've even heard about abandoned underground highways and forgotten subway stations. But the real problems are the mains. They're huge pipes filled with water or highly explosive natural gas. There's no way to tell exactly where they are unless we have a map. We could use DeeDee's explosives to blow a hole in a wall, but if we were anywhere near a gas main, we could destroy half the city."

"Can't we find a map of all the mains?" I asked.

"No," said Luz with an air of finality.

"Yes, we can," DeeDee jumped in.

Luz glared at her. "Maps like that are guarded like the Declaration of Independence. And anyway, there's only one place we'd be sure to find one."

"Where?" asked Kiki.

"The gas company," said DeeDee.

"You mean Con Edison?" I cut in. "They're not going to let us have something like that."

The second I spoke, I noticed Betty begin feverishly drawing on her pad.

"Of course they won't," Luz agreed.

"We'd have to break in," said DeeDee, surprising

everyone but Luz. I had pegged DeeDee for the law-abiding type.

"We are *not* breaking into Con Edison," said Luz firmly.

"Hold on a second," said Kiki. "Oona, do you think you could hack into their computer system?"

"No," Oona admitted. "Not from the outside. I've tried, believe me. But it might be easier if I were inside their building."

"Have you ever seen the main Con Edison building? It's a fortress," said Luz.

"It has a door, doesn't it?" I asked.

"Yeah, but the security's incredible. It has to be. Don't you know what could happen if a terrorist got his hands on those maps?"

"Security passes are my specialty," said Oona dismissively.

"Okay, genius, but do you think they'll let a bunch of little girls with security passes through?" snapped Luz.

"I have an idea," said Betty, who had been silently finishing her drawing as the rest of us fought. The room grew quiet and we all looked at Betty, who turned the color of a ripe pomegranate. She flipped her pad around to face us. On the page were elderly versions of Luz and Oona, both dressed in cleaning ladies' uniforms.

"I don't look like that!" cried Oona angrily, glaring at a wrinkled version of her twelve-year-old face.

"I c-could make you," Betty stammered.

"What are you trying to say?" Oona threatened.

"A disguise . . . ," Betty tried to explain.

"Brilliant," said Kiki, ignoring Oona and beaming at Betty. "Absolutely brilliant."

"No one would ever question you if you were disguised as little old ladies," said DeeDee with admiration. For once, even Luz couldn't argue.

⭐ ⭐ ⭐

Luz sulked for the rest of the evening. Clearly, she wasn't accustomed to being wrong. As the rest of us plotted, she sat at the end of the sofa, her feet tucked beneath her, her right hand yanking her ponytail tighter and tighter. Even without her help, we had a plan in short order. Oona would make security passes and hack into the Con Edison computer system from the inside. Betty would provide the disguises. There was just one problem. Luz would have to go along. She was the only one who knew exactly what to look for.

"Forget it. There's no way I'm going," Luz insisted.

"You have to go," Oona urged, looking a bit worried. "I can't do it by myself."

"We'll get caught."

"Are you worried about your probation?" asked Kiki.

"You're on probation?" DeeDee asked.

Luz turned on her ferociously. "You don't get it, do you, rich girl? Not all of us are lucky enough to have tons of money and our own private laboratories. Some of us have to make it on our own."

DeeDee sat back in stunned silence. I tried to give her a reassuring look, but she was busy staring at the wall in front of her, looking like she might cry.

"What did you do, Lopez? Steal something?" asked Oona.

"No, I didn't *steal* anything," said Luz. "I was walking

down the street one day, and I saw a television sitting on the curb. I thought I could make something out of it. So I took it. I thought it was garbage. I didn't know someone had left it on the sidewalk for a minute while they were moving into an apartment."

"You got probation for *that*?" I scoffed.

"Yeah, and if I get caught doing anything else, they'll ship my butt off to jail."

"I'll go to Con Edison instead," offered DeeDee quietly, but Luz ignored her.

"Luz, we can't do this without you," said Kiki.

"No way. I can't go to jail. And I don't have the money to pay some fancy lawyer to get me out of trouble," said Luz, sending another furious glance in DeeDee's direction.

"When you joined the Irregulars, you knew there would be risks involved," Kiki told her. "There's no point in exploring the Shadow City unless we have the equipment we need. And if what you've said is true, we might not get very far without a map of the mains. But, Luz, if we're able to map the tunnels, everything down there will belong to us. There's a chance we could all walk out rich. If you do this one thing for the Irregulars, you may never have to go through other people's garbage again."

The rest of us waited for Luz's response.

"My mother's strict. She'll never let me out of the house at night," she announced.

"Tell her there's a slumber party at my house," said Kiki. "Verushka will cover for us."

"Okay," Luz reluctantly agreed. "But if we need to break any more laws, don't expect me to do all the dirty work."

We were all so relieved that Luz had decided to go along with the plan that none of us realized that we had skipped Kiki Strike's presentation.

🔲   🔲   🔲

Two weeks later, Kiki Strike and I watched from a diner across the street from the gas company as Luz and Oona, in full disguise, mingled with the Con Edison night staff on their way into the building. I held my breath as the girls approached the security desk, and let out a sigh of relief as they sailed past without attracting any notice.

Not that Luz or Oona would have been in danger had anyone given them a good once-over. In the course of three hours, Betty had aged them fifty years and supplied both with cleaning ladies' uniforms she had sewn herself. When we left for the gas company, Betty stayed behind in her apartment, cleaning up before her parents came home from work. DeeDee claimed to have schoolwork to finish, but I suspected that her feelings were still hurt by Luz's outburst. Kiki had come along to make sure everything went as planned, and I had joined her only because I was too nervous to stay at home. I knew Oona would be fine, but I felt sorry for Luz, who had prepared for the operation as if she were headed for the guillotine.

Kiki and I waited at the diner for three long hours until Luz and Oona emerged with a half-dozen cleaning ladies, all taking a coffee break and chatting amongst themselves. When the coast was clear, Luz and Oona slipped away from the others and made their way to the diner. Earlier in the evening, I had hidden a bag of clothing and face soap in a trash can in the diner's bathroom.

There, Luz and Oona removed their disguises and washed the makeup from their faces. When they had finished, they met Kiki and me on the street.

Once we were a safe distance from Con Edison, Kiki broke the silence.

"Did everything go as planned?" she asked.

"Not exactly," said Oona.

"We almost got caught," Luz explained. "Another cleaning lady came in just as we were downloading the map."

"What did you do?" I asked.

"It was brilliant," said Oona, and Luz smiled proudly. "Luz told her we'd spilled some cleaning fluid on the keyboard and that we turned the computer on to make sure it was still working."

"She bought it?" asked Kiki.

"Yeah," said Oona. "She said we were lucky. A maid got fired for accidentally destroying a computer last week."

"So you found a map of the mains?" I asked.

"Yeah. It's on a CD," replied Luz. "We should have everything we need. In fact . . ."

"What?"

"We hit the jackpot." Luz paused before explaining.

"Do I look psychic to you? Do you expect me to *guess* what you found?" huffed Kiki.

"Go ahead and try," Luz laughed. "You wouldn't stand a chance. When Oona and I were going through the computer files, we found something. Something amazing. It's called the nice map."

"The nice map?" I asked. "What's so nice about it?"

"No, that's just how it's pronounced," said Luz. "It's really N-Y-C-M-A-P. It stands for New York City Map. It's a map of Manhattan, but in three layers. The bottom layer shows everything belowground. It has all the gas pipes and water mains. It even shows the location of all the sewers, electrical lines, and subway tunnels. The only thing it doesn't have on it is the Shadow City. My guess is no one's ever discovered the tunnels because they're too far underground. In the part of town where you found the Shadow City, even the subway lines aren't more than forty feet below the street.

"But that was just the layer of the NYCMap we could download. There were two other layers of the map that we couldn't get to. We could only read the descriptions. Supposedly, the second layer of the NYCMap shows everything at street level—that means every fire hydrant, every manhole, every park bench, and every tree. And the third level of the map shows everything above the ground, including the floor plans of every building in the city. Every room in every building in New York City is on it."

"So what? As long as it doesn't show the Shadow City, who cares?" I asked.

"*We* care. There's never been a map like this before. If you had all three layers, you could do just about anything. You could place a small bomb in just the right spot and blow up an entire city block. You could even plan a robbery without ever casing the building."

"What stopped you from downloading the other two layers?" Kiki asked Oona.

"Whoever made the NYCMap won't let Con Edison

have access to all the layers," she replied. "It's *that* dangerous. They're keeping it secret for a reason."

"It's the sort of map that terrorists dream about," added Luz.

"So how can we get the whole thing?" asked Kiki.

"It's impossible," said Oona. "Don't you think I'd have already tried?"

"Nothing's impossible," replied Kiki.

"Why do you want it?" I asked. It sounded like the sort of thing that should be left under lock and key.

"You never know when you might need a good map," Kiki said with an evil grin.

❧   ❧   ❧

Two months after the Con Edison break-in and a week before summer vacation began, the Irregulars were almost ready for the Shadow City. We met one last time to try on the jumpsuits Betty had designed. They were so flattering that Oona kept hers on for over an hour. When she saw me in mine, she nodded with approval.

"You could be kind of cute if you tried a bit harder," she told me. I took a look in the full-length mirror in Betty's bedroom and wondered where she thought I should start.

After our fitting, Luz and I spent the afternoon testing two Reverse Pied Pipers she had crafted from spare parts. (I didn't dare ask where she had gotten them.) For the first time since I'd met her, she seemed genuinely happy as we traveled from alley to alley looking for rats to scare. The first test took place behind a seedy restaurant on the Lower East Side, a rat Shangri-la with overflowing garbage cans and a faint stench of sewage.

Luz put one of the Pipers up to her lips and gave a quick puff. We heard nothing, and for an uncomfortable second, it seemed as if the device had failed. Suddenly, dozens of frantic rats appeared out of nowhere, scurrying away from us as fast as their legs could carry them. A deliveryman happened to step out the back door of the restaurant and into the rat-filled alley. When he felt the swarm of rats weaving between his feet and trying to climb his legs, he issued a shrill scream and performed a dance not native to any country. Luz and I ran out of the alley and down the street, laughing so hard, we nearly threw up.

Within a week, each of the Irregulars had her own Reverse Pied Piper, uniform, and set of lock-picking wires enclosed in a pretty silk case. DeeDee had crafted several small but effective packets of explosives, and Kiki had used the CD that Luz and Oona had stolen from Con Edison to make a waterproof booklet out of the NYCMap.

We had all the supplies we needed, but there was one last obstacle to overcome. Our explorations were to take place under the cover of night. For most of us, this didn't pose a problem. Kiki was an orphan, and none of us knew if Oona had a family or not. Betty's parents were costume designers who worked nights at the Metropolitan Opera and rarely made it home before seven in the morning. My mother and father could sleep through a hurricane, which meant I'd be able to leave my apartment through the fire escape outside my bedroom window without fear of waking them. DeeDee made a deal with her beloved housekeeper to keep her parents away from her room at night. But Luz's overprotective mother was going to be a problem.

Fortunately, Luz's mother had insisted that Luz find a summer job, so we invented one for her. Posing as Luna Actias, a renowned entomologist, Verushka placed an ad in the paper, looking for a young person with a keen scientific mind to help her study the nocturnal behavior of moths. The pay was good, and the job suitably respectable, so after a two-hour meeting with the very persuasive Luna Actias, Luz's mother reluctantly allowed her daughter to work the night shift.

With Luz finally free to roam the city, we chose the first day of summer break to enter the Shadow City. We truly believed we had thought of everything. Little did we know that exploring the Shadow City was like being on the first expedition to Mars. We did what we could to make ourselves feel better, but there was no way to prepare for what we would find.

HOW TO BE A MASTER OF DISGUISE

Most people think that a master of disguise needs a vast collection of wigs, masks, false teeth, and makeup. If you have the time, money, and talent to acquire such a collection, I won't counsel you against it. However, the essential tools of a master of disguise are already in most people's closets. Just follow these simple guidelines, and you may find there's no need to waste your money on fake noses or prosthetic chins.

Look as Bland as You Can
The most common mistake when donning a disguise is to make yourself appear too conspicuous. Bright red lipstick, platinum wigs, and tacky sunglasses are all no-no's unless you're trying to blend in at a Las Vegas

casino. The last thing a true master of disguise wants to do is turn people's heads.

Camouflage Your Most Distinctive Features

We all have certain features that make us unique. Perhaps you have gorgeous brown eyes, curly hair, rosy cheeks, and a huge nose. If you're going incognito, you'll want to start by disguising these traits. A clunky, unattractive pair of nonprescription glasses can divert attention from both your eyes and nose, and some drab foundation makeup can hide your beautiful complexion. Take a few minutes to straighten your hair, and you may not recognize yourself!

Change the Shape of Your Body

Although your face is what people will remember most clearly, they can also identify you by the shape of your body. If you're curvy, choose clothing that doesn't emphasize the fact. If you're skinny, a little extra padding here and there can transform you into a whole new person. (Although avoid giving yourself an ample bosom, or you run the risk of breaking rule #1.) You can also use shoes to change your height. Opt for platforms if you're short, flats if you're tall.

Don't Wear Your Own Clothing

People will recognize that pretty blue sweater you wear all the time before they even have a chance to see your face. Leave it at home and spend a few dollars at your local Goodwill store. Choose clothing that you wouldn't ordinarily wear. Stay away from clothes that are brightly colored or clearly belong to your grandmother.

Take Advantage of a Uniform

Your friendly neighborhood thrift store should be packed to the rafters with discarded uniforms of all varieties. Choose wisely, and you may have the perfect disguise. Uniforms by nature are meant to hide one's individuality. (Think about it. A man in a brown uniform comes to your door. Do you say, "There's a guy with blond hair, green eyes, and a pug nose outside" or "Hey, it's the UPS man"?)

Choose a uniform that's appropriate to your age and setting. If you're young, a nurse's uniform may look a bit strange, but a school uniform could work nicely.

A Few More Tricks and Suggestions
Now that you know the basic rules, here are a few simple suggestions:

- Avoid letting people look you in the eyes. If they do, you're more likely to be remembered.
- Try wearing multiple layers of clothing. Shed a layer every now and then so your disguise will remain fresh. Carry a large handbag, and use it to carry the clothing you've removed.
- Don't dye your hair—you'll just destroy it. Instead, experiment with different hairstyles or wigs.
- Place a couple of cotton balls in either cheek. You'll look puffy and your face will have a different shape. A piece of cardboard hidden under your tongue can change the sound of your voice.

Chapter 7

Curiouser and Curiouser

The sun had only just set by the time Kiki Strike turned the key to the gates of the Marble Cemetery, but once we were inside, it might as well have been midnight. The moon was missing from the sky, and our only light came from the buildings beyond the cemetery walls. We could see the faint outlines of trees and the glow of the marble slabs set into the grass, but we could barely see one another. In our black uniforms, we blended into the shadows, all but invisible to human eyes.

"Here." Kiki's voice cut through the silence. She had located the right slab. Guided by her white hair, which shone like a beacon in the darkness, we gathered around her. Silently, six crowbars dug beneath the edge of the slab. "Now," ordered Kiki. We each pulled back on our crowbars, and the slab rose above the ground. A foul, musty odor issued from the hole, and I heard one of the girls gagging.

"I didn't know it was going to smell like that," someone whispered.

"What do you expect? It's a grave. The people who live here don't care what it smells like," someone else quipped.

"Shh," said Kiki. "It's time. I'll go first."

She turned on a flashlight and illuminated a narrow stairway that led into the ground. The Irregulars followed single file behind her down the stairs. I had been assigned the job of making the map of the Shadow City, so I kept an eye on my glow-in-the-dark compass, and used a pedometer to measure the distance we traveled. At the bottom of the stairs, we found ourselves in a cramped marble corridor. Once we were safely out of view, we flipped the switches on our miner's hats. The vault was suddenly as bright as day, and the unflattering light hollowed our eyes and washed out our skin, making us appear pale and cadaverlike. Only Kiki's naturally bloodless complexion remained unchanged.

"The entrance to the Shadow City should be at the end of the hall," Kiki announced, leading the way. The spikes on the bottoms of our fly-fishing boots clicked softly against the marble floor. As we walked, we passed a dozen small rooms, each furnished with a sarcophagus and decorated with piles of long-dead flowers. The graves hadn't been visited for more than a century, and it seemed to me that the dead preferred their own company. We were trespassing on sacred territory—going where we weren't wanted and didn't belong. I couldn't help but find it thrilling . . . at first.

Then, as I paused in front of one of the rooms to

check my compass and make a quick sketch, I thought I sensed movement. I aimed my light into the darkness and saw two sets of wild and beady eyes peeking through a cemetery wreath. They appraised us for a moment before they vanished from sight. But as the Irregulars marched toward the empty tomb of Augustus Quackenbush, I knew we were still being watched. Something was hiding amongst the graves.

At the end of the hall, we reached a chamber identical to all the others, save for the absence of flowers and wreaths. The Irregulars crowded inside.

"Well, hello, Augustus," said Oona, slapping the side of the coffin and speaking a bit too loudly. Her voice echoed throughout the vault. Kiki put a finger to her lips.

"Where's the tunnel?" Betty whispered.

"In there, I think." Kiki pointed at the marble coffin, which was covered with delicately carved images. When I bent to examine the carvings, I saw that they told the story of Theseus and the Minotaur. A fearsome monster—half human, half bull—lay in wait for a young man who was making his way through a labyrinth. I felt goose bumps sprouting up and down my arms.

DeeDee regarded the coffin nervously. "Are you absolutely sure there's no one in there?"

"I guess we'll find out, won't we?" said Kiki. "Maybe we should make you have the first look." It was then that I began to wonder if our leader had a bit of a mean streak.

Together, we pried the heavy lid off Augustus Quackenbush's sarcophagus. Peering over the side, we saw that the coffin was not only empty, it had no bottom. A ladder descended into the darkness.

"Wow," whispered Betty.

"Don't be so easily impressed," Kiki scolded her. "You haven't seen anything."

"How far down are we going?" asked Oona.

"At least fifty more feet," I told her.

One by one, each of the girls climbed down the ladder, the lights on their miner's hats flickering and fading as they neared the bottom. At last we arrived in a crude tunnel dug out of the earth. Two bolts of cloth, remnants of Augustus Quackenbush's misadventures, leaned against one wall. As we waited for Luz to reach the bottom, Betty brushed the dirt from one, revealing a swatch of bright red silk.

"This is nice stuff," she said, taking off her glove to caress the fabric. "Did you know this red dye is made from crushed beetles?"

None of the other girls paid her any attention. They were all gazing in wonder at the tunnel before them.

"Amazing, isn't it?" said Kiki. "And this isn't even the Shadow City."

"It's not?" asked Luz as she jumped off the ladder. Kiki and I laughed.

"Just wait," Kiki told her. "You're in for quite a treat."

We followed Augustus Quackenbush's tunnel down-hill, deeper and deeper into the earth. Tree roots poked their withered tentacles through the ceiling, and sections of the walls had crumbled away.

"This doesn't seem very safe," said DeeDee after a tree root knocked her hat to the ground.

"Maybe not, but if you're *that* clumsy, I'm surprised your parents let you cross the street by yourself," said Kiki.

"Good point," admitted DeeDee as she stooped to retrieve her hat.

We traveled for several minutes through the treacherous tunnel until we reached a wooden door.

"This is it," said Kiki. My hands were shaking with excitement, and I found myself reaching out to turn the knob. The door wouldn't budge, and it was only then that I noticed four different locks lined up along its side.

"Allow me, ladies," said Oona, reaching into her pocket and fishing out a lock-picking packet.

"What about your precious nails?" Luz teased.

"I'd say this is worth the price of a manicure," Oona replied, kneeling in front of the locks. As she worked, we heard a peculiar whooshing. It was as if a powerful wind were converging on us from every direction, though the atmosphere remained still and stale. We looked about in bewilderment. The noise abruptly stopped the moment Oona sprang the last lock.

"Since I opened the door, I get to be the first inside," insisted Oona, standing and twisting the doorknob. She stepped through the door and disappeared into the Shadow City.

Not a second later, a scream of pure terror bounced off the walls. It wasn't the reaction any of us had expected. We hurried to Oona's aid only to see both sides of the tunnel rushing toward us. Suddenly everything was quiet. Thousands upon thousands of enormous rats stood before us, all perched on their hind legs like a miniature army. They had known we were coming, and I could have sworn I saw one licking its lips.

We shared one loud scream before the rats charged, clambering up our legs and chewing on our uniforms. If it hadn't been for Betty's wise choice of fabrics, I'm sure we would have been consumed in seconds.

"Stay still," ordered Kiki, ignoring the large rat that had climbed on top of her head. She withdrew her Reverse Pied Piper and held it to her lips. As she blew into it, the army of rats froze and issued an ear-shattering shriek. The fat one nibbling at Kiki's hat tumbled to the ground and raced to join his comrades, who were stampeding away from the noise like a herd of monstrous lemmings.

Within seconds, the tunnel was practically rat-free. Only a handful of scruffy beasts remained. Somehow, the Reverse Pied Piper hadn't bothered them at all. A dozen beady eyes glared up at us, as if the last six survivors were willing to fight to the death. But when Kiki kicked a small rock in their direction, their courage deserted them. The last of the rodents fled the tunnel.

Once they were gone, we straightened our hair and checked ourselves for bites. None of us had been seriously harmed, though Luz's cheek bore a nasty scratch.

"That worked rather well," said a pleased and perfectly composed Kiki. She stretched her arms wide, like a tour guide at the Grand Canyon. "Welcome to the Shadow City."

For the first time, we were able to take a good look at our surroundings. Unlike the tunnel I had found, this section of the Shadow City was stone-lined and arched, resembling illustrations I had seen of ancient Roman sewers. From where I stood, I spied three closed doors, along with the rat-picked skeleton of a small dog. Water dripped from between the stones and bled down the sides of the walls. The air was cool and damp.

"Where should we start?" I wondered out loud. Both ends of the tunnel stretched as far as I could see. Suddenly struck by the size of the Shadow City, I realized that mapping it would be no simple task.

"How about at the beginning?" Kiki marched over to the nearest door. She twisted the handle and found it unlocked. We followed as she hopped up a short set of stairs and into a room the size of a school auditorium. The floor was lined with rough wooden planks that would have been at home in any barn, but the walls were painted a beautiful blue. The ceiling, where it hadn't collapsed and fallen to the ground, was decorated with scenes of women dancing, and a dusty chandelier dangled above our heads. In one corner of the room sat a bar, and wooden tables circled a dance floor. A woman's satin shoe lay in the center of the floor as if waiting for its owner to return to retrieve it.

"Where *are* we?" asked DeeDee.

"I think it's a dance hall." I consulted my compass and the map I had been sketching since we first entered the vault in the Marble Cemetery. "We're under Broadway."

"A dance hall?" Luz asked.

"They were places where people could go to drink and party."

"But why would anyone build a *dance hall* seventy feet underground?" Oona wondered.

"Why not?" Kiki answered. "At least there weren't any neighbors around to complain about the noise."

Like delinquents set loose in a deserted amusement park, the Irregulars fanned out in every direction to explore the ballroom. Luz and Oona performed a mad jig around the forgotten shoe, the beams of light from their hats casting crazy spotlights about the room. DeeDee was opening bottles behind the bar, smelling their contents and taking samples for later study, while Betty examined the costumes of the women on the ceiling. Only Kiki seemed unimpressed.

"This is a dead end," she noted with disappointment as we stood watching the others.

"No exits to above," I agreed. "But it's still pretty amazing."

"It's not what we came here to find," she said. "Let's go," she called out to the others.

The Irregulars began to slowly regroup, but DeeDee was hesitant to leave.

"Just a few more minutes?" she pleaded, holding up a miniature test tube that she had filled with a fuchsia liquid. "There's some interesting stuff in these bottles."

"We're not down here on a field trip, DeeDee," Kiki said hotly. "If you want to play scientist once we've finished making our map, go right ahead. But in case you've forgotten, we're here to find all the entrances and take control of the Shadow City. Now, what do you say we go do it?"

Without further discussion, Kiki stomped out of the room. The rest of us followed silently as she headed down a tunnel that my compass informed me snaked to the south.

✦ ✦ ✦

Though I tried not to show it, I dreaded leaving the cheerful dance hall. Even with the rats vanquished, I hadn't been able to shake the sensation that we were not alone. The feeling slithered over my skin and bored itself into my brain. Every time I paused to plot our path on the map, I could feel the darkness trailing close behind me. Somehow I knew that if I spun around, I would catch a glimpse of the people who had spent their lives in the gloom. In my imagination, I could see the spotlight of my miner's hat capturing a set of hardened eyes, a featureless face, or the twirl of a ghostly dress. I tried not to make too much of the images that flashed through my mind, but there was one thing I knew for certain. At least some of the people who had called the Shadow City home had never left. They were still down there, waiting for someone to stop by for a visit.

My excitement at exploring the Shadow City had turned to fear. Whenever Kiki rounded a corner or stepped through a door, I held my breath. And every time we opened a door to find nothing but a brick wall or packed earth, I sighed with relief. But while we found many dead ends, there were far more doors that swung open and beckoned us into the darkness they had long guarded. As I nervously stepped out of the tunnel and into one of the Shadow City's gloomy chambers, I saw Kiki watching me out of the corner of her eye. Her nose twitched, and I wondered if she could smell my terror.

Within four hours, we had discovered three saloons, a gambling parlor, a room crammed with barrels of gunpowder, and an elegant boudoir furnished with a wardrobe packed with delicately ruffled dresses tailored to fit a monstrously large woman. In the back of the wardrobe, hidden behind all the lace and tulle, was an escape tunnel that circled back to another part of the city. What function that particular chamber had served was anyone's guess, but there seemed to be at least one room devoted to every kind of mischief. With the exception of sunlight, everything a hard-living villain might have needed or desired could be found in the Shadow City. It was a carnival for criminals.

Hidden in the darkness seventy feet below the surface, the people of the Shadow City must have believed that their fun would never end. But before the night was over, the Irregulars would discover the terrible price they had paid for their pleasure.

☆ ☆ ☆

In the early-morning hours, Betty called our attention to a door that was padlocked from the outside and marked with a hastily painted red cross. Above the cross, the word MERCY had been scrawled in an unsteady hand. As usual, Oona insisted on being the first inside. She picked the lock and aimed her light into the room.

"I think I know what happened to the people who used to hang out down here," she said, her voice lacking any of its usual sarcasm.

The room was crammed with so many teetering bunk beds that it resembled a giant set of monkey bars. To our horror, none of the beds were empty. Each held at least one skeleton, some of them three or more. Leg bones dangled between wooden slats. A long blond braid, miraculously preserved, clung to the skull of a woman dressed in the bright red costume of a dance hall girl. Her fleshless arm reached out to us.

"What happened?" I heard someone ask.

"They were locked inside to die," I muttered to myself.

"Someone murdered them?" whispered Betty.

"No, I don't think so. Not so many at once. They must have died from a plague. I think they were locked in this room so they couldn't spread the disease."

Luz made a dash for the exit.

"Don't worry," DeeDee assured her. "There's no danger now. Whatever killed them would have died with them."

"There was a plague in New York?" asked Oona.

"Sure, lots of them," I replied. "Cholera, smallpox, yellow fever. You hardly hear about them anymore, but they killed thousands of people in New York. All of the parks downtown are crammed with bodies. So many people died, there wasn't anywhere else to bury them. The whole city is one big graveyard."

"So this is why the Shadow City was deserted," Kiki said thoughtfully.

"Anyone who escaped would have never come back," I said. "But it looks like a lot of them never made it out."

We closed the door and tried to erase the horrible image from our memories. But no matter how desperately we wanted to forget, the Shadow City wouldn't allow it. Before our first adventure in the tunnels came to its unexpected and unfortunate end, we came across dozens of doors with the same red cross. We chose not to open them, but instead passed silently by. There was no point in disturbing the dead to check for exits. After all, the rooms had been chosen because there was no way out.

☆　☆　☆

The discovery of the plague that had swept through the Shadow City left us all feeling homesick for the world above. Though Kiki kept pushing us forward, none of us had much heart left for adventure. Fortunately, we had to summon the courage to face only one more locked door that first night. We found it in a forlorn branch of the Shadow City—a wooden door with the image of a fierce-looking rabbit painted on its exterior. Kiki jiggled the handle. The door wouldn't open, and there was no lock to pick.

"Maybe it's time to go home," DeeDee offered with a yawn. With the exception of Kiki, we were all exhausted.

"Not yet. This is important," Kiki insisted, staring intently at the door. "It's barricaded from the inside."

"So?" asked Oona.

Kiki didn't appreciate the challenge. "Don't be stupid. If it's barricaded from the inside, it means that the last people in there got out some other way."

"Or died in there," Oona shot back. "Haven't you seen enough dead people tonight?"

Sensing that things were about to get ugly, I decided to step in.

"Look, Oona, there's no red cross on the door, and if there's an exit, we need to note it on the map," I tried to explain, though I, too, would have preferred to start for home.

"You'll have to blow the door open," Kiki instructed DeeDee.

Happy to have the opportunity to try out her explosives, a reenergized DeeDee reached into her knapsack and carefully took out two small test tubes. The liquid inside one of the tubes was a hot pink not known to nature; the other tube contained a gloopy substance the color of rotten lemons.

"Stand back," she told us with evident glee.

"Wait!" cried Luz in alarm. "We have to check for mains first."

Luz and I carefully compared my map of the Shadow City with the NYCMap. According to my calculations, we were beneath Pearl Street just south of Chinatown. The NYCMap showed no dangerous pipes in the vicinity.

"We're good to go," I informed DeeDee, feeling like the hero of an action movie.

We all stood at a distance while DeeDee uncorked the two test tubes and attached them at their mouths, leaving only a thin layer of paper to separate the two liquids. With remarkable speed and precision, she duct-taped the two vials to the door just below the knob and then sprinted in our direction.

"The blast shouldn't be too powerful," she said when she reached us, panting softly, "but the last thing I need is a splinter the size of a wooden stake. So get ready. As soon as the layer between the two test tubes dissolves, you're going to hear a big bang."

Sure enough, within ten seconds the vials exploded,

leaving a cloud of blue smoke and a gaping hole the shape of a shark bite where the lock had once been. Kiki smiled triumphantly as the door swung open.

Inside were three dark chambers. I had secretly feared that they, too, would be stacked with corpses, but the first room featured little more than a soiled mattress, a couple of chamber pots, and a pair of men's overalls hanging from a nail in the wall. The second room, however, was in utter disarray. A chair had been smashed against a wall and shards of glass littered the floor. A large black stain coated one of the dingy plaster walls.

"I'd bet you anything that's blood," said Oona, taking a closer look. "If somebody died here, it wasn't a plague that got him."

The final chamber was filled with crates stamped with the word *cargo*. Kiki reached into the straw packing that lined one of the crates and pulled out a tarnished silver teapot and matching creamer. Another crate held moth-eaten cashmere shawls in every imaginable plaid.

"Ladies, we've found ourselves a thieves' den," said Kiki.

"Look, there's an exit!" Betty cried, pointing to a ladder on the side of the room that led to an opening in the ceiling.

"Why don't you check it out, Ananka?" Kiki casually suggested as she continued to root through crates. "But try to be careful. There's no telling what's up there."

She could have spared me the warning. The last thing I wanted to do was crawl into a dark space by myself. Unfortunately, I couldn't decline the offer. Kiki Strike had noticed my nervousness and had decided to test me. So despite my misgivings, I mounted the ladder and climbed through the opening in the ceiling. Surrounded by a circular wall of crumbling earth, I realized I was at the bottom of a deep hole. I counted sixty rungs before the top of my head hit a wooden trapdoor. I took a deep breath and reluctantly raised the trapdoor an inch. Looking through the crack, I saw a spacious, dimly lit room that clearly belonged to the twenty-first century. We had found our first exit to the world above.

A pale green light issued from a digital display on one wall. Icy air streamed down and froze my nostrils. I listened carefully for any sound of activity. Once I was certain that the room was empty, I raised the trapdoor a bit farther. What I saw delivered such a shock that I nearly tumbled headfirst from the ladder. Hundreds of large animals were suspended from the ceiling, their glossy fur gleaming in the light. Having nearly been consumed by rats earlier in the evening, I was in no mood to come face-to-face with any more members of the animal kingdom.

"What'd you find?" someone called up from below. The question brought me to my senses. The animals hanging from above were minks, and though I'd read that minks can be surprisingly ferocious, these hadn't been able to attack anyone for quite some time.

"It looks like a cold storage room for furs," I shouted down to the others.

I climbed into the room, and Kiki followed close behind. Inside, it was the dead of winter, and though I stood shivering in the cold, Kiki showed no sign of discomfort. She marched around the perimeter of the room, examining the merchandise.

"Verushka has a picture of my mother wearing a coat just like this," Kiki said as she lifted a gleaming coat off the rack. I was thinking of my own mother's threadbare overcoat, when alarms began to ring throughout the building.

"That was dumb," Kiki said, showing no trace of panic. Spying my terrified expression, she offered a superior smirk.

"Don't be such an old lady, Ananka. It's not like we don't have an escape route. And I'm sure no one knows about that trapdoor. Look how well disguised it is. We won't even need to block the entrance."

"I think we should go," I practically pleaded. The police could arrive at any moment.

"What's the hurry?" Kiki lingered longer than she had to before finally placing the mink back on the rack. "Okay, then," she said as if humoring a whiny child. "If you *insist*."

We climbed down to the thieves' den to discover Luz rummaging through one of the crates and shoving fistfuls of silver forks into her pockets. Kiki's sense of humor evaporated, and she reached into Luz's uniform and pulled out the purloined silverware.

"What are you doing?" complained Luz. "Where else am I going to get this much silver? Besides, it's ours."

"Yeah, *ours,* not *yours,* Luz. Do you have to be so greedy? When we've finished the map, you guys can come back for the silver. But if we stop to hunt for treasure in every room, it will take us forever to find all the entrances to the Shadow City. We can't slow down now."

"Oh come on, Kiki, I need some silver for one of my

inventions. And I'm just taking a few extra forks for my mom."

"I don't care if you're making silver bullets to defend the city from werewolves," said Kiki. "The forks are staying here. It's time to go home."

Luz threw down the silverware she still held in her hand. But as Kiki turned her back, I saw Luz pick up two fish knives and shove them into her pocket. I gave her a smile and decided to say nothing.

By the time we emerged in the Marble Cemetery, it was five o'clock in the morning, and after eight full hours of exploring, we were all dead tired. It took our last bit of strength to restore the marble slab to its proper place over the vault's entrance. The sun was starting to rise, and as we removed our dirty uniforms, the sky burst into a brilliant orange. We left the cemetery and dragged our exhausted bodies along the deserted streets, lured by the promise of breakfast at Kiki's house.

The moment we arrived, Betty collapsed on the couch. The rest of us forced ourselves to stay awake long enough to scarf down the platter of cherry blintzes that Verushka had prepared. As my stomach began to strain against my waistband, I noticed that Kiki's plate remained empty. Instead, she drank countless cups of milky coffee as Verushka grilled her on the evening's discoveries. The housekeeper wanted to know everything—how far we had traveled and what we had seen. But like Kiki, she seemed particularly interested in the passages that connected the Shadow City to the world above.

"The exit you found, Ananka. Where did it lead?" Verushka asked me without warning. I stopped shoveling food long enough to grab my map.

"A fur storage facility," I told her.

"And what was the street?"

"Pearl Street," I said.

Verushka seemed disturbed by my answer. "That is very far away," she said to no one in particular.

I turned to Kiki in confusion. "Far away from what?"

"Far away from the Marble Cemetery," she answered curtly. "The Shadow City is bigger than we expected, Verushka. Ananka's going to find the building with the exit this morning. Then we'll know for sure just how far away we were."

Looking dangerously cranky, Kiki leaned back on the couch and sipped her coffee. I took advantage of the lull in conversation to serve myself another blintz.

"Are you sure you need that?" Oona asked, pointing at my bloated belly.

I dropped my fork, and it fell onto the serving plate with a loud clang.

"Nice manners, Oona," snipped Kiki. "Were you raised by wolves?"

"What? I'm just trying to help her out," Oona said, casually licking her fork.

Before I could say anything in my own defense, Betty jolted out of sleep.

"What time is it?" she asked, looking panicked and confused.

"Almost seven," Luz told her.

"I've got to go!" Betty exclaimed, running for the door. "My parents will be home from work any minute now!"

Betty's panic spread like a bad case of head lice. Within minutes, DeeDee and Luz were sharing a cab uptown, and Verushka was on the phone with Luz's angry mother, apologizing for letting their moth watching run late. Not long afterward, Oona disappeared without any explanation, leaving me alone with Kiki and her housekeeper. I still had at least three hours before my mother and father rolled out of bed, so I borrowed Kiki's laptop computer—a high-tech model with features I could never afford. As I spread out my notes in the living room and began crafting my map of the Shadow City, I heard Kiki and Verushka whispering furiously in the kitchen.

Eager to leave them alone to argue, I hurried through my work and set out to find the building with the entrance to the Shadow City. By then, I was so exhausted that I fell asleep in the back of the cab I'd hailed and was rudely awakened by the driver when we reached the address I'd given him. I got out of the car to find myself standing in front of an empty parking lot. My calculations had been off. The map would need to be revised. One block south of the parking lot, I came across an old building with a dry cleaner on its ground floor. The walls of the shop were lined with hundreds of anonymous packages wrapped in plain brown paper, and a neon sign in the window flashed the words *Fur Storage*.

Examining the map I had printed out, I hastily sketched a few corrections. Then I took out a large rubber stamp I'd made and a pad of ink. After making sure no one was watching, I stamped a golden *i* on the sidewalk in front of the building, marking the entrance to the Shadow City with the Irregulars' logo in case we needed to find it in an emergency. Once I had finished, I used a camera that DeeDee lent me to snap several pictures of the building. Finally, almost twelve full hours after I had snuck out of my bedroom window, I started on my way home.

A middle-aged couple joined me on the corner of Pearl and John streets as I waited for the light to change. I tucked the camera into my pocket and tried to look innocent, but neither of them seemed aware of my presence.

"Did you hear about the rats?" I heard the woman ask. My stomach flip-flopped.

"What rats?" replied the man in a bored voice.

"It was on the news this morning. They said that a ship in the middle of the Hudson River was attacked by thousands of rats last night."

"Rats can swim?"

"Apparently," said the woman.

I had to bite my tongue to avoid offering the bit of trivia that sprang to mind. According to *The Devil's Army,* rats are champion swimmers. During the plagues that laid waste to old New York, the dead were often buried in mass graves on islands in the East River. Whenever the graves were left unfilled, the city's rat population would swim across to picnic on the exposed corpses.

"But what were a bunch of rats doing in the Hudson River?" asked the man.

"Nobody knows," the woman answered. "The reporter said they might have been swimming to New Jersey."

"That makes sense. New Jersey's a good place for them."

"They said the boat just got in the way."

"What happened to it?"

"Well from what I could gather, the crew abandoned the ship and escaped in life boats."

"That bad?" At last he was really intrigued.

"I guess. The reporter said they ate the crew's dog."

"Rats eat dogs?"

"They eat anything, don't they?" said the woman.

The light changed, and the happy couple strolled off, arm in arm. I reached in my pocket for my Reverse Pied Piper. I had never imagined it could be quite so powerful, and I suddenly felt a little guilty. I wondered how my grandfather would have felt about what we had done. He probably would have packed up his bags and followed the rats to New Jersey.

Chapter 8

The Big Bang

My mother's voice dragged me out of a dream filled with rodents, pirates, and plagues. I opened my eyes and was instantly blinded by a bright beam of sunshine.

"It's one o'clock in the afternoon," my mother announced, reminding me that I had forgotten to lock my bedroom door. As my eyes adjusted to the light, I could see her standing in the doorway with several books tucked under her arm. She had a pencil stuck behind her ear and another pinning her hair in a loose bun. "Are you planning to spend your summer vacation in bed?"

"I was up late reading," I informed her, knowing she'd approve. "I've been studying the history of New York City."

"Oh, Ananka, how wonderful!" my mother gushed. I doubt she had been so excited since the day I was potty trained. "I've dabbled a little in that subject myself. The Revolutionary period is particularly fascinating, don't you think?" She looked over at the pile of books and papers on my desk. Sitting on top was my map of the Shadow City. "What's this?" she asked, bending down for a closer look. "Is it part of your research?"

I considered lying until I realized that nothing would be harder for my mother to believe than the truth.

"It's a map," I told her, sitting up in bed. "There's an underground city beneath downtown Manhattan. Only six people know about it, and I'm one of them."

My mother looked crestfallen. "You're twelve years old, right?" she asked in the same sad voice she used whenever I brought home a report card filled with C's.

"Twelve and a half," I reminded her.

"Well, I don't know what you've been reading, Ananka, but you should know the difference between fiction and nonfiction by now. It's time to start using your brain for something other than daydreaming. If you're interested in history, I can give you the right books."

"Thanks, Mom, but I've already found all the books I need."

"Are you sure?" she asked, trying to hide her disappointment. "I'd really love to help."

"Positive," I said.

My mother shut my bedroom door with a weary sigh, and I smiled to myself. Someday, I thought, I'd tell my parents what their dimwitted daughter had discovered.

As soon as it was dark once more, I climbed down the fire escape outside my bedroom window and walked to Kiki's house to meet the Irregulars for our second night of explorations. Before we left for the Marble Cemetery, Kiki asked to take a look at my map. I made a few quick corrections and printed out a copy for her. She studied it for several minutes, tracing her finger along the thick red line that indicated the Shadow City.

"Looks good," she told me. "Tonight, we'll try to walk north."

From the moment the words left her lips, I could feel a question dangling on the tip of my tongue. Why north? I wanted to ask her. Who cares which way we go when we have an entire city to explore? Of course, now I wish I'd been brave enough to ask.

In my defense, I did keep a closer eye on Kiki Strike from that point forward. I began to notice that she chose the routes we took with care, and it didn't take long for me to reach the conclusion that Kiki was leading us to something. The other girls detected nothing unusual. They were too thrilled by the discoveries we continued to make. But every time we stopped to explore a room, Kiki would grow impatient if Luz lingered over some pirate's booty or Oona and DeeDee played a quick game of blackjack in an abandoned gambling parlor. Instead of joining in on the fun, Kiki would pace the room, stopping only to snap at anyone who dared to raise a ruckus. She seemed to grow crankier as the hours passed, until nothing we did could please her.

Each night, Kiki pushed us deeper into the Shadow City. Whenever we spied a trapdoor, her mood would magically lighten. Luckily, we discovered enough of them to keep her from getting truly nasty. New York was peppered with entrances to the Shadow City. Following hidden passages, we found ourselves in fancy wine cellars, dungeonlike basements, and steam-filled boiler rooms. We even discovered an exit from the Shadow City that led to a dingy broom closet in the bowels of City Hall. But it wasn't until we climbed up a ladder and into the cash-filled vaults of the Chinatown Savings and Loan that we finally understood the importance of our mission. Until then, it had felt like a game. But suddenly Kiki Strike's warnings made sense to us all. If criminals were allowed to take control of the Shadow City, there was no doubt they could cause plenty of trouble.

Fortunately, most of the entrances to the Shadow City were well camouflaged and unlikely to be discovered by anyone from the world above. In fact, our explorations uncovered only one entrance that seemed too dangerous to remain open. It was located in Chinatown, just one block away from the Chinatown Savings and Loan.

★　★　★

If it hadn't been for Luz's tireless treasure hunt, we might never have found the entrance. She insisted on rifling through every trunk, box, or crate we discovered, and waiting for Luz could make Kiki furious. But while our leader threatened, ordered, and pleaded, Luz continued to tear open crates like a kid ripping apart a pile of birthday presents.

Though her heart seemed to break each time she discovered a horde of porcelain chamber pots or a stash of pickled pigs' feet, Luz refused to give up. In her eyes, every dank and smelly chamber held the promise of untold riches. So the night we came upon a cramped storage room that was filled to the rafters with shabby straw mats and dirty pillows, she ignored Kiki's orders to move on and set about trying to topple a stack of crates in a corner of the room. After several good pushes, the top two crates crashed to the ground, spilling a million worthless chopsticks across the floor and revealing an opening in the room's ceiling.

Luz pouted while Oona, Kiki, and I climbed up the crates. A long ladder led to a bizarre room, its walls lined with dark cubbyholes just large enough to hold a human body. We saw no evidence of an exit to the world above, but another ladder leaning against a wall told us that we hadn't reached a dead end. Kiki and Oona searched the cubbyholes while I thumbed through *Glimpses of Gotham* for clues. Skimming a chapter on Chinatown, I found we had stumbled upon one of Pearcy Leake's favorite haunts—an opium den with a secret entrance located in the basement of a Chinatown warehouse.

"Hey, Ananka. Mind sharing your expert opinion for a moment?" Kiki called. "Take a look at this."

I turned in time to catch a small bottle with a Chinese label. It was filled with a greasy liquid. I unscrewed the cap and was overwhelmed by a sickly sweet odor.

"I found it in one of the cubbyholes. Does it look a hundred years old to you?"

"Not unless the Chinese were using bar codes back then. And there's a sell-by date in English. Whatever this stuff is, it's good 'til next month."

"Hey, let me see," said Oona, snatching the bottle. "I read Chinese."

Her brow furrowed as she examined the label.

"What is it?" I asked.

"Devil's Apple Wart Remover," she read. "Who would leave a bottle of wart remover down here?"

"Someone with a wart problem, probably," Kiki said. "It doesn't matter who left it. It means someone's been in here. We need to have a look upstairs."

After a long search, we located a camouflaged trapdoor and climbed into the warehouse above. There, we came upon a sight that could make any girl weak in the knees. Cobwebs curtained the warehouse's windows, and dust bunnies the size of cabbages tumbled around tall towers of shoeboxes. In all, there were thousands of boxes, each filled with a pair of the most beautiful designer shoes I had ever seen.

"Fake," said Kiki.

"Fake? They look like real shoes to me," I said.

"That's not what I mean. They're counterfeit." She ran her finger across the soft leather of a pair of black boots. "All this attention to detail, and then they screw it up by misspelling Italy."

I peeked at the sole of one of the shoes. It was stamped with the word *Italie*.

"Who left them here?" I wondered.

"Smugglers, who else? They must be using this warehouse, and they've already found the opium den underneath it. We'll have to close off this entrance if we want to keep them out of the tunnels."

Before we left for home, we barricaded the trapdoor that led from the opium den to the storeroom below. Back at Kiki's hidden house, we listened as Verushka made an anonymous call to the police, tipping them off about the counterfeit footwear. The next day, a scandal erupted when the authorities announced that a wealthy real estate magnate named Oliver Harcott owned the warehouse. Unfortunately, no one could prove that Oliver Harcott was in league with the smugglers. The building had been rented to a Chinese businessman who had fled the city. With no leads left to follow, the police were forced to close the case and distribute the shoes to Manhattan's homeless.

The Irregulars celebrated our little victory with more of Verushka's cherry blintzes, though in an amazing show of restraint, I limited myself to one. We were all thrilled that our mission to control Shadow City was proving to be a success. For the moment, the tunnels were safe. And Kiki Strike was pleased she'd caused trouble for Oliver Harcott. As far as she was concerned, a man who had looked the other way while his son, Jacob, had harassed people in Central Park couldn't be entirely innocent. That morning, as Kiki drank her coffee and laughed along with the rest of us, I wondered if I might have misjudged her. Maybe she isn't so dangerous, I thought to myself.

I had almost begun to believe it, when everything went horribly wrong.

✫   ✫   ✫

We had been exploring the Shadow City for more than two weeks when a remarkable change came over Kiki. One evening before we departed for the Marble Cemetery, she asked again to see the map. By that point, my masterpiece was impressively detailed, and I was proud of my work. I had taken great pains to perfect the image of the snakelike city that lay coiled beneath Manhattan.

As Kiki held the printout in her hands, a small smirk played across her lips. She flipped through the photos of the buildings with exits and lingered on the last one, which showed an ordinary brownstone with a little blond girl playing on the stoop.

"Where did you say this building is?" she asked.

"It's only a couple of blocks from your house, actually. It's on Bethune Street."

"I thought I recognized that kid," she said, staring at the photo and grinning like a maniac. I suspected we were close to whatever it was she was after. But once again, I didn't ask. Let her find it, I thought, and then we can get back to the business of mapping the Shadow City. It was wishful thinking of the most dangerous sort.

That night, Kiki was eager to return to the part of the city where we had left off the night before. We practically ran through the tunnels, despite the fact that our boots were not built for speed. Finally, we arrived at the door that led to the house on Bethune Street. Several more doors lay just beyond. Kiki stopped abruptly.

"We're under people's houses now, so you've got to be quiet," she told us, her order making very little sense. We were too far underground for anyone to hear us. But rather than argue, we all nodded obediently.

"Okay, then, let's see what we've got." Kiki walked to the next door and tried the handle. It was locked. Oona took out her lock-picking kit, and after a few seconds, the door stood open. Inside, a skeleton dressed in the remains of a colorful three-piece suit lay splayed across a bed.

"Don't mind him," Kiki instructed. "Look for an exit." I scanned the ceiling, but there was nothing to be seen. A frown darkened Kiki's face. "We're done here," she announced.

"Wait," called Betty, who had been examining the dead man's suit. We turned to see her pointing at the skeleton. "There's something hidden under his jacket."

I moved closer to the bed and peered down at the man.

"It's some sort of sack," I confirmed.

"Well, see what it is and let's get out of here," said Kiki.

I reached over and pinched the sack's fabric, careful not to come into contact with the hand that still clutched it tightly. When the skeletal fingers refused to release the sack, I tugged with frustration. The rotten fabric ripped, and a shower of golden disks rained down on us. One bounced off Betty's forehead and fell at her feet. She bent down and grabbed it.

"It's gold," she said, holding up a coin the size of a quarter.

"We're rich! We're rich!" Luz shouted, jumping up and down as if she'd won the lottery. Everyone but Kiki scrambled to recover the gold pieces.

"Leave the coins. We'll come back for them later," Kiki demanded, but there was no way to stop Luz from claiming her prize. She walked up to Kiki and shook a finger in her face.

"You told me that if I joined the Irregulars I'd never have to go through anyone's trash again," Luz snarled. "Well, I'm sick of waiting. Sit your butt down and shut up while we take what belongs to us."

Rather than argue, Kiki took a seat next to the skeleton and studied my map while we collected the coins, many of which had fallen into cracks or rolled into crevices. By the time we were finished, we had found almost two hundred of them. We loaded them into DeeDee's backpack, which sagged with the weight.

With our newfound wealth stashed away, we returned to the main tunnel of the Shadow City. Kiki approached the next door. It opened to reveal nothing but dirt. Slamming it in frustration, she headed for the third door along the side of the tunnel. Unlike the others we had encountered, the door was made not of wood but rather a dull, dense metal. Although there was no lock to be seen, the door refused to open. Kiki turned to DeeDee.

"This one's locked from the inside. Get your explosives ready. Luz, Ananka, check for mains."

Luz and I studied our maps. According to the NYCMap, there was a water main that stretched through the middle of the block and a smaller gas main that ran alongside it. If my map of the Shadow City was to be trusted, we were far enough away from the pipes to safely detonate the explosives. But I was well aware of my map's shortcomings.

"It's not safe," I informed Kiki. "We may be too close to a water main."

"We *have* to open that door," she replied, daring me to disagree. She wasn't going to let the rebellion Luz had started get out of control.

"It's too dangerous," I said. "The pipes are old. Any strong vibration could cause them to burst."

"It's only a small explosion, Ananka," said Kiki.

"I don't think it'll cause any problems," added DeeDee.

"What about you? What do you think?" Kiki turned to Luz.

"If the maps are right, it should be okay," she said.

"My map could be off," I confessed. "I've had to correct it every time we've found an exit."

"We're only a few doors down from the last exit," Kiki insisted. "So the map should still be accurate."

"Why do you want to open that door so badly?" I asked, tired of her orders and feeling a sudden surge of courage. I heard somebody gasp.

Kiki's voice turned icy cold. "Our job is to find all the exits. If a door is locked from the inside, there's a good chance there's an exit behind it."

"You know what I think? I think you're full of it," I told her. "You've never been interested in mapping the Shadow City. You've been leading us here all along. What is this place?"

For a brief moment Kiki was taken aback, then her wolflike eyes narrowed.

"It doesn't really matter what *you* believe, Ananka. You're not in charge, are you? DeeDee, get your explosives ready."

DeeDee hesitated.

"If you don't trust me, why are you here?" Kiki shouted. With her brow furrowed, nostrils flared, and white locks sticking out in every direction, she looked wild and dangerous.

DeeDee reluctantly pulled out two small vials. "Sorry Ananka," she apologized. "I'm sure we'll be fine."

There was nothing more I could do. I sullenly followed

behind the others as they moved a safe distance away. We watched from the doorway of the skeleton's room as DeeDee connected the two vials and taped them to the locked door. As she dashed to meet us, the chemicals exploded. The blast was deafening, and a pale blue ball of fire raced down the tunnel, engulfing DeeDee as she ran. Then the walls of the tunnel rumbled, and stones began to fall from the ceiling. Where the metal door had stood, the tunnel collapsed in a mound of rubble and a cloud of dust. DeeDee lay on the floor in front of us. Her uniform had protected her body from the flames, but her hat had been knocked from her head and what little was left of her hair was smoldering. A long red gash stretched across her forehead. She wasn't moving.

"DeeDee!" I shrieked. As I ran for DeeDee's body, I heard a loud *crack* followed by the roar of raging water. I grabbed one of DeeDee's legs and began dragging her to safety. Kiki took the other leg and tried to help.

"Look what you've done!" I yelled. If I'd had a free hand, I would have punched her. "I hope you're satisfied!"

Kiki said nothing, and together, we managed to move DeeDee from the wreckage. I dropped to my knees and took DeeDee's pulse. It was very faint.

"She's alive," I informed the others. "But we have to get her to a hospital."

"Take off her backpack. It'll make it easier to carry her," Kiki said. I pulled the backpack filled with gold from DeeDee's shoulders and shoved it at Kiki.

"You take it, then." I turned to the others. "Okay, let's

get her out. We'll have to go through the nearest exit. We don't have time to make it back to the cemetery."

Together, the four of us were able to lift DeeDee quite easily, but when we reached the ladder that led into the basement of the nearby building, we seemed to be stuck.

"Let me do it," insisted Kiki. She hoisted DeeDee fireman-style over her back and carried her fifty feet up the ladder and through the trapdoor. Although I couldn't have been angrier, I had to marvel at Kiki's strength.

With DeeDee's limp body in tow, we hurried for the front door of the brownstone. The house was dark and difficult to navigate. Adding to the ambience, the people who owned the building were avid collectors of ceremonial masks from around the world. Wherever we turned, another bug-eyed monster or hideous hyena god was there to greet us. As we neared the front door, we heard little footsteps on the stairs that led to the upper floors. I half expected to see that one of the demons had sprung to life, but it was only a tiny blond girl, dressed in pink pajamas with feet. We all froze.

"You're awfully short for robbers," the little girl noted calmly.

"Shh. We're not robbers," Kiki told her as Oona scrambled to open the locks on the front door.

"Then what are you?" she asked.

"Elves," said Kiki.

The little girl looked briefly puzzled.

"See?" Kiki took off her hat and shook out her unnaturally white hair.

"Where did you come from?"

"The basement," Kiki said. "But we're leaving now."

"Okay," said the girl, apparently satisfied. "Have a nice night."

Oona opened the door, and we carried DeeDee out of the building. A cab was driving past and Oona sprinted to hail it.

"St. Vincent's Hospital," I demanded once we had carefully loaded DeeDee into the backseat.

"You girls got cash?" asked the very hairy man behind the wheel.

"Of course we do," I snapped.

"Okay, then, but don't let your friend bleed all over the upholstery."

"Just drive!" I screamed at him.

"No need to be rude," he muttered as he stepped on the gas.

As the cab neared the hospital, we stripped out of our uniforms, revealing our regular clothes underneath. We didn't need to make the situation any worse by showing up dressed like a band of miniature ninjas. When the cab stopped in front of the emergency room, someone threw a twenty-dollar bill at the driver, and we pulled DeeDee from the car. As soon as we entered the hospital waiting room, a swarm of doctors surrounded us.

"What happened?" one asked, but none of us could think of an answer. "Never mind," the doctor huffed in exasperation as he loaded DeeDee onto a stretcher and wheeled her through two swinging doors.

"It's time you explained yourself," I said, spinning around and expecting to see Kiki behind me.

"What are you talking about?" said Oona.

"Where is she?" I asked the group.

We looked around the waiting room. Betty ran to the window and Oona checked the ladies' room. Kiki Strike was gone. And so, we soon realized, was the gold.

HOW TO CARE FOR AN INJURED COLLEAGUE

While I'm certain that you are the very picture of caution, by now you must have learned that in any good story, there's always a character who's a bit accident-prone. And unless you intend to abandon your stumbling sidekick or clumsy companion in the middle of all the fun, I recommend that you learn how to care for her.

Fortunately, many injuries can be easily dealt with if you have a little common sense, a well-stocked first aid kit, and an expert knowledge of CPR. But for those of you who've already learned how to bandage a bullet wound or kick-start a heart, I've included a few helpful guidelines for dealing with some of the injuries common among adventurers.

Teeth Knocked Out in a Brawl

Your colleague is probably too charming to get into a fight. But just in case, you should know what to do. It would be a shame to ruin that pretty smile.

1. Get to a dentist or a hospital FAST. You have only thirty minutes before the tooth dies and can no longer be returned to its proper place.
2. Gently rinse the tooth under water, and never touch the tooth's roots.
3. Keep the tooth from drying out. To do this, you have three options. If your colleague is conscious, she can reinsert the tooth in her mouth and hold it there with a finger. If not, you can place the tooth in a glass of milk, which should keep it nice and fresh. However, if your colleague is woozy and there's no milk around, you only have one option left. You'll have to tuck the tooth underneath your own tongue or in between your gum and cheek. Yes, it's disgusting, but it's still more appealing than hanging around with someone who's missing her front teeth.

Attacked by Wild Animals

Let's face it. This could happen to any of us. One bright spring day, you and your colleague are strolling through the woods picking mushrooms that you're absolutely certain aren't poisonous, when an angry creature darts out from behind a tree stump and bites your friend on her exposed pinky.

1. Try to identify the animal. If it was a bat, raccoon, skunk, or fox, start heading for a hospital as quickly as possible. These cuddly woodland creatures are the most likely to transmit rabies.
2. Wash the bite with soap and water, and don't pour any antiseptic on the wound. Apply pressure with sterile gauze or a clean cloth. (I hope you took some with you when you went into the woods.)
3. Cover any broken skin with a bandage.
4. Seek medical attention. On the way, be sure to mentally prepare your friend for the many, many unpleasant shots she's about to receive.

Frozen Alive

You're trekking through the Andes in search of a forgotten Incan city when a nasty blizzard slows your progress. Of course *you're* prepared for such unfortunate twists of fate, but your colleague has left both her hat and her mittens back at the motel. Only an hour into the blizzard, her ears and fingers are white, waxy-looking, and can't be moved. You'll have to act quickly to save them.

1. Wrap her ears and fingers with warm, dry cloth.
2. Strike up a campfire and soak the frozen areas in warm water for ten to thirty minutes.
3. Avoid direct heat, and don't thaw her ears and fingers if there's a chance they might be refrozen.
4. Don't rub the frozen areas and don't apply snow.
5. Give her aspirin to ease the pain.
6. Apply sterile dressings and wrap between the fingers.
7. Find medical help or start praying.

Bitten by a Rattlesnake

There is simply no excuse for getting bitten by a rattlesnake. After all, how many creatures are nice enough to warn you before they attack? But just in case your companion is hard of hearing, couldn't find her snake-proof leather hiking boots, or likes to stick her fingers into dark rock crevices, here's what you can do to save her.

1. Wash bite with soap and water as soon as possible.
2. Help the victim stay calm and keep the bite lower than her heart.
3. Remove any jewelry or tight clothing near the bite in case the area begins to swell.
4. Don't let her eat or drink anything.
5. Do not apply ice or a cold compress.
6. Ignore the old cowboy who tells you to make a cut around the wound and try to draw the venom out with your mouth. Making yourself sick isn't going to help anyone.

Chapter 9

The Case of the Vanishing Villain

Once the sun began to rise through the waiting room window, we lost all hope of Kiki Strike returning. At the time, her disappearance was the least of our concerns. The doctors had whisked DeeDee into surgery hours before, and we'd had no news since. The Morlocks' housekeeper had phoned DeeDee's parents at a chemistry conference in Austria, and they had jumped on the first plane back to New York. But their flight wouldn't land until late afternoon, so we were left alone with the unpleasant task of explaining what had happened.

After dismissing several potential stories involving sadistic thugs or exploding manholes, we finally told the doctors that DeeDee was the victim of a chemistry experiment gone wrong. As it turned out, it was an excellent choice. DeeDee's medical history was filled with chemistry-related injuries, including several vicious acid burns and a life-threatening shrapnel wound from a shattered beaker. One look at DeeDee's chart, and even the most suspicious nurse had no difficulty believing our story.

When the paperwork was done, there was nothing left to do but nervously follow the hands of the clock. As New York's sick and injured arrived at the emergency room, every possible malady was paraded in front of us. We saw an actor who'd been skewered in a sword fight, a woman whose head had swollen to the size of a beach ball, and a young man who was suffering from a condition known as Black Hairy Tongue. But even with a steady stream of medical oddities to distract me, I couldn't sit still. I stood up to pace the hall. I took one turn up and down before I found myself walking through a set of automatic doors and out onto the sidewalk. Without any thought of my destination, I kept on going, thoroughly exhausted but fueled by fury.

I walked west until I felt water filling my shoes. When I snapped to attention, I realized I was standing on the edge of a lake that hadn't existed the day before. Ducks blissfully paddled around dozens of buildings that were partially submerged, feeding off the exotic plants in the window boxes and ignoring the people who leaned from the windows calling for help. According to the street sign, I was on the corner of Bethune and Hudson streets, less than a block away from the site of the explosion.

I stared at the water that sloshed around my feet. Whatever had happened, there was no doubt that the Irregulars were responsible. Somehow we had flooded an entire neighborhood—damaging people's homes and endangering their lives. And although the thought was too terrible to contemplate, I knew the Shadow City might be flooded as well. In one night, we had managed to destroy the tunnels we had tried so hard to protect. At first I felt sick, but then a powerful, poisonous rage began to spread through my body. I swore to myself that Kiki Strike would pay for what she had done.

A canoe piloted by a weathered man dressed like a cowboy arrived at the edge of the lake a few feet from where I stood. The boat was packed with sodden paintings and dripping sculptures. The man jumped from the canoe and pulled it ashore.

"What happened?" I asked, though I already knew the answer.

"Earthquake," he responded, conserving his words as he unloaded his canoe. "Ruptured a water main."

"Was anyone hurt?"

"Nah," said the old man with a dismissive flip of his wrist. "Just a darn big mess, that's all. Couple of my paintings didn't make it. And that fellow over there lost his collection of masks. Not that it's any big tragedy. Most of 'em were pretty dang ugly, if you ask me." He pointed at the brownstone from which the Irregulars had escaped just hours before. I saw the little girl who lived there poking her head through a window and reaching out to snatch one of the ducks.

My eyes scanned the row of houses. One of them had to be the building that Kiki had been desperate to enter. As I searched for clues, a rowboat rounded the corner of Bethune and Greenwich streets and pulled up in front of the second floor balcony of a building three doors down from the little girl's house. Although its window boxes were a bit fancier than its neighbors', there was little remarkable about the house itself. A woman and her daughter greeted the boat and began shoving luggage at the man. Once the suitcases were safely stowed, the woman and the girl stepped daintily into the boat, and the man began to row toward the water's edge.

My mind was racing with anticipation. As the boat drew closer to where I stood, I could see its occupants more clearly. The man at the oars was beefy and dressed in a tight dark suit that didn't seem at all appropriate for seafaring. Seated by his side was a flashy woman wearing a thick mask of makeup. There was scarcely a part of her body that wasn't covered in gems, and she sparkled brilliantly whenever the boat hit a patch of sun.

Tucked away behind them was the girl I had taken to be the woman's daughter.

"It was her. I know it was," I heard the hidden girl complain.

"Shush, darling," the woman replied in an impenetrable accent as she smoothed her elaborate hairdo. "Sergei has gone to investigate, and we will know soon enough. But now is not the time to discuss such things."

The girl issued an obnoxious sigh just as the boat stopped in front of me.

Oblivious to my presence, the giant in the navy suit stepped from the boat and dragged it onto the asphalt. He helped the woman onto land, where she straightened her skirt and shot me a withering look. The girl in the boat saw me standing by the water's edge and rose to her feet. Dressed in a lovely white summer dress with her black hair streaming down around her shoulders, she would have been the picture of innocence had her yellow eyes not had the gleam of a wild beast's. It was none other than the Princess.

"*You,*" she growled, her voice swimming in hatred. As she pointed a finger at me, she lost her balance and fell backward, landing with a thump on one of the suitcases. Her dress flew over her head, exposing a pair of white panties embroidered with little pink crowns.

I couldn't help myself. I snickered at the sight. The Princess was beside herself with rage.

"Little girl," said her confused mother, "what are you laughing at? Who do you think you are?"

"That's her friend!" the Princess screamed from the bottom of the boat. The man trudged toward me with a scowl on his face. Realizing I was about to be throttled, I turned and sprinted for safety.

A few blocks later, a stitch in my side forced me to slow down. Thankfully, the large man had given up the chase. As I sat on the stoop of a building to rest, a flood of questions caught up with me. Kiki must have been trying to break into the Princess's house. But why? What had she been looking for? Having seen the look in the Princess's eyes, I knew she had figured out who was responsible for the flood. But how? And more importantly, could she prove it?

As I pondered these questions, a pair of old ladies in summer dresses stopped in front of my stoop. Stepping around me, they walked up the stairs, both struggling under piles of books. I looked up to see a sign over the door of the building that read: "New York Public Library, Abingdon Branch." Just then, one of the ladies missed a step and lost her footing. I caught her before she tumbled down the stairs, but I couldn't stop her books from flying in every direction. As I helped gather them, I stole a glimpse at a few of the titles. The first I recovered was *Homemade Booby Traps,* the second was entitled *Defending Your Home Against Invasion,* and the third bore the unsettling heading *1001 Deadly Devices.*

"My sister and I used these books to catch a burglar," one of the old ladies boasted.

"Yes, poor fellow," her sister tittered. "I'm afraid he never knew what hit him."

The first lady leaned toward me and whispered, "Take it from us, if you're ever in need of a deadly device, you can certainly rely on number two hundred and thirty-five."

"That's right, young lady," her sister added, "and it doesn't even make enough noise to wake up the neighbors."

"Isn't the library just wonderful?" the first asked, her innocent eyes beaming up at me. "You can learn absolutely anything here!"

I helped the ladies return their books, and once I was inside the library, I figured I might as well learn a thing or two for myself. I headed for the computer terminals set against the back wall. A man was hunched over one of the desks. Hearing my footsteps behind him, he glanced over his shoulder and quickly tapped one of the keys. An image of three little puppies frolicking about a garden popped up on his computer screen. I sat down at a terminal and tried to get to work.

"Say, cutie pie, do you like puppies?" hissed the very creepy man at the next computer.

"Only if they're cooked medium rare," I informed him. I've found that in certain situations, it's best to come across as a little loony. "Now get lost before I ask the librarian to have a look at the Web sites you've visited today." I was only acting on a hunch, but the man jumped out of his seat as if I had set him on fire. Avoiding my eyes, he snatched his belongings and scurried out of the library.

Alone at last, I typed in the Princess's name and scanned the results. For a fourteen-year-old, she had an impressive number of listings. I clicked one of the links and entered a Web site called the *New York Society Journal*. The face of the man who had created the site was plastered on every page. With his plastic-surgery-enhanced features and his too-white smile, he looked every bit as sinister as the puppy lover. I scrolled down, and a picture of the Princess in a much better mood popped onto the screen, along with a profile entitled (*yech*), "The Little Princess."

Royal families who have found themselves unjustly uprooted from their ancestral lands have always been welcomed into the Manhattan social set with open arms. Today, our fair isle is so rich in royalty that no gathering of any consequence is complete without an exiled prince or two.

So, I'm delighted to report that the beau monde will soon be graced with an entrancing new face. A mere fourteen years old, Sidonia Galatzina, Princess of Pokrovia, is set to make one of the most stunning debuts in recent memory. Rarely has fate blessed one with such a rare combination of beauty, blood, and fortune. Heir to the crown of Pokrovia and an honors student at the prestigious Atalanta School for Girls, the Princess arrived in New York five years ago with her mother, the enchanting Queen Livia. With all the wit and whimsy of royalty, they shunned the Upper East Side and chose to settle instead in the quaint and bohemian West Village.

Though still so young and innocent, the Princess has been no stranger to tragedy. Her once peaceful kingdom withstood countless attacks by neighboring Russia in the twentieth century, only to be destroyed in the twenty-first by a bloody war. Revolutionaries poisoned the Princess's aunt and uncle, and less than a year later, Queen Livia and her three-year-old daughter were forced to flee from the murderous masses. But destiny was on their side, and they managed to wrest the royal jewels away from the clutches of Pokrovia's pushy peasants . . .

I had to stop reading. Not only was the profile making me nauseous, I could see that it wasn't going to tell me much that everyone at the Atalanta School didn't already know. But there was no time to sort through the other sites I had found. According to the clock on the computer, I had been absent from the hospital for more than an hour. I deleted all traces of my search and ran back to join the others.

I arrived to find Luz asleep. Her legs were stretched across the lap of an elderly woman in a fencing uniform whose arm was bandaged with a ripped purple towel.

Betty, wearing a pair of bejeweled sunglasses, was numbly flipping through a five-year-old copy of *Vogue* as Oona interrogated one of the nurses at the front desk. The Irregulars looked terrible. Even Oona's hair was disheveled and her clothing wrinkled and dirty.

"Where the hell have you been?" Oona demanded when she saw me. "These people won't tell me anything about DeeDee."

The nurse looked frazzled. "We'll tell you as soon as we know," she said with a sigh. "Now please stop cursing and have a seat. You're offending the other patients."

"She's not offending *me*," called the woman in the fencing uniform. "I'm eighty-six years old, and you can bet your skinny butt I've heard a few curse words in my day. Even used a couple here and there." Apparently, the woman had been sitting in the waiting room long enough to make friends with the Irregulars.

"Thanks, Maude," said Oona, giving the nurse a righteous stare. Then she turned the stare on me.

"So where *have* you been?"

"Returning to the scene of the crime."

One of Luz's eyes popped open.

"Crime?" asked Maude, her eyes widening.

"It's just a figure of speech," Betty assured her.

"Maude Sandborn?" called the nurse in the nick of time. "You're next." Maude stood up and looked us over.

"You girls stay out of trouble," she told us, winking at Oona.

"You bet, Maude," Oona replied.

The moment Maude was gone, the others gathered around me.

"What did you find out?" asked Luz sleepily.

"We ruptured a water main. Four whole blocks are under water. I think the Shadow City may be flooded, too."

The others looked horrified, and I saw tears in Betty's eyes.

"Are the tunnels gone?" she asked.

"I don't know. But it's too dangerous to go back now to find out. The good news is that no one was injured," I said. "And people think an earthquake caused the flood."

"Did you at least find out where the exit led to? Do you know where Kiki was trying to go?" asked Oona.

"That's the best part. Ever heard of Sidonia Galatzina?"

"The Princess of Pokrovia? One of the richest girls in all of Manhattan, whose mother rescued the family jewels from a bunch of pushy peasants?" Betty quoted flatly.

"I see you're a fan of the *New York Society Journal*," I noted.

"Isn't everyone who's anyone?" said Betty.

"So what does Princess whatshername have to do with the exit?" Luz wanted to know.

"It led into her house." I paused to let the information sink in.

"I'm confused. Why would Kiki want to get into some dumb princess's house?" Oona asked.

"I can think of one reason," I said.

"She wanted to rob it, didn't she?" asked Luz.

"I don't believe it!" Betty exclaimed.

"Luz is right," I said. "Kiki tried to steal something from the Princess once before. A diamond ring. And I was stupid enough to believe her when she pinned the crime on someone else."

"She took the gold, too," Luz added. There was more than a hint of bitterness in her voice. "And she was supposed to be *our* friend."

"I think we're going to have to face the fact that Kiki isn't who we thought she was," I told the Irregulars, though I was still finding it hard to believe myself.

Oona was nibbling on her lower lip and looking uncomfortable. She opened her mouth to say something, but shut it quickly as a doctor rounded the corner and stopped in the waiting room.

"Your friend is out of surgery," he informed us.

"Is she going to be okay?" asked Betty.

"We think so, but it's still too soon to tell. She'd like to see you." We followed the doctor down the hallway. He stopped in front of DeeDee's room. "You have three minutes. Miss Morlock needs her rest."

I poked my head around the door. DeeDee lay on a hospital cot. With her head wrapped in bandages and IV tubes sprouting from her arms, she looked like a soldier who had barely survived a fierce battle. She waved feebly from the bed, and we stepped inside.

"I'm sorry," DeeDee whispered hoarsely once we were standing by her bedside.

"What are *you* sorry for?" I asked. "We've been worried sick about you."

"It was all my fault," she said, her eyes tearing up.

"No, it wasn't. It was Kiki's fault. She made you do it," Oona said angrily.

"No," insisted DeeDee. "Something went wrong with the explosives. They must have been too powerful. Was anyone hurt?"

"Just you," I assured her. I didn't have the heart to tell her about the flood.

"Good," she said, slowly drifting out of consciousness. "Where's Kiki?"

The rest of us looked at one another.

"She had to run home," Betty lied sweetly. "She'll be back."

"Tell her I'm sorry," DeeDee mumbled as she fell asleep.

"She's the one who should be sorry," I said, but DeeDee was already snoring.

"There's something you should know," Oona whispered to me.

We left DeeDee's room and found our way out of the hospital. On the street, Oona stopped us. She was practically squirming with discomfort.

"Remember when you said that Kiki isn't who you thought she was?"

"Yes." I could tell that something big was coming.

"She's not."

"What are you saying?" asked Luz.

"Okay. Don't be mad. I know I should have told you guys before, but I couldn't. You know, professional confidentiality. A forger's only as good as her secrets."

"Spill it, Oona," demanded Luz.

"Well, before I joined the Irregulars, Kiki asked me to do a job for her. Two jobs, actually. First she wanted me to create a computer file for her at the Atalanta School. And then she asked me to forge a birth certificate."

"So she wasn't actually enrolled at Atalanta?" I asked.

Oona shook her head.

"That explains a lot. But why would she need a forged birth certificate?"

"She never told me, but I figured it out. She needed the birth certificate so she could pretend to be Augustus Quackenbush's granddaughter and get a key to the Marble Cemetery."

"She's not his granddaughter?"

Oona shook her head.

"Then who is she?" asked Betty.

"I don't know," Oona admitted.

"I *knew* there was something weird about that girl," Luz said, nodding. "Did you ever notice that she never ate anything? Remember all those times when we were eating like pigs, and she just sat back and watched."

"Maybe she was poisoning us," said Oona.

"No," I said. "She wouldn't have poisoned us. She needed us to do her dirty work."

Even as I uttered the words, I was beginning to realize that everything had changed. Over the course of a single night, the girl who had picked the Irregulars out of the crowd and shown us the greatest adventure of our lives had been demoted from hero to villain. We may have been too tired to think straight, but there was one thing we all knew for sure. There wouldn't be any naps in our future. We had no choice but to pay a visit to Kiki Strike.

We had planned to pick the lock on the gate that led to Kiki's hidden house, but we arrived to find it swinging in the wind. The knocker in the shape of a severed hand pounded loudly against the wood. When we shut the gate behind us, the yard was eerily quiet. The only sound was the creaking and groaning of the giant weeping willow as it whipped the sides of the old cottage with its branches. Oona and Luz sneaked around the house to the back door while Betty and I made for the front entrance. There was no sign of movement, and the windows were dark.

Once I was certain that Oona and Luz had the back of the house covered, I knocked on the front door. There was no answer. After a pause, I knocked more firmly. Again, there was no answer. I tried the knob, and to my great surprise, the door was unlocked.

"Hello?" I called. The house was silent. "Verushka?"

Betty and I stepped into the living room. The morning light spilled through the windows and onto a scene of total devastation. The video monitors had been smashed. The couches were split open to reveal their fluffy innards. Even the fireplace was now nothing more than a pile of rubble. Something terrible had taken place.

As Betty and I stood speechless, the front door suddenly slammed behind us, and we heard the sound of someone sprinting down the stone path that led to the gate. Before I could run to the window, I heard more footsteps crunching over broken glass. A dark figure appeared in the hallway. I grabbed a brick from what was left of the fireplace and prepared to smash the intruder.

"Hey!" I heard Oona yell as I reared back to hurl the brick. "Do you want to send someone else to the hospital?"

"How did you get in here?" I asked, dropping the brick and trying to keep my heart from exploding.

"Back door was open. Wow," she said, looking around the living room. "Looks like there was one heck of a party."

"Someone was in here," I panted. "He ran out the front door. Did you see him, Betty?"

"No," she admitted. "It all happened too fast."

Oona hurried to the window and looked out at the yard.

"Whoever it was, they're long gone," she said. "But I have a feeling it wasn't Kiki. Come on, you guys, there's something you should see back here."

We stepped past the disemboweled couch and into the hallway. At the back of the house was a tiny bedroom. Other than a bed, a lamp, and a dresser stacked high with books, there was only a cavernous closet filled with black clothing.

Usually, one can learn a great deal about someone by examining her possessions. The legendary detective Sherlock Holmes was fond of remarking that no person can use an object every day without leaving her mark upon it. But even Sherlock would have been baffled by Kiki's bedroom. There were no personal items of any sort—no photos, no mementos, no knickknacks. I couldn't put a finger on it, but the whole setup seemed somehow temporary, like a hotel room or a jail cell.

"She has a fantastic wardrobe," observed Betty as she rifled through Kiki's closet. "It's all handmade."

"Yeah, but it doesn't look like she took much of it with her," I said. There wasn't a single empty hanger.

"Uh-oh," said Luz, who was stooping to examine a pile of twisted metal and wires by the side of Kiki's desk.

"What's that?" I asked.

"I think it's her computer," said Luz.

"Oh, no," I moaned. "She had our maps on it." All of my hard work was lying smashed on the ground.

"You guys didn't have a backup?" Luz asked.

"Of course we did. I burned a new CD every time I updated the map of the Shadow City. But I don't see a CD in that mess, do you? Now all we have are the last copies I printed out, and they're covered in DeeDee's blood."

"Forget about the maps," said Oona. "What good are they if the Shadow City is flooded? Here, take a look at this." She pointed at the wall behind us. We turned to see three bullet holes in the plaster. "This is what I wanted to show you. Whoever left *these* was pretty serious."

"Do you think they killed Kiki?" asked Betty.

"There's no blood," I said. "If they got her, they must have taken her alive."

As I checked the walls for more bullet holes, a book on the dresser caught my eye. *Unlocking the Secrets of Diamonds* was one of the books Kiki had been eyeing at my house the night we prepared for the Shadow City. I glanced at the other books on Kiki's dresser. There was a Russian-English dictionary and a medical text on poisons, but the rest were devoted to precious gems.

"Interesting bedtime reading," said Oona, thumbing through the medical text. I picked up my parents' books and tucked them under my arm. Villain or not, Kiki Strike certainly appeared to be a thief.

★ ★ ★

Dazed and confused by what we had seen, the Irregulars left the hidden house and walked across town to my apartment. We arrived to find a note written in my mother's hand tacked to the kitchen door.

> *Ananka,*
>
> *I was surprised to wake up and find you missing. I can't imagine where you had to go so early in the morning, but a more thoughtful girl might have left her parents a note. However, your father and I will not allow your bad manners to interfere with our plans. We're visiting the library in New Haven today, and we should be back this evening. I expect you to be at home when we return, and I suggest you spend the day thinking up a brilliant explanation. Let's just say that I had better be impressed.*
>
> *Love,*
> *Mom*

It was only then that I remembered we'd been out all night. The Irregulars were in serious trouble. We collapsed in a miserable clump in the living room and tried to come up with a plan, but we hadn't been home for more than five minutes when there was a knock at the door. I stood on tiptoe to see through the peephole. Standing in the hallway was a very dapper man.

"Who is it?" I called through the door.

"FBI," answered the man.

I motioned for the other girls to hide out of sight.

"May I see some identification, please?" I asked.

The man flashed a badge in front of the peephole.

"Who are you here to see?"

"Ananka Fishbein," said the FBI man.

"I'm sorry, but my parents aren't at home. Can you come back later?"

"I'm afraid I can't, Miss Fishbein. This is urgent."

Had I been alone in the house, there's nothing he could have said that would have persuaded me to open the door. But since I had backup, I figured it was probably best to get any questioning out of the way before my parents came home. I opened the door, and the man stepped inside. He was a little slicker than I would have expected, with a complicated haircut and carefully manicured fingernails.

"Would you like to have a seat?" I asked, showing him into the living room.

"Yes, thank you." He lowered himself onto the couch, taking pains not to wrinkle his suit.

"What's this all about?" I asked, sitting down and trying to sound casual.

The man leaned toward me menacingly.

"We're looking for a friend of yours, Miss Fishbein. A girl your age. Four feet tall, white hair, pale complexion. Ring any bells?"

"What happened to her?" I asked, wondering how the FBI could know that Kiki was missing.

"We'll get to that in a minute. Could you tell me her name, please?"

I hesitated for a moment too long and the man detected my nervousness.

"I could take you in if I need to, Miss Fishbein."

"Her name's Kiki Strike," I said, and instantly hated myself for saying it.

The man jotted the name down on a pad of paper.

"Do you know where I could find her?"

I shook my head.

"When was the last time you saw her?"

"Not for a week, at least," I said. I was done with the truth until I figured out what the man was aiming for.

"Any idea where she might have been last night?"

"No."

"Where were you?" His eyes had locked on mine, and he stared at me without blinking. It was a run-of-the-mill interrogation technique, and I wasn't going to fall for it.

"Spending the night with some friends." I'd always heard that the best way to lie was to stay as close as possible to the truth. "Could you please tell me what this is all about?"

The man settled back on the sofa. As he crossed his legs, I saw that his shoes were handmade. His suit was also surprisingly flamboyant for a government employee. He looked more like an international playboy than someone paid to uphold the law.

"So tell me how you met this . . ." He looked down at his notes. "Kiki Strike."

"We go to the same school."

"Ever noticed anything unusual about her?"

"Not really," I said, trying to look innocent.

"Well, your friend isn't who she says she is. Her name isn't Kiki Strike. In fact, she isn't even an American."

The conversation was getting quite interesting.

"Okay, then, who is she?"

"She's an international assassin."

I'd thought I was ready for anything.

"She's twelve!" I uttered in disbelief.

"I didn't say she was in it alone." He reached into his pocket and pulled out a grainy photo. For a moment I expected to see one of the Irregulars. "Recognize her?" he said, holding up a picture of a young Verushka. She was wearing military fatigues and aiming a machine gun at the camera.

"This is your friend's mentor, a woman named Verushka Kozlova. Ms. Kozlova was once a member of the Pokrovian royal guard, but she betrayed her employers and joined the revolution. Now she's wanted for numerous crimes, including the assassinations of Princess Sophia of Pokrovia and her husband.

"Verushka Kozlova is a very dangerous woman, Miss Fishbein. She's an accomplished sniper, she speaks a dozen languages, and she's mastered most of the martial arts. She's been training your friend for more than a decade."

"Training her?" I managed to mumble. "To do what?"

"Eliminate her targets."

"Targets?"

"Yes, I believe you're familiar with one of the targets of the operation as well. Princess Sidonia of Pokrovia?"

My head was swimming.

"She goes to my school, too."

"As long as Princess Sidonia and her mother are

alive, there's a chance they could return to rule Pokrovia. Ms. Kozlova will stop at nothing to kill them. In fact, she and your friend came very close to accomplishing their goal last night. Are you sure you know nothing about it?"

"About what?" I asked.

The man watched me silently for what seemed like ages. I made an effort not to squirm.

"Miss Fishbein, are you aware of the trouble you'll be in if you choose to aid a known assassin?"

"Yes, sir. I am." I wasn't, but I had a feeling that it wouldn't be good.

"If you hear from Kiki Strike, I want you to call me immediately." He rose from his seat and handed me a business card with the FBI logo stamped on the top and the name Bob Goodman written across the bottom.

"I will," I promised.

I walked him to the door. When he stepped into the hallway, he stopped and turned to face me.

"One last question, Miss Fishbein. Do you know how Kiki Strike might have gotten underneath the Princess's house?"

I tried my best to look confused.

"Underneath her house? No, sir. I have no idea."

"Thank you for your cooperation, Miss Fishbein," said the man.

"Any time," I responded, hoping he didn't take the offer seriously. I watched him walk to the stairway. Only when the sound of his footsteps had faded away did I close the door of my apartment.

As soon as they heard the door slam shut, the other Irregulars rushed into the living room.

"How much did you catch?" I asked.

"All of it," whispered Betty, who was trembling with anxiety. "We were hiding in the hall closet."

"Kiki's an assassin?" muttered Oona in disbelief.

"That's what the man said." I still hadn't decided what to believe.

"Do you think he was telling the truth?"

"I don't know. Kiki was up to something, that's for sure. But there was something strange about that FBI guy. His shoes weren't right. I'm pretty sure they were handmade."

"There's a rule against wearing handmade shoes in the FBI?" Luz scoffed, but Betty was nodding.

"Awfully expensive for a civil servant," she said. "I wish I could have seen them."

"Anyway, it doesn't matter whether he was lying or not," I said. "I know what we have to do."

"What?" asked Oona.

As the others waited eagerly for the answer, I experienced my first taste of power.

"Whether she's an assassin or just a lowly thief, we can't let her cause any more trouble. We have to stop Kiki Strike."

HOW TO TELL A LIE

As you learned in chapter 2, there are many tricks you can use to expose a liar. Unfortunately, you're not the only one who knows them. So when you find yourself in a position where telling a little, tiny, insignificant fib or two is in the interest of the common good, it's an excellent idea to stick to the following guidelines.

1. **Always try to be yourself.** Your friends and family know how you usually behave, so they'll be quick to spot it if you start sweating, talking too quickly, or gesturing wildly—unless that's what you're usually like.

2. **Practice makes perfect.** If you have to tell a fib, practice in front of a mirror until it's so familiar that you could repeat it in your sleep. That way, when the time comes, you'll feel perfectly in control and you won't end up stumbling over your words.

3. **The more detailed your story, the better.** It may sound a little suspicious if you say, "I couldn't have stolen that priceless artifact from the museum because I was with my friend Betty all day." Instead, try to make your fib a little more interesting. "I was with my friend Betty Bent at the library looking for books on puppies." For additional credibility, feel free to add further details that can't possibly be checked. For instance, you might go on to elaborate, "I've been thinking about getting a Chihuahua, because I've read that they bite more people than any other dog." Of course, don't add so many details that you won't be able to memorize your story. There's always a chance that you will have to repeat it at a later date.

4. **Make it embarrassing.** Few people will doubt a story if it sounds like something you'd rather not admit. So instead of telling the principal you missed class because you were at the doctor, try telling her you went to see the doctor because you had a terrible case of diarrhea. She probably won't ask too many questions.

5. **Most importantly, try to stay close to the truth.** If you don't feel like you're lying, you won't look like it, either.

ChAPTER 10

A Visit from Lady Luck

Joan of Arc, France's favorite girl warrior, was only fourteen years old when she left home to fight for her country. Some say the voice of God was whispering in her ear, urging her to take up arms. Others claim that the voices inside her head were clear evidence that the girl was a little loopy. Whatever you choose to believe, there are certain facts that can't be disputed. She was fourteen. She was a girl. And she was about to lead the French army against their mortal foes, the English.

What many people don't know is that the voices had been egging Joan on for more than two years before she finally summoned the nerve to kick some English butt. You can hardly blame her for stalling. After all, Joan was little more than a scrawny peasant lass, and she lived at a time when goats were more valued than girls. But Joan was no coward. She just wasn't certain she was the right person for the job.

Of course, these days it's hard to take a pleasant stroll

in France without stumbling across a statue of a tiny girl dressed in knight's armor. There's little doubt that Joan was indeed the right girl for the job. She just needed a little convincing. And therein lies the moral of this side trip to the fifteenth century. Not everyone is born with a desire to lead. But in times of crisis, even girls who would rather stay at home and tend to the pigs should answer the call of duty.

☆   ☆   ☆

If you had come to me in the hours after Kiki Strike's disappearance and asked me to choose the next leader of the Irregulars, I wouldn't have nominated myself. At the time, I thought Oona would make a much better choice. She had the confidence it takes to get people to sit up and pay attention—and the temper to make sure they did. In fact, if anyone had actually offered me the role, I probably wouldn't have taken it. I might have preferred to spend my time catching rabid raccoons with my bare hands or defusing bombs while blindfolded. But once we knew that Kiki was gone, somebody had to take charge. The subject wasn't discussed, and there was never a vote, but somehow I ended up with the job.

I never dreamed that the Irregulars would take me seriously. I had none of Kiki Strike's charisma, and the only thing I'd ever led was a lunchroom line. Standing in front of the other girls, I felt like the pudgy, line-fumbling understudy of a brilliant Broadway actress. But though I longed to step out of the spotlight, I knew the Irregulars were looking to me to come up with a plan. So I did. If Kiki Strike is still alive, we have to find her, I informed the group, trying to keep a tremor from my voice. And we aren't going to turn her in to an overdressed FBI agent. Assassin or not, Kiki needs to answer to *us* first. We deserve to know what she was after and why she chose to betray us. Once she answers our questions, I said, we can then decide how to punish her.

To my surprise, no one argued, although I suspected that a couple of girls would have preferred a plan with a little more violence. Luz was eager to recover the gold by any means necessary. Oona just wanted to make Kiki pay. And while sweet-tempered Betty refused to believe that Kiki had abandoned the Irregulars, she had to agree that Kiki owed us an explanation. By the time the Irregulars left my apartment, they not only had a new leader—they had a new mission.

Unfortunately, I didn't foresee how long it would be before the Irregulars could put my plan into action. DeeDee spent three long weeks being poked by doctors and prodded by nurses. Her faithful housekeeper kept quiet and never told DeeDee's parents about the mysterious circumstances surrounding her accident, but DeeDee was still forbidden from conducting experiments until her head wound healed. Her parents locked up her laboratory and confiscated her chemicals. She may have survived an explosion, but for a while, I worried that the boredom might do DeeDee in.

The rest of us weren't much luckier. When my mother and father returned from New Haven, I met them at the door with a carefully crafted fib that involved an early-morning trip to the library. I even slyly suggested they check my story with the librarian at the Abingdon branch of the New York Public Library. My parents nodded along, but I could tell they didn't believe a word of it. For several weeks, they paid an annoying amount of attention to my comings and goings. They also decided they preferred a tidy house and kept me mopping and scrubbing for hours each day. But aside from the unsightly calluses I developed, I suppose I got off easy. Betty's parents grounded her and paid a sadistic babysitter to make sure she stayed in bed at night. And of course, Luz fared the worst. When she hadn't shown up from her summer job, her mother had called the police. They had already put out an all-points bulletin and were trying to locate a missing entomologist by the time Luz showed up covered in dirt and soot. However ingenious her excuse may have been, she wasn't allowed out of her bedroom until the beginning of school.

Fortunately, Luz's cruel imprisonment couldn't prevent her from breaking the law. While her mother slept, she built five illegal police scanners and lowered four of them out her bedroom window to Oona, who was stationed on the street below. Having mysteriously escaped all punishment, Oona was able to deliver the goods to the rest of us. Luz's handiwork allowed the Irregulars to eavesdrop on the New York police department and listen for news of Kiki Strike. But other than an amusing encounter between a SWAT team and an escaped Komodo dragon, we heard little of interest.

It was late July before my parents stopped ordering me around like the family maid. Oona and I spent our last weeks of summer break staking out Sidonia Galatzina's house, waiting for Kiki to strike again. We weren't interested in protecting the Princess. As far as I was concerned, the obnoxious brat and her haughty mother deserved whatever was coming to them. We just wanted to find Kiki, and the Princess and her jewelry seemed to be the perfect bait. But it soon became clear that we were wasting our time. From what I could tell, Kiki Strike was done with diamonds.

By the time DeeDee, Betty, and Luz were free to join the hunt for Kiki Strike, I had already begun to believe she was gone for good. After two months of watching and waiting, we were still no closer to finding her. Summer break ended, and the Irregulars started the eighth grade. With Kiki missing, our lives felt almost normal—too normal. Then, on a Saturday in early November, just after my thirteenth birthday, there came an unexpected knock at my apartment door.

✦   ✦   ✦

Peering through the peephole, I could tell that the man on the other side of the door wasn't with the police or the FBI. His face was hidden, but I could see he was short, unkempt, and wearing a tweed suit that was fraying at the lapels.

"Hello?" I called through the door.

"Ananka Fishbein?" squeaked the man in a harsh New York accent.

"Who's asking?"

"My name is J. Willard Katzwinkle. I'm from the Capybaras Corporation."

"The what?" I asked.

The man cleared his throat nervously.

"The Capybaras Corporation? We, ah, we specialize

in environmentally friendly rodenticides. You know, rat traps, poisons, that sort of thing. If you've got a minute, I'd like to talk to you about your Reverse Pied Piper."

"Do you have any identification?" My heart was thumping painfully inside my chest. If the man knew about the Reverse Pied Piper, the information could only have come from Kiki Strike. Though he was short and slovenly, I couldn't dismiss the possibility that he might be a killer. So, as he slid a business card under the door, I ran and grabbed a can of oven cleaner from beneath the kitchen sink. If the little man had come to do Kiki Strike's dirty work, he was in for a nasty surprise.

I opened the door, holding the can of oven cleaner behind my back. The man standing in the hall resembled a large rodent. His nose was long and pointy, his teeth were stained a dark yellow, and his mustache grew like a set of bristly whiskers.

"Who told you about the Reverse Pied Piper?" I demanded to know. Mr. Katzwinkle began to fidget with one of his lapels.

"I got a letter from a friend of yours. She said you had an invention you might wanna sell."

"What friend?"

The man shook his head and smiled meekly.

"Sorry, I shouldn't have said anything. I'm not supposed to tell you until after we've talked."

I almost slammed the door, but my curiosity got the better of me.

"Okay. Then tell me this. The postmark on the letter," I said. "Where was it from?" I already knew who had sent it, but I needed to know where she was.

"You know, it's funny you should ask. I don't usually pay attention to those kinds of things, but this one was unusual. It was shaped like a tea bag. I think it said Hong Kong." His answer left me a little stunned.

"Come in, Mr. Katzwinkle," I said, hoping I could learn more about Kiki Strike's whereabouts. "And please, have a seat."

I slid the can of oven cleaner between two sofa cushions as I settled in the living room. Mr. Katzwinkle looked around nervously, as if scanning the surroundings for predators, and I realized I had nothing to fear. The rat man was too jittery to do me much harm and too preoccupied to realize I was only thirteen years old.

"The letter said you had, ah, invented a powerful rodent removal device."

"I didn't invent it. My grandfather did."

The man looked bewildered and began fidgeting again.

"Oh? In that case, I should talk to your grandfather. Where can I find him?"

"You can't. He's been dead for years. A friend of mine built a few Reverse Pied Pipers using my grandfather's sketches."

"You've got prototypes?" asked Mr. Katzwinkle. "Do you have one handy?"

"Sure." I retrieved a Reverse Pied Piper from my backpack and handed it to the rat man.

"Looks like a kazoo," he noted, turning the device over and over in his hands. "How does it work?"

"It works like a kazoo, too. You just turn it on and blow into it. Rats can't stand the noise."

The rat man looked skeptical.

"Mind if I try?"

"Go ahead. But blow it out the window. We have a mouse in the cupboard that I don't want to disturb."

The man threw open the window and leaned outside. I wasn't sure if he would get any results. There were no creatures of any kind to be seen in the little park below. After wiping the mouth of the Reverse Pied Piper on his shirtsleeve, the man put it to his lips and gave a quick puff. Six enormous rats emerged from beneath a shrub in the park and ran as fast as their filthy legs could carry them toward a building across the street. A young man entering the building with two bags of groceries fainted when he saw the rats heading in his direction. As he dropped to the ground, his bags exploded on the sidewalk. Eggs, oranges, and a smoked trout flew through the air as the rats scrambled over the man's body. One of the rodents jumped up and caught the trout in its jaws before it disappeared into an alley. The rat man thrilled at the sight.

"Not bad, not bad," he said. "It works pretty good with *Rattus norvegicus*. But who's to say they ain't gonna come back?"

"I wouldn't worry about that," I assured him. "My grandfather's experiments showed that rats find the sound so unpleasant that just the memory of it keeps them away."

The rat man paced the living room as he quietly studied the Reverse Pied Piper. He tried to keep a straight face, but he couldn't conceal the gleam in his eyes. He was ready to make a deal.

"Would you mind excusing me while I call the office?" he asked.

I nodded and went to the kitchen, where I attempted to eavesdrop with my ear against the door. I could hear Mr. Katzwinkle whispering into the phone, but I couldn't decipher a single word. When the conversation was over, I allowed a few minutes to pass before I returned to the living room.

The rat man was pacing the room again, his eyes caressing his new love. When he saw me, he cleared his throat and tried to make his voice sound as official as possible.

"Pending thorough testing of your Reverse Pied Piper, the Capybaras Corporation is prepared to make you a very generous offer."

"Really?" I said, hoping I didn't sound too eager. "How much?"

The man looked up at me with a sheepish grin. "I've been authorized to offer you two million dollars," he said. "Oh yeah, I almost forgot. Kiki Strike says to wish you a very happy birthday."

★ ★ ★

"Two million dollars!" shouted Luz, who had suddenly transformed from a sullen scientist into the happiest girl in the world.

I had called a meeting of the Irregulars at a coffee shop near Kiki's hidden house. A nosy waiter craned his neck, trying to listen in on our conversation.

"It's not all ours," I whispered, knowing there could be spies anywhere. "About half goes to taxes. And I'm not old enough to sign contracts, so I had to make a deal with my parents. They get half of what's left over. It's only fair, I guess. The blueprints were in their house, and it was my mother's father who invented the Reverse Pied Piper. But the other half goes to me, which means there's a little more than a hundred thousand dollars for each of us."

"You're giving us a hundred thousand dollars?" Oona asked. Her eyes were as wide as my parents' had been when I had given them the news. They still couldn't believe that their daughter, a straight C student, had managed to make them a fortune.

"I'm not *giving* it to anyone," I told the group. "You've all earned it. And I didn't set this whole thing up. Kiki Strike did."

At the mention of her name, the conversation turned serious.

"What does *she* want?" sneered Luz.

"I don't know," I admitted. "She doesn't want money, or she could have sold her own Reverse Pied Piper and cut us out of the deal."

"Maybe she wants to pay us back," said Betty. "Maybe she wants to be friends again."

"She's trying to buy our goodwill," said DeeDee, shaking her head thoughtfully. Her hair had at last grown to an attractive length, but the scar on her forehead would turn a vivid red whenever she was excited. "She probably wants to lower our defenses."

"I think DeeDee's right," I agreed.

"If that's what she wants, she'll need to give me more than a hundred thousand dollars," snarled Luz.

"Does this mean Kiki's back?" Betty whispered, pushing

her sunglasses back and adjusting the curly red wig that made her look like a crazed Little Orphan Annie.

"I don't think so," I told her. "The postmark on the letter she sent Mr. Katzwinkle was from Hong Kong."

"I have a hunch she'll be staying there for a while," said Oona. "Here, I brought something to show you guys." She pulled a roll of paper out of her bag and spread it across the table. It was a poster for an Asian kung-fu movie. "Look what I found in a video store in Chinatown."

The poster showed a girl in a plaid school uniform standing triumphantly over an assassin's whale-sized carcass. Above her head she held a double-edged *jian* sword dripping with blood. Despite a black wig and glittery makeup, the girl's arched eyebrow and ice blue eyes were all we needed to identify her as Kiki Strike.

"Want to hear something funny? In Chinese, the movie is called *Cute Little Demon Girl*. Pretty dead-on, wouldn't you say? But get this. The clerk in the video store said it's coming out in Asia in a few months. Our sweet little Kiki Strike is going to be a movie star."

"Oona?" said Betty, looking a little pale beneath her makeup. "Are you sure this movie was filmed in Hong Kong?"

"Pretty sure, why?"

"They've been making martial arts movies in Chinatown. Right before school started, I heard my parents talking about a costume-designing job. They said it would be a challenge because the lead actor was really short. Do you think it could have been Kiki?"

"She must have spent all our gold if she's taking acting jobs," said Luz.

"Get over the gold, would you, Lopez?" Oona said, rolling her eyes.

"I don't think Kiki's back in New York yet," I said. "Why would she leave Hong Kong if she's going to be a movie star?"

The other girls looked unconvinced.

"I didn't know Kiki was a kung-fu master," said DeeDee, rubbing her fingers against her scar. "Maybe that's how she got away from the people who were after her."

"Maybe," I said, desperate to change the subject. "But if you're worried that Kiki will come after us, just think of how many kung-fu lessons we can buy."

No one laughed. What should have been a day of celebration had turned out to be as cheerful as a puppy's funeral.

❧   ❧   ❧

Within a week's time, Oona and Luz started martial arts training with a sushi chef who claimed to be a former ninja. But as the months passed and Kiki Strike failed to reappear, we all began to focus less on self-defense and more on spending our fortunes. Oona paid an unemployed actress to help her open a manicure shop. At first we thought she might have lost her mind, but Oona assured us she had a plan. And judging by the evil glimmer in her eyes, we knew it had to be a good one. Luz bought Mrs. Gonzalez's apartment and converted it into a private workshop, while Betty used her share of the money to start a business that sold designer Kevlar vests to women who wanted to be both fashionable and bulletproof.

DeeDee, the most pragmatic of the Irregulars, tripled her stash by investing in the Capybaras Corporation and a company that had developed a super-powerful kitty litter.

All in all, the Irregulars spent their money well. If you're ever lucky enough to come into a fortune, you should try to follow their example. A lot of girls would be tempted to throw their cash away on shoes, lip gloss, and new clothes. That's exactly what I did with my share of the money.

Before you start questioning my sanity, please let me explain. Every day, each of us comes into contact with hundreds of people who haven't had the opportunity to learn how intelligent, charming, and kindhearted we are. Whether these people are teachers, shopkeepers, or unpleasant young princesses, they have only one way to determine what kind of people we might be. It sounds terrible—and it is unfair—but the fact of the matter is, they judge us by how we look.

The good news is, with the right attitude and attention to detail, you can become whoever you want to be. For instance, if you want to proclaim yourself a rebel, a few carefully placed tattoos and some strategically ripped tights can go a long way. On the other hand, if you'd prefer to be the darling of authority, I would recommend a plaid headband and pleated knee skirt to go along with your eager smile. As for myself, I wanted a look that reflected my new power. For the first thirteen years of my life, people had always looked right through me. But now that I was the leader of the Irregulars, I wanted to make it clear to the world that I was not a girl to be ignored.

With Betty's help, I spent a day trawling the finer department stores of New York, choosing items that made me appear more formidable. With a new wardrobe stuffed into a dozen shopping bags, we made our way back to Betty's basement apartment in the East Village. Her parents were designing costumes for two new operas, and their apartment was crammed with headless dressmaker's dummies displaying the latest in Viking fashions and Venetian finery. The walls were decorated with detailed sketches of devious geishas, fat men in lederhosen, and Southern belles imprisoned in whalebone corsets and frilly hoopskirts.

Betty's room was large, dim, and cavelike. A weak beam of sunlight entered the room through a tiny window with iron bars. It landed on a row of featureless Styrofoam heads, each sporting a different wig. Betty sat me down at a vanity in front of her collection of prosthetic noses, ears, and lips.

"Are you sure you couldn't use a beauty mark?" she asked, pointing to a plastic box that held hundreds of fake moles, many of them sprouting long hairs.

"Just a haircut, please," I laughed.

"Well, then here's something to look at while I get to work." She tossed a supermarket tabloid into my lap. "I recommend the cover story."

The cover featured a photo of the Princess kissing her latest boyfriend—a famous actor who everyone agreed (behind her back, of course) was way too old for her. Alongside the picture was the caption: *New York's New "It" Girl*. It wasn't the first cover the Princess had graced. At age fifteen, she was already famous, though she'd done nothing to deserve it. Swarms of paparazzi waited outside the Atalanta School each afternoon, hoping for a new snapshot of the Princess to sell. She pretended to be annoyed but always offered them one of her six well-rehearsed poses.

Inside the magazine I found a picture of the Princess wearing a stunning silver dress and carrying a beautiful blue handbag.

"How much would a bag like that cost?" I asked Betty, thinking I might like one of my own.

Betty paused from her work and studied the photo.

"Twenty bucks," she announced.

"Oh come on, I've seen bags like that in other magazines. It's got to cost more."

"The ones you saw were real. That designer doesn't make handbags in blue. The only place you can get one like that is in Chinatown. It's counterfeit."

"Really?" I snickered.

"Yeah. You can't hide anything from the paparazzi these days," said Betty.

I put down the magazine and watched as Betty snipped at my hair with a pair of dangerous-looking scissors. For the first time, I realized how pretty she was with her own nose and hair. If I looked like Betty, I thought, I wouldn't change a thing.

"Why did you start disguising your appearance?" I wondered aloud.

Still concentrating on my haircut, Betty didn't look up.

"I used to be really weird-looking. I had a birthmark

in the shape of Florida on one side of my face. It just got removed a couple of years ago."

"But what's with all the wigs and things? Couldn't you cover the birthmark with makeup?"

"I tried, but I still got picked on. I was sick of being called a mutant or a monster or having kids ask me what was growing on my face. I complained to a teacher once, and she said I should just 'turn the other cheek.' She thought that was really funny. So at some point, I realized it would be easier to become someone else altogether. If nobody could figure out who I was, they wouldn't be able to give me a hard time."

"But why do you still do it? The birthmark's gone. You look great."

"It's nice of you to say so, but inside I'll always be a mutant." Betty spun me around and began rummaging through a tool chest filled with makeup. "All right, we're almost done here. Just a dab of lip gloss, a touch of rouge, and a quick brush of mascara and your new look will be complete. Not too much makeup, though. That's the mistake everyone makes. We don't want you to end up looking like some old floozy."

When she was done, I avoided the mirror and chose a new outfit from the shopping bags. In the bathroom, I exchanged my ratty old clothes for a new skirt, sweater, and boots.

"Wow," said Betty when I emerged. "This may be my best work yet."

At first I thought she was humoring me, but when I saw my reflection, I had to agree. I would never be as pretty as Betty, but I looked better than I ever had. My hair was no longer mousey, my clothes fit me perfectly, and running around the city had helped me lose my last bit of baby fat.

"Do you think I look dangerous?" I asked.

"I'd say you look downright deadly." Betty grinned.

My transformation wasn't lost on my classmates at the Atalanta School. Girls who had snubbed me since kindergarten started inviting me to sit with them at lunch or study together after school. Remarkably, few of them seemed to remember my days as a pudgy misfit. A couple of girls even assumed I was new to the school, and sometimes, when I caught sight of my reflection, I barely recognized myself. More had changed than my hair and my clothing. My posture was straighter, my eyes were brighter, and my smile was more confident. I finally looked like someone interesting.

At first I was flattered by all the attention, but once I had visited my classmates' mansions and taken part in their giggly gossip sessions, I discovered that my new friends were hopelessly dull. None of them wanted to talk about books, and they changed the subject whenever I mentioned giant squid. I started to spend more time alone, watching the Princess and her friends, and wondering if Kiki Strike would ever show up.

I followed the Princess though the Atalanta hallways as she yammered away on her cell phone and tossed insults at scholarship students. She grew meaner by the day, treating The Five like servants and humiliating

Naomi whenever she could. She flirted shamelessly with Naomi's boyfriends, and insisted her friend wear only last season's fashions. Behind Naomi's brown-nosing smile, I could see hatred beginning to bubble up to the surface. If Kiki Strike didn't get to the Princess, I figured her best friend might. In fact, had Naomi decided to seek her revenge, I might have helped. But Naomi appeared to have been born without a spine.

As the months passed, I grew desperate for something exciting to happen. For ages, it seemed as if nothing ever would. After the kung-fu poster, our last clue to Kiki Strike's whereabouts came from a photo Betty found in a copy of *Town & Country*. It showed Prince Egon of Lichtenstein and a mysterious girl entering an exhibit of Russian royal jewels at the Metropolitan Museum of Art. The picture had been taken from behind, and although the girl in question was very small and her hair unusually light, it was impossible to say for sure if it was Kiki Strike.

Sadly, with Kiki missing, the Irregulars began to go their separate ways. Betty and I had grown close, and DeeDee phoned at least twice a week, but once I called an end to our weekly meetings, I rarely saw the other girls. DeeDee kept me up to date on Luz. They often collaborated on experiments and had become unlikely friends. But all of us lost track of Oona, who spent long hours at her nail salon and rarely had time to chat. Where she went after business hours remained a mystery. None of us knew where she lived, and Oona seemed to like it that way.

I spent an entire year doing little more than shopping with Betty and keeping an eye on the Princess. Many nights, I had nothing better to do than my homework. I tried studying the plague to help ease the boredom, until I found that the subject made me hopelessly nostalgic. Even a walk through the streets of New York could send me into a deep despair. Whenever I passed a building that was stamped with the fading logo of the Irregulars, I'd return home misty eyed and melancholy.

The day I turned fourteen, I began to worry that my life would always be dull. The night before, I dreamt of Kiki Strike and the Shadow City and woke up with my heart racing and a smile on my face. Then I remembered that my adventure was over.

Or so I thought.

HOW TO MAKE THE RIGHT IMPRESSION

(I hope you noted the title of this section. It's not about making a *good* impression, it's about making the *right* impression—which in many cases may not be good.)

Each day before I hop out of bed, I decide what kind of impression I'd like to make. If it happens I'm on trial for a crime I didn't commit, I might want to impress the jury with how young, innocent, and harmless I am. If, on the other hand, I plan to spend the day confronting villains, I would likely opt for a look that lets them know that I'm no pansy. But no matter what kind of person the day calls for, all it takes is one trip to the closet to assume the ideal identity.

Choose Your Colors Wisely
The colors you wear say a great deal about you. Pink, for instance, is a fantastic color if you want to appear sweet and harmless. But if you'd prefer to look powerful and mysterious, black is a far better option. Politicians have closets full of navy suits because the color helps them seem honest, even when they're lying through their teeth. Gray is good if you're going incognito, while red is certain to attract attention.

Pick the Right Clothes

Forget about looking "good" or "bad." Instead, ask yourself how you want other people to react. If you're going undercover, you'll want them to ignore you, so a frumpy pair of sweatpants and an old T-shirt will be ideal. If you want an older person to think you're trustworthy, slip into a crisp button-down shirt and pleated skirt. But if you're trying to intimidate a foe, search your closet for an outfit that makes you look a little unhinged.

Accessorize

Accessories can give your look a bit of a twist. Pearl earrings make any outfit look more prim and proper. Glasses can help you seem smarter. Pin layers of ordinary clothing together with several dozen safety pins, and you're sure to appear unstable. And never underestimate the power of temporary tattoos. They're easy, painless, and give any ensemble an edge.

Don't Forget the Details

This is where most people go wrong. Their clothes say one thing, but their makeup, hairstyle, or manicure says something else. So if you've chosen to be a rebel for a day, make sure you remove the baby pink toenail polish before you leave the house. And if you're trying to convince someone that you really are a responsible person no matter what everyone says, remember that a nice manicure (skip the red nail polish) and simple hairstyle can make your argument more believable.

Chapter 11

The Chinatown Incident

One Saturday morning in June, almost two years after Kiki Strike's disappearance, I was jolted out of a
peaceful sleep by the sound of my cell phone playing
the polka.

"Ananka?" said a quivering voice. "It's DeeDee."

"Who?" I muttered with a mouth full of pillow.

"It's *DeeDee*. Get up and turn on channel three.
Quick. There's something you've got to see."

With my eyes still half shut, I groped for the remote
control and flipped on the television. A young reporter
stood in front of the Chinatown Savings and Loan. Bright
yellow crime scene tape stretched across the bank's front
door, and a crowd of tired policemen and eager reporters
mingled outside.

I jumped out of bed and turned up the volume, keeping my eyes trained on the screen. It was clearly the
young reporter's first big news story, and he was grinning

like a rabid hyena. Several old Chinese ladies stood nearby, making obscene gestures in his direction.

"Good morning, Janice! I'm here in Chinatown at the Chinatown Savings and Loan, site of one of the most daring bank robberies in recent memory! Sometime last night, thieves broke into an underground vault and made off with more than half a million dollars in cash. Police have been examining the crime scene all morning, but a source tells me that they haven't been able to determine how the crooks made it into—or out of—this heavily guarded building.

"In related news, a nearby fur storage facility was also robbed last night, the thieves absconding with more than four dozen mink coats. Police are still searching for clues as to how the thieves gained access to the building, and it's believed that the two crimes may be related. I'll be coming back to you with more information as this exciting investigation progresses! Reporting live from Chinatown, this is Adam Gunderson for News Channel Three."

As an ad for a revolutionary new hair removal system took over the screen, I closed my eyes and tried to breathe deeply. Adam Gunderson had no idea just how big his story really was.

"Ananka!" DeeDee was still on the phone. "Ananka? Are you there?"

"Yeah," I said, wishing I could take a minute to think things through.

"Those buildings have entrances to the Shadow City, don't they?"

"Yes. They do."

"So do you think we were wrong? Do you think Shadow City survived the flood?"

I couldn't help but smile at the thought.

"I guess it must have. Someone's been down there. How else could thieves get inside the vault at the Chinatown Savings and Loan without being seen?"

"Do you think it could be her?"

"Kiki Strike? It's possible," I said, though my instincts told me it was *probable*.

"What should we do?" asked DeeDee.

"Call the Irregulars. Tell them there's a meeting at my house tonight," I ordered. "I'm taking a walk down to Chinatown."

I slid into a pair of jeans and a T-shirt. On my way out the door, I caught myself humming a happy little tune. Finally, life was about to get interesting again. The Shadow City hadn't been destroyed. The Irregulars would soon be reunited. But what pleased me most was the fact that we might have a chance to capture Kiki Strike. I was giddy with excitement.

As I made my way toward Chinatown, I daydreamed about the adventures that lay in store for the Irregulars. We could finish mapping the Shadow City. Luz could search for treasure and DeeDee could take all the scientific samples she wanted. But if we managed to catch Kiki quickly, I hoped I could convince the Irregulars to take another case—one that had the whole city talking. A week earlier, a kidnapping had taken place. The victim was one of my classmates at the Atalanta School—a high school sophomore by the name of Melissa "Mitzi" Mulligan.

☆　☆　☆

At the Atalanta School for Girls, kidnappings weren't as rare as they might be at other educational facilities. Over the years, several of my classmates had been abducted, then returned for record ransoms. Just a few years earlier, three women disguised as perfume samplers had snatched Dylan Handworthy from a department store. They kept her imprisoned in an abandoned sewage treatment plant until her music mogul father (a notorious penny-pincher) reluctantly exchanged five million dollars in unmarked bills for his only daughter. Dylan returned home unharmed, though somewhat poorer and smellier than before.

But Mitzi Mulligan's kidnapping was not the usual Atalanta abduction. Her father worked for the city as a subway engineer, and his salary could never pay for her freedom. What made her disappearance even more remarkable was the fact that Mitzi was the school's kickboxing champion. Whoever had taken her must have wanted something badly, for they couldn't have done so easily. Mitzi's perfectly executed kicks had hobbled some of the country's best kickboxers and were said to be powerful enough to take down a sumo wrestler.

Although I was upset to hear she'd been kidnapped, Mitzi Mulligan and I had never been the best of friends.

She was a member of the wannabes—the scholarship girls who wasted their time sucking up to rich girls like The Five. As far as the Princess and her cronies were concerned, there was no lower form of life than people like Mitzi Mulligan. They snickered at Mitzi's less than fabulous footwear and told anyone who would listen that Mitzi's father trapped rats in the subway tunnels and cooked them for his daughter's dinner. Eventually, the rumor even reached Mitzi's ears. Had she decided to kick the Princess's scrawny butt, few people would have stopped her. But Mitzi couldn't learn her lesson. She just took her punishment and kept coming back for more.

Then, much to my surprise, Mitzi's social climbing had begun to pay off. On at least two occasions, I had overheard the Princess speaking to her in what passed for civil tones. It looked like Mitzi might finally be making some progress up the social ladder. It was her bad luck to be kidnapped just as she was starting to become popular.

I may not have cared much for Mitzi Mulligan, but her kidnapping intrigued me. On the night she disappeared, Mitzi had snuck out of her parents' house. The security cameras in her apartment building had captured an image of Mitzi dressed in a flimsy party dress and tottering on a pair of stiletto heels. The police questioned her friends and classmates, but no one knew where Mitzi had been going or whom she had set out to meet. She had been missing for two days before her parents received a cryptic note written on elegant stationery. It informed them that Mitzi had been kidnapped, but it didn't mention a ransom.

Hoping for a clue to the kidnapping, I listened to the

rumors that floated about the school like scraps of trash over a subway grate. One girl claimed that Mitzi had been taken by a band of subway-dwelling mole people who wanted revenge against her father—the man who had evicted them from their underground homes. A strange girl in my chemistry class tried to convince me that Mitzi had been abducted by aliens, but I doubted whether beings from an advanced civilization would have anything to learn from probing Mitzi Mulligan.

My guess was that Mitzi Mulligan's kidnapping had been an accident. Since Mitzi spent her days trailing after the Princess and her friends, I wondered if the kidnappers had mistaken her for a rich girl. It was even possible that the kidnappers had been after one of The Five. I suppose I could have warned them, but I didn't. After all the suffering The Five had caused, a week in a sewage treatment facility was exactly what they deserved.

★ ★ ★

As I drew closer to the Chinatown Savings and Loan, an image of the Princess held captive in the New York sewers flickered through my mind. I burst into laugher, forgot to look where I was going, and knocked over a barrel of fingerlike roots that stood in the middle of the sidewalk. Several other barrels containing hairy seedpods and foul-looking fungi formed an obstacle course that blocked my path. They belonged to a Chinese herbalist shop with yellowing posters of wild ginseng in its windows. A little white porcelain cat with one raised paw waved to me from the windowsill.

As I stooped to toss the roots back into the barrel,

I heard an angry voice inside the shop. I peered between the hanging scrolls and into a dim room. Dozens of antlers dangled from the ceiling, and an enormous wooden cabinet with hundreds of tiny drawers stood against the back wall. A batch of dried shark fins and what looked like the claw of a giant bird poked out of an open drawer. Standing in front of the cabinet was an elderly man who was shouting in Chinese and shaking his fist at a dark-haired girl in a black cotton dress.

The girl listened quietly, drumming her fingers on the shop's counter until the force of the man's rage began to dwindle. When at last he was quiet, she said something softly in Chinese. Her words had a magical effect on the man. He nodded curtly and turned to the cabinet. Opening a drawer marked with a Chinese symbol, he retrieved a small glass bottle. The girl dropped the bottle into a black pouch and started for the door.

In an instant, the girl was looking directly at me. A sly smirk spread across her lips and she raised an eyebrow high above one of her icy blue eyes. She spun around, whispered to the man behind the counter, and disappeared through the shop's back door. It all happened so quickly that I barely had time to think. I ran into the shop and out the back. The old man shouted ferociously and snatched at my T-shirt, but I barreled past him without even pausing.

I followed the girl through the cluttered backyard of the shop, under a clothesline filled with dripping men's underwear, over a small fence, and out onto the street on the other side of the block. I arrived just in time to see her toss her black wig into a trash can and slam a helmet over her own long white hair. Then Kiki jumped on a black Vespa motor scooter parked on the sidewalk. As I watched her run a red light and turn the corner, it occurred to me that I had no idea what I would have done had I caught her.

☆ ☆ ☆

That evening, Oona was the first to arrive for the emergency meeting of the Irregulars. She was still wearing her smock from the manicure shop when she knocked at the door.

"You look good, Ananka," she said, examining me from head to toe. "No more pudge. And you got some new clothes. I always said you had potential." She took off her smock, revealing a stunning dress that looked better suited for a cocktail party than a nail salon.

"Do you always dress like that when you're working?" I asked her.

"Sure," she said. "It helps me remember why I'm there."

"Why *are* you there?" I asked.

"So I can buy more dresses like this," she answered.

Oona took a seat in the living room, and I handed her a drawing of the symbol I had seen on the drawer in the herbalist's shop.

"Can you tell me what this means?" I asked.

Oona examined the sheet of paper.

"Your calligraphy sucks, but if I squint my eyes and tilt the page to one side, it kind of looks like it says Devil's Apple."

"Devil's Apple," I mused. "Where have I heard that before?"

"It's wart remover, remember? We found a bottle of it in the Shadow City."

I was just about to search my library for information on Devil's Apple when Luz barged through the door with DeeDee and Betty following close behind.

"Did you see the news?" Luz demanded.

"Nice to see you again, too, Luz. And yes, we've all heard about the robberies," I said.

"I'm not talking about the robberies. They're ancient history by now."

"What, then?"

"You don't know?" Luz smiled and pretended to brush at one of the oil stains that speckled the overalls she wore around her workshop.

"Know *what*?" I hadn't seen Luz in over a year, and she was already driving me crazy.

"You heard about Mitzi Mulligan, that girl who was kidnapped?" asked Luz.

"Sure, she goes to my school," I said.

"Well, there was another kidnapping last night."

"We'll talk about the kidnappings later," I told her. "Right now we have more important things to discuss."

"I doubt it," said Luz, yawning annoyingly.

"What could be more important than the fact that the Shadow City wasn't destroyed?" asked DeeDee. "Did someone we know get kidnapped?"

"No, the girl goes to school at Bronx Science," Luz said.

"Would you get to the point, Lopez?" said Oona.

"I know why they took her. And I don't think anyone else has figured it out." Luz looked pleased with herself.

"Would you care to share?" I sighed.

"The girl's name is Penelope Young. Her mother works for the city—just like Mitzi Mulligan's father. But they mentioned one interesting fact in the news report. The new girl's mother works for the New York City Parks Department. I thought it sounded weird. Why would anyone kidnap two girls with no money? So I did some research on Penelope's family. Her mother was one of the original designers of the NYCMap."

"You mean *our* NYCMap?" asked Betty as the pieces of the jigsaw puzzle began to come together in my head. "The map with the gas and water mains? The one we took from Con Edison?"

"Yeah, except we could only find the bottom layer. Penelope Young's mother has access to the middle layer—the one that shows everything at street level."

"I remember," said DeeDee. "You said that if someone put all the layers together it would be a terrorist's dream."

"That's right. Anyway, Mitzi Mulligan's father must have access to the bottom layer. Penelope Young's mother can get the middle. I'd bet you a billion dollars that the NYCMap is what the kidnappers are after," said Luz.

"You mean what *she's* after," I said, more to myself than to the group. The other girls fell silent. "Don't you see?" I asked them. "It can't just be a coincidence. First someone finds a way inside the Shadow City and then someone else decides to steal the NYCMap? No. I think the same person's behind the robberies *and* the kidnappings."

"Are you talking about who I think you're talking about?" asked Betty.

"Who else could it be?" I asked.

"Why would Kiki want to kidnap Mitzi Mulligan?" asked Oona. "She already has the bottom layer of the NYCMap."

"We don't know that for sure," said Luz. "Kiki's computer was destroyed by the people who raided her house. She could have lost the maps, too."

"Wait a second," said DeeDee. "Aren't we getting a little carried away? Isn't she supposed to be in Hong Kong?"

"That's why I wanted to talk to you," I told the Irregulars. "Kiki Strike is back. I saw her in Chinatown this morning, less than three blocks away from the Chinatown Savings and Loan."

HOW TO PLAN AN ESCAPE ROUTE

Whether I'm crossing the North Sea on a luxury liner or spying on an enemy at the local Gourmet Garage, I always know what path I'll take should anything go wrong. But you don't have to wait for disaster to make use of an escape route. They also come in handy when you're avoiding an annoying suitor, evading the authorities, or running from a furious sibling.

Know Your Surroundings. Take a moment and look around you. Find out where all the exits, lifeboats, or hidden trapdoors are located, and figure out how to get to them quickly. It's always best to have at least two routes planned in case one is blocked. You should also make a mental list of possible hiding places and know how long you'll need to reach them.

Prepare in Advance. If you have time, practice your escape routes. That way, you'll be able to act quickly and confidently when you need to. (You should be able to escape from your own house in a matter of seconds.) And always know where you'll go once you've made it out.

Wear the Right Things. Unless you're attending a ball, try to wear clothes that will allow you to move comfortably. In particularly dangerous situations, you may want to choose fabrics such as wool or silk that won't easily catch on fire or melt under extreme heat.

Have the Tools You Need at Hand. If your escape route involves climbing out a window, it's always best to have a rope at the ready. A small flashlight can help you navigate in the dark, and a cell phone will allow you to call for help. But don't bother searching for unnecessary items. Take only what you need and get out fast.

Act Fast, but Move with Caution. As any horror movie will teach you, running blindly won't get you anywhere. Listen carefully and, in case of fire, check doors for heat before you open them—if they're hot, choose another path.

Smoky Conditions. If you find yourself in a real emergency, there may be smoke. Tie a wet cloth over your nose and mouth, and crawl on your hands and knees to an exit. Don't let your head drop too low, or you may breathe in toxic fumes.

CHAPTER 12

The Return of Kiki Strike

Most people think of maps as simple tools that can guide them from one place to another. (Of course, these tend to be the same dimwits who will tell you that disguises should only be worn to costume parties and that all good stories come with a moral.) But for those who know the right way to read them, maps can reveal remarkable secrets. Even the most ordinary road map can show you where to find dusty ghost towns, dangerous mountain passes, and swamps blooming with rare orchids. But there are other kinds of maps as well—maps that can lead you to hidden gold mines, lost Mayan cities, or the caves in the Oregon forest where Bigfoot resides.

Unlike maps of Wisconsin, these kinds of maps can't be purchased at your local gas station. They're usually kept locked away in bank vaults or tucked beneath your grandmother's mattress. That's because the guardians of such maps know they must be protected at all costs. The secrets they hold can be dangerous in the wrong hands. And there's no shortage of people who would be willing to kill or die for the chance to possess them.

Of all the maps ever created, the NYCMap was among the most powerful. Even the Irregulars' map of the Shadow City couldn't compare. Put the three layers of the NYCMap together, and the secrets of the greatest city on Earth would be laid bare. With the bottom layer of the NYCMap to guide her through New York's sewers and subway tunnels, the middle layer to help her find the perfect shrub to hide a bomb, and the top layer to show her the way into every building aboveground, a criminally inclined fourteen-year-old could break into any museum, destroy any building, or kidnap any Princess. And she wouldn't have to stop there. She'd have all the information she needed to bring millions of New Yorkers to their knees.

I hadn't forgotten the feverish look in Kiki Strike's eyes when Luz first told us she had found the NYCMap. For me, it had been a bit like discovering an alien spaceship. Though I'd found it fascinating, I didn't have the foggiest idea what to do with it. But Kiki had always understood the true power of the NYCMap. And once it was no longer possible to break into the Princess's house through the Shadow City, the NYCMap became Kiki's last hope. It alone could guide her to the one thing she really wanted.

I knew that if Kiki was after the map, the Princess, the Irregulars, and the entire city of New York could all be in serious danger. We needed to find her before she found us. But searching for a single girl in a city the size of New York is like looking for a diamond ring that you've flushed down the toilet. In other words, we had no clue where to start, and we knew it might turn nasty. Finally, Oona suggested we pay a visit to Kiki's hidden house. Of course, I doubted we would find her there. Few sane people would return to a place they've been forced to flee in a hail of bullets. But we couldn't afford not to follow every lead. If she was after the NYCMap, Kiki Strike was more dangerous than I had ever imagined. And unless we could stop her quickly, I'd be forced to take drastic action. I didn't want to do it, but I was prepared to call the police.

✦   ✦   ✦

The Irregulars waited until dark and set out through the streets of Greenwich Village. We arrived at the wooden gate at 133½ Bank Street to find that the knocker in the shape of a severed hand had been replaced with a bronze smiley face engraved with the words *Have a Nice Day!* With an effortless flick of her wrist, Oona picked the lock, and the gate creaked open. The little garden was in full bloom, and warm light streamed out the windows of the cheerful storybook cottage. Hiding behind a bush in the yard, I took out my trusty binoculars and aimed them toward the house.

Sinking into the cushions of an overstuffed sofa were angelic dark-haired twins sporting pretty purple party dresses. One girl's dress was embroidered with the name Emily, while the other girl's dress bore the name Charlotte. Apparently, even their parents had a hard time telling them apart.

Without so much as a warning, Emily pounced on her sister, and soon the two girls were beating each other senseless. Charlotte sat on top of Emily, her fingers entwined in her sister's curly hair, yanking with all her might. Emily's hands were locked about her twin's throat. The two girls seemed intent on killing each other, and I had a feeling we were witnessing just one battle in a long and bloody war.

A tired-looking man whom I took to be their father entered the living room from the kitchen, carrying a newspaper under his arm. He stepped over the twins, who were locked in mortal combat, and took a seat in an armchair by the fire. As Charlotte turned blue and began to lose consciousness, he opened the newspaper and started to read, ignoring the struggle taking place at his feet.

"Kiki must have sold the house." I shoved the binoculars at Oona and silently thanked my parents for allowing me to remain an only child.

"Yeah, but look on the bright side. If we ever need to hire an assassin, we'll know where to come," Oona remarked with a note of respect in her voice. "That Emily's a real killer."

We slid out of the bushes, and tiptoed through the yard to Bank Street. Though the hidden house had been a long shot, I had secretly hoped we would find Kiki Strike sitting on the sofa, wearing a mink coat and counting the cash she had stolen from the Chinatown Savings and Loan. Now those foolish hopes had vanished. I said nothing to the other girls, but I wondered how long we should look for Kiki before I took our story to the authorities.

With no time to waste, we started our search imme-diately. That very night, in a flurry of caffeine-fueled ac-tivity, Luz crafted two miniature video cameras, each no bigger than a bonbon. The next afternoon, Oona care-fully tucked the cameras inside a pair of stuffed pigeons that Betty had discovered in her parents' prop collection. Before the sun had time to set, one of the cyborg pigeons was keeping a silent watch over the gates of the Marble Cemetery. The other recorded all the comings and goings at the Princess's brownstone on Bethune Street.

In case Kiki Strike made it past the pigeon guard at the Marble Cemetery, DeeDee and I rigged Augustus Quackenbush's vault with Deadly Device #575. Should Kiki try to pry the lid off his coffin, she would trigger a cloud of noxious gas that would render her unconscious for hours. Before we assembled the booby trap, DeeDee warned me that it would be difficult to deactivate. If the Irregulars wanted to return to the tunnels, we would first have to get our hands on some gas masks. After a mo-ment's thought, I decided to proceed with the plan. Gas masks or no gas masks, I reminded DeeDee, none of us had time to explore the Shadow City.

For a week, in the lonely hours between dusk and dawn, I monitored the snowy feed from the cameras and waited for Kiki to appear. The other Irregulars took turns patrolling the entrances to the Shadow City, searching for signs of breaking and entering at the dozens of buildings that were still marked with our logo. When we slept, we dozed with our cell phones next to our ears. Mine never rang, and each morning I left for school dazed and disappointed. Panic and caffeine kept me alert for signs of Kiki during the day, though I fell asleep twice during biology, and my hands shook so badly that the frog I was dissecting looked like he'd had a date with Jack the Ripper.

Apparently, the Irregulars weren't the only ones who were worried. One Saturday evening as I guzzled a tumbler of coffee, I saw a man in a dark suit arrive at the Princess's door. A thunderstorm was making the video from the pigeon cameras sputter and crackle, but I recognized the dapper FBI man who had come to my apartment after the explosion in the tunnels. The following Monday, the Princess was escorted to school by two large bodyguards who, judging by their jailhouse tattoos, had spent their formative years behind bars. After school, they followed the Princess wherever she went, happily shoving menacing senior citizens and dangerous toddlers out of the Princess's path. I watched the two hulks viciously manhandle enough innocent civilians to realize that even Kiki Strike, kung-fu movie star, would be no match for them.

According to school gossip, the Princess's mother had hired the bodyguards to defend her daughter from the danger of stalkers. But the main person they kept at a distance was Naomi Throgmorton. Naomi had been dismissed from The Five the day her father, an accountant to the stars, was arrested for stealing millions from his celebrity clients. It wasn't the crime that offended the Princess, but rather the fact that the last of Naomi's fortune had been used to pay her father's lawyers. A poultry heiress replaced Naomi as the Princess's new "best friend," and whenever Naomi tried to cozy up to The Five, the Princess's bodyguards escorted her back to her proper place.

Once, just before summer vacation began, I saw Naomi try to speak with the Princess. Ignoring her old friend, the Princess stepped into the Bentley waiting for her outside the school gates and slammed the door. When Naomi tapped on the car window, a bodyguard grabbed her by her designer belt and dropped her into a puddle that reeked of something other than rainwater. Inside the Bentley, the Princess roared with laughter. A scholarship girl tried to help Naomi to her feet, but Naomi angrily pushed the girl's hand away. Watching her walk down the sidewalk, leaving a trail of sodden footprints behind her, I felt sorry for Naomi. She may have been despicable, but I knew what it felt like to be betrayed by a friend.

While the Princess's bodyguards shielded her from social climbers, I continued to keep an eye out for Kiki Strike. By the time summer vacation began, I was starting to wonder if Kiki knew we were watching. Since we had started our search, the robberies had stopped and not a single girl had been kidnapped. As the days passed and my exhaustion grew, I began to see Kiki everywhere. I'd catch a glimpse of her peeking out from between the curtains in a building I passed. Ahead of me on the street, someone in black would duck around a corner. The loud rattle of a Vespa motor followed me, and several times I heard footsteps on the fire escape outside my bedroom. I still don't know whether any of these phantoms were Kiki Strike, but I could sense her presence wherever I went.

One night, Betty offered to monitor the pigeon cameras while I stepped outside for some fresh air. Strolling through Chinatown, I turned down Doyers Street, a narrow lane that curves in unexpected ways and never lets you see more than a few feet ahead. In the days when gangs ruled Chinatown, Doyers Street had been the scene of countless murders, and it was still an ideal place to ambush an enemy. I was thinking of all the blood that had trickled down that tiny street when I heard someone singing "Ring Around the Rosie." For a second, I wished I had chosen a different route.

As I rounded the corner, I saw a girl about my age sitting on the dark stoop of an old building. I hid in a nearby doorway and watched her. Her face was obscured by the shadows, but the girl's outfit struck me as familiar. She wore a dress smeared with grime and a single stiletto heel. As I inched closer, I saw why she had stopped. She held the other shoe in her hand and was staring at its broken heel, which dangled by a thin strip of leather.

The girl looked up as I approached. Her face was filthy, and her hair was greasy and matted. She leaned heavily against the stoop's railing.

"It's broken." Her words came out slurred, as if her tongue were too thick to move. She held out the mangled shoe like a child handing a ruined toy to her parent. The word *Italie* was stamped on the bottom. "Fix it, Ananka? Please?" she pleaded pathetically. It was Mitzi Mulligan.

There was no mistaking it. Something was wrong with Mitzi. The pupils of her eyes were the size of dimes. Having watched enough hospital dramas to know that this could be the sign of a serious head wound, I examined her scalp for bumps and cuts. Other than a dead bug or two, there was nothing to be found. I could think of only one other thing that might be responsible for her condition, and at first it seemed too ridiculous to consider. Girls like Mitzi Mulligan did not take drugs. But there she was, petting her ruined shoe and singing mixed-up nursery rhymes.

"Can you stand up?" I asked her.

Mitzi giggled. "Of *course* I can, dummy." She dragged herself up by the railing and managed to stand for a few seconds before she began to teeter, and then finally slumped back down on the stairs.

"Where have you been?" I asked.

"Fighting dragons," she giggled. She reached behind her and grabbed an unfashionably large handbag. She turned it upside down and a heavy metal object and a scrap of golden paper fell out. "See?" Mitzi handed the object to me. It was a bronze five-toed dragon, roughly half a foot in length. "Be careful. It bites," she warned.

The dragon's head wobbled from side to side. I gave it a gentle twist and the head popped off in my hand. The body of the dragon was hollow. A tiny amount of liquid trickled out, and a familiar, sickly-sweet odor rose to my nose.

"Where did you get this," I asked Mitzi.

"Party favor," she said, swooning. "You weren't invited." Her eyes fluttered, and it looked as if she might pass out on the stairs.

"Come on, Mitzi," I said, giving her a vigorous shake. "It's time for rehab."

"You're letting me go?" she asked, looking up at me in surprise.

The unmistakable rattle of a motor scooter appeared out of nowhere and began to travel slowly down Doyers Street.

"Get up now!" I demanded, grabbing Mitzi's arm and dragging her off the stoop. The urgency in my voice brought her around. "Kick off your other shoe," I ordered. No sane person would walk barefoot through Chinatown, but it was the only way to get Mitzi moving, and I figured she couldn't get much dirtier. Mitzi draped her arm around my shoulder, and I pulled her into an entrance at 5 Doyers Street. A staircase led to an old underground tunnel lined with tiny shops. Together we made our way toward Chatham Square at the other end of the passage.

When we emerged, I could still hear the scooter drawing closer. Ten different streets fed into the square, and it was impossible to tell which direction the scooter was coming from. As I fought off a surge of panic, a taxicab swung around Bowery and into the square. I waved frantically with my free arm, and it pulled to the side of the street. I shoved Mitzi inside, but before I could jump in beside her, a Vespa appeared on the opposite side of the square. The driver wore a black T-shirt, black leather pants, and a helmet with a visor that concealed her face. A shock of white hair stuck out from beneath the helmet. The Vespa stood motionless, the driver watching me from behind her visor. I bent into the cab and squeezed in beside an unconscious Mitzi.

"St. Vincent's Hospital," I told the driver. "As quickly as possible." As soon as the cab began to move, I remembered Mitzi's purse and the bronze dragon. I had left them sitting on the stoop.

✮ ✮ ✮

Once Mitzi had been wheeled into the emergency room, I settled down to wait for the police. Flipping through an old newspaper, I came across the story of a group of second-grade girls who had captured a mugger. The girls had chased the man into an alley, tied him up with a jump rope, and dragged him to a nearby police station. I smiled at the thought of justice being served and looked up in time to see Mitzi's father run past me. Shortly afterward, a nurse guided two middle-aged men with thinning hair and protruding beer bellies into the waiting room.

"Ananka Fishbein?" inquired one of the men in a brusque tone.

"Yes?" I offered an exaggerated smile to show I wasn't scared.

"You the girl who found Mitzi Mulligan?"

"Are you the police?"

"FBI, Miss Fishbein. We're investigating the kid-nappings," the bully's partner answered. He was the more pleasant of the two. "I'm Agent Baynes, and this is my partner, Agent Bellow."

"The nurse said you're friends with Mitzi Mulligan," the gruff agent barked.

"I wouldn't go *that* far. We just go to the same school."

"Still, it's some coincidence, don't you think? What are the odds *you'd* find her?"

It suddenly dawned on me that I was the only suspect they had.

"I couldn't tell you what the odds are. I've never been very good with numbers," I replied.

"And just what, may I ask, was a girl your age doing wandering around Chinatown in the middle of the night?"

"Taking a walk. I assume that's still legal in New York."

"Don't you know that it's dangerous for young women to be out alone after dark?" His gruff voice had assumed a fatherly tone that made me want to vomit—preferably on his shoes. I've always wondered why strangers feel they have the right to offer this kind of advice to girls—or why they don't seem to be as concerned about boys. I struggled to reply in a civil tone.

"It's dangerous for everyone, sir. Not just young women. Now, if you would stop interrogating me, I'll be happy to tell you what I know."

The two men glanced at each other and decided to adopt a different strategy.

The good cop took over the questioning. "Okay, Miss Fishbein. Please start at the beginning."

Without mentioning Kiki Strike or the Shadow City, I recounted how I had stumbled upon Mitzi Mulligan. I repeated everything that Mitzi had said, and even told them about the dragon I had accidentally left behind.

"You say Miss Mulligan had been drugged?" asked Agent Bellow.

"I think so."

"And what makes you think she hadn't taken the drugs voluntarily?"

"Don't take my word for it. Ask her yourself."

"I'm afraid Miss Mulligan either can't or won't tell us anything," Agent Baynes explained.

"Mitzi's the school's kickboxing champion," I sighed.

"She's about the last person on Earth who would ever take drugs. Besides, she gets tested before every competition. You can check for yourselves."

One of the men scribbled a note.

"So that's it?"

"Pretty much," I told them.

"Sure you don't want to tell us about the person on the scooter?" The bully had been waiting to spring this on me, and he looked quite pleased with himself.

"Who?" I asked, trying to play dumb.

"We just spoke with your cabdriver. He told us you were running from someone on a scooter when he picked you up. Mind telling us what that was all about?"

These guys knew what they were doing.

"It was someone I know."

"Oh, yeah? And who might that be?"

I thought for a moment before I spoke. I hadn't intended to turn Kiki in so quickly, but with the FBI sitting right in front of me, it seemed as good a time as any. All I knew was that Kiki needed to be stopped, and I desperately needed some sleep.

"A girl named Kiki Strike." I waited for a look of recognition to flash across the agents' faces, but neither seemed familiar with the name. Something wasn't right.

"Should we know this Kiki Strike?" asked Agent Bellow.

"I thought you already did."

"Agent Baynes, why don't you run that name?" The pleasant agent pulled out a cell phone and turned away while the other continued to grill me. "What makes you think we know her?"

"I heard a rumor she was in trouble."

"What kind of trouble?"

"I couldn't say, sir. I don't pay attention to gossip," I said, deciding not to volunteer any more information.

"Do you think she might be involved in the kidnappings?"

"No," I told him, acting on instinct. Why was I protecting Kiki?

The agent stepped toward me. He was close enough that I could smell his dinner on his breath. Chicken vindaloo, if I recall correctly.

"You know what I think? I think you're afraid of this Kiki Strike."

"I'm not *afraid*," I snapped at him. "I just didn't want to talk to her."

The agent on the cell phone hung up.

"We don't have anything on anyone by that name," he said to his partner.

"Do you know where this Kiki Strike lives?" asked Agent Bellow.

I almost laughed. "I wish I knew."

"In that case, is there anything else you'd like to tell us?"

"You know everything I know," I assured him.

"You're sure about that?"

"Absolutely, sir."

"Okay, then, Miss Fishbein. You're free to go. We know how to reach you."

I bent down to pick up my bag and happened to catch a glimpse of the agents' shoes. Both men wore wingtips that were polished to a shine, but clearly of inferior quality. Their suits, though carefully pressed, had also seen better days. Suddenly, inspiration struck.

"Do you have a business card?" I asked. "Just in case I remember anything."

With Agent Bellow's card in hand, I hurried out of the hospital. As soon as I was out of sight, I phoned Oona and asked her to meet me at my apartment. When she arrived, I placed two business cards in front of her. The first was Agent Bellow's. The second belonged to Bob Goodman, the first FBI agent to pay me a visit. Suspecting it would someday come in handy, I had tucked it away inside *Glimpses of Gotham*.

"What do you think?" I asked, handing Oona a magnifying glass. She examined the two business cards I'd given her.

"You're right, they're different," Oona finally said. "I wouldn't have guessed unless I had the other to compare it to, but this one's a fake." She held up the card that the first FBI agent had given me. "The FBI would never pay for paper this fancy, and the ink is far more refined than the stuff they use. But like I said, whoever forged this is a real pro. I don't know if I could do any better myself."

"I should have known," I muttered.

"How? Even I couldn't tell at the time. Anyway, you did have a hunch about Bob Goodman—if that's even his real name. Remember his shoes?"

"Yeah, but this changes everything," I said. "The real FBI isn't after Kiki. They don't even know who she is."

"What are we going to do?" asked Oona.

"I have no idea," I told her.

✿ ✿ ✿

There was only one thing I *could* do. The next evening, I stopped by St. Vincent's Hospital during visiting hours to check in on Mitzi Mulligan. I was surprised to find Mitzi freshly showered and shoving her belongings into a plastic bag.

"I take it you're feeling better?" I asked. Mitzi jumped at the sound of my voice. There was something different about her and it wasn't just embarrassment. Mitzi knew something.

"Hello, Ananka." Mitzi's hands were twitching, and she couldn't meet my eyes.

"So you've been released?"

"Yeah. I'm sorry, but I don't have time to talk. My dad's waiting for me in a cab. But thanks for bringing me to the hospital."

"Don't mention it," I said.

"I'm sure I acted like an idiot."

"It's not your fault," I tried to assure her. "You'd been drugged."

"It's still embarrassing." She grabbed her plastic bag, eager to escape from the room. I stopped her at the door.

"Mitzi, there's something I need to know. Can you tell me anything about the people who kidnapped you?" I asked.

Mitzi's face went blank. "No," she announced in a slow, steady voice that sounded rehearsed. "I already told the police everything I know."

A nurse popped into the room with an exquisite bouquet of flowers in her arms.

"Just in time," she sang, handing the flowers to Mitzi. "Better late than never, they say."

Mitzi tore open the envelope that was tucked between two lilies. Inside was another tiny envelope.

"It has *your* name on it," said Mitzi, passing me the envelope with a trembling hand.

I pulled out the card. There was no signature, but the handwriting was unmistakable.

350 Fifth Avenue. 86th floor. 21:00, it read.

I checked my watch. It was eight o'clock.

☆   ☆   ☆

An hour later, I was standing on the eighty-sixth-floor observation deck of the Empire State Building, looking out over the city. A thunderstorm was rolling in from the south. All the tourists had moved inside, leaving me alone, assaulted by raindrops that pelted my body from every direction. Leaning over the edge, I watched the city lights disappear as dark clouds surrounded the skyscraper. Soon, the observation deck was an island in the sky. Every few seconds, the clouds exploded with light. A gnarled bolt of lightning struck the needle that rose from the tip of the building. For the briefest of moments, it coursed with blue veins of electricity. A bird that had been seeking shelter from the storm fell from the upper reaches of the building. It landed with a thud at my feet, stone dead and faintly smoking.

A figure was standing at one of the telescopes that ring the observation deck. Wearing a slick black trench coat and dark hat, it bent over and peered though the lens of the telescope. As I approached, it glanced up at me.

In all the excitement at the herbalist's shop, I hadn't noticed how much Kiki had changed in the two years since I had seen her. She wasn't more than a few inches taller, but somehow she looked older than fourteen. Her colorless hair fell past her shoulders and her face had lost its elfin appearance. With her translucent skin and dramatic cheekbones, she was bewitchingly beautiful. The only makeup she wore was a lip gloss the same shade as the rubies in her ears.

"Want a look?" Kiki beckoned me over to where she stood, and I peered into the eyepiece of the telescope. Through a break in the clouds, I could see the statue of Washington Irving, which stood in the park in front of my apartment building more than forty blocks away.

"It's funny. Every time I see that statue I always think of him lying in the mud at the bottom of that hole." There was a hint of nostalgia in Kiki's voice. I looked up and saw the rain streaming down her pale face.

"When did you get back from Hong Kong?" I asked.

"Hong Kong? I haven't left New York in years." Then she laughed. "I guess you fell for it after all."

"Fell for what?"

"The postmark on the letter I sent to the Capybaras Corporation. I made a movie in Chinatown with a director from Hong Kong. I asked him to mail it when he got back to China. Pretty smart, don't you think?"

"Brilliant. How did you know I was at the hospital?" I demanded.

"The same way I always know where you are." She laughed again. Then seeing the serious expression on my face, she added, "You don't really expect me to tell you *all* my tricks, do you? Wouldn't that ruin the mystery?"

"Fine. Don't tell me. I don't care. What do you want?"

"Your help," she said.

"If you wanted my help, you shouldn't have run away when I saw you in Chinatown."

"Sorry about that, Ananka. It wasn't the best time for a reunion."

I looked away from her and into the clouds.

"Look, Kiki. I know you robbed the Chinatown Savings and Loan, and I know you're after the NYCMap now. In case you've forgotten, we aren't friends anymore. I have no interest in joining you in your life of crime. I'll turn you in to the police if I have to."

Kiki sighed. "I'm not a crook, and I *am* your friend. You just don't know it. I haven't been inside the Shadow City since the explosion, and I've never robbed anyone. What would I want with a bunch of mink coats? I don't even wear fur."

"What about the kidnappings?"

"Do you honestly think I'd kidnap Mitzi Mulligan? Even on drugs, she'd bore me to tears. I can't think of anything I want *that* badly."

"So you had nothing to do with any of it?"

"On the contrary, my dear Miss Fishbein. I'm planning to rescue Penelope Young, the girl who's still missing. Who better to find a fourteen-year-old girl than another fourteen-year-old girl?"

"Penelope's parents have the FBI and practically every police officer in New York looking for her. Why would they need *you*?"

"Because the Youngs want their daughter back, and they may be willing to pay the ransom. And if the FBI knew what the ransom was, they'd never let that happen. That's why the Youngs haven't turned over the ransom note to the authorities."

"The ransom is the NYCMap, isn't it?"

"I see you've been doing your research. Penelope's mother has access to the middle layer of the map—the one that shows everything street level in Manhattan."

"Let me guess—Mitzi Mulligan's father had the bottom layer. That's why they let her go. He delivered the ransom."

"Precisely."

I walked to the edge of the observation deck and watched the lightning strike in the distance. I hated to admit it, but everything Kiki had said made perfect sense.

"There's still one thing I don't understand," I announced. "Who robbed the Chinatown Savings and Loan?"

Kiki came to stand beside me. "I don't know yet. But you were right to think there was a connection between the crimes. It just isn't me."

"If you're not the link, what is?"

"This," said Kiki, pulling from her pocket the same vial I had seen her take from the herbalist shop. "When I found the dragon that Mitzi Mulligan left behind on Doyers Street, I recognized the disgusting smell inside. It was Devil's Apple."

"I thought it smelled familiar," I admitted, wishing I had figured it out myself. "But why was Mitzi carrying wart remover?"

"Devil's Apple isn't just wart remover. The main

ingredient is a powerful narcotic called mandragora. It's illegal, but it's smuggled into Chinatown and sold at herbalist shops. I have a hunch that the kidnappers are using it to drug their victims. There's no way someone like Mitzi Mulligan is going to willingly use drugs. But Devil's Apple can be slipped into a sweet drink without the victim suspecting a thing. And it wouldn't take more than a couple of teaspoons to knock someone out."

"So let me get this straight. You think the smugglers who almost found their way into the Shadow City are after the NYCMap now?"

"No, I'm just saying there may be a connection between the robberies and the kidnappings. We'll have to ask DeeDee to run a few tests if we want to make sure it was Devil's Apple inside Mitzi's dragon."

A jolt of anger hit me at the mention of DeeDee's name. Just because Kiki wasn't responsible for the robberies and kidnappings didn't mean she was entirely innocent.

"You think DeeDee's going to help *you*? Come on, Kiki. You nearly killed her."

"That was a mistake," Kiki said quietly. "I never meant to put any of you in danger. There was something I thought I had to do, and I forgot what was really important. You guys were the only friends I've ever had. I should have put your safety first."

I felt the anger draining out of me. Kiki's remorse seemed genuine, and it was the evidence I had been looking for—proof that she was a real human being. Still,

I wasn't going to make it easy for her. She was down, and I couldn't resist giving her a little kick.

"Friends?" I snorted. "You didn't even wait to see if DeeDee would be okay. You just disappeared. And you took our gold. You're crazy if you think Luz will ever forgive you for that."

"I didn't *leave*," Kiki insisted. "I was in hiding. I didn't have a choice. And I know it doesn't make any difference, but I did keep track of DeeDee. I called the hospital every day to check on her progress."

"How were we supposed to know that? None of us have heard from you in two years. Don't you think you could have called or sent an e-mail?"

"There are dangerous people after me, Ananka. I couldn't put you at risk. If they thought you knew anything, they'd come after you, too."

"What do you mean? Who's after you? And why are you willing to put us at risk now?"

"I can't tell you who's after me, but it doesn't matter anyway. Don't you see? There's more at stake this time. This isn't just about the Shadow City anymore. If the wrong people get their hands on the NYCMap, everyone in Manhattan could be in serious trouble."

"This is all too dangerous, Kiki. Stick to making kung-fu movies and let the police do their job."

"How can the police do their job when they don't even know what the kidnappers are after? We both know Penelope Young's mother isn't going to tell them about the ransom note. She just wants her daughter back. And can you imagine the cops believing *us*? Think about it,

Ananka. Could you live with yourself if the criminals get the NYCMap and you know you did nothing to stop them? That you didn't even *try*?"

"Why am I supposed to trust you?" I asked. "You lied about being Augustus Quackenbush's granddaughter. You lied about attending Atalanta. As far as I know, you haven't told us the truth about anything."

"I guess Oona snitched. So much for forger-client confidentiality. I can't make you trust me, Ananka. All I can do is tell you what I know and let you make the decision for yourself."

"But why do you need *me*?"

"I can't find Penelope without you," Kiki said. "You've got something I need."

"What? The map of the Shadow City?"

"No, though the map might come in handy. I need the Irregulars. And you're the only one who can convince them to help."

"Are you sure you're not after the Princess again?" I asked.

Kiki frowned. "Ah, Sidonia. How is she?"

"Mean, boring, shallow, stupid. A total waste of your time."

"That's what *you* think. But if you're worried about Sidonia, I promise she's the furthest thing from my mind right now."

"You swear?"

Kiki raised one tiny hand.

"On my mother's grave," she said solemnly.

ChAPTER 13

The Bannerman Balls

If by now you're a little confused, don't be too hard on yourself. Life is confusing, and anyone who claims that she has all the answers has probably uncovered the wrong ones. Was Kiki Strike a dangerous criminal or just a well-meaning vigilante? I hate to admit it, but I hadn't a clue. By the time we left the observation deck of the Empire State Building, the only thing I knew for certain was that I didn't know Kiki at all.

As our elevator plunged toward the street, I wondered how long it would take Luz to assemble a lie detector. I even considered asking DeeDee to whip up a batch of truth serum. But when we landed in the lobby, I knew there was no avoiding the biggest decision of my life. I could either help Kiki or hinder her. As the leader of the Irregulars, it was a decision I would have to make on my own.

"How do I get in touch with you?" I asked.

"If you're going to help, you can meet me on the northeast corner of Fifty-sixth Street and Third Avenue tomorrow at noon," Kiki said. "That's where Penelope Young lives. I've got a meeting with Mrs. Young. She thinks I have information about her daughter."

"I still don't know why I should trust you," I repeated.

Kiki's response was blunt. "Don't trust me, Ananka," she said. "Trust yourself."

The elevator doors opened, and Kiki vanished.

I thought she might be joking, until I realized it was excellent advice. Although it's often spoken of in jest, there's a peculiar form of ESP known as women's intuition. Every female on earth is born with it. Simply put, women's intuition is the little voice inside your head that whispers that your new boyfriend may be bad news, that you shouldn't take the shortcut through that dark alley, or that your sister has been snooping though your stuff again. If you learn to pay attention to the voice, you're likely to find that it's often accurate. Of course, I'm not suggesting that all women have supernatural powers. Unfortunately, only a few of us can predict the future or read people's minds. But I like to think that the rest of us are natural detectives. By paying attention to the little details, we notice when something's not quite right—even if we can't pinpoint what it is.

As I waited for a downtown subway, I took Kiki's advice and listened to my intuition. When the train pulled into the station on a gust of hot air, the little voice inside my head told me to get ready for another adventure.

☆ ☆ ☆

Penelope Young's parents lived in one of the glittering skyscrapers that form the famed Manhattan skyline.

From a distance, the building looked perfectly solid and reliably modern, but appearances are often deceiving. According to an elderly doorman in a threadbare uniform, the electricity in the lobby had been out for days. He guided us by flashlight to an elevator that jerked, jolted, and shook with the kind of mysterious thuds that you'd rather not hear while suspended hundreds of feet above the ground. When we reached Penelope Young's floor, we found that the hallway carpet was spotted with ancient spills, and several knockers had been ripped from apartment doors.

We tapped at the Youngs' door, and a tall woman with orange hair answered. Her eyes were bloodshot and her nose swollen. She caught a tear with a handkerchief.

"Hello, Mrs. Young," said Kiki. "Thanks for seeing us."

"It's nice to meet you girls. Please, come inside." She led the way through the apartment and gestured to a sofa in the living room. A breeze was blowing in through a large crack in the window. "You say you know something about Penelope's disappearance? Are you friends of hers?"

"No," said Kiki. "We've never met Penelope. But we do know why she was kidnapped, Mrs. Young, and we'd like to ask *you* a few questions."

Penelope's mother stopped sniffling.

"If this is a joke, it isn't very funny. Maybe you two girls should leave," she said.

"We'll leave if you ask us to, but unless you tell us what we need to know, our next stop is the FBI. They may find it interesting that you've been keeping the ransom note from them," Kiki replied.

"Ransom note?" said Penelope's mother, trying to look surprised. Her acting needed some practice.

"Yes, Mrs. Young. The one that demanded the NYC-Map."

"How do you know that? Did you come here to blackmail me?"

"Blackmail is such an ugly word, Mrs. Young," said Kiki. "I assure you that we only have Penelope's best interests in mind. If you're willing to talk to us, we can help you find her."

"But I don't have anything to tell you," the woman moaned. "Penelope just disappeared."

"On the night Penelope was abducted, the doorman saw her leaving the building wearing a yellow party dress. Do you have any idea where she might have been going?" asked Kiki.

"Noooo." The woman paused to sob. "Penelope would never go anywhere without my permission. She's such a good girl. A perfect child. So quiet and shy. I've never had a moment's trouble from her." Mrs. Young broke down, and we spent five unpleasant minutes watching her cry. "I'm afraid I'm just not up for being blackmailed today," she told us between sniffles.

"I understand, Mrs. Young. In that case, let's get right to business. May I take a look at the ransom note?"

Mrs. Young managed to retrieve an envelope from a nearby desk before breaking down again. The note was handwritten on expensive stationery.

We, the kidnappers, are pleased to make you this offer: Penelope Young in exchange for

layer #2 of the NYCMap. Instructions will
be delivered forthwith.

"Have they made any further contact?" Kiki asked.

"Nooooo," the woman wailed.

"Thank you, Mrs. Young," said Kiki, rising from the sofa. "We'll be in touch. In the meantime, I'd like you to call me if you hear from the kidnappers."

She handed Mrs. Young a business card. I almost laughed when I saw that it read: *Kiki Strike, Detective.*

"So you're a detective now?" I teased Kiki once we were inside the creaking elevator. "Like Nancy Drew?"

"Nancy Drew was just an amateur," Kiki sniffed, as if insulted by the comparison. "I'm the real thing. What did you make of Mrs. Young? Any thoughts?"

"A couple. First of all, anyone who thinks her daughter is the perfect child hasn't been paying much attention. Penelope was sneaking out of the house just like Mitzi Mulligan," I said.

"My conclusion exactly," Kiki agreed. "Anything else?"

"Our kidnappers aren't exactly run-of-the-mill. The paper the note was written on was pretty pricey. The penmanship was superb. And what kind of wacko uses the word *forthwith*?"

"So you think you'll be able to convince the Irregulars to help?"

"I hope so," I told her, crossing my fingers inside my pocket and praying we'd get lucky.

Since Luz was likely to make a scene, addressing the Irregulars as a group would not have been the smartest move. Instead, I opted for the strategy of statesmen and warlords around the world—divide and conquer. We would visit each of the Irregulars separately to make our case. Kiki's powers of persuasion would be put to the test, but two on one, we might have a chance of convincing them.

Oona was first on our list. I didn't think she would put up much of a fight, and Kiki thought she might be able to tell us something about the dragon that Mitzi Mulligan had been carrying the night I found her on Doyers Street. So after our brief interview with Mrs. Young, Kiki and I headed to Oona's place of business—the Golden Lotus nail salon.

As with many upscale businesses in the city, there was no sign marking the entrance, and only those in the know were welcome to drop by for a visit. Inside, the salon resembled the sort of spa where you might find a Roman empress getting her mustache waxed. The walls were decorated with ancient-looking murals, and a mosaic on the floor depicted an oracle lost in a trance. Wealthy clients lounged in plush chairs, trading gossip with their friends as young women dressed in simple white smocks painted their nails in garish colors.

An elegant woman stopped us at the door.

"May I help you?" she asked in an accent that shifted between Northern Italian and North Dakotan. Although everything about her appearance was designed to communicate snobbishness and style, I knew she was merely an actress that Oona paid to front the salon.

"We're here to see Oona. We're associates of hers," I informed the woman. Those appeared to be the magic words. A smile flashed across her face.

"Certainly," she cooed. "Miss Wong is with a client at the moment. Please have a seat, and I'll let her know you're here. Is there anything I can get for you?"

"Two café au laits, if you don't mind," said Kiki, staring ahead with a sly smirk on her face. I followed her eyes and discovered Oona hunched over the nails of a woman in a Chanel suit who was whispering with a friend at the next table. Both of the older women had indulged in so much plastic surgery that they no longer appeared quite human. One resembled a giant, wig-wearing insect and the other could have passed for a homely extraterrestrial.

As the hostess glided past Oona on the way to make our coffees, she gave her boss an almost imperceptible nod. Oona glanced up and spotted us waiting. She betrayed no surprise at seeing Kiki sitting on her couch, though I thought I saw her stifle a grin.

"I always suspected that Oona might be a financial genius," Kiki said.

"Yes, her business seems to be doing well," I noted. There wasn't an empty seat in the house.

"So she hasn't explained her scheme to you?" Kiki's raised eyebrow told me that she knew something I didn't.

"Scheme?" I asked. "She hasn't said anything about a scheme. You know how secretive Oona can be. I've known her for more than two years, and I still don't know where she lives."

"Well, it's pretty easy to figure out what she's up to.

Take a look at all the girls who work here. Other than the woman at the door, what do they all have in common?"

I glanced around the shop.

"They're all young and they're all Chinese," I said. "But so is Oona. It's hardly out of the ordinary."

"Maybe not. Now take a look at all of the women who are here to have their nails done. See anything unusual?"

My eyes passed over dozens of wealthy clients. They were all chatting as if there were no one else in the room.

"They brought their friends?"

"Yes. And why do they feel so free to gossip in front of the women who work here?" I watched Oona, who was mutely applying the finishing touches to her client's manicure. Suddenly, I knew what she was doing.

"Oona's clients don't think the Chinese girls who work here speak English," I said. "So they'll say *anything* in front of them."

"Exactly. Oona's not just painting that woman's nails, she's listening to everything the woman says. Gossip, stock tips, you name it. Oona's just a fly on the wall. So are the rest of them, for that matter. This room has more flies than the city dump. And they're all gathering information that Oona can use. I bet she even has her employees wired."

"My God, you're right," I said as the faux Italian woman returned with two steaming café au laits. "Oona *is* a genius."

We sipped our coffee and watched Oona bow to her client and accept a tip with a smile. The insect and her alien friend marched past us on their way out the door. Oona trailed behind them.

"You come?" Oona asked in a thick accent, gesturing toward the back of the shop. We followed behind her, past scores of women deep in conversation, and into an office in the rear of the building. As soon as the door was closed, Oona stripped out of her smock.

"Well, well. Look who's all grown up now," she said to Kiki. "Long time no see. Can you believe that old biddy gave me a two-dollar tip? Rich people can be so cheap."

"Still, I suspect the experience was worth your while." Kiki grinned.

"She did tell a funny story about her daughter getting kicked out of school. The idiot hired someone to take the SATs for her. She might have gotten away with it if it hadn't been a forty-year-old guy with gray hair and a beard. I had to hold my breath to keep from laughing at that one. Oh yeah, and you might want to purchase some stock in a company called Fem-Tex Pharmaceuticals. Her ex-husband says it's about to introduce a miracle drug that cures female baldness. And the size of my bank account is proof that he's rarely wrong."

"It's quite an operation you have here," I said.

"You guys didn't really believe that I was just sitting around painting nails every afternoon, did you?"

"I guess I should have known better."

"Yeah, you should have," agreed Oona. Suddenly her expression turned serious and she glared at Kiki. "But I don't think that's the point of your visit. What are *you* doing here?"

"Never one to mince words, were you, Oona?" said Kiki.

"I don't like to waste time. It's money, after all."

I let Kiki explain herself, listening with amusement as Oona barraged her with questions. Eventually, Oona started to come around.

"So what do you think, Ananka?" she finally asked me.

I shrugged. "I'm here, aren't I?"

"Luz isn't going to like this."

"Luz knows better than anyone just how dangerous the NYCMap can be. She'll understand."

Oona didn't look terribly convinced.

"I'm glad I'm not the one who has to win her over. So how can I be of service?" she asked Kiki.

"Take a look at this." Kiki reached into her backpack and pulled out Mitzi Mulligan's bronze dragon. Oona's face turned gray.

"I'm guessing you've seen this sort of thing before," said Kiki.

"It's Fu-Tsang," Oona said somberly. "There are nine Chinese dragons. Fu-Tsang is the dragon that guards hidden treasures. You're saying Mitzi Mulligan had this?" she asked.

"Yes."

Oona took the dragon from Kiki.

"This could be more than a thousand years old. I've seen similar bronze figures that have been stolen from ancient tombs in China and smuggled into the United States. Most of them are priceless. But this one's even more interesting. There's a gang in Chinatown that does most of the smuggling. Their leader's an old man named Lester Liu, and they use this dragon as their symbol."

"Do they smuggle anything other than dragons?" asked Kiki.

"Yes," Oona said.

"Drugs?" Kiki prompted.

"Sure. The Fu-Tsang gang will smuggle anything they can sell. One week it might be drugs. Another week it could be counterfeit designer handbags. And that's just the start of it. You'd be amazed at what people are willing to buy in New York."

"Do you know where to find them?" We waited for Oona to answer. I could tell from the look on her face that there was something she wasn't telling us.

"No," she said. "Lester Liu skipped town a few years ago. They say he runs the gang from Shanghai. And I don't know if we should go looking for the rest of the Fu-Tsang, either. They're not very friendly."

"I'll keep that in mind. Oh, one more thing." Kiki pulled out a scrap of gold paper. I remembered seeing the same scrap flutter to the ground when Mitzi dumped out her bag. "Mitzi was carrying this as well." She handed it to Oona. Only the letters *BANN* could be read.

"It's an invitation," Oona informed us, her mood lightening. "There were two girls in here yesterday. They must have been about sixteen. One of them had an invitation just like this. From what I've heard, there's a series of elite parties called the 'Bannerman Balls.' They're top secret. Only the crème de la crème is invited. It sounds strange, but the girls kept talking about boats. I think the parties may be held on an island."

"That makes sense," I said. "There's a Bannerman's Island in the middle of the Hudson River just north of the city. It has a castle on it that's been abandoned for years. But how did Mitzi Mulligan or Penelope Young get an invitation to a party like that? They're more like skim milk than the crème de la crème."

"The parties were the bait," said Kiki. "That's where they were kidnapped. Do you know who's throwing the Bannerman Balls?" she asked Oona.

"I don't think my client knew who sent the invitation."

"What was the girl like?" I asked.

"A total pain in the butt. She kept changing her mind about what color of nail polish she wanted. But other than that, she wasn't that remarkable. Just another blonde with a bad attitude. We get about two dozen of them in here every day. I think her father's a fire chief."

"Wow," said Kiki. "Talk about getting lucky."

"Yeah, how does a fireman's daughter come up with enough cash to hang out with the Bannerman Ball crowd?" I asked.

"*We're* the ones who got lucky, Ananka," Kiki corrected me. "A fire chief might not be a millionaire, but he *would* have access to the top layer of the NYCMap."

"So his daughter could be the next victim," I said.

"Do you remember the girl's name?" Kiki asked Oona.

"Not off the top of my head, but it should be in the appointment book."

"Did she say when the party was?" Kiki asked.

"Yeah. This Friday."

"It's already Tuesday," I moaned.

"We've got to get to her first," said Kiki. "One of us has to go to the Bannerman Ball in her place."

The girl's name was Tyler Deitz. Oona called the number she'd left to confirm her appointment at the Golden Lotus. In her thickest Chinese accent, Oona told the girl's mother that Tyler had forgotten a schoolbook at the salon. If she could only have their address, she'd be happy to send a messenger to return it. The woman thought nothing of giving her address to a perfect stranger, and within five minutes, we were in business.

The three of us headed over to Tyler's building on the Upper East Side, and waited across the street for her to emerge. Oona would identify the right girl, and Kiki's Vespa would allow us to follow her wherever she might go. That way we could get her alone. There was no point in talking to the girl if her parents were around.

After an hour of not-so-patient waiting, we saw an unpleasant-looking girl with long blond hair exit the lobby of the building and hail a cab.

"That's her," said Oona. "Good luck."

Kiki and I jumped on the scooter.

"Tomorrow night. Eight o'clock. Ananka's house," Kiki called to Oona. Then, with a quick wave, we roared off in pursuit of our prize.

If you plan to follow people in crowded urban environments, I would recommend investing in a scooter. While even the smallest car can get cut off or stalled in traffic, a scooter allows you to avoid any obstacles. She may have been too young for a driver's license, but Kiki was already a master of the Vespa. With little effort and no apparent fear, she zipped around kamikaze cabs, lumbering bicyclists, and men with baby carriages. I held on as we sped through the streets, trying to keep pace with a taxi hack who had missed his calling as a professional getaway driver.

Just as I was beginning to lose all sensation in my rump, Tyler's cab screeched to a halt in front of a midtown department store. Kiki pulled the Vespa to the curb, and we saw Tyler jump from the car and disappear into the store. I pulled off my helmet and started to follow her, but Kiki caught my arm.

"Slow down, Ananka," she told me. "There's no rush. It's not like we don't know where to find her. She's not going anywhere for a while."

We caught up with Tyler on the fifth floor. It was midday on a summer Wednesday, and the store was almost deserted. Only a couple of saleswomen drifted aimlessly among the racks of clothing. Tyler was making her way to one of the dressing rooms, followed by a salesman whose arms were straining beneath a pile of party dresses. Kiki grabbed several random items from one of the racks and shoved them at me.

"What do you say we try a few things on?"

One look at her wicked grin, and I knew she was up to no good. A saleswoman directed us to the fitting room next to Tyler's. As soon as we were alone with our new friend, Kiki knocked on her door.

"I found a few more dresses you might like," she called to the girl on the other side. The door opened a crack and Tyler peeked out.

"Who are you?" she demanded rudely when she saw the two of us.

"Your fairy godmothers." Kiki shoved the door open, pushing the girl onto the bench at the back of the stall.

"What the—" Tyler started to shout, but Kiki raised a finger to her lips and slowly shook her head.

"I wouldn't if I were you. One quick call to your parents regarding your plans for Friday night, and I doubt you'll ever find the need for one of these dresses again."

Tyler glared at us from the bench. She had a lot of nerve for someone who was wearing only her underwear.

"What do you want?" she spat, keeping her voice low.

"The invitation," said Kiki.

"How . . . ?"

"Don't waste my time. It doesn't matter how I know. Just hand it over."

"No way," said the girl. "I mean, even if I wanted to give it to you, I couldn't. I left it at home."

"You're dumb, that's for sure, but you're not stupid enough to leave something like that behind where your nosy mother could find it. Hand me your purse," Kiki ordered.

Tyler snorted. "Get out or I'll call for help."

Kiki leaned in close to the girl until their noses were almost touching.

"If you don't hand me that purse, you're going to *need* help." There was no doubting Kiki Strike's sincerity. The girl thrust the handbag at Kiki. Mixed in with the credit cards, lip gloss, and chewing gum wrappers was a golden invitation. Kiki pulled the envelope out of the bag, never letting her eyes stray from Tyler's. "If you don't mind my asking, how did you get this?"

"It came in the mail," said the irate girl.

"Return address?" asked Kiki.

"There wasn't one."

"Did you know about the Bannerman Balls before you got the invitation?"

"I heard people talking about them at school. Only the most popular people get an invitation."

"Wow. Dumb *and* deluded. Your parents must be so proud."

"You don't know what you're talking about," Tyler said. "For your information, I'm an honors student."

"Who isn't? A talking monkey could make the honor roll at most schools. Now, we're going to leave and let you get dressed. I recommend you keep your mouth shut until we're gone. Otherwise, my genius friend, this little slip of paper will find its way into your mother's hands, along with a suggestion that she keep a closer eye on her little girl."

"Go ahead. Take the invitation. You'll never get in," taunted Tyler with her last bit of moxie. "There will be people I know at the party, and you don't look anything like me."

"Oh, right. That reminds me," I chimed in.

"What?" snapped our half-naked friend. I pulled out a camera I had borrowed from Oona.

"Say cheese," I told her.

By the time we hopped on the Vespa, the clock on the dashboard read 1:30. Betty was expected at my house for coffee at 2:00. She was the second Irregular on our list, and now she was the most important person to convince. Without the use of Betty's unusual skills, we would have little chance of attending the next Bannerman Ball.

Not two minutes after we'd parked in front of my building, Betty arrived at the door dressed as a sultry flamenco dancer. When she saw Kiki Strike standing behind me in the hallway, she froze. For a moment, I thought she might turn around and leave, but instead she walked up to Kiki and gave her a hug.

"I knew you'd come back," she said. "I never believed you were an assassin."

"What? In less than twenty-four hours I've been accused of being a thief and a kidnapper, and now I'm an assassin?" Kiki arched an eyebrow and looked to me for an explanation. But if she wasn't going to tell me everything, I certainly wasn't going to open up to her, either.

"It's a long story," I said.

"I bet. I'd love to hear it someday," said Kiki.

It took only a few minutes to fill Betty in on what we had learned so far. The kidnappers were after the NYCMap and had already gotten part of it from Mitzi Mulligan's father. And we believed that Mitzi and Penelope Young may have been lured to the Bannerman Balls and drugged with Devil's Apple.

"How are we going to find out where Penelope's hidden?" asked Betty.

"One of us is going to the next Bannerman Ball disguised as one of the guests," said Kiki.

"This is Tyler Deitz," I told Betty, handing her the camera with Tyler's picture. "She may be the next victim."

Betty studied the screen for a moment. "There's only one of us who could pass for this girl."

"Who?" I asked.

"Me," said Betty.

"Thanks for offering, but that wasn't what I had in mind," said Kiki. "I've learned my lesson. I'm not putting any of you in danger if I can help it. I'll be taking all the risks this time."

"Wait a second, Kiki. How tall was this girl? Five six? Five seven?" asked Betty. Kiki nodded. "There's only so far that a disguise will go. I'm really sorry, but I just don't think you're tall enough. And the other girls would require a lot of effort. It's always best if a disguise doesn't have to work too hard."

"In that case, you've got the job," said Kiki. "And it'll be our duty to make sure you don't get drugged and kidnapped."

"I'm not worried. I trust you," said Betty.

Kiki grinned.

"Okay, then. Get to work," I told Betty. "We'll all meet here at eight o'clock tomorrow night to make the final arrangements. But first Kiki and I need to pay a visit to DeeDee."

☆   ☆   ☆

We found DeeDee alone in her bedroom laboratory, sitting on a stool surrounded by beakers that belched foul-smelling smoke and Bunsen burners that never rested. Clothes had been flung randomly about the room, and most were covered in substances that no detergent could banish. A month-old bowl of cereal left behind on a windowsill had begun the fermentation process and was bubbling like a witch's cauldron. And one corner of the room was dominated by a heap of rotten apple cores tossed aside by someone too busy to locate a trash can.

When she saw us, DeeDee dropped a test tube on the

floor, where it burst into flame. A thin stream of water shot from a system of pipes attached to the ceiling and doused the fire. The targeted sprinkler system had been a gift from Luz and had saved DeeDee's laboratory on more than one occasion.

Once the fire was out, there were no hugs or words of forgiveness. DeeDee pushed her safety goggles back on her head, showcasing the ugly scar that marred her pretty face. She invited us to take a seat, trying very hard to assume the character of a sober scientist. Kiki took her through the facts of the case one by one. As she finished, her voice grew softer.

"There's one more thing I have to say," Kiki told her. "I'm very sorry for what happened to you in the Shadow City. I let things get out of control."

"You weren't the only one to blame," sighed DeeDee. "I should have listened when Ananka said we were too close to the mains. You gave the order, but it was my decision to set the explosion."

"It won't happen again," said Kiki.

"That's not what concerns me," said DeeDee pensively. "We've all gotten older and wiser. We won't make the same mistakes. But before I risk my life again, I want to know one thing. Why are you doing this? Last time you didn't tell us what you were after. We deserved to know."

Kiki fixed DeeDee with her best snake-charming stare. "I still can't tell you what I was after the last time. I wish I could, but I can't. But believe me when I tell you that this time, my motive is simple. By keeping the NY-CMap out of the wrong hands, we could be saving New York from a terrible fate."

"That's it?" asked DeeDee.

"That's it," Kiki assured her.

"If Ananka's going to give you a second chance, I'll support her. But if it turns out you're just using us again, I will personally dedicate my life to making you suffer."

Coming from DeeDee, it sounded serious.

"Fair enough," said Kiki.

"All right, then. What do you need me to do?"

Kiki Strike handed DeeDee the bronze dragon, along with the vial of Devil's Apple she had taken from the herbalist's shop in Chinatown.

"Two things," Kiki said. "First, we need to know if the substance inside the dragon matches the Devil's Apple. If it does, we'll have solid proof that the robberies and kidnappings are connected. Second of all, when we send Betty undercover into the Bannerman Ball, there's a good chance she's going to be drugged. We need an antidote for Devil's Apple."

"I don't know about an *antidote*, but I think I may have something that will work. I'll do a few tests to make sure," said DeeDee. "When do we need it?"

"Eight o'clock tomorrow evening," I told her. "The Irregulars will be meeting at my house."

✯ ✯ ✯

Kiki and I had saved the hardest task for last. Convincing Luz to help us would not be easy. Leaving DeeDee's townhouse, we rode east, traveling along the wild northern border of Central Park. I was not looking forward to the encounter, and I hoped we didn't run into Luz's new boyfriend, Attila. According to DeeDee, his personality was every bit as challenging as Luz's, and his arrest record much lengthier.

We stopped in front of a building with a fresh coat of paint and a lovely little garden. A label on the buzzer simply read: *The Shop.* I pressed the button and Luz's voice called down.

"It's Ananka," I shouted into the speaker, and the door popped open. Luz's workshop was on the third floor, and we walked up a staircase that had been decorated with colorful paintings of tropical landscapes. The door to the workshop was open, and we entered without knocking. The former living room of the apartment was filled with appliances in various stages of dissection. The silicon brains of several computers lay exposed upon a workbench. In one corner of the room sat a half-assembled robot. Luz had been working on it when we arrived. Her welding equipment lay hastily discarded nearby and the room smelled of molten metal. Luz was nowhere to be seen.

"Luz?" I called, taking a few steps toward one of the bedrooms and leaving Kiki standing alone in the middle of the living room. A flash of light nearly blinded me, and I spun around to see Kiki trapped by a net of lasers that issued from a device planted in the ceiling. Luz emerged from the kitchen, a remote control device in one hand and a cell phone in the other.

"I wouldn't move, if I were you," she informed Kiki. "Those lasers can cause some nasty burns."

"Luz, turn that thing off," I demanded.

"And let a dangerous fugitive go free?" she asked menacingly. "I don't think I could live with myself. It's a good thing I have the FBI on speed dial." She held up the phone for us to see.

"Don't even think about it," I warned her. "Aren't you curious to hear what she has to say?"

"Nope," said Luz. "Once a liar, always a liar."

"True," said Kiki. "And once a juvenile delinquent, always a juvenile delinquent."

"*You're* insulting *me*?" demanded Luz. "You've got *some* nerve."

"All I'm saying is that you can call the police if you like, but they'll probably be more interested in you than me."

"What do you mean?"

"You own this apartment?" asked Kiki.

Luz nodded.

"Well, I can count at least a dozen serious fire code violations just standing here. Really, Luz, you're not supposed to be welding in your apartment. You're putting everybody in the building at risk. The police don't usually like that sort of thing."

"I've got a sprinkler system to deal with any problems."

"Of course you do, Luz. But as you and I both know, the law's the law. And I don't think you're going to be able to convince anyone that this laser device is safe."

Luz pressed a button on her remote control and the laser net vanished in an instant.

"You win," Luz said. "But if you want me to help you with one of your schemes, you can go ahead and leave right now."

"Luz," I pleaded. "We're here because you were right about the NYCMap. That's what the kidnappers are after, and nobody seems to know it but us. I don't care whether you ever forgive Kiki. But this is serious. It's not just the Shadow City that's in danger this time. Who knows what these people can do if they get all three layers of the NYCMap? You're the one who said it was a terrorist's dream. We could wake up one morning and find out that they've looted the Guggenheim Museum or bombed the Empire State Building."

"Where's the gold?" Luz asked Kiki.

"Lost," she responded. "But if you agree to help us, I'll pay you back every last cent."

"That's all you care about?" I asked.

"Of course not," Luz snapped. "But this is a matter of principle."

"I know it is. I know you had something stolen before." Kiki's voice was soothing and patient. "When your family left Cuba, everything they had was taken by the government. I can understand why you're angry about the gold."

"How do you know that?" snapped Luz.

"How *do* you know that?" I asked.

"I have my sources," said Kiki. "But I promise that I will make sure that what's rightfully yours is returned to you."

"It better be," said Luz, who looked on the verge of tears. "Now what do you want?"

I explained the situation, adding in as many hard facts as I could.

"We're going to need a tracking device that we can

plant on the kidnappers. That way they'll lead us back to their hiding place," Kiki said once I had finished.

"I guess I can do that," said Luz, already rummaging through a box filled with wires and microchips.

"Good," I told her. "We'll go and let you get started. There's a meeting of the Irregulars at my house. Tomorrow night at eight."

Kiki Strike and I left Luz's apartment and jumped on the Vespa that was waiting for us at the corner. As we cut through Central Park on our way downtown, I caught sight of a man in a dark suit standing on a boulder at the top of a hill, looking down at the traffic below. From a distance, he resembled Bob Goodman, the overdressed FBI agent. As we sped past, his sunglasses caught the afternoon sun, and his eyes seemed to burst into two balls of fire. I saw him raise a cell phone to his ear, and I got the impression he had been watching us. He disappeared from sight as the Vespa dove beneath the trees of the North Woods. I closed my eyes and hoped I was doing the right thing.

HOW TO GET WHAT YOU WANT

Some people are born with a gift for getting what they want. They always know just what to say, and other people seem desperate to please them. Unfortunately, most of us don't have the power of persuasion. But winning people over isn't always as hard as it seems. Follow these six simple rules, and you may find it remarkably easy to convince anyone of anything.

Rule One: Know What You Want
This sounds simple, but you'd be surprised how often people lose sight of what they're after. So always have a specific goal in mind (whether it's a boyfriend or bail money) and don't settle for anything less.

Rule Two: Know What Scares the Other Person

Figure out why the other person may hesitate to give you what you want. Once you know what her fears are, it will be easier to convince her that she has nothing to worry about.

Rule Three: Let the Other Person Think She's in Control

Don't be a brat. Making demands isn't going to get you anywhere. Instead, get the other person talking and listen to every word she says as if it were the most fascinating thing you've ever heard. If she thinks she's in charge of the situation, she'll be more likely to listen to what *you* have to say.

Rule Four: Stay Calm and Confident

It's important to be able to think quickly and clearly. Never get angry or defensive. Instead, smile sweetly, and don't let her see an ounce of weakness.

Rule Five: Pile on the Praise

People instinctively like people who like *them*. It's hard to refuse your biggest fan. But remember, flattery can backfire, so try your best to sound sincere.

Rule Six: You Can't Get Something for Nothing

Give them something little, and they'll be far more willing to give you something much bigger in return.

Chapter 14

Damsels in Distress

By eight o'clock the following evening, the Irregulars had assembled in my apartment. Betty arrived lugging two large shopping bags and immediately set off for the bathroom to try on her party disguise for our approval. Oona and DeeDee were sitting on the living room sofa, trading stock tips and beauty advice. Luz paced the perimeter of the room, shooting poisonous glances at Kiki, who was busily making notes in a small black notebook. I could see that twenty-four hours hadn't done much to improve Luz's attitude. It was going to be an interesting evening.

I set six cups of coffee down on the dining room table. Luz drained hers in one gulp.

"Are we ready to start?" I asked. The Irregulars took their seats at the table, while Kiki remained standing. We waited anxiously for her to address the group.

"Thanks for coming," she began. "I couldn't do this without you."

"That's for sure," Luz muttered under her breath.

"Oh shut up, Lopez." Oona's voice was one decibel short of a shout. "Don't you know when to stop?"

"I don't blame Luz for being angry," said Kiki. "I just hope she'll consider the facts. The city is in danger, and the Irregulars are the only ones who know it. I need all of your help. Whether or not you offer it is your decision."

Luz examined the sludge at the bottom of her coffee cup, refusing to meet Kiki's eye. She said nothing, but looked unmoved. After an awkward pause, Kiki continued.

"By now you know most of the story. The two kidnapped girls share a single thing in common: They each have a parent who has access to a layer of the NYCMap. Mitzi Mulligan's father has given the kidnappers the bottom layer of the map—the layer that shows everything in New York belowground. If the criminals can get their grubby hands on the other two layers, the city will be theirs. They'll be able to rob any house, destroy any building, and bring life in New York as we know it to a halt. And no one will be able to stop them. Not even us.

"But we *can* prevent the kidnappers from accomplishing their goal. We just need to rescue Penelope Young before her mother hands over the second layer of the map. I can only hope that she hasn't done so already. Ananka, do you want to fill them in on the rest?"

I rose from my seat to address the group.

"When I found Mitzi Mulligan in Chinatown, she had a scrap of paper in her handbag. It was part of an invitation. An invitation like this." I held up Tyler Deitz's ticket to the Bannerman Ball.

"Half the girls in New York would kill to get their hands on this. It's an invitation to a Bannerman Ball—the latest in a series of secret parties that are held on an island north of Manhattan. We believe that Mitzi Mulligan and Penelope Young were drugged and kidnapped at one of these parties.

"Lucky for us, Oona remembered seeing one of these invitations in the possession of a girl named Tyler Dietz. Her father's a fire chief, and he may have access to the third and final layer of the NYCMap. There's a good chance she's the kidnappers' next victim. So we convinced Tyler Deitz to lend us her invitation to the ball. All it took was a little 'persuasion.'"

I slapped a picture of Tyler Deitz in her underwear down on the table. Oona snickered.

"Betty's in the bathroom right now transforming herself into the lovely Miss Deitz," I said.

I laid the invitation beside the photo. The Irregulars pored over the golden card, which read:

The Pleasure of Your Company is Requested at:
THE BANNERMAN BALL
June 21st
Pier 54
9:30 P.M.
No invitation, no admission.

When they had finished, Kiki scanned the room.

"If you haven't figured it out by now, here's the plan. We're going to crash the party. And we've got to act fast. We only have two days to prepare."

Luz picked up the invitation and studied it.

"Pier Fifty-four? I thought you said the parties were held on an island."

"We think Pier Fifty-four is where the guests are being picked up," I said, trying my best to remain patient. "They've got to get to the island somehow, and most people in New York don't own a boat. But you're right about one thing. It's an odd place for a rendezvous."

"Why?" asked DeeDee before Luz could jump in.

"Pier Fifty-four is a run-down pier on the west side of Manhattan. It used to be owned by the White Star Company, but it hasn't been used in decades. Some people say it's cursed."

"Cursed?" asked Oona.

"It's where the *Titanic* was supposed to dock when it arrived in New York. Of course, it never made it."

"Okay, so they're meeting at the pier. But how do we know where they're going?" Luz asked. "There's got to be more than one island around New York."

"Actually, there are dozens. But in this case, there's only one that fits the bill."

THE ISLANDS OF NEW YORK

Hart Island
There are two ways to gain passage to Hart's Island, and I can't recommend either. The only people allowed on board the ferry that stops at this small island in the waters off the Bronx are unidentified corpses and the prison inmates who are forced to bury them.

Rikers Island
Not far from Hart Island, Rikers Island is the last place you'd want to be shipwrecked. For years, the island was used as a garbage dump, and its

sole inhabitants were a herd of giant rats. In the 1930s, after a long and fierce battle against the rodents, a different kind of vermin took up residence. Today, the island is home to thousands of convicted criminals, and its ten jails are tastefully decorated with miles of razor wire.

Roosevelt Island

Originally known as Blackwell's Island, this two-mile-long island located off the east side of Manhattan was once the final destination of New York's unwanted citizens. Crowded with insane asylums, prisons, and hospitals housing people with contagious diseases, Blackwell's Island was a miserable and foreboding place. In 1887, Nellie Bly, a twenty-year-old journalist known as the "intrepid girl reporter" went undercover to expose the cruel treatment of the women confined to the island's asylum. Her story made front-page news around the world. Today, most of Roosevelt Island's institutions are gone, but you can visit the ruins of a former smallpox hospital on the southern tip of the island.

Randall's Island

Throughout the nineteenth century, juvenile delinquents were sent to Randall's Island for "improvement." Today, unwitting kids play soccer on the same ground where their unfortunate predecessors once suffered. Randall's Island is also home to what looks at first to be a rather ordinary town. But looks can be deceiving. The peaceful village is a pyromaniac's paradise. As home to the Fire Department Training Academy, it's the site of more explosions and fires than any other place on earth.

North Brother Island

This small, overgrown island in the East River was once home to one of the most feared women of the twentieth century. Mary Mallon was a cook who worked for families, restaurants, and hotels throughout New York City. Each dish she prepared came with a special ingredient—a deadly disease known as typhus. Until she was captured by authorities and imprisoned on North Brother Island, Mary Mallon was responsible for starting at least eight typhoid epidemics, earning her the nickname "Typhoid Mary."

I unrolled a map of New York State and spread it across the table.

"There." I pointed to a small speck of land in the middle of the Hudson River. The Irregulars leaned in for a closer look.

"Pollepel Island?" asked DeeDee.

"Otherwise known as Bannerman's Island, site of Bannerman's Castle."

"I've lived in New York my whole life, and I've never heard of a castle in the middle of the Hudson River," said Luz.

For a second, I wondered how badly we needed Luz's help, but a look from Kiki warned me to remain calm.

"Would you just take my word for it, Luz?" I groaned. "A man named Francis Bannerman built the castle over a hundred years ago. He used it to store his collection of military equipment—guns, cannons, suits of armor, stuff like that. But one day it got really hot, and his stockpile of ammunition exploded. It blew a big chunk out of the building. Not long after that, the castle was abandoned. Seems someone's found a new use for it."

"Oh please," sneered Luz. "Next you'll tell us there are alligators in the sewers."

"You think you know everything, don't you?" I snapped. "For your information, there *have* been alligators in the sewers!"

"Just ignore her," Oona advised. "The girl's got issues. So you think the kidnappers are throwing the Bannerman Balls?"

"It's too soon to jump to conclusions," said Kiki. "All we know is that the girls are being kidnapped at the balls, and that there's a Chinatown connection. DeeDee's tests showed that the drug used on Mitzi Mulligan was Devil's

Apple—the same substance we found in a hidden room in Chinatown. And it's only sold at Chinese herbalist shops."

"This is starting to sound dangerous," Oona said. "And you say we're sending *Betty* to the party? Is she really the best choice? I mean, I don't want to say anything bad behind her back, but wouldn't it be better if one of us went?"

"You're underestimating Betty," said Kiki. "She's a lot stronger than you think."

"Sure, Betty's great," Luz snarled at Kiki. "But why should we send her to the party to be drugged and kidnapped? Why shouldn't *you* go instead?"

"Because I volunteered to go," a confident voice called from behind us.

An unfamiliar girl was standing in the doorway of the dining room, wearing a swan-white cocktail dress.

"Do you like it? I thought a white dress might make it easier for you to keep an eye on me while I'm at the party."

I grabbed the picture I had taken of Tyler Deitz in the department store dressing room. Betty was the spitting image of the girl. I passed the photo around the table, putting an end to the argument.

"Amazing," DeeDee muttered. "You're a real artist, Betty."

"Good work," said Kiki. "If the rest of you have done your jobs as well as Betty has, we won't have to worry about anyone getting drugged or kidnapped." She pulled out her notebook and sat down with the rest of us at the dining room table. "What do you say we go over the plan?

The first step is to follow Betty to the island. Verushka and I have already rented a boat. Luz, we'll need you to come up with a way to silence the motor. We don't want to tip anyone off by making a lot of noise."

"Piece of cake," said Luz.

"I thought so," Kiki replied matter-of-factly as she returned her gaze to the notebook. "Now, Betty. Let's go through your part. Once you're inside the castle, what are you going to do?"

"Mingle," Betty answered.

"Correct, but don't move too far away from the castle's windows, or we won't be able to see you from the boat. Okay, so you're mingling, then what?"

"I wait for someone to offer me a drink."

"We're pretty sure that's how they drug the girls," I reminded the Irregulars. "Devil's Apple is a powerful narcotic. And when it's mixed with other liquids, it can be difficult to detect."

"And what do you do when they offer you a drink?" Kiki continued to drill Betty.

"I tell them no thanks. But if they keep insisting, I'll know it's one of the kidnappers."

"That's right. So what then?"

"After he hands me the drink. I spill it all over myself. Then I run to the ladies' room to clean myself off. But I accidentally leave my handbag behind."

"We'll get back to the handbag in a minute, but let's keep in mind that the kidnapper may not be a 'he.' Okay, what next?"

"I slip outside, strip down to the bathing suit I'll be wearing under my dress, and swim to meet the boat."

"Fantastic," said Kiki. "There's nothing like a simple plan."

"Wait a second," said Oona, as if something wasn't making sense to her. "Betty will see the person who offers the drink, but how will we know how to find him after the party? Maybe we should kidnap one of the kidnappers."

"We'd be crazy to confront the kidnappers on their own turf," said Kiki. "First of all, we don't know how many of them there are. Second, they'll be on guard. It will be better to strike when they least expect it. We'll find the right moment."

"Yeah? And how are we going to know when we've found that perfect moment?" asked Luz.

"Well, Luz, that's where you come in again. Did you assemble the tracking device we discussed?"

"Of course." Luz held up one hand. Pinched between her thumb and index finger was a metal object the size of a baby pea. "It's even smaller and more powerful than the ones used by the CIA. But if the kidnappers are on guard, how do you expect to plant a tracking device on one of them?"

"We're not going to plant the device on the kidnappers," said Kiki. "We're going to plant it in something the kidnappers will want to take with them."

"Other than Betty, what do we have that they would want?" asked Luz.

"This." Kiki dug into her knapsack and pulled out Mitzi Mulligan's bronze dragon. "The figure is hollow. We're going to glue the tracking device inside and leave the dragon in Betty's handbag, where the kidnappers are sure to find it. I doubt they'll want to let it out of their sight again."

"From what I can tell, the dragon is really old," I butted in. "I read that one like it just sold at a gallery in New York for half a million dollars. This one's probably stolen."

"If it's worth so much, why don't we sell it and find some other way to plant the tracking device?" asked Luz.

"Luz, you were the one who just pointed out that there's no other way," said DeeDee. "And *I'm* not interested in selling stolen goods."

Luz sat back and twirled a strand of hair around her thumb until the tip started to turn blue.

"Whatever. Dragon or no dragon, the plan's too risky. What if they find some other way to drug Betty? Or what if they force her to drink it?"

"That's where *I* come in." DeeDee held up a glass bottle filled with a thick, chalky liquid. "I call it Morlock's Miracle Mixture. I developed it last year after I came down with a bad case of food poisoning. I got the idea from a Pepto-Bismol commercial. Just a tablespoon coats the lining of the digestive system and keeps poisons from being absorbed. So forget wart remover—they could serve Betty a tumbler of drain cleaner and she'd never feel a thing."

"Yeah, but what if that gunk doesn't work?" asked Luz. "What are we going to do then?"

"I took some before I got here, Luz," DeeDee said calmly as she pulled the Devil's Apple out of her pocket, opened it up, and gulped down the greasy liquid inside. "I'm pretty sure it works."

DeeDee smiled triumphantly and the rest of us laughed in amazement.

"Well, I guess that settles it. We have a plan." Kiki rose from the table. "Let's get started, unless anyone has something else to add."

"I've got something," said Oona, turning to Betty. "Sorry for what I said earlier. I'm just jealous that you get to have all the fun." She held out a card. "Here, I made this for you. It's a driver's license for Tyler Deitz. You never know when you might get carded."

"Thanks, Oona," said Betty, looking genuinely touched.

"I've got one for you, too, Strike," said Oona, tossing a laminated card to Kiki. "I don't want to bail your butt out of jail when you get caught riding that scooter without a license."

"Who knew you could be so thoughtful?" Kiki laughed.

"I had a moment of weakness," said Oona. "Don't get used to it."

★ ★ ★

Kiki Strike and I anchored our boat in the middle of the Hudson River, the current pushing softly against its bow. The city before us shot out of the water in a blaze of lights. The Empire State Building rose above it all, illuminating the sky and painting the clouds silver. From where we sat, New York looked like a magical realm—glittering and dangerous.

On the river, the shadowy shapes of other boats moved about in the darkness. A hundred years earlier, they might have been pirate ships invading the harbor under cover of night. Now they were garbage barges ferrying New York's toothpaste tubes, dirty diapers, and half-eaten pupu platters to less magical places. I held my breath as a barge the length of three football fields glided noiselessly by. Piled high with mountains of rancid garbage, it made its way toward the Atlantic Ocean, leaving an indescribable odor in its wake. As it passed, something bumped against the side of the boat. Leaning over the side, I saw a pale, fleshy object bobbing in the water. I gasped and hopped toward the middle of the boat. Kiki took one look and burst into laughter.

"It's only a fish," she said, poking it with an oar until I could see the fins. "Did you think it was a floater?" she asked, referring to the human corpses that are regularly fished out of the rivers that encircle Manhattan.

"Of course not," I insisted, trying to save face and hoping it was too dark for her to see me blush. "But who'd have thought there were fish in the Hudson River? Isn't the water supposed to be poisonous around Manhattan?"

"It is a *dead* fish," Kiki noted, picking up her binoculars and training them on Pier 54.

I checked my watch. It was 9:28, and a well-dressed mob had assembled at the pier. Letting my eyes drift across the crowd, I recognized a few of the more popular older girls from the Atalanta School, each wearing a stunning dress and a dangerous set of heels. A diamond mine's worth of bracelets, rings, and necklaces sparkled in the moonlight. But even surrounded by a swarm of beautiful people, Betty stood out from the crowd. And to my surprise, she was making no effort to blend back in. Beneath the city lights, her simple white dress glowed with the cold fire of an opal. That night, Tyler Deitz looked devastatingly lovely—a fact that wasn't lost on the half-dozen young men who were chatting with her impersonator. It was hard not to feel a twinge of envy.

The cell phone vibrated, and Luz's number appeared on the caller ID. She, Oona, and DeeDee were stationed on the George Washington Bridge, keeping an eye out for the boats that would ferry the guests to the Bannerman Ball.

"A bunch of boats just passed under the bridge," Luz reported. "Get ready."

"Good luck!" called Oona in the background.

"Time to turn on the tracking device," whispered Kiki. I flipped a switch, and the screen illuminated. A green dot identified Betty's position on a fuzzy map of Manhattan.

The drone of a dozen motors arrived with a gust of wind that rushed down the river and through our hair. A line of boats was headed for the pier. They were Venetian water taxis—elegant, wood-paneled boats designed for racing through canals. They looked as out of place in New York waters as a herd of antelope galloping across the meadows of Central Park.

One by one, the boats stopped at the edge of the pier and left laden with partygoers. A muscular young man in a dark suit helped Betty into the third boat to stop at the pier.

"There's something familiar about the guy with Betty," I told Kiki.

"That's because you've seen him before. I'm surprised you've forgotten, but I guess it was a long time ago."

I racked my brain, but I still couldn't come up with an answer. "Okay, who is he?"

"That happens to be Thomas Vandervoort, known at one time as the scourge of Central Park."

"That's one of the guys you beat up when you saved the man in Central Park?"

"Bingo. He may look tough, but he cries like a baby and loses control of his bladder if you give him a good kick. He really wasn't much of a challenge. I bet you could take him, too."

"I'll keep that in mind," I told her, wondering if she remembered how little experience I had with hand-to-hand combat.

When the last of the boats had departed from the pier, Kiki fired up the engine. Rather than the ordinary roar, it emitted only a pleasant purr that was too soft to attract any attention.

"Luz may be a pain in the butt," Kiki remarked as we took off in pursuit of the boats, "but you can't say she's not a fantastic mechanic."

We skimmed noiselessly across the black water of the Hudson River, navigating between the massive legs of the George Washington Bridge and beneath the steep rock cliffs of the Palisades, where the heads of captured pirates were once displayed on spikes. We kept the headlights of our boat off to avoid detection and followed the wakes of the Bannerman boats. Outside of the city, our only light came from the moon above and the mansions perched high on the hills overlooking the river.

An hour into our trip, an eerie fog engulfed our boat, and we traveled blindly for more than a mile before we spotted lights flickering in the distance. As we drew closer, an enchanted fairy-tale castle floated on the water before us. Candlelight spilled from dozens of enormous glassless windows. Kiki slowed the motor and angled our boat toward a shadowy section of the riverbank.

"I doubt they'll anchor a dozen boats around the island," she explained. "They'll probably return to one of the towns downstream and come back later to pick up the guests. If we pull over now, we won't be spotted. Once the other boats have gone, we'll steer closer to the castle."

As the party guests began to set foot on dry land, I raised my binoculars to take my first look at the island. According to my research, Native Americans had believed that malevolent spirits haunted the island. The first European explorers had also returned home with stories of the fiends and goblins that made Pollepel Island their home. In fact, until Francis Bannerman chose the spot for his castle and renamed the island in his own honor, most people went out of their way to avoid it. Only shipwrecked sailors and pirates looking to stash their booty had been willing to brave the isle, which, aside from the resident demons, was said to be crawling with ticks and snakes.

The sight of the ruined castle that covered most of the island should have kept most trespassers at bay. Its turrets, towers, and guard walls didn't seem terribly inviting, and I suspected that, without the support of the poison ivy vines that crawled along its sides, the castle would have disintegrated into a pile of rocks. But inside the crumbling fortress, a party was raging. I was too far away to see through the open windows, and my curiosity was killing me.

I set my binoculars aside and watched the screen of the tracking device. I followed Betty's movements, keeping an eye out for anything unusual. When the last water taxi passed our hiding place and disappeared around a bend in the river, Kiki steered us into the open water. We stopped just beyond the reach of the castle's lights— close enough to enjoy the festivities through our binoculars, but too far away to be seen.

I peered through the open door of the castle and into a cavernous room that was filling with guests from the boats. The line into the castle stalled as each person who entered took a moment to gape in disbelief at the castle's décor. Just one foot inside was enough to convince them that the party had been worth the trip.

As I stared up at the castle from the middle of the Hudson River, one thing quickly became clear. The hosts of the party were loaded. The sumptuous furnishings would have delighted the most discerning of decorators and emptied an emperor's pocketbook. Bloodred silk draped the stone walls of the castle. Hundreds of round white lanterns floated down from the ceiling, each trailing tendrillike ribbons that swayed in the breeze. From where I stood, they looked like a swarm of jellyfish floating through a tranquil sea.

Guests reclined on chaise longues covered in plush velvet and stared up at statues of handsome gods and fierce goddesses that stood about the castle like silent sentries. In the center of the room, a ten-foot Chinese dragon carved out of glacier ice crouched on a table, a

ball of fire suspended in its frozen belly. The pale blue
ice dripped into a pool of water on which platters piled
high with delicacies appeared to float. Stunning waitresses in shimmering cheongsams wound through the
crowd, dispensing exotic drinks trimmed with tapioca
pearls. Guards were stationed at every exit. Each wore
the bronze armor of an ancient Chinese warrior and carried a long, thin sword that looked as if it had been designed for lopping off heads.

I scanned the castle for Betty and found her standing
in front of a window, chatting with Thomas Vandervoort,
who refused to leave her side. Though I had held my
tongue, I had questioned the wisdom of sending Betty to
the party. But seeing her engaged in pleasant chitchat
with a dolt like Thomas Vandervoort, I had to admit I'd
been wrong. It couldn't be easy to hold a conversation
with someone whose interests, I imagined, were limited
to his hair and his bank account.

A waitress slinked up to the pair. Thomas Vandervoort
selected a pale drink with three lychee nuts perched on
its rim, but Betty held up her hand in polite refusal. The
waitress simply nodded and moved to the next group.

"Now there's something you should see," I heard
Kiki say.

"Where?" There was so much going on, I had no idea
where to look first.

"Standing at the main entrance."

Greeting the last of the guests as they entered the
castle was an unpleasantly familiar face. Her strapless
jade dress was embroidered with a golden dragon that

complemented the castle's décor and identified her as the party's hostess. Piles of yellow curls were artfully arranged about her face, and an insincere smile was plastered on her lips.

"Naomi Throgmorton?"

"The one and only," said Kiki. "And my, my, my. Look who's escorting the lovely Miss Throgmorton this evening." I barely recognized the young man standing at Naomi's side. In the two years since I had seen him, he had grown even taller and more handsome. Standing side by side, he and Naomi looked like a prince and princess from a sinister fairy tale.

"That's one of the guys I saw with Thomas Vandervoort that night in Central Park."

"Jacob Harcott." Kiki nodded. "Heir to the Harcott smuggling fortune and all-around bad seed."

"I don't suppose it's a coincidence that he's escorting Naomi while his best friend has been glued to Betty's side all night."

"We both know there are no such things as coincidences," chided Kiki.

"But Naomi can't be behind the kidnappings," I argued. "She's too dumb to mastermind something like this. And from what I've heard, she doesn't have enough money to pay for the hors d'oeuvres."

"Maybe not, but her date does. Jacob Harcott's father is swimming in cash. Remember the warehouse we found packed with counterfeit shoes? It belonged to Oliver Harcott—Jacob's father. He's our connection to Chinatown. They're working with the Fu-Tsang gang."

It was only then that I began to get anxious. We may have identified the kidnappers, but Betty's life was still in danger. It seemed pointless to continue the stakeout.

"Maybe we should get Betty out of there. We can find out where Jacob and Naomi live. We don't need to plant a tracking device."

"Are you insane?" said Kiki, looking at me as if she already knew the answer. "They're not hiding the girls under their beds. We still have to find out where they're taking them. Don't be so nervous. Nothing's going to happen anytime soon. All their boats are gone. Even if they manage to drug Betty—which they won't—they can't take her anywhere until one returns. So sit back and enjoy the party. It may be a long night."

Once all the guests had been greeted, Naomi started to mingle. Everyone was desperate to suck up to her, and she basked in their admiration. I followed her as she glided across the castle. Along the way, she was stopped by a waitress who whispered in her ear. Naomi nodded and carefully chose an unappetizing drink the color of seaweed from the waitress's tray. With the drink held out in front of her, she made a beeline to the far corner of the room, where Betty stood trapped by Thomas Vandervoort.

"Heads up," I told Kiki, who was casually cleaning the lenses of her binoculars. "They're going in for the kill."

I shuddered as Naomi greeted Betty warmly, even planting a little kiss on her cheek. Betty flushed, but she handled herself like a professional. I could see her fawning over Naomi's dress, and I knew she was tossing out compliments like confetti. My eyes focused on the toxic liquid sloshing about the glass in Naomi's hand. I held my breath, waiting for the moment of truth. The offer of a drink, the spill, the transferred handbag. I knew that in a few short minutes, Betty would be swimming out to greet us, and I couldn't wait until we were speeding away from the castle.

Instead, a different silent movie played out before my eyes. The manicured hand clasping the green drink rose. Naomi offered the glass to Betty. Betty shook her head. And then, most unexpectedly, I saw Naomi take a prim sip from the crystal glass. A wide smile spread across her face as she looked out the window and over the dark water. Although I knew she couldn't see us, I felt the urge to duck.

"What's going on?" I asked Kiki.

"Who knows?" Kiki didn't sound terribly concerned.

Naomi placed a hand on Betty's arm, smiled sweetly, and disappeared into the crowd with Jacob Harcott by her side.

"She didn't do it," I mumbled, utterly confused.

"She didn't have to. Like I said, she's got all night. I hope you weren't expecting something to happen in the first thirty minutes. Stakeouts are always a lot longer and duller than you think they'll be." With that, Kiki sat down in the boat and began fiddling with her binoculars. "There's something wrong with these things. Let me know if anything happens."

I remained standing, watching Betty.

She was leaning against the window frame when I

saw her spine stiffen in alarm. She muttered something to Thomas Vandervoort, who headed off toward the drinks table. As soon as her companion was gone, Betty faced the open window and pretended to gaze out over the river. I could see her mouth moving, but my binoculars weren't powerful enough to let me read her lips.

"Hey, hand me the telescope," I said to Kiki.

"Do you see something?" she asked.

"Maybe," I told her, taking the telescope from her outstretched hand.

With the telescope to my eye, I could see Betty's face more clearly. She was mouthing the same two words over and over. *The Princess*. My heart seemed to stop.

"Is something happening?" asked Kiki.

"Not yet," I told her. Why did all of my adventures with Kiki seem to end with the Princess? I grabbed the binoculars and scanned the crowd in the castle, hoping that Betty was mistaken. There, in the center of the room, stood Sidonia Galatzina.

Never one to blend into a crowd, the Princess was wearing the most stunning dress I had ever seen. It was the color of fine champagne and decorated with a million tiny crystals that captured the candlelight and surrounded the Princess with a golden aura. It hung from her shoulders by two delicate straps and stopped several inches short of her knees. Snaking about one of her thin, pale arms was a golden armlet in the shape of a serpent swallowing its tail. Surrounded by a circle of admirers, the Princess was putting on a show for the crowd—laughing, flipping her ebony hair, and making sure that all eyes were on her. As far as I could tell, only two sets of eyes were missing. Her two hulking bodyguards were nowhere to be seen.

As I watched, Naomi and Jacob Harcott joined the Princess's group. While the other guests rushed to say hello, the Princess met Naomi with the superior sneer she reserved for servants and scholarship students. She turned her back on her old friend, and began chatting with another girl, snubbing Naomi at her own party. Even I was shocked by the Princess's appalling manners, but Naomi seemed untroubled. She smiled at the insult and signaled to a waitress across the room. The waitress nodded and slithered toward the Princess with a tray of drinks. The Princess chose a pink concoction garnished with a flower, and took a small sip before continuing her conversation.

I was beginning to suspect that we had made a terrible mistake. As the Princess took a second sip of her drink, the signs began to appear. First she dropped her handbag, which Jacob Harcott gallantly retrieved. Soon, her legs began to wobble atop her stiletto heels. Finally, she stumbled, dropped her glass, and landed in Jacob's arms. Holding her upright, he guided the Princess away from the crowd. With Naomi there to entertain them, the Princess's friends barely noticed her departure. Only one person at the party appeared worried. Betty was trailing behind Jacob Harcott and the woozy Princess. When they disappeared through a door at the back of the castle, Betty brazenly followed behind them.

"No!" I called out through the darkness, but there was no way for Betty to hear my warning.

"What's going on?" Kiki heard the alarm in my voice.

I looked down at her sitting on the boat's bench. Either she was a gifted actress or she had no idea that the Princess was at the party.

"They took another girl!" I cried. "They never wanted Tyler Deitz. They were after someone else all along."

"Who was it? Was it anyone you recognized?"

"You could say that," I spat.

"Well?"

"It was your friend the Princess of Pokrovia. The one you swore wasn't involved."

When Kiki Strike jumped to her feet, I could see every vein in her forehead.

"Why didn't you tell me that Sidonia was at the party?" she demanded.

I didn't know what to say. Should I confess that I still didn't trust her? Should I lie?

"Forget it. You've got to be wrong. Tell me *exactly* what you saw," she insisted.

"Naomi sent a waitress to give the Princess a drink . . . the Princess drank it . . . the Princess started to wobble, and then she nearly fell. Jacob Harcott practically dragged her through the party and out a door at the back of the castle. Is that convincing enough for you?"

"Where were Sidonia's bodyguards?"

"I guess they were too big to fit on the boats. I didn't see them anywhere."

"This isn't good," said Kiki.

"You bet it's not good. And it gets a lot worse."

"How could it get any worse?" asked Kiki.

"Betty saw the whole thing happen. She followed Jacob Harcott and the Princess. I think she's trying to rescue her."

"How could she be so stupid?" asked Kiki.

"We've got to do something!" I was starting to panic.

"Stay calm, and let me think," she said. "We haven't seen a boat come back, so we should have a few minutes to figure things out."

Just as she closed her eyes and took a deep breath, a motor roared, and a boat sped around the back of the castle, where it had been hidden from sight. It was no water taxi, but a super-powered speedboat, and it was headed straight for us.

"They're taking the Princess!" I shouted over the din. "Start the engine!" Kiki dropped into the driver's seat, turned the key, and our little boat came to life. "They don't see us! They're going to hit us!" I screamed as the larger boat neared.

Kiki turned hard on the boat's wheel and we steered out of the speedboat's path. A spray of water drenched us and soaked our surveillance equipment. Kiki pushed forward on the throttle. I grabbed the tracking device out of a pool of water on the floor of the boat. As I wiped it off, I saw something that made me feel faint. The little green blip was moving steadily southward. The kidnappers had taken Betty.

"They've got Betty, too!" I shouted to Kiki. I looked up to see the speedboat vanishing in the distance.

"Their boat's too fast," said Kiki. "We can't keep up."

"What are we going to do?" I moaned, dropping my head into my hands.

"Call the Irregulars," said Kiki. "Tell them to get ready. We have to rescue Betty *tonight*."

HOW TO FOIL A KIDNAPPING

Anyone with half a brain can recognize many of the tricks that kidnappers play. Strangers offering candy, puppies, or modeling advice should be avoided at all costs. No one's that friendly.

But if someday you find yourself in trouble, keep your wits about you and think mean. Forget all those lessons you learned in finishing school. When it comes to a kidnapping, the worst thing you can do is mind your manners.

1. **Run.** If you're being followed by a car, run in the opposite direction. The car won't be able to turn around as quickly as you can. If you're being followed on foot, duck into the nearest public place and ask for help. If you're followed inside, pull items off the shelves, break things, and try to get yourself into as much trouble as possible.
2. **Kick, Scream, Bite, Fight.** Even if the kidnapper has a weapon, try to escape. If you can't, make as much of a racket as possible. Do your best to inflict serious damage.
3. **Disable the Kidnapper's Vehicle.** Pull a small button off your shirt and wedge it into the car's ignition. (A piece of chewing gum will also work well.) If the vehicle won't start, you aren't going anywhere. If you lack the appropriate supplies, reach beneath the car's steering wheel and pull out any wires you can grasp.
4. **Cause a Minor Accident.** Step on the gas pedal when you're at a stoplight. Turn off the headlights. Do whatever you can to get other people involved without hurting them.
5. **Take Inventory of Your Weapons.** Do you have a pen or pencil? A pointed hair clip? A heavy schoolbook? A belt or umbrella? Find a weapon and use it.

6. **Call Attention to Yourself.** Write *help* in lipstick on the rear window. Bang on the windows. If you're in the trunk of a car, rip out any wires you can find along the sides of the car or under the carpeting. These may deactivate the taillights and even pop the trunk. Or you can kick out the brake lights and shove your fingers through the hole. A car following behind may notice and call the police.

7. **Never, Ever Do What You're Told.**

Chapter 15

The Little Princess

One Christmas when I was small, my great-aunt Beatrice gave me a book filled with stories of princesses in peril. Their stepmothers were determined to murder them, wicked witches cast spells on them, and frogs demanded to kiss them. The message of these stories was usually the same. If you work hard, act humble, and are kind to animals, a handsome prince will arrive to rescue you. As far as I was concerned, that approach didn't seem like much fun. Instead, I decided that the real lesson to be learned from fairy tales is that things are rarely what they seem. Beautiful queens can be nasty villains. Beggars might be princes in disguise. Gingerbread houses may look tasty, but are best left uneaten. And if, like most people, you see only what you expect to see, you could find yourself in a great deal of trouble.

As our boat raced toward Manhattan, I watched Kiki Strike out of the corner of my eye. If she felt my gaze, she didn't show it. She stared straight ahead, her eyes on the water, and her white hair floating behind her in the wind. For a moment, I wondered if the real mastermind might be sitting beside me. Perhaps the robberies and the NYCMap had been a red herring—a way to draw the Irregulars' attention away from the Princess. As the lights on top of the Empire State Building flickered into view, my stomach began to churn. I didn't want to believe that Kiki was responsible, but either way, Betty's life was in my hands, and I couldn't bear to make another mistake.

We returned to the rotting pier from which we had set sail. I tied the boat up while Kiki ran to retrieve her Vespa from its hiding place behind an overflowing Dumpster. She climbed on and revved the motor.

"Get a cab and go meet the other girls. I've got to go home to get a few things."

"Forget it," I told her, shaking my head. "You're not giving the orders anymore. I'm coming with you." There was no way I was letting her out of my sight. Kiki raised an eyebrow in surprise, and I prepared myself for an argument. Instead, she shrugged and handed me a helmet.

"Jump on," she sighed.

We sped through the nighttime streets, skidding around corners and running red lights. Whenever we hit a patch of traffic, Kiki hopped the curb and steered the Vespa onto the sidewalk, scraping fire hydrants and denting mailboxes. I was just recovering from a near collision with an oil truck when Kiki turned a sharp corner onto Third Avenue and headed straight for a metal garage door set in the side of an apartment building. I was certain my time on Earth was about to come to an unpleasant end, when Kiki pulled a remote control out of her pocket. She pressed a button and the door began to rise.

"Duck!" Kiki shouted, and we made it under the door with an inch to spare. Kiki drove the Vespa down a steep ramp and into a dark parking garage, where she slammed on the brakes and spun around to watch the door shut quickly behind us.

We were in the basement of one of the bland apartment buildings that line the lower reaches of Third Avenue. Of all the places I had imagined Kiki's secret lair might lie, I would never have picked this one. I swallowed my disappointment and tried to focus on the mission at hand.

"Sorry for the fancy driving." Kiki removed her helmet and shook out her hair. "I never know when I'm being followed, and there's no point in making it easy for them."

"Followed?" I asked "Who's following you?"

"I don't have time to explain," she said. "Let's move."

We rode an elevator to ground level and stepped into a lobby decorated with fanciful murals of old New York. A handsome doorman in an old-fashioned uniform was there to greet us.

"Hello, Boris," Kiki said to the doorman.

"Good evening, miss," he replied in a Russian accent. He selected a key from the hundreds that dangled from a ring on his belt, walked over to one side of the lobby, and unlocked a door that had been disguised to look like part of the mural.

Beyond the door was a set of fire stairs. Kiki bolted up two flights and paused briefly in front of a window on the third-floor landing. Before I had the chance to catch up, she threw open the window and hopped outside.

"Are you coming or not?" I heard her call.

I peered out the window and saw Kiki standing on the fire escape of the building next door. Its metal railing was only a couple of feet from the window. I stepped onto the window ledge and leaped toward the fire escape. I landed with a thud and started climbing. Twenty torturous flights later, I reached the top, where a simple rope ladder dangled from the roof of the building. My muscles were burning, and I stood against the wall, catching my breath, as Kiki scaled the rope ladder and disappeared. Once I had recovered enough of my strength, I dragged myself up the side of the building and onto the roof. When I stood up, I found myself in the middle of a well-tended lawn.

Grass sprang up around my sneakers, and the leaves of a cherry tree brushed against my hair. A rustic wooden house sat in the middle of the lawn, far enough from the edge of the building to be all but invisible from the street below. Looking out into the night, I realized I had a bird's-eye view of the entire city. The skyscrapers of Midtown grew like a forest of lights in the distance, and a helicopter circled the financial district like a lone vulture.

As we walked through the grass toward the house, the front door swung open. Verushka stood in the doorway, dressed in an olive-green robe and leaning on a gnarled wooden cane. I forced a smile to hide my shock. In the two years since I had seen her, Verushka had grown old. Her hair was mostly gray, and all that was left of its once vibrant color was a single streak of red. Her left leg appeared all but useless.

"You are back!" she called out cheerfully, but once she caught sight of Kiki's expression, she knew the operation had not gone as planned. A flicker of disappointment passed across her face before she turned and greeted me with a heartfelt smile.

"My dear Ananka. It has been a long time—long enough for me to become an old woman." She put a hand to my cheek and whispered in my ear, "I was pleased to hear that you are on our side again."

She ushered me into a living room teeming with a jungle of exotic plants.

"Please excuse my hobby. I cannot leave the house as I once did, so I am forced to bring nature inside." She stopped to tenderly stroke the leaves of a giant orchid covered with tiny purple blooms. "Did you know that an orchid, if properly cared for, will never die? They are immortal. If only we were all so fortunate."

Verushka sighed and sank into a sofa that was in danger of being swallowed by an overgrown Virginia creeper.

"Now you must tell me. What has happened?"

"We know who's behind the kidnappings," Kiki informed her. "It's Naomi Throgmorton and Jacob Harcott. They're working with the Fu-Tsang gang."

"The Atalanta girl and the boy from the park? No," Verushka said, shaking her head in disbelief. "I cannot believe they could organize such an ingenious plan."

"I wouldn't have thought so, either. But there's no doubt now. Ananka saw them in action."

"And were you able to plant the tracking device?"

"Yes. But not in the way that we had hoped."

"No? Then how did you plant it?"

"Something went wrong, Verushka. They weren't af-ter Tyler Deitz. They wanted another girl."

"How is this possible? Who did they take?"

Kiki grimaced, unable to find the right words.

"They kidnapped the Princess," I told Verushka.

"Sidonia?" The horror in Verushka's voice told me two things. The first was that Kiki was not behind the kid-nappings. The second was that they knew the Princess well.

"Yes," Kiki admitted.

"I do not understand. What do they want with Sido-nia? She cannot give them the map."

"No, but she has enough money to fund their little get-togethers. And she's tortured Naomi for years," I said, offering the only solution I had been able to find. "I guess this was Naomi's revenge."

"Stupid children," said Verushka sadly.

"There's more," Kiki told her. "Betty tried to save Sidonia. They took her, too."

"You will have to find them," Verushka insisted. "To-night. You will not be the only ones looking. You must get to them first."

"We're already on the case. The Irregulars are meet-ing us at Ananka's house. I'm just here to collect some supplies."

Kiki set off down the hall and disappeared into an-other room. Verushka leaned back on the sofa, lost in thought. An opportunity had presented itself. With Kiki gone, I could ask the question that was bouncing around in my head.

"Verushka?"

"Yes, my dear?" she replied absentmindedly, still distracted by the news.

"How do you know the Princess?"

Verushka snapped to attention and looked at me with an amused expression.

"Two years ago you were too shy to ask such a question." She pulled herself up with her cane. The effort was clearly painful. "You ask how I know Sidonia? This is not a story I can tell in a few minutes. Just remember that all are not cooks who walk with long knives. If I tell you more, I will put you in terrible danger."

"As far as I can tell, I'm already in danger."

"This is true," she agreed. She studied me for a moment, then walked to a bookshelf, where she retrieved a small red book. "Kiki has told me you like to read," she said enigmatically.

I nodded.

"This is a very important book. You must keep it in a safe place and never let anyone see it. Even little books can be very dangerous."

I scanned the cover, but the book had no title. I slipped it into my knapsack.

"What's it about?" I asked.

I could tell that I wasn't going to get a straight answer.

"Do you know why you were chosen for the Irregulars?" Verushka asked instead. It was a question for which I had never found an answer.

"Because of my library?" I guessed.

"No," Verushka said, chuckling softly and shaking her head. "There are other libraries. Maybe they are not so good, but . . ." She shrugged. "You were selected because you were the only one Kiki did not have to find. You found *her*. That makes you very special." I didn't know what to say. "Take care of my book," she said.

"I will," I promised, and Verushka reached out and hugged me with her free arm.

Kiki walked into the living room stuffing a flashlight and a handful of hypodermic needles into a black knapsack.

"How touching," she said. "You've gotten awfully sentimental in your old age, Verushka. Let's go, Ananka. It's getting late."

We left the house, and I began to cross the lawn, heading for the fire escape.

"Not so fast," instructed Kiki. "We may have been spotted on the way here. We'll have to take the fast way down. Here, put these on." She tossed a pair of heavy gloves at my feet.

"Spotted? Who could have spotted us?" I asked.

"Bad guys," said Kiki.

"What kind of bad guys? And why are we running from them?"

"Did you see Verushka's leg? They shot her. She'll be crippled forever."

"I don't understand. When was Verushka shot?" I asked.

"After the explosion in the Shadow City. Now stop asking questions and move faster. If we get caught, they'll be happy to shoot us, too."

My hands trembled as I pulled on the gloves. Kiki walked to the edge of the building and threw two ropes over the side. She grabbed one, and without waiting for me, began rappelling down the building's wall. I took the other in my hands, muttered a short prayer, and hopped over the side. But my feet never made contact with the wall of the building. Instead, I swung in through an open window and landed with a crash inside a dark bedroom where a teenage boy was sleeping in his underwear.

"No, I don't want to go to your spaceship," he mumbled, tossing in his sleep. "I want to stay here on Earth."

I jumped back out the window, skinning both knees in the process. A few minutes and a panic attack later, I slid off the end of the rope and landed in a courtyard in the back of the building.

"What took you so long?" asked Kiki with an arched eyebrow.

"I dropped in on one of your neighbors," I said, feeling a little light-headed.

"Yeah, I saw that. Betty's been kidnapped and you're making social calls. Come on, we have to leave the Vespa," Kiki said. "We'll go out the back way." She climbed over a fence that separated the courtyard from the backyards of several buildings. I scrambled behind her as we made our way to the other end of the block. Peeking out of a narrow alley, we checked Second Avenue for suspicious vehicles. A battered taxi sped through a cloud of steam that billowed out of a manhole in the middle of the road.

"All clear," said Kiki. "Let's go."

I found the door to my apartment unlocked and a figure pacing the center of the room. I flipped the light switch, ready to confront the intruder. When my eyes adjusted to the light, I saw it was Oona. DeeDee and Luz were seated on the couch.

"You don't mind, do you?" whispered Oona. "It's past midnight. I didn't think we should wake your parents up, so I picked the lock."

I made a mental note to change the locks.

"Just be quiet," I warned them. "My parents think I'm spending the night with Kiki. If they hear us, we'll be stuck here 'til morning."

"What's going on?" whispered DeeDee. "Where Betty?"

I couldn't think of a thing to say.

"They got her, didn't they?" snarled Luz, jumping to her feet. "I knew something bad was going to happen. I can't believe I snuck out of the house for this."

"Didn't the Miracle Mixture work?" DeeDee was distraught.

"It didn't have a chance to work," I assured her. "They never tried to drug Betty. They weren't after Tyler Deitz. The kidnappers wanted the Princess. They got her."

Every eye in the room turned to Kiki.

"Then where's Betty?" demanded Oona.

"She tried to save the Princess. They took her, too."

Luz pointed a finger at Kiki. "Don't you see? She's behind all of this. She's a liar and a thief, and you guys were idiots to believe her. I'm out of here."

I stopped Luz before she got to the door.

"This is all about the gold, isn't it, Luz? Are you really that greedy? Betty's been kidnapped, and we don't have long to rescue her. If they find out she's a spy, she could die."

"Oh, come on, Ananka. Don't you know when you're being had? You can't tell me that *she* didn't set this whole thing up."

"Actually, I *can* tell you that. I know who's responsible for the kidnappings. It's Naomi Throgmorton and Jacob Harcott. I saw them drug the Princess with my own eyes."

Luz and I stared at each other. Any sign of uncertainty in my face, and she'd walk out the door. Finally, she sighed and tugged on her ponytail.

"We need your help, Luz," I begged.

"Okay. I'll do it for Betty. But as soon as we find her, I quit. Now give me the tracking device."

I reached into my knapsack and handed it to Luz. She turned it on and studied the screen. "The signal's faint, but it looks like they're in Chinatown," she said.

"Do you think they could be in the Shadow City?" I asked.

"They're not that far underground. The signal would be much weaker. But they could be in one of the hidden rooms with an entrance to the Shadow City."

"What are we waiting for?" asked Oona. "Let's go!"

"Hold on. I need to get the map," I said.

"The map of the Shadow City?" asked Oona.

"Are we going back?" whispered DeeDee.

"I'm not sure we have a choice," I told her.

I left the Irregulars in the living room and went to retrieve the map from its hiding place. I shut the door of my bedroom and scanned the towers of books that lined the walls. I snatched a book of fairy tales and shook it.

The map of the Shadow City fell to the floor, its paper stiff with DeeDee's dried blood. I grabbed *Glimpses of Gotham* and opened my knapsack. Inside was Verushka's book. There was no time for reading, but I couldn't stop myself from flipping past dozens of pages handwritten in Russian. One of the few entries in English was marked with a small photograph.

It is the anniversary of the death of Princess Sophia. Ten years ago, she and her husband were poisoned, and Livia became queen of Pokrovia. Today, Livia and her men continue to search for us, and the world believes I am guilty of Sophia's murder. When you are older, we will make sure that the truth is told. It is my duty to punish Livia for the terrible things she has done.

I looked down at the photo of a stunning woman dressed in royal robes. Standing by her side was a tall man in a military uniform. He smiled down at an infant cradled in his arms. I turned the picture over to find the inscription *Sophia and Her Family* written on the back.

The floorboards outside my bedroom creaked, and I tucked the little book under a pillow.

"What's taking you so long?" Kiki Strike stuck her head through the door. "Don't tell me you forgot where you hid the map."

"No, I've got it," I said. For a moment, I found myself unable to move.

"Well?" Kiki demanded. "What is it, Ananka?"

"Nothing," I said, ignoring a little voice that was whispering in my ear.

☆ ☆ ☆

The green blip on the tracking device grew stronger as the Irregulars slinked through Chinatown. According to Oona's watch, it was one thirty in the morning. At the corner of Bayard and Elizabeth streets, Kiki grabbed Luz's arm.

"How close do you think we are?"

"The building's got to be nearby. It's probably around the next corner," Luz answered.

"Okay, ladies," Kiki called out to the rest of us. "The street's too dangerous here. We're going to have to travel across the rooftops," Kiki said. "The buildings here are so close together, we should be able to step from one to the next."

"I don't know. That sounds pretty risky," said DeeDee.

"We'll be fine," I told her. "When these buildings were built, the streets were far more dangerous. People used to travel around on the roofs all the time. If you lived on the top floors, you only went downstairs if you had to."

Kiki scanned the street, then pointed at a run-down tenement building across the street.

"Do you think you can pick the lock on that door?" she asked Oona.

"You're kidding, right?" Oona marched over to the building. Within seconds, the front door was standing wide open, inviting us inside. We climbed a set of steep, rickety stairs, kicking trash and cockroach carcasses out of our way.

"I can see why people stayed on the roof," said DeeDee, struggling to catch her breath as we neared the sixth-floor landing.

At the top of the stairs we opened the door to the roof and stepped out into the nighttime air. The smell of tar was overwhelming, and our feet stuck to the ground as we moved.

"This way," Luz directed us, pointing east. We quietly stepped over the low walls that separated the roofs of half a dozen buildings and ducked under clotheslines draped with damp sheets that floated like ghosts in the breeze. Finally, we stood at the edge of a building, looking down on Bayard Street. A streetlight illuminated the entrance to a warehouse where four men stood smoking cigarettes and chatting. To the casual passerby, the scene would have appeared perfectly innocent. Kiki took out her binoculars.

"Have a look." She passed the binoculars to me. One of the men had a telltale bulge beneath his jacket.

"They're armed," I said. "And a couple have dragons tattooed on their arms."

"That means they're members of the Fu-Tsang gang," said Oona.

"I guess we're not going in through the front door," noted DeeDee.

"We wouldn't stand a chance," said Kiki. "What about the building, Ananka? Does it have an entrance to the Shadow City?"

"The building has an entrance, all right. Look, you can still see our logo stamped on the sidewalk. The problem is, we nailed the trapdoor shut. This is Oliver Harcott's warehouse—the place where we found the counterfeit shoes. There's a secret room under the building. That must be where they're hiding the girls."

I flipped through *Glimpses of Gotham*.

"Here it is," I said, placing my finger on a passage I had highlighted two years earlier. "Pearcy Leake heartily recommends a visit to the Jade Monkey Salon, located on Bayard Street but also accessible through the Shadow City. It says it was an opium den that was secretly owned by one of New York's finest families."

"How appropriate," muttered DeeDee.

"So that's where they're holding Betty and the Princess?" asked Oona.

"That's my bet," said Kiki. "Which means we'll have to take them out through the Shadow City."

"But how are we going to get back into the Shadow City?" DeeDee wondered. "The Marble Cemetery's booby-trapped, and we don't have any gas masks."

Realizing what she had just let slip, DeeDee bit her lip and we all looked nervously toward Kiki. None of us had told her about our efforts to keep her out of the tunnels.

"You booby-trapped the Marble Cemetery?" Kiki asked. "To keep me out?"

"Well, you did lie to us about being Augustus Quackenbush's granddaughter," said Luz defensively. "What did you expect us to do?"

"I guess I thought you might trust me," sighed Kiki Strike. "But it doesn't matter now. It's a good thing I know another way into the tunnels."

We followed Kiki to Greenwich Village. At three o'clock in the morning, we reached Bethune Street. The

Princess's house sat at the end of the block, its windows dark. I would have expected a flurry of activity and perhaps a police car or two. But the Princess's mother didn't seem to know her daughter was missing. Kiki walked up the stairs of a brownstone three doors down from the Princess's house. I noticed a little golden *i* stamped on the sidewalk, and I realized it was the same house we had escaped from two years earlier.

"I can't pick that lock." Oona pointed to a sticker in the corner of one of the windows. "They've installed an alarm system. The police would be here in no time."

"Believe it or not, Oona, there are other ways of getting inside a building." Kiki knocked at the door.

Several seconds later, the door opened and a little head popped through the crack.

"Hello, elf," said a cheerful face.

"Hi, Iris," replied Kiki. "Are your parents still out of town?"

"They won't be back from Borneo 'til next week," said the little head.

"And the nanny?"

"Sleeping off a bottle of tequila and a half-dozen wine spritzers. Want to come in?"

We stepped into the foyer of the brownstone. The walls were covered with ceremonial masks, and two shrunken heads sat propped on a little table next to a stack of mail. The door shut behind us, and a girl wearing pink pajamas embroidered with ladybugs stepped forward to greet us. She was almost as small as Kiki had been when I first met her, with hair only a shade or two darker. In fact, her resemblance to the young Kiki Strike might have been uncanny if it hadn't been for her healthy complexion and hazel eyes.

"Ladies," said Kiki, "this is Iris McLeod. Iris, you remember the Irregulars, don't you?"

"Sure," said Iris, stepping forward to shake our hands. "They're kind of hard to forget."

"You can't be the little girl on the stairs," said Oona. "She was just a baby."

"It's been a long time. People grow up. I'm eleven now," huffed Iris, who seemed a little offended.

"What's with the masks?" asked Luz.

"My parents collect them," said Iris. "They're anthropologists, experts on cannibalism. My dad thinks the masks keep burglars away."

"So how long have you two known each other?" I asked Kiki.

"About a year now," said Kiki. "Iris helps me out with a few things."

"I keep an eye on the neighbors," added Iris enthusiastically.

Kiki shot Iris a disapproving look. "She's usually more discreet."

"Sorry," said Iris. "I guess you guys are here to see the basement. It's this way."

Iris guided us down a set of stairs and into a basement that reeked of mildew.

"We haven't been able to get rid of the smell since the flood," noted Iris.

"We're really sorry about that," said DeeDee.

"Oh, don't worry," Iris laughed. "If you ask me, it was all worth it."

She walked over to an empty trunk that sat against one wall of the basement. She heaved it to the side and studied the floorboards beneath it for a second.

"The handle's around here somewhere," she said.

"Wait, Iris, let me . . . ," insisted Kiki, stepping forward to raise the trapdoor. But Iris had already reached down and grasped an upturned board. As she struggled to open it, her fingers slipped and she fell backward into Kiki, who stumbled a few steps before she tripped over the trunk. As she fell, Kiki's backpack flew across the room, its contents spilling out along the way. A roll of duct tape bounced across the floor and came to a stop at my feet.

"I'm sorry," Iris said quickly, rushing to help Kiki gather her things. Kiki ignored her as she shoved her possessions into her backpack. "I'm really sorry," Iris tried again.

"This is serious business, Iris. You've got to start thinking before you do things." Kiki threw her backpack over her shoulder and returned to the trapdoor. As she pulled upward, a section of the floor rose, revealing a hole beneath.

"The Shadow City," murmured DeeDee.

"Are you sure you're feeling up to this?" I asked.

"You don't have to go if you don't want to," added Oona.

"Of course I'm feeling up to it," DeeDee insisted.

"I'll go!" offered Iris.

"Forget it, Iris," Kiki told her.

"But it was an accident!" pleaded Iris.

"We can't afford any accidents tonight," said Kiki as she flipped her flashlight on.

"Next time," I whispered to Iris.

"Ready?" Kiki barked at the rest of us. I saw the others nod solemnly. "Okay, then. Let's go."

And with that, Kiki dropped into the darkness.

HOW TO BE A GOOD DETECTIVE

Anyone who regularly watches the local news may have noticed a curious fact. Each time a bank robber, kidnapper, or garden-variety bad guy is hauled out of his house in handcuffs, there's always a group of neighbors milling about who swear that they never noticed anything unusual. As far as they knew, the man who knocked off the local Stop & Shop was just an average upstanding citizen who took good care of his lawn.

After seeing so many surprised neighbors, you might come to the conclusion that criminals are an exceptionally clever bunch. But that's simply not the case. Neighbors rarely see anything strange because they just aren't paying attention. A good detective, however, makes a habit of looking for the clues that other people miss.

Open Your Eyes!

Most people walk through the world in a daze, seeing only what they expect to see. They never bother to notice that the mailman never stops at the house down the street or that the shades in one of its bedrooms are always drawn. The fact is, most clues are hidden in plain sight. All you have to do is keep your eyes peeled and never assume that there's a harmless explanation for everything you see.

Know that Little Things Can Mean a Lot

Even everyday objects can offer important information. For instance, if you were to find an ordinary fountain pen at the scene of a crime, you might conclude from the bite marks around the top that the owner was either a nervous nellie or desperately trying to quit smoking. By examining the tip of the pen, you might be able to determine whether the person was right- or left-handed. And if the ink in the pen were a pale shade of purple, you would know that the owner had a bit of a flamboyant streak.

Listen for What People *Don't* Say

In many cases, the subjects that people avoid are far more interesting than the ones they choose to talk about. Has the new girl down the street never mentioned what her parents do for a living? Perhaps you should find out. Does she try to change the subject whenever you ask where she lived before she moved to your town? If a subject is off limits, there's bound to be a reason.

Read Their Body Language

People communicate far more with their body than they do with words. Often a person will say one thing while his body tells you the opposite. And while you can't always trust the things people say, their bodies never lie. A good way to teach yourself to interpret body language is to watch television with the sound off.

Chapter 16

Sugar & Spice
& Not Very Nice

i was the last of the Irregulars to make the descent into the Shadow City. Iris closed the trapdoor from above, and the weak light that had guided the others down the ladder was suddenly extinguished. All I could see were the beams of four flashlights flickering like fireflies far below me in the darkness. Each time my feet searched for another rung, my heart pounded hard and fast against my chest. Dizzy with fear, I prayed that my sweaty fingers wouldn't lose their grip.

I reached the bottom and immediately grabbed for the flashlight tucked into the waistband of my pants. My eyes followed its spotlight as it illuminated one small section of the room at a time. Stacked high along the walls were simple wooden boxes, each filled with dozens of bottles labeled *Angus McSwegan's Finest Scotch Whisky*. There must have been hundreds of boxes and enough whisky to give half of Manhattan a vicious hangover. Judging by the skeleton slumped in one corner of the room, Angus McSwegan had guarded his fermented fortune to the very end.

"Okay, ladies," said Kiki Strike. "We're not here to enjoy the scenery. We've got to move fast. There will be no sightseeing this time. Without our uniforms, we're extremely vulnerable. So it's there and back again—nothing more. Got it?" She shined her flashlight in each of our faces, searching for signs of opposition. She wasn't going to get an argument from any of us. Oona was chewing nervously on one of her nails. DeeDee's scar was flushed, and little beads of sweat had appeared on her forehead. Even Luz had momentarily forgotten she was angry at Kiki and was nodding along in agreement.

Kiki opened the door to the Shadow City and stood aside to let us pass. On the other side, we found an avalanche of rubble that blocked one side of the tunnel. Two years earlier, I had stood in the very same spot and watched DeeDee running for her life.

"The tunnel looks exactly like we left it," Luz marveled. "Why wasn't it flooded?"

"Maybe all the rubble kept the water from coming in from the Princess's house," I guessed.

"But what about Iris's basement?" Luz asked. "It was totally soaked. It *still* smells like mildew."

"The trapdoors must be watertight," said Kiki. "The river's only a couple of blocks away. In the days when the tunnels were built, it must have flooded all the time. The Shadow City would have been destroyed pretty quickly unless the builders had found a solution."

"So this is what happened," said DeeDee. Her eyes drifted across the destruction. "Now that I've seen it, there's no doubt in my mind. This was my fault. I made the explosives too powerful. They never should have caused this much damage. It must have been a bad batch." She turned to Kiki. "I let everyone blame you. I can't tell you how sorry I am."

"It was a long time ago," Kiki said, taking DeeDee's arm and steering her away from the rubble. "It's over now. All that matters is that we all got out alive. I just hope we'll be able to say the same tonight."

As Kiki and DeeDee started to walk away, I saw Luz heading toward the spot where DeeDee had fallen after the explosion.

"What are you doing?" I asked.

"Wait a second," she said without looking back. She stopped in front of one of the large rocks that lay scattered about the floor of the tunnel. Bending down, she reached out and brushed it with her fingertips. It wasn't a stone, but rather a backpack sprinkled with gray dust. Luz looked up at me. Her eyes were wide and her jaw slack.

"It's DeeDee's backpack. It's the gold," she whispered in a voice that was barely audible.

"The gold?"

I heard the other girls stop and turn back.

"It's been here all along." Luz looked as if she might burst into tears. I turned in time to see Kiki drop DeeDee's arm.

"You didn't take it?" Oona asked, staring at Kiki in astonishment.

"No," admitted Kiki.

"But why did you leave it here?"

"I had to. It was too heavy to carry. And saving DeeDee was more important. I thought I'd come back for it later. But I never got the chance. I was too busy trying to stay alive."

"I don't understand." Luz was struggling to keep her voice even. "We thought you had stolen it."

"It was better to let you think I was a thief than to let you risk your lives going back for it. After the flood, I didn't want you to return to the Shadow City unless it was absolutely necessary. It just wasn't worth it. There are easier ways to make money. When I had to disappear, I wrote to the Capybaras Corporation and told them about the Reverse Pied Piper. I assumed that would make up for the lost gold."

"I thought . . . I mean, I've said so many horrible things. I nearly turned you in to the FBI," Luz sobbed, her face now slick with tears.

"There's no time for any of that," Kiki said softly. "We're all friends again, right?" Luz nodded. "So forget the gold. Let's rescue Betty."

"Okay," said Luz. She wiped her face on her sleeve and set off down the tunnel, leaving the bag of gold lying on the ground.

✪ ✪ ✪

We walked south toward Chinatown. The tunnel was colder and much smellier than I remembered. A putrid odor assaulted our senses, and we shivered in our light summer clothes. My bare arms were covered with goose bumps, and I longed for the uniform that was now several sizes too small for me.

For what seemed like miles, we followed the tunnel's twists and turns. Then, after choosing a fork in the path, I saw something scamper across the beam of my flashlight.

"Did you see that?" I asked the others.

"Uh-huh," said Oona.

"Was that what I think it was?"

"Uh-huh," Oona confirmed.

"What was it?" asked DeeDee.

"A rat the size of a cocker spaniel," I told her.

"But there can't be any rats in the Shadow City. We got rid of them all," said Luz.

"That doesn't mean that a few haven't moved back in," said Kiki. "I brought my Reverse Pied Piper just in case."

We huddled closer to one another. I linked arms with Oona and checked the map with my free hand. We weren't far from our destination. Another half a mile and we would be under the warehouse. Just then, I tripped and dropped the map. As I scrambled to retrieve it in the darkness, I felt a warm furry body brush against my arm. I screamed and grabbed my flashlight, pointing it toward the section of the tunnel we had just walked through. The others aimed their beams in the same direction. For a second, I fought the urge to faint. There behind us were thousands of rats, their teeth gleaming in the light.

"Don't move," ordered Kiki, pulling a Reverse Pied Piper out of her knapsack. She put it to her mouth and blew. Nothing happened. The army of rats stared at us in anticipation, waiting for us to make the first move. Kiki tried once more. Again, nothing. Growing restless, the rats began to inch toward us.

"What's going on?" DeeDee wailed.

"It's not working," said Kiki, examining the Reverse Pied Piper with her flashlight. "It must have broken when I dropped my backpack."

Suddenly, the whole horrible situation made sense to me.

"It's not broken. It doesn't work because the rats are all deaf."

"Tell me you're joking," pleaded Luz.

"Remember the first time? A few of the rats weren't bothered by the Reverse Pied Piper. They must have been deaf, too. They were left behind in the city and now they've had two years to breed. These are their descendants. There could be thousands of them by now."

"Well, I guess we only have one option," said Kiki, tucking the Reverse Pied Piper into her pocket.

"What?" I asked.

"RUN!" she shouted.

With the rats behind us, I led the way as we sprinted through the tunnel. There was no time to check the map. I let my intuition guide me past a dozen identical doors and through featureless forks in the tunnel. Once or twice, I worked up the courage to look over my shoulder. The thundering herd of bloodthirsty rodents was hot on our heels. A giant rat was running alongside Luz, nipping at her shoe. With one well-aimed kick, she sent it flying into a wall. Her moment of victory didn't last long, however. It was only a second before an even bigger and hungrier specimen took its place. I picked up speed and hoped I was leading the Irregulars in the right direction. One misstep, one wrong turn, and we'd all be eaten.

As we neared the warehouse, the ground became soft and slippery. Dozens of dirty mink coats lined the floor of the tunnel, along with two human skeletons, their bones picked clean by rats. A third skeleton wearing a jacket decorated with the Fu-Tsang dragon lay just outside the door I had been searching for. I darted inside and waited for the others to file in behind me before I slammed the door as hard as I could. There was no lock, and I hoped that the mutant rats hadn't learned to turn doorknobs. We could hear hundreds of furry bodies hurling themselves against the wood and the squeals of frustration when the door refused to budge. Once we knew we were safe, we collapsed on the floor of the room.

"I thought we were dead for sure," DeeDee panted.

"Don't worry," said Kiki with a grin. "It will take more than a bunch of rats to get rid of us."

"Oh, yeah? Did you see those skeletons? And all of the coats?" Luz asked. "The rats got rid of *somebody*."

"Now we know why the robberies stopped," Kiki said. "The Fu-Tsang gang couldn't get past the rats. They didn't have enough bullets to kill them all. And it's hard to run fast when you're carrying stolen goods."

"At least we're safe now," said DeeDee.

"Sure, as long as Ananka's brought us to the right place," said Oona.

I looked around the room. The ceilings were low and the space was crammed with crates, rolled floor mats, and dirty pillows. The floor was strewn with wooden chopsticks. Above the crates was a hole in the ceiling.

"Yeah, this is it," I said. "We're in the storeroom under the opium den."

Kiki and I slowly climbed through the opening in the ceiling and up a long ladder that led to a wooden trapdoor. The boards we had used to close off the entrance had been removed. We pushed the trapdoor open an inch and the too-sweet odor of Devil's Apple drifted down to us. The walls of the opium den were lined with shadowy wooden cubbyholes the size of coffins. Most were filled with old silk cushions, but two were hidden from view by brightly colored screens on which miniature dragons danced. The room was dark and cavernous, but a lantern on a table at the far end of the room illuminated an unexpected scene.

Seated at the table less than twenty feet away from the trapdoor were Jacob Harcott and Thomas Vandervoort, both dressed in the expensive suits they had worn earlier in the evening. Jacob was boasting of the time he'd forced a boy to walk the plank on the way to a Bannerman Ball. When he finished with his story, they both slumped over the table, their bodies heaving with laughter.

"Idiots," spat Kiki. "They should take better care of the few brain cells they were born with."

"What are you talking about?" I asked, not entirely certain of her meaning.

"Just look at them. They've been sampling the Devil's Apple. Even those oafs wouldn't act that stupid without a little help. But I guess it makes it easier for us."

"They may be high on wart remover, but they're still dangerous," I cautioned her.

"Not as dangerous as I am," she said, climbing into the room.

"Hey, look," said Thomas Vandervoort, shaking his friend's arm and pointing in Kiki's direction. "It's the leprechaun!"

"How'd it get in here?" asked Jacob, looking up in confusion at the camouflaged trapdoor that led from the opium den to the warehouse above.

"Must have followed the rainbow," said Thomas Vandervoort, cracking himself up.

Kiki walked over to the table. "Having a good time?" she asked with the syrupy politeness of an overeager waitress. "I really hate to interrupt your fascinating conversation, but I just wanted to thank you."

"Thank us?" asked Thomas Vandervoort, his evil smile fading quickly.

"Yes. I want to thank you for making this so easy. I mean, look at me. I'm just a girl, and as you can see, I'm not a very big one at that. So thank you for going out of your way to make it so easy to kick your butts."

Jacob Harcott stood up from the table, knocking his chair over backward. A snarl deformed his handsome features as he towered over Kiki like an angry ogre.

"We spent six months in jail thanks to you," he growled. "We know who you are, and we've been looking forward to meeting you again. It's not going to be easy this time."

"Oh, I beg to differ," said Kiki. "This is going to be another walk in the park. By the way, how was juvie? I hear the food's not bad, but the maid service leaves something to be desired."

"Do it, Jacob. Bash her head in," Thomas Vandervoort cheered. Jacob Harcott reached down, grabbed Kiki by the throat with one giant hand, and lifted her off the ground.

"Your luck just ran out, leprechaun," he sneered, clenching his free fist and rearing back to punch her in the face. Kiki didn't struggle. Instead, she looked him calmly in the eye and rammed her tiny foot into his gut. Jacob Harcott dropped her to the ground, clutching his wounded stomach.

"Who needs luck when you can do this?" asked Kiki as she landed on her feet. She spun around, jumped high in the air, and kicked him in the side of his head. His eyes rolled back and he crashed to the floor like a toppled statue.

Thomas Vandervoort leaped from the table and scurried toward the trapdoor that led to the warehouse above. Kiki was on him in no time. With one quick move of her feet, she tripped him and sent his body sliding across the floor.

"Going somewhere?" she asked as she stood over him.

"Don't hurt me!" Thomas Vandervoort begged, curling his body into a tight ball. His voice quivered as if he might cry, and a puddle of liquid began to form beneath his body.

"Oh, don't you worry your pretty little head. I'm an expert. This isn't going to hurt a bit." She landed a karate chop on the base of his neck with surgical precision. Thomas Vandervoort's body went limp.

"All done, Ananka," Kiki called out to me. "Want to give me a hand?"

I climbed out of the hole in the floor and walked across the opium den toward the two massive bodies.

"Are they dead?" I whispered, prodding Thomas Vandervoort's carcass with the toe of my sneaker.

"I'm dangerous, not homicidal. They're just unconscious. We're going to have to tie them up." She grabbed a roll of duct tape from her bag and tossed it over to me. "Make sure you wrap their hands and feet tightly. And put a strip over their mouths as well. I don't want to listen to them blubbering like a couple of babies when they wake up."

Luz, DeeDee, and Oona crawled into the opium den, and we wrapped Jacob Harcott and Thomas Vandervoort in miles of duct tape until they both resembled metallic mummies. Just as I finished placing a strip of duct tape over Jacob Harcott's mouth, his eyelids fluttered. He looked up at me, and a fat tear rolled onto his cheek.

"You big crybaby," I whispered into his ear. "Now you know why your mother warned you not to hit girls. Sometimes they hit back."

"Hey, everybody, I found Betty!" Oona called out behind me. She had moved one of the screens and was standing in front of a wooden cubbyhole. "She's out cold!"

I dropped the duct tape and ran to where Oona stood. Inside the cubbyhole lay Betty. She was gagged and her hands were tied. Someone had removed the blond wig, and her dark hair spilled across a silk pillow. Her white dress was torn and dirty, but she still looked astonishingly beautiful—like a fairy-tale princess under the spell of a wicked queen.

"Take the gag off and untie her hands," Kiki ordered. Oona bent down and removed the ropes that bound Betty's hands. Luz lifted the gag over her head.

"Betty," Luz whispered in her ear. "Betty, wake up!" She shook Betty's arm and pinched her softly on the cheek, but there was no reaction. "What's wrong with her?" Luz moaned.

"MMMUMPH!" came a voice in response.

"What?" said Luz, looking around at the rest of us in confusion.

"MMMMUMPH!" said the voice again.

"It's coming from down there," said DeeDee, pointing to a cubbyhole below the one where Betty lay.

We dropped to our knees. There, lying on a bed of pillows, was a redheaded girl wearing a filthy yellow cocktail dress. She, too, was gagged and bound.

"It's Penelope Young," said Kiki, reaching in to untie the girl's gag.

"Who are you?" asked the girl once she was free to speak.

"It doesn't matter. We're here to rescue you."

"Oh, thank goodness, because I'm *dying* for a shower. They've made me wear this same dress the whole time I've been here. They never even let me wash my face or anything. And you wouldn't *believe* where they made me go to the bathroom. I must smell awful, and I can't stand to be smelly, even in gym class. I mean, I feel gross if I don't take at least three showers a day," said the girl, rambling on.

"No wonder they gagged her," whispered Oona.

"I can't smell anything," Kiki lied. Penelope was as ripe as a chunk of Gorgonzola cheese. "Do you know what happened to the other girl?"

"Who? Oh, right. Her. The pretty one in the white dress. They brought her in a few hours ago. At least I think it was a few hours ago. It's so hard to tell, you know, without a watch or anything."

"Get to the point, Penelope," warned Kiki.

"Oh, okay. Um, they brought her in, and she was fighting to get free. She kept yelling something about how they'd never get away with this and that her friends would come and that they'd all be really sorry. So those two guys I heard you beat up tried to make her drink the stuff they give me every day. It tastes pretty good—kinda like candy—but it makes you sleep forever and your head really hurts when you wake up."

"*Please*, Penelope. Just tell us what happened to her," pleaded Kiki, trying not to lose her patience.

"Yeah, so anyway, they got her to drink some of the stuff, but it didn't seem to work at all. At first, she pretended to be asleep, but then she made a break for the ladder. One of those guys caught her by the back of the dress, and she fell off and hit her head on the floor. I don't think she's moved since then. Hey, you guys don't have any food, do you? I'm practically starving. But only if it's not Chinese food. That's all I've eaten for days, and I swear I'll vomit if I ever see another egg roll."

"We have to get Betty out of here," said Kiki to the rest of us. "Untie Penelope. Luz, you and DeeDee will have to carry Betty out through the Shadow City. Do you think you can handle that?"

"What about the rats?" asked DeeDee.

"Shouldn't we just take her out the front door?" Luz asked. "I mean, what's the point of saving Betty if she's just going to end up as rat food?"

"You can't go through the front door. We don't know who's waiting for us up there. But don't worry. You don't have to go out the same way we came in. There's a closer exit. The rats can't hear you coming, so if you move fast, they won't have time to regroup."

"Another exit? You mean the Chinatown Savings and Loan?" I asked, finally catching on. "She's right. It's only two doors down in the Shadow City."

"If it's so close, why didn't we come in that way and save a lot of time?"

"It's a bank, Luz. They have a pretty good alarm system—especially after the robbery. We would have tripped it," Kiki explained.

"But we'll set it off on the way out, too, won't we?"

"That's the idea. Betty needs help and nothing's going to bring the cops faster. Leave Betty and Penelope in the bank, break a window, and get out. The cops will find them and take them to the hospital. But you two stay close by and keep your cell phones on. If we need help, you can send the police to the warehouse."

"What do you mean if we need help?" asked Oona. "We've got Betty and the other girl. Let's just get out of here."

"You're forgetting someone," I told her. "There's still one person we haven't rescued."

"Who?" asked Oona. In the excitement, she'd forgotten.

"The Princess."

"You mean Sidonia Galatzina? Princess of Pokrovia?" Penelope squealed. "Is she here, too? Can I meet her?"

"I'm afraid you won't have the pleasure," snapped Kiki.

"That's too bad," sighed Penelope. "I've heard she's the most popular girl in New York. But where's this city we're going to? Is it big? Is it dangerous? Is it out-of-state?"

"We can't let Penelope see the Shadow City," I whispered in Kiki's ear. "That girl couldn't keep a secret if her life depended on it."

"You're going to have to blindfold her," Kiki said to Luz and DeeDee.

"Blindfold me? Why do you have to blindfold me?" whined Penelope.

"Do you want to be gagged, too?" snapped Kiki. "Or perhaps you'd prefer to stay here."

Penelope opened her mouth to argue, but seeing the icy look in Kiki's eyes, she wisely opted to sulk quietly.

Together, we helped Luz and DeeDee lower Betty down to the main tunnel of the Shadow City. Kiki wrapped the blindfold around Penelope's head and guided her down the ladder. Then Kiki, Oona, and I set off in search of the Princess.

✿ ✿ ✿

Kiki Strike climbed up to the warehouse above the opium den, and Oona and I followed behind her. One by one, we pulled ourselves into a narrow space, surrounded by towering piles of counterfeit handbags, wallets, shoes, and luggage.

"This way," said Kiki, pointing toward a light that issued from a corner of the warehouse. We walked softly down a hall lined with wooden crates, all stamped with a cross-eyed dragon.

"Look at all this," I whispered, picking up a perfect copy of an eight-thousand-dollar Hermès Kelly bag. "The Fu-Tsang must make a fortune."

Oona snorted. "This is just small stuff," she said. "Trinkets. I'm surprised they even bother."

"Why? What sort of things do they usually smuggle?" I asked.

"They'll smuggle anything. They aren't very picky. But mostly they deal in people."

"People?" I asked.

"Yeah. People who are so poor, they'd do anything to have a better life. So they allow themselves to be smuggled into the United States. Of course, no one ever tells them that they're selling themselves into slavery. The Fu-Tsang gang brings them here and sells them to sweatshop owners who make them work for nothing. That is, if the people make it here alive."

"How do you know so much about the Fu-Tsang?" I asked.

"How do you think I got here?" Oona said.

"Shh," Kiki hushed us. "We're getting closer."

The light had grown stronger, and we could hear voices, and occasionally a sinister giggle or two. We peeked between a gap in the crates and spied a group of girls seated in a circle. In a gilded chair fit for an empress sat Naomi Throgmorton, still dressed in her gown from the Bannerman Ball. Seated nearby were three other members of The Five, all looking a little haggard. Naomi was doing her best to entertain the group.

"Did you see what Gwendolyn was wearing at the party? That pink dress made her look like an enormous piglet. I kept expecting her to climb up on the buffet table and root around in the lychee nuts like a little oinker." Naomi wrinkled her nose and snorted like a pig, and the rest of The Five cackled cruelly. It was hard to believe that these were the masterminds behind the plot to steal the NYCMap.

One of the other girls jumped in. "Everybody said you had the best gown at the party, Naomi. I heard Lila Livingston say that you were the most beautiful girl she'd ever seen."

"It's true. Next to her, I'm a goddess. When is she going to get that nose fixed, anyway? I don't know if we can afford to be associated with her if she insists on keeping that beak of hers. I don't care *how* much money she's got."

"Naomi," a third girl whined. "Do you think we'll have to wait much longer? We've been here for hours."

Naomi turned on the girl with a malicious sneer. "Why? Don't tell me you have something better to do. Oh, no," she said, her face suddenly contorting into a mask of mock concern. "Is today the day you have your mustache waxed? Are you growing hairier as we speak?" The other girls giggled. "No wait, I know. You have to run home to take your pills."

"Pills? What pills?" asked the whiny girl.

"You know—the ones for that nasty case of toenail fungus that you caught from your maid."

"I don't have nail fungus!" insisted the girl, her face the color of a boiled beet.

"That's not what I've heard. But if you'd care to take

off your shoes and prove you're fungus-free, I'll be happy to admit that I'm wrong."

"Why d'you have to go and tell everybody?" screamed the girl at another member of The Five.

"Because it was funny," her friend replied. "Besides, what if one of us had caught it from you? I couldn't have slept at night."

"You're evil—all of you," whimpered the fungus-ridden girl.

"It's true," admitted Naomi. "Isn't it great?"

Kiki shook her head in disgust. "They don't know what they've gotten themselves into. You two stay here. I'm going to have a word with Naomi."

"What are you going to do that for?" asked Oona. "Shouldn't we just save the Princess and get the hell out of here?"

"We're not here to save the Princess," said Kiki. "We're here to save her kidnappers. Now, if anything goes wrong, call Luz and DeeDee and have them alert the police. But whatever happens, don't try to rescue me yourselves." With that, she marched out into the open area.

The girls looked up at the new arrival. Surprise registered on the faces of The Five, but Naomi merely smiled as if she had been expecting Kiki all along.

"Kiki Strike," she said, standing up and extending a hand like a queen to a subject. "I've heard so much about you. I can't tell you how thrilled I am to meet you." Kiki stood her ground and refused to accept Naomi's hand. Naomi shrugged off the insult and kept on smiling.

"Where's Sidonia?" asked Kiki.

"Oh, I wouldn't worry about our favorite princess," said Naomi. "She's quite safe."

"You've made a big mistake, Naomi," warned Kiki. "You have no idea who you're dealing with. You're lucky I found you before Sidonia's people did. They won't hesitate to kill you and your stupid friends. But if you hand Sidonia over to me, I'll make sure you get out of here alive."

One of the girls giggled ominously.

"Mistake?" scoffed Naomi. "I don't make mistakes anymore, munchkin."

"You're wrong, Naomi. I can't decide whether you're incredibly greedy or just not very bright, but somehow you always seem to choose the wrong girl to steal from."

"Greedy?" Naomi giggled. "You don't know what you're talking about. I don't want Sidonia's money."

"Then I guess you must be dumb, because there's no way Sidonia can help you get your hands on the NYCMap."

"What? Oh, that silly old thing? The map's just a bonus. That's not what we're really after."

"Okay, Naomi, what is it you really want?"

"You," said a voice from behind a crate. A girl dressed in black stepped out of the darkness and into the light. Her yellow eyes shone like gold, and a vicious smile stretched across her pretty face. In one hand, she clutched the bronze dragon we had left in Betty's pocketbook. In the other hand was an electric stun gun. It was the Princess.

"Call Luz and DeeDee," I whispered frantically to

Oona. "Tell them to send the police." I heard nothing, and I spun around to find Oona in the clutches of a man with a cross-eyed dragon tattooed on his burly bicep. The man wrenched the cell phone out of her hand and crushed it under his heel.

"Take them to the opium den," I heard the Princess call. "It's time we all got to know each other better."

HOW TO KICK SOME BUTT

Imagine for a moment that a thug has grabbed you from behind. You struggle and scream, but your arms are pinned down by someone much bigger and stronger than yourself. It's hopeless, right? But if you think you're a goner, think again. When it comes to kicking butt, size isn't really an issue. Bruce Lee, the legendary kung-fu fighter, was only five foot seven and weighed less than your average cheerleader. Yet Bruce could take out guys twice his size with a single kick.

So, even if you're the shortest, daintiest, most delicate girl on the planet, don't think you're incapable of putting up a fight. If someone grabs you from behind, just stay calm and use your head.

1. Bend your head forward, and slam it back into your attacker's face. It may hurt you a bit, but since your skull is much denser than someone else's nose, you'll be able to cause far more damage to your attacker than you do to yourself.
2. If your attacker refuses to let go, pull one of your legs up to your stomach, then deliver a powerful mule kick to the man's shin. If you're in the habit of wearing high-heeled shoes, the kick will be *extremely* painful. The attacker's grip may loosen, and you'll be able to break free from his hold.
3. The attacker may grab your wrist as you're trying to escape. There are plenty of ways to break free in such situations, but one of the easiest is to take the man's pinky

finger and snap it back. The attacker will let go, and you
should be able to run to safety.

Of course, there are many effective techniques you can use, and any
good martial arts instructor can teach them to you. But don't forget that
in many situations, a bad attitude may help as much as a black belt.

ChapTER 17

Death by Chocolate

One Fu-Tsang guard dragged me across the warehouse while another carried Oona kicking and screaming into the hidden opium den. It took three more guards to subdue Kiki Strike, who landed a few good punches before someone pummeled her with the heel of a counterfeit shoe. Kiki's tiny body crumpled and blood trickled down the side of her face. One of the assailants—a goon whose skin was speckled with warts— spat two teeth onto the floorboards before tossing Kiki over his shoulder. For one dreadful moment, all hope deserted me. The girl I'd believed was invincible had finally been beaten.

Inside the opium den, the three of us were tied to chairs with the same duct tape we had used to bind Jacob Harcott and Thomas Vandervoort. A mold-flavored gag was thrust into my mouth, and I had to summon my powers of concentration to avoid throwing up. When the urge subsided, I searched my surroundings for any means of escape. I wanted out—and every brain cell I possessed was dedicated to finding a way.

Naomi and the other members of The Five flitted about the room like murderous butterflies. One of the girls arranged six martini glasses and a pitcher filled with a milky blue liquid on the table in the center of the room, while Jacob Harcott and Thomas Vandervoort remained wrapped like mummies on the floor.

"Shouldn't we untie Jacob and Thomas?" one of The Five asked Naomi.

"Not yet. Sidonia said to wait," Naomi responded in a businesslike fashion. Hearing this, the two boys grunted loudly in protest, and thumped their heads against the floor. But nothing could entice the girls to disobey the Princess and come to their rescue.

Naomi glided across the room to where Kiki was strapped to her chair. Leaning over, she slapped Kiki's injured cheek.

"Wake up, sleepyhead," she sang. "This is your big day—you don't want to miss any of it!"

Kiki's eyes flickered open. She stared at Naomi, showing no sign of fear. Then she lowered her head and peered down at the floor. I followed the path of her gaze and realized that my chair sat just inches from the edge of the trapdoor that led to the Shadow City. Kiki's head snapped up and our eyes met. I knew she had seen something, and I wished I could read her mind. If she had a plan, I had no idea what it might be. She arched an eyebrow, gave me a wink, and turned to face Naomi.

"I wouldn't start celebrating, Naomi. You're in as much danger as we are," Kiki whispered in a raspy voice.

"If you let us go, we can help you escape before it's too late."

"Danger?" giggled Naomi. "Look around you, Thumbelina. This is my boyfriend's warehouse. I don't see any danger here, do you? And even if I did, why on earth would I let you go?"

"You're out of your league, Naomi," Kiki warned. "Sidonia's more dangerous than you know. This is a stupid way to stay popular."

"Oh, shush," said Naomi playfully. "You're talking about my best friend."

"Don't tell me you're taunting the prisoners, Naomi." The Princess's voice echoed through the opium den. She was slinking down the ladder from the warehouse, her movements as graceful as a cat's.

"Sorry, Your Highness," said Naomi. "The albino doesn't know when to shut up."

"She'll be quiet now," the Princess said in a cool, confident voice as she stepped off the ladder. Her eyes took in everything in the room. "I have a feeling she wants to hear what I have to say. Tell the guards to leave us."

Naomi nodded to the Fu-Tsang, and they climbed up the ladder to the warehouse and shut the trapdoor behind them.

Once they were gone, the Princess crossed the room, her eyes glinting like gold and her long black mane swaying behind her. Her perfect posture and confident stride were as regal as any queen's. She stopped in front of us and peered down at her captive with a self-satisfied smile.

"Kiki Strike . . . that is what you're calling yourself

these days, isn't it?" the Princess asked. "I suppose it's not a bad choice. Your real name is a bit of a mouthful."

Real name? I looked over at Kiki, who was staring at the Princess defiantly, refusing to speak.

"Try not to look so glum, Kiki. You should feel flattered!" exclaimed the Princess. "I planned all of this for *you*. The kidnappings, the robberies—even the parties. All of it just to get *your* attention. Oh, look," she said, pointing at Naomi. "You've hurt Naomi's feelings. You have to admit she's a wonderful actress. She's given the performance of a lifetime hosting my Bannerman Balls."

Kiki Strike showed no interest in the Princess's performance. Instead, she was staring at the pink diamond ring on her captor's hand.

"I see that you like my ring," the Princess said, with a nasty smile. She held the diamond up to the light and sprayed Kiki's face with tiny rainbows. "They say the diamond's cursed. Most people who've worn it have met with a terrible fate. But I consider it my personal good luck charm. After all, it's what brought the two of us together."

The Princess pulled a chair toward us and sat down across from Kiki.

"It's a remarkable story," she said, crossing her long legs and toying with the diamond on her finger. "Two years ago, this ring was stolen. As you might imagine, I was terribly upset. It's a family heirloom, and I thought it was gone forever. Then suddenly it reappeared—under *very* mysterious circumstances. Just as I was about to punish the wrong person, I received a letter that told me where to find the missing ring. When Naomi described the strange girl who had written the note, I knew it could only be *you*.

"You see, my mother had always warned me that one day a sickly child and an old woman might try to kill us and steal our jewels. Do you know how terrifying it is to believe you might be murdered at any moment? My mother couldn't tell me what you looked like, of course, but she told me to keep an eye out for anyone unusual. And the white-haired ghost girl who told me where to find the ring was nothing if not *unusual*.

"It's funny, though," the Princess laughed. "I might never have known you were in New York if you had only let Naomi keep the ring."

"Me? Keep the ring?" Naomi squealed. "What are you talking about, Sidonia? I didn't steal your ring."

"Oh, shut up, Naomi," said the Princess pleasantly. "I always knew it was you. You'd robbed half the lockers at Atalanta before you finally got round to mine."

I stopped searching for escape routes and tried to make sense of it all. Kiki had been after the Princess all along? And Sidonia was responsible for the kidnappings and robberies? Were there any good guys in this story?

The Princess stood up and began to pace the room.

"I waited for you to come back to school," she continued, "but you must have known I'd identified you. If you were smart, you would have disappeared for good. But you just couldn't bear to leave me alone. The night my house was flooded, I knew you had caused the explosion. I insisted that my mother's men search the neighborhood. One of them found that dismal little shack where you and Verushka Kozlova were living. But somehow you both escaped. That's when I knew I had to come up with a plan of my own. I had to kill *you* before you could kill *me*. Thank goodness I found *this*."

I gasped when the Princess held up a disk with my own handwriting on the front. It was the CD with the maps.

"I was dying to know more about you," said the Princess, "so I dropped by the house where you had been hiding. My mother's men had left the place in an awful mess. I found pillows ripped open, bullet holes in the walls—and this CD lying on the floor. I had just picked it up when your friends arrived. I'm afraid I ran off without saying hello.

"When I got home, I took a look at the files on the disk. The minute I saw it, I could tell the map of the tunnels was important. It explained how you had gotten under my house. But there was a second map on the CD that didn't seem terribly interesting. All it showed were water pipes and subway stations.

"If it hadn't been for Mitzi Mulligan, I might never have realized how important the NYCMap map really was. I suppose I should thank the little brown-noser. Without Mitzi, none of us would be here today."

I remembered Mitzi's strange behavior at the hospital. She had known something after all. I promised myself I'd make her pay if I ever got out alive.

"For ages, Mitzi had been bragging about a top-secret map that her father had developed," the Princess continued. "At first I couldn't have cared less. Who needs maps when you have a chauffeur? But then I realized that she was talking about the map on your disk. Of course, Mitzi had told me how dangerous the NYCMap could be. She said that anyone with all three layers could destroy New York. That's when I came up with my plan. I knew the NYCMap would make the perfect bait. If someone were to steal it, you'd come out of hiding to find it. Then I'd be able to get you out of the way once and for all.

"I already had the bottom layer of the map, but I knew kidnapping Mitzi would get your attention. Her father would have given me anything in exchange for his little girl. But when you didn't take the bait I realized I'd have to kidnap two more people to get the other layers. Unfortunately, I was a little short on cash. I hadn't anticipated how expensive the first Bannerman Ball would be. So I used your map of the tunnels to rob the Chinatown Savings and Loan. By the way, I'm impressed that you made it past the rats in the tunnels tonight. Five members of the Fu-Tsang gang were eaten alive during the Chinatown Savings and Loan robbery alone. Perhaps you'll be kind enough to tell us how you did it?"

Kiki Strike arched an eyebrow and shook her head.

"It doesn't matter," said the Princess with a shrug. "I already have what I want."

"How did you know I'd come after the NYCMap?" asked Kiki.

"She speaks!" exclaimed the Princess, clapping her hands together with excitement. "I'm *so* glad you asked. I was beginning to think you were deaf as well as dumb. You see, your problem is that you're terribly predictable. Think about it. You followed my mother and me all the way to New York, but once you were here, you couldn't stop yourself from helping every little nobody who crossed your path. So I knew you wouldn't be able to sleep at night if someone stole the NYCMap. You'd have to go after them. All I had to do to get your attention was kidnap a few silly girls. Then, to make sure no one suspected *me*, I simply kidnapped myself. I'm still surprised by how easy it's been.

The Princess sauntered over to Naomi and threw an arm around her friend's shoulder.

"But what am I saying? It must sound like I'm taking all the credit. I could never have done this alone. Thanks to all your noble deeds, there was no shortage of people who were willing to help me. Naomi, Mr. Harcott, and Mr. Vandervoort were all dying to lend a hand. And when Jacob told his father we were going to punish the person who'd tipped off the police about the counterfeit shoes in his warehouse, the Harcotts even put this wonderful room at our disposal. Of course, the Fu-Tsang gang didn't want to miss out on the fun, either. They lost a *fortune* when the warehouse was raided. We have them to thank for the Devil's Apple. They'll be delighted when you're dead. And I must say, I'll find it a bit of a relief myself."

"It's a brilliant plan, Sidonia," admitted Kiki. "But you're wrong about one thing. I never wanted to kill you," said Kiki.

"No? Well you must have wanted *something* badly," said Sidonia. "Wait a second. It can't be *this* old thing, can it?" Her dimples flashed as she held up the diamond ring.

"That ring was my mother's," Kiki stated calmly. "I will get it back."

"Why would I let *you* have it, when my own mother went to such trouble to take it?" asked the Princess. "Do you have any idea how risky it is to poison an entire royal family? Particularly when one of them is your own sister? Things like that can get a girl hanged."

The Princess glanced over at Oona and me and laughed. "Just look at your little friends. Their eyes almost popped out of their heads. I suppose you never told them they were in the presence of royalty. That's right," she said, addressing us, "the midget is my cousin. Her mother was Princess Sophia, my mother's older sister."

"Your mother is a murderer and a thief," snarled Kiki. "She poisoned my parents so she could be queen. Every penny you have, every single thing you own, she stole from us."

"Yes, Mother's an amazing woman, isn't she? Someday, I hope to follow in her footsteps. But first I have to clean up one of the loose ends that she left. You see, Mother made one dreadful mistake. She let a lowly servant escape with the littlest member of the royal family."

"Verushka's no servant," Kiki said as if stating a simple fact. "She was a member of the Pokrovian royal guard. And if I don't return home by morning, she'll hunt you down."

"A crippled old woman is hardly a challenge. From what I hear, she couldn't even dodge a bullet when she was still in her prime. But your point is well taken. Once I watch you die, she'll be next on my list. That little house of yours should be easy to reach by helicopter."

I thought I saw Kiki flinch. "Don't tell me you're going to kill me in front of all these witnesses," she said. "That wouldn't be smart, Sidonia. They don't look very trustworthy."

The Princess tied a gag across Kiki's face, then knelt

down between us to whisper in her ear. "There aren't going to be any witnesses," I heard her say. "Once you're dead, there's going to be a terrible fire. *Everyone's* going to die."

The Princess walked to the table in the center of the room. She put her stun gun down, picked up the pitcher, and poured five glasses of the pale blue liquid. One by one, she handed the drinks to Naomi and The Five. The last she kept for herself.

"A toast!" cried the Princess, and all five girls raised their glasses to the ceiling. "For years, she's been the bane of my existence, the fly in my ointment, the worm in my apple. But today, we're here to bid a fond adieu to the remarkable Kiki Strike. From this day forward, this city will be ours for the picking, and there won't be a soul who can stop us.

"For me, this day is bittersweet, for I say good-bye not only to my archenemy, but to my only cousin—the true heir to the crown of Pokrovia. So here's to you, Princess Katarina. It's a shame the world isn't big enough for both of us."

The girls clinked their glasses, and all but the Princess lifted the drinks to their mouths. Naomi had only just swallowed when the glass slipped from her hand and shattered on the floor. Her knees buckled, and she grasped for the edge of the table to steady herself. One by one, the members of The Five began to drop to the ground like overripe fruit. Their eyes swam inside their heads before they fell into a deep, drug-induced sleep. Naomi struggled to stand, but her head wobbled around on her neck and her legs refused to straighten.

"Why?" she asked the Princess, but before she could hear the response, Naomi fell face-first onto the straw mats, her beautiful green dress spread out around her and her golden hair sweeping the ground.

"Why?" asked the Princess, stepping over the bodies of The Five as she walked toward us. "Why not? By the way," she said to Kiki, "you were right about Naomi. She would have done anything to stay popular. It impaired her judgment. Popularity isn't the object of this game. You and I know what's really important. It's power—and the fact of the matter is, I'd rather not share mine with anyone."

The Princess pulled the gag out of Kiki's mouth.

"You won't be needing this anymore," she said. "As you can see, there's no one left to warn."

"Did you kill them?" asked Kiki.

"Oh, no. I just gave them a dose of their own medicine, that's all. That'll teach them to get mixed up with drugs.

"No, you're the only person I plan to kill with my own two hands," the Princess told Kiki. "The fire I set will take care of the rest of them. With all these straw mats and pillows, the place should burn in no time. But I'm getting ahead of myself. Family first, I always say."

The Princess bent down in front of Oona and me.

"Now. As for you, squid girl, I'll bet you're wishing you had never gotten mixed up with this midget. Just look at all the trouble she's gotten you in. But don't worry. She's going to pay for it, and you lucky girls get to watch. I bet you're wondering how I'm going to do it, right? Well, I'm not going to leave you in suspense any longer.

"I want you to close your eyes and think back. Do you ever recall having seen your friend eat? Now, think hard. Maybe a sandwich? A piece of fruit? A candy bar? No? I didn't think so. You see, when your friend was just a baby, my mother poisoned her entire family. She may have survived, but according to our royal physician, she was left with what's called an Achilles' heel—a fatal weakness. You've never seen your friend eat because she's allergic to almost everything. Even a breath mint could kill her. That's why she's such a miserable runt.

"So. Now for the good part. You've heard of death by chocolate? I bet you always thought it was just a meaningless turn of phrase. Well, you're about to witness it firsthand. They say anaphylactic shock is a gruesome way to go. The tongue swells, the airways close, and then the heart practically explodes. Not very pretty, and extremely painful. The perfect ending for a little princess, wouldn't you say?"

The Princess reached into her pocket and retrieved a bar of chocolate wrapped in gold foil. She tore it open and snapped off a square.

"I've chosen the very best for your last meal, Katarina. They claim this Belgian chocolate is worth its weight in gold. So go ahead. Open wide."

I expected something to happen. At the very least, I thought Kiki would have a few last words. Instead, she obediently opened her mouth and allowed the Princess to pop the chocolate inside.

"Don't forget to chew," laughed the Princess.

Kiki chewed slowly and swallowed.

"Delicious," she said, licking her lips, which were

beginning to swell. Within seconds, her face had turned a deathly shade of blue. She gasped for breath, her chest heaving against her restraints. Her eyes rolled back in her head, and her body began to shake violently. Watching her struggle, I felt as if my own breath were being sucked out of my body. I fought against the duct tape, desperately trying to help her. If I couldn't break free, Kiki would die.

Suddenly, someone in the warehouse above began pounding on the entrance to the opium den.

"Dayb got choo," whispered Kiki, her tongue too swollen to speak.

"Oh, I don't think so," said the Princess. "That's what's so brilliant about my plan. By now mother has reported my kidnapping. The police think I'm a victim, too. Unfortunately, my kidnappers will die in a terrible fire before anyone can find their hiding place. I'll be the only one to escape."

She left Kiki writhing in her chair and climbed up the ladder to the warehouse. I heard her speaking with one of the guards. The police had surrounded the building. DeeDee and Luz must have gotten suspicious when they couldn't contact us. As the Princess issued her terse instructions, I heard a faint crack from beneath my chair. I looked down to see the hidden trapdoor to the Shadow City rise six inches. Two small hands emerged, one holding a butcher knife. With a quick swipe, the knife cut through the duct tape that bound my hands. Before I could move, what felt like a long glass tube was pressed into my palm. The hands then freed Oona's arms and passed the knife to her.

While the Princess's back was still turned, I examined the object in my hand. It was a hypodermic needle filled with a colorless substance. I had no idea what it was, but I knew what to do with it. I pulled off the syringe's protective cap and plunged the needle deep into Kiki's arm. As the liquid gushed into her bloodstream, her body stopped shaking, and Oona was able to cut the tape that bound her to the chair. Kiki's lips began to deflate, and she took a breath so deep that it sounded as if she had just swum the English Channel—under water.

"It's about time," she gasped. "That was getting unpleasant. Ananka, grab the stun gun!"

The Princess was climbing back down the ladder, the trapdoor closing behind her. I pulled off the tape around my ankles and sprinted for the table where the Princess had left the stun gun, strands of duct tape fluttering about my body. Her head turned at the sound of my frantic footsteps, and she sprang from the ladder. We reached the table at the same moment. I grabbed the weapon, but before I could make use of it, the Princess's hand locked around mine. We struggled furiously, and she scratched at my face while I tried to pry her fingers away.

At first, I figured I was no match for the Princess. I'd witnessed enough fights to know that winning such contests often has nothing to do with strength or stamina. Sometimes, pure meanness gives one fighter the advantage. The devil himself was glaring at me through the Princess's yellow eyes, and I knew she'd stop at nothing to win. But then I remembered the punch that Kiki had given one of the guards. I tried my best to imitate her, rearing back with my free hand and slamming my fist into the Princess's perfect nose.

"Nice one!" Oona cheered as the Princess crashed to the floor with a demonic cry, clutching her face with both hands. I took a glass of the pale blue liquid off the table and thrust it toward her. The Princess took the glass reluctantly, and I pulled the gag out of my mouth.

"Drink up," I demanded.

"You'll never get out of here alive," the Princess growled. I noticed her regal nose now leaned to one side. I must have broken it with a single punch. I gazed at my own hand in awe. "There are dozens of guards in the building, just waiting for someone to make a run for it. They won't be as nice as I was."

"I wouldn't worry about me, Sidonia," said Kiki, who had come to my side. "I always manage to escape. But before you take a trip to dreamland, why don't you give me the ring."

An evil smirk spread across the Princess's blood-splattered face. She wrenched the ring from her finger and threw it at Kiki.

"Go ahead and take it," she laughed.

Kiki caught the ring and held it up to the light.

"This is glass," she said. "Where's the real ring?"

"You'll never know, will you?" said Sidonia.

"Don't be so sure," Kiki said. "Bottoms up."

The Princess looked at the glass and hesitated.

"Do it, Sidonia, or we'll wrap every last inch of your body in duct tape," Kiki warned. "The police might not find you for a while. And once they do, removing the tape should be pretty painful. You may never have to wax again."

Sidonia put the glass to her lips and emptied it with one quick gulp. Not three seconds passed before her yellow eyes rolled back in her head and she collapsed into a stupor.

Kiki took a pen and a piece of paper out of her backpack.

Dear Police, she wrote.

I am responsible for kidnapping Mitzi Mulligan and Penelope Young. Naomi Throgmorton and her friends were kind enough to help. We were after the NYCMap, which we planned to use for nefarious purposes. The bottom layer can be found in my computer files. We have been very, very bad and we deserve to be punished severely. Sincerely, Princess Sidonia of Pokrovia.

P.S. We also robbed the Chinatown Savings and Loan.

She pinned the note to the front of the Princess's shirt.

"That should do the trick," she said.

A deep sigh escaped from my mouth, and I felt suddenly exhausted.

"Let's get out of here," I said.

Kiki and I walked toward the trapdoor, but Oona remained standing perfectly still in the middle of the room, her eyes glazed over.

"Oona?" I asked.

"Was all of that true, Kiki? Are you really a princess?"

"Yes," Kiki admitted.

"Why didn't you tell us?" asked Oona.

"Sidonia and her mother would have killed anyone who knew their secrets. Livia would be in prison if the truth were known. And she wants Sidonia to become queen of Pokrovia, but that can't happen if I'm in the way. Livia's men have been hunting me since the day they found out I was still alive."

Oona absorbed the information, and a twinkle returned to her eyes.

"We don't have to call you 'Your Highness,' do we?"

"Pokrovia is a democracy now, and I'm an American citizen," Kiki said in a humorless voice. "So I guess you'd better call me ma'am."

At first, we didn't know how to respond. Then Kiki grinned, and we all burst into laughter.

"Who set us free?" I asked.

"You don't know?" asked Kiki. "You're telling me that neither of you heard someone making a racket in the room below?" Both Oona and I shook our heads. "We were being followed all along."

"By who?" asked Oona.

"You'll see soon enough," laughed Kiki. She opened the trapdoor to the storeroom and called down. "You can come up now."

A terrible odor rose from below. It was the same smell that had followed us through the Shadow City.

"It's that disgusting smell again." Oona gagged. "It's like a farting pig in a men's locker room. Where's it coming from?"

"It's me," came a little voice. A blond head poked through the hole in the floor.

"Hello, Iris," said Kiki.

Iris climbed into the opium den. She was still wearing her ladybug pajamas.

"It's a potion my parents brought back from Borneo last year. The people there use it to keep animals out of their villages at night. I knew there might be rats in the tunnels, so I dabbed a little behind each ear."

"That's some powerful stuff," I said. "It's a wonder it doesn't keep the people out of the villages, too."

"You get used to it after a while," said Iris.

"So *you're* the person who rescued us," said Oona. "I thought you were supposed to stay at home."

"I would have, but these dropped out of Kiki's bag," she held up two more hypodermic needles. "I thought they might come in handy."

"Yeah, come in handy as an excuse to follow us," said Oona.

"What are they?" I asked Kiki.

"Adrenaline," she replied. "It's the only thing that can stop the seizures. When you're allergic to everything, it's good to be prepared."

"What if I hadn't injected you in time?"

"I would have thought of something else," she said. "But I knew Iris was behind us. I could smell her a mile away." She looked at Iris and smiled. "When we were tying up those two oafs, I realized the needles had fallen out of my bag. I figured Iris must have found them, and I knew she'd bring them. That seemed like a pretty good backup plan to me."

"So you really are allergic to everything?" asked Oona. "That must suck."

"I don't know what it's like *not* to be allergic to everything," said Kiki. "All I can tell you is that I'm hungry all the time. And as Iris knows, that can make me a little cranky."

It was the closest Iris was going to get to an apology, but it was more than enough.

"Cranky?" she said. "I've met cannibals with better personalities. I'm just glad that I didn't miss all the fun."

"What do you mean, all the fun?" I asked. "There's still more to come."

"There is?" asked Oona.

I owed Kiki Strike. Not only had I been willing to believe the worst of her, I was responsible for everything that had happened. If she hadn't written the note that rescued me from public humiliation, the Princess would have never known she was in New York. The way I saw it, there was only one way to repay her for what she had done.

"We've got one more stop to make," I informed the group. "Before we go home, we need to pay a visit to the Princess's house. It's time to return the royal jewels to their rightful owner."

HOW TO SPOT A FAKE DIAMOND

It makes no difference if you're a gullible young heiress, a budding cat burglar, or just a sucker for stones that sparkle, every girl should learn how to tell a real diamond from a fake.

The next time you come face-to-face with a pricey pebble, remember to think first and swoon later. Don't risk your freedom or your fortune on a common crystal or piece of glass. Instead, put your stone to the test. While none of the following seven methods is entirely foolproof, together they may help you spot a fake—and avoid making a terrible mistake.

1.   **Give It the Scratch Test.** Before evil scientists began

making fakes in labs, diamonds were known to be the hardest substance on Earth. A real diamond will scratch a mirror or a piece of glass, but so will many impostors.

2. **Check for Signs of Aging.** Although most diamonds are over a billion years old, they tend to age more gracefully than their wearers. So take a magnifying glass and examine the surface of your stone. If you see scratches or chips, there's a chance it's a fake. Cracks *inside* the diamond, however, may be a sign that it's real.

3. **See Through Imposters.** Write the word *fake* in tiny letters on a piece of paper. Place your "diamond" facedown on top of the word. If you're able to read through the stone, odds are you've found your answer.

4. **Drop It in Water.** Some fakes, such as cubic zirconium, will appear to vanish when placed in a glass of water. A real diamond will always remain visible.

5. **Get It Steamy.** Turn on your teakettle and wait until it starts to boil. Use a pair of tongs to carefully pass your "diamond" through the steam. If the stone fogs up for more than a second or two, it's a fake.

6. **Make It Glow.** Most diamonds will either turn blue or glow when you put them under a black light. If your diamond doesn't glow, it's either a stone of exceptional quality—or a fake.

7. **Weigh It.** A real diamond will weigh far less than a cubic zirconium of the same size.

Chapter 18

Diamonds Are a Girl's Best Friend

We left the Princess drooling on the floor of the opium den and prepared to climb down to the Shadow City. Above us in the warehouse, we could hear dozens of frantic Fu-Tsang guards waging a losing battle against New York's Finest. Eventually, the police would have arrived to rescue us, but we had no intention of waiting around. There was still work to be done—the kind of work that the police might not understand. If we wanted to finish what the Princess had started, our only choice was to make our way through the tunnels back to the exit in Iris's basement.

We had already cheated death twice that night, and there was no reason to believe that our luck would continue to hold. A herd of deaf and famished rats could be lurking in the tunnels, eagerly awaiting a bedtime snack. As I opened the door to the Shadow City, I silently prayed for a rat-free escape route. Shining my flashlight through a crack in the door, I spied a single mangy rodent. He bared his fangs and scurried toward the door, willing to take on the four of us. But when the scent of Iris's repulsive perfume wafted past his snout, he squealed in disgust, turned tail, and ran.

With no beasts left to battle, I spent the long walk briefing Iris on the history of the tunnels and telling her about our discoveries. She wanted to know everything, and if we hadn't been in a rush, she would have insisted on opening every door.

"How did you guys find the Shadow City?" she asked.

"Sheer luck for the most part. But this book helped." I showed her my copy of *Glimpses of Gotham*. "When this is all over, you can read it if you like."

Iris shined her flashlight on the cover.

"Pearcy Leake III wrote that?" she squealed in surprise.

"Know him?" asked Oona with a condescending laugh.

"Maybe I do," Iris shot back.

"Pearcy Leake disappeared more than a hundred years ago," I informed Iris. "I doubt he's still up for making friends."

"Disappeared? Well, he's not missing anymore."

"What do you mean?" I insisted.

"I found him," Iris said.

"Where did you find a hundred-and-fifty-year-old man?" Oona laughed.

"When I was following you guys, I had to sneeze. I didn't want you to hear me, so I stepped inside one of the rooms along the way. There was a skeleton lying on a bed. I needed something to wipe my nose with, and I saw that the skeleton had a handkerchief in the pocket of his suit. So I took it."

"You stole a handkerchief from a skeleton?" I asked.

"To wipe your *nose* on?" added Oona.

"I don't see what the big deal is. *He* didn't need it. But here, take a look." She pulled a rumpled handkerchief out of her pocket and offered it to me.

"No offense, Iris, but there's no way I'm touching something you've sneezed on."

"Oh, right," she said sheepishly. She spread the piece of cloth out in her hand and pointed to a name embroidered along one edge.

"Pearcy Leake III," I read in astonishment. "So he didn't disappear after all. The plague killed him. He died here in the Shadow City."

"It was his gold we found," said Kiki, snapping out of a thoughtful silence. "It must have been the money he made smuggling fabric for Augustus Quackenbush."

"I think he would have wanted us to have it," I said, surprising everyone, including myself.

"You won't hear *me* arguing," said Oona. "As a rule, I never turn down treasure."

"No, I'm serious," I said. "We were the first people in more than a century to explore the Shadow City. We used his book as our guide, and we made it out alive. He would have been impressed."

"In case you haven't noticed, we haven't made it out yet," Oona said.

"But when we do, I think we should take the gold with us," I said. "What's the point of leaving it down here again?"

I looked at Kiki. Since we had all accused her of stealing the gold, it seemed only fair to let her make the call.

"If you want the gold, take it." She shrugged. "No one can say you haven't earned it."

☒   ☒   ☒

Before leaving the Shadow City, we grabbed the backpack filled with gold and paid a brief visit to Pearcy Leake to offer our thanks. I would have spoken a few words in his memory, but we hadn't a minute to spare. By the time we emerged in Iris's basement it was already six o'clock in the morning. The nanny was awake, and we could hear her thundering footsteps as she stumbled around the kitchen on the first floor. Something shattered, the nanny cursed, and Iris winced.

"We're not going to have any dishes left at this rate," she muttered to herself. "Don't worry about her," she told the rest of us. "Sounds like she has one of her hangovers. She won't even know we're here."

We hid Pearcy Leake's gold inside a trunk in Iris's basement and crept up the stairs to the ground floor of the brownstone. The morning light hit us as we reached the top step, and I saw that the four of us were filthy. Oona's hair was gray with dust and her arms and legs were red and irritated from the duct tape. Black, greasy smudges covered Iris's pajamas. But Kiki had fared the worst. Her bloodshot eyes were the color of cherry tomatoes, and dark bags drooped beneath them. Whole patches of white hair shot straight into the air, as if she'd stuck a fork in a toaster. Her black pants had ripped across one knee, and a stretch of frighteningly pale flesh flashed whenever she moved. If it hadn't been for the wicked little smile on her face, she could have been mistaken for one of the undead.

"Iris," she whispered. "Get the supplies we talked about and meet us outside."

The rest of us tiptoed out of the house and slid behind a parked car across the street. From where we were hiding, the Princess's house looked dark and deserted.

"Looks like we got lucky," said Oona. "I don't think anyone's home."

"Don't be so gullible. They never leave the house unguarded. If it were that easy to get inside, I wouldn't have bothered trying to break in through the Shadow City," snapped Kiki, pulling a cell phone out of her bag. Oona looked at me and rolled her eyes. Now that we knew the cause of Kiki's crankiness, it was easier to ignore.

"What are you doing?" I asked.

"I'm going to see if I can reach DeeDee and Luz while we're waiting," she responded.

I felt a twinge of guilt when I realized I'd forgotten about the others. I peered over Kiki's shoulder as she typed.

8 AM. Coffee shop. Hudson St. Betty?

The response was instantaneous.

Betty safe. C U @ 8.

"So far, so good," said Kiki, switching the phone off.

Minutes later, Iris emerged from her house and ran across the street, sporting a pink ruffled dress that made her look like a giant cupcake. In one hand was a brown paper sack.

"What do you think?" She curtsied to Kiki. "My grandma made this dress for me."

"Your grandmother has unusual taste. Does she work for the circus?"

"No, and her taste is fine," said Iris. "She just wants me to look seven years old for the rest of my life. I *really* hope nobody sees me wearing this."

"But you're adorable," Oona joked.

"Not funny, Wong," Iris warned.

"Quit bickering. Did you get the supplies?" asked Kiki.

"One large onion. One sharp knife." Iris took the items out of the brown paper bag.

"Excellent. Time to see if you're as good an actress as you claim to be." Kiki cut open the onion and held it under Iris's nose. Iris's eyes blinked rapidly, and plump, juicy tears began to roll down her pink cheeks. She sniffled and adopted a miserable expression. "What's wrong, little girl?" prompted Kiki.

"I locked myself out of the house," Iris sobbed. "The nanny's asleep, and she won't open the door. May I use your telephone, please?"

"A little more snot next time, but otherwise excellent," said a proud Kiki. "Okay, get going."

A bawling Iris ran across the street and up the stairs to the Princess's front door. She pressed the doorbell and then stood back looking small and helpless. It was a brilliant plan, and Iris was the only one who could pull it off. She was still young enough to appear harmless, and the Princess's guards would be used to seeing her in the neighborhood.

A man opened the door of the Princess's house and glared at the little cupcake on the stoop. I gasped when I saw his slicked-back hair and perfectly polished footwear gleaming in the sunlight. It was Bob Goodman, the fake FBI agent.

"Friend of yours?" asked Kiki.

"He came to my house after you disappeared," I admitted. "He said he was with the FBI. He told us you were an international assassin."

"That explains a lot," said Kiki. "For your information, that man's name is Sergei Molotov. He's my aunt's right-hand man. The same right hand, I might add, that put a bullet in Verushka's leg. I've been looking forward to catching up with him."

At first the man shook his head and refused to let Iris use the phone. But when she turned up the volume on her sobs and threatened to make a scene, the man ushered her inside and shut the door. I worried that it might be the last time we would see our brave little friend, but a few seconds later, Kiki's cell phone vibrated. She let it ring a few times before answering it.

"Hello?" she asked in a tired voice in case Sergei was listening.

"Hello, nanny, it's me," I could hear Iris's teary voice. "I locked myself out of the house. Can you come downstairs and let me in?"

"What a stupid thing to do," Kiki scolded her. "Why do you always run off when we have a busy day ahead of us? What time is your macramé lesson?"

"One o'clock," whimpered Iris. This was the code we

had devised. It meant Iris had seen only one person in the house.

"All right, then. Give me a second and I'll meet you at the front door."

Kiki Strike, Oona, and I leaped out of our hiding place and raced toward the Princess's house. As Sergei opened the door to let Iris out, the rest of us barged inside. We found ourselves in a spacious marble foyer, standing beneath a crystal chandelier large enough to house a family of tree-dwelling monkeys. Surrounding our quarry, we backed him up against a wall. Sergei reached under his jacket, his hand fishing for his gun. It was missing. He patted himself down and frantically scanned the room.

"Looking for this?" Iris tossed him a gun. She had taken it from its holster as he led her to the phone. "Don't worry. I removed all the bullets. Didn't anyone ever warn you not to play with loaded firearms?"

"I taught her how to do that," said Kiki Strike proudly. "She's a natural."

Sergei threw the useless gun across the floor and laughed.

"Get out of this house or I will tear you all to pieces."

"Talk, talk, talk," said Kiki, circling the well-groomed man like a hungry dingo. "You know, I think I've been threatened enough today. So let's just skip all the chitchat and get right to business. Or does the idea of a fair fight not appeal to you?"

"I'm not going to fight a little girl," Sergei uttered with a look of disgust. "It's beneath me."

"How remarkable. You refuse to fight a little girl, but you don't have any problem shooting an old lady in the leg."

"Of course I do," Sergei said, leering at the four of us. "I would have preferred to hit her in the head."

Kiki stepped toward Sergei and gazed up at his face, which towered two feet above her own. Without taking her eyes off of him, she raised one foot and brought it crashing down on his shiny Italian shoe. When he instinctively bent over, Kiki smashed an elbow into his left eye and followed the move up with a quick punch to his right eye. Temporarily blinded, the man staggered about the foyer, bellowing at the top of his lungs and crashing into furniture. Kiki stood back, her bloodshot eyes watching the scene with amusement.

"So what do you think? Should I put him out of his misery?"

"You might as well," said Iris with a yawn. "He's going to destroy the whole house if you don't do something."

"In that case, here's a move I invented on the set of my movie. I call it the Taiwanese Tumble. Watch closely."

As Sergei passed in front of her, Kiki stuck out one foot. Unable to see the obstacle in his path, he tripped and banged his head against a marble table. Sergei groaned once, and then the room was silent. In a flash, Kiki pulled a roll of duct tape out of her bag and hog-tied the large man.

"That concludes our lesson for today," she said, standing up and brushing herself off.

"Then what do you say we search the place?" I asked.

"What are we looking for?" asked Oona.

"Anything that sparkles," I told her.

⋆ ⋆ ⋆

We set out to inspect the ground floor of the Princess's house. As we stepped out of the foyer and into the house's grand parlor, Oona started to snicker. The parlor had been decorated by someone with a flair for the downright ugly. Throughout the room, hundreds of floral patterns battled one another for attention. It was hard to look at the sofa, with its mismatched cushions, without becoming a little dizzy. Anything in the room that wasn't decorated with flowers had been dipped, sprayed, or painted in gold. Above a hideous golden fireplace was a portrait of the Princess's mother wearing a crown and petting a Pekingese dog that was perched on her ample lap. An identical dog sat stuffed on the mantel, gazing at us with glass eyes. Dozens of tacky knickknacks cluttered every surface, but there wasn't a single book to be seen.

"Wow. Looks like they spent a million dollars at one of Liberace's garage sales," said Oona, checking her hair in a gilded mirror.

"And to think it could have all been mine," Kiki added.

Oona and Iris laughed, but I was too anxious to join in.

Kiki walked around the room, examining every object as if searching for an elusive clue. She shook porcelain figurines and crammed her fingers inside vases. She paused in front of an empty glass case on top of the fireplace mantel.

"Strange," she said. "This case was designed to hold

Fabergé eggs," she noted. "Livia took three with her when she fled Pokrovia. But the case is empty."

"Maybe they're redecorating," offered Iris.

"Let's hope," Oona joked, but Kiki didn't laugh along.

After checking out the kitchen and dining room, we headed upstairs. The second floor of the house was devoted to Livia's bedroom. Pictures of Livia in golden frames were everywhere, and an enormous white bed with a frilly canopy sat at the end of the room. A long row of closets lined one entire wall of the building. Kiki threw open the closet doors, revealing countless outfits for every conceivable occasion. Thousands of shoes in a rainbow of colors lined custom-built shelves. Behind the last closet door we discovered a huge metal safe, its door ajar. There was nothing inside.

"Look what I found," called Iris, stooping down beneath a vanity to pick up a glittering object. She handed it to Kiki, and the rest of us gathered round.

It was a brooch with a hundred bloodred rubies arranged in the shape of a pomegranate. Their color matched the two rubies in Kiki's ears. Kiki's fingers closed around the brooch, and her hand tightened into a fist.

"This looks like something that belonged to my mother, but it's a fake. Where did you say you found it?"

"On the floor. Over there." Iris pointed. Kiki walked over to the vanity and flipped open a golden jewelry box. It, too, was empty.

"Something's wrong," muttered Kiki, looking down at the brooch in her hand. "All the real jewels are gone. And it looks like Livia left in a hurry. She didn't even take her clothes."

"Where do you think she went?" I wondered.

"She must be in New York," said Kiki. "She wouldn't have left the city without Sidonia."

"This is getting really creepy," Oona said. "Maybe we should get out of here."

"Yes." Kiki nodded. "You should go. But I can't. This could be my last chance. I can't leave until I've found what I'm looking for."

"We're not going anywhere," I insisted. "From now on, we're all in this together."

⚔ ⚔ ⚔

On the top floor of the brownstone lay the Princess's lair. The walls had been painted a pale yellow, and the antique furnishings were simple and tasteful. Hanging near the Princess's bed was a painting of a dark and beautiful sorceress standing on a hill overlooking the sea. A herd of unhappy pigs milled around her legs.

As in Livia's room, a row of closets lined an entire wall. Inside, we found only a custom-built shelf filled with shoes and handbags, many of them designer knock-offs. Oona picked up a leather-bound scrapbook that lay on the Princess's bedside table and began to flip through it. She grabbed my arm as I walked past, on my way to inspect the Princess's bathroom.

"Hey, take a look at this," she said.

Carefully arranged on each page of the scrapbook was a memento from the life of Kiki Strike. The book began with a series of pictures of a rosy-cheeked infant with a shock of pale blond hair. Later in the book, we discovered copies of old stories that the Princess had pulled off the Internet. There was the *New York Post* article about the Central Park Vigilante and a dozen clippings describing the raid on Oliver Harcott's warehouse. The Princess had even salvaged the note that Kiki had written the day she saved me from public humiliation. While I had been watching the Princess, she had been keeping track of Kiki Strike.

"Hey, Kiki," Oona called. "I think you have a fan."

Kiki didn't answer. Something on top of the Princess's dresser had caught her eye. It was a porcelain doll in a colorful dress that I assumed was the national costume of Pokrovia. Kiki picked up the doll and examined it, even peeking under its skirts. Then she seized the doll by its legs and with one quick flip of the wrist, smashed the doll's head against the wall. The porcelain head shattered, and a black object the size of an apricot pit rolled across the floor. Oona picked it up.

"It's a video camera," she sputtered. "Someone's been watching us."

"I knew this was too easy," said Kiki. "Let's go find our Peeping Tom. Where's Iris?"

As soon as she spoke, I realized that Iris was missing. A bolt of panic shot through my body. Kiki and I raced downstairs to check Livia's bedroom while Oona stayed on the third floor to search the Princess's bathroom. Iris was nowhere to be found.

"Oona," Kiki called. "Did you find her?" There was no answer. "Oona!" Kiki called louder. Not a peep. Kiki and I looked at each other and rushed back upstairs. Oona was gone.

"She couldn't have gone downstairs. We would have

passed her. But how could she disappear from the third floor?" I wondered. "There's something strange about this house. How did you know it had an entrance to the Shadow City?"

"It was mentioned in *Glimpses of Gotham,*" she said.

I took out my copy of the book.

"Here it is," I told Kiki. "It says it was a lodging house. There's a hidden room under the building that used to have an entrance to the Shadow City. According to Pearcy Leake, it was a thieves' den. But how do we get into the room?"

"I don't know," Kiki said. "I didn't see a trapdoor, did you?"

"No," I admitted. "But there must be a way inside."

I sat down on Sidonia's bed and tried to think like a criminal. Why would a gang of thieves build a hidden room under a *lodging house*? It didn't seem very smart. They wouldn't have been able to get in or out of the building without being seen by the guests. Suddenly, the answer was clear. The thieves had used the hotel as their own private gold mine, stealing from out-of-towners who stayed the night. If they had a way to sneak into the rooms while the guests were sleeping, they could have made a fortune.

Examining the shelves in the Princess's closet, my eyes were drawn to a pair of prim Mary Janes that the Princess wouldn't be caught dead wearing. I tried to pick them up, but the shoes were anchored to the shelves. Reaching inside the first shoe, I felt nothing but dust. But inside the second, all the way at the toe of the shoe was a small button. I pushed it and part of the wall popped open, revealing an empty space behind it.

"I think we've found the way to the secret room," I told Kiki.

Behind the closet was an ancient staircase. As we quietly descended, we passed two more camouflaged entrances to the main house. At the bottom of the staircase was a metal door. My heart sank. If it was locked, we might not be able to find a way inside without Oona. But when I reached out to turn the handle, the door opened.

Inside the dungeonlike room was a wall filled with flickering video monitors. One monitor was dark, but the rest showed black-and-white images of the parlor, dining room, and kitchen. Several computers sat on a steel table that rested against one wall. I heard a muffled cry come from one corner of the room, and I realized we were not alone. Oona and Iris were in the clutches of the giant man I had seen rowing Livia and the Princess the day the water main had burst beneath their house. Both of the girls had put up a fight. Oona's lip was bleeding and Iris's pink dress was shredded. Now the two of them were hanging from the bodyguard's arms like a pair of rag dolls. Seated nearby on a plush chair was Livia Galatzina, wrapped in a mink coat.

We must have interrupted Livia in the middle of her morning beauty ritual. One cheekbone was spackled with a thick layer of rouge, while the other remained as pale and gray as a corpse. Her hair was perfectly coiffed, but her clothing looked as if she'd been attacked by badgers. By the side of her chair was a small Louis Vuitton suitcase.

"Going somewhere, Livia?" asked Kiki. "You might want to fix your makeup first."

"You nasty little changeling." Livia's face wrinkled into a hideous sneer. "You should be dead."

"Sorry to disappoint Your Highness." Kiki dipped into a sarcastic curtsy. "As you can see, I'm still very much alive."

"No matter," sniffed Livia. "I am a patient woman. I can wait another minute for you to die."

"I don't intend to go so quickly. But even if I do, you'll still have to postpone your trip. It could be a while before Sidonia gets out of jail. My guess is that the police are probably fingerprinting her right about now. Or maybe she's enjoying a friendly strip search."

Livia's cold eyes studied Kiki's face.

"You remind me of my sister, Sophia. You inherited none of her beauty, of course, but you have grown to be just as foolish. And like your mother, you will find out what happens when someone stands in my way."

"Give it a rest, Livia. I've already won. If you're smart, you'll hand over the jewels."

"Jewels?" scoffed Livia. "Is that what you've come for? There are no jewels left, you little fool. Do you think I would allow my own daughter to stoop to robbery if there were? I sold the jewels to pay for this house, for these guards, for these clothes. New York is a very expensive place to live, you know."

Kiki looked devastated.

"You're lying Livia. You're wearing some of them now. Don't you think I'd recognize the royal jewels?"

"These?" Livia held up a necklace, then let it drop. "These are copies. A woman in my position must keep up appearances. But I am afraid they are made out of ordinary glass."

"And my mother's ring?"

"The pink diamond?" Livia smiled, revealing a smear of red lipstick on her two front teeth. "It paid for the bullet in your guardian's leg. Now it will pay to put one in you, too."

"You might want to switch to plan B, Livia. The police have Sidonia. They'll be coming here next."

"In that case, I should leave them a welcoming gift. What do you say, Igor?" Livia asked the giant beside her. "Would four dead little girls be appropriate? Kill them all." Livia leaped from her chair and grabbed her suitcase. As Igor's two meaty arms flexed, strangling Oona and Iris, Kiki hurled herself at him. Livia pushed past me on her way toward the staircase.

"Out of the way, you filthy peasant," she snarled.

Livia's rudeness brought me to my senses. I jumped at her and wrenched the suitcase out her hands. It popped open, and a fortune in cash spilled out on the floor. Livia roared like a furious warthog and slapped me across the face. Stumbling backward, I grabbed hold of one of her gaudy necklaces to steady myself. It snapped off in my hand, and I slipped on a pile of hundred-dollar bills. Livia rushed for the exit, and by the time I got to my feet, she was already at the door. I snatched at her hair, trying to prevent her escape. But the hair came away in my hand, and Livia issued a blood-curdling shriek. Confused, I looked down at the wig in my hand, then up at a bald Livia, who was bounding up the stairs. I started to go after her, when I heard people laughing behind me. I turned to see Kiki, Oona, and Iris standing beside the fallen bodyguard.

"Let her go," said Kiki. "She won't get very far. And

being seen in public like that is punishment enough for now. I can't wait to see the mug shot."

Kiki stepped over Igor's bloated body and bent down and picked up the necklace I had ripped from Livia's neck.

"Worthless," she sighed after examining it. "For once, the old bat was telling the truth."

"We may not have found your jewels, but we still have Pearcy Leake's gold," I said, trying to cheer her up.

"And think of how much fun we can have with this wig," said Iris, joining in. She picked up Livia's silver wig off the floor and set it on top of her head. For a moment, she looked like one of DeeDee's old Scout leaders.

"Hold on, Iris," said Oona, plucking something out of Iris's wig. "There's a piece of jewelry hidden in your hair." She held the bauble up to the light. "Not bad for a fake," she said. "I can see why she wanted to keep it. Mind if I take it?"

I stopped breathing when I saw what Oona was holding.

"May I see that?" asked Kiki quietly, taking the pink diamond ring from Oona's hand. She held the ring carefully between her fingers, studying not the diamond, but the band.

"This one's real," she said.

"How do you know?" I asked.

Kiki Strike passed the ring to me. There, engraved into the gold, were six Russian words.

"It's a set of directions," said Kiki. "It's what I've been searching for."

"Does it lead to a treasure?" asked Oona.

"It depends on what you'd call treasure," said Kiki.

"I don't understand," I said.

"I never really cared about money or jewels. These are directions to a letter my mother wrote. One that will prove that Livia murdered her."

HOW TO EXPERIENCE THE REAL NEW YORK

Most people who visit New York return home with the same boring pictures of the Empire State Building and the Statue of Liberty. But those of you who are willing to leave the tour groups behind can see a side of the city that few really know.

Stone Street. If you're dying to know what New York looked like in the days of the Shadow City, this tiny, easy-to-miss lane in lower Manhattan should give you a good idea. A crooked, 400-year-old Dutch road, Stone Street is lined with buildings that were built just after a fire destroyed most of the city in 1835.

Wall Street. Anyone can tell you that Wall Street is the financial center of America, but few know that it was the site of a deadly anarchist bombing in 1920. The bombers were never caught, but you can still see evidence of their work—just look for pockmarks in the façade of the building at 23 Wall Street.

Bridge Café and Ear Inn. Two of the oldest establishments in New York, these restaurants have dark and dangerous pasts. Built in 1817, the Ear Inn (326 Spring Street) has been a brothel, a bar, a boardinghouse, and a hiding place for runaway slaves. The Bridge Café (279 Water Street) has been serving patrons since 1794 and was once at the heart of the most dangerous neighborhood in Manhattan.

Doyers Street. The site of battles fought among rival Chinese gangs in the nineteenth century, it's said that more people have been murdered on this short, narrow street in Chinatown than on any other block in the city. The area is also riddled with underground passages. Take a walk through one such tunnel—located at the bottom of a staircase at 5 Doyers Street.

Burial Grounds. There are only a few true cemeteries to explore in Manhattan. (Make sure to visit the two Marble cemeteries—one on Second Avenue between Second and Third streets, the other on Second Street between First and Second avenues.) However, if you feel like paying a visit to the dead, just stop by the nearest park. Many were built on top of long-forgotten burial grounds, and underground crypts are often unearthed by hapless city workers.

Washington Square Park. This famous park was also a burial ground, and is the final resting place of many a plague victim. When the land was first converted into a public park, the graves had a nasty habit of collapsing and revealing their occupants. Walk to the northwest corner of the park, and you'll find a 300-year-old elm tree from which dozens of criminals were hanged.

Haunted Places. Clinton Court (420 W. 46th Street between Ninth and Tenth avenues). Originally used as a stable, this hidden house dates from the early nineteenth century. According to legend, it was built on top of a cemetery and is haunted by Old Moor, a mutinous sailor who was hanged in the courtyard. The Merchant's House Museum on Fourth Street is also reputed to be haunted, and the catacombs under Old St. Patrick's Cathedral are said to be visited by the ghost of Pierre Toussaint, a hairdresser and possible spy for George Washington.

Hidden Houses. More than seventy-five hidden houses can be found in Greenwich Village. (There are seven on the west side of Cornelia Street alone.) Though they can't be seen from the street, you can find clues to their existence. Street addresses marked with an A or a $1/2$ may indicate that a hidden house is nearby. Also look for wooden doors that might lead to "horse walks"—passages just wide enough for a horse.

Chapter 19

The Legend of Kiki Strike

a t eight o'clock in the morning, we emerged from the home of Sidonia Galatzina. We stood on the stoop of the building and took in the peaceful morning scene. The air had a fresh, clean smell, as though sometime in the early hours, invisible hands had scrubbed the streets, sidewalks, and gutters. The sun sparkled in a puddle of rainwater, and the pansies in a window box danced in the breeze. The birds were chirping, the street was empty, and everything seemed right in the universe.

It was a new day. There was no need to protect the city from evil princesses. There were no social climbers left to rescue. No hungry rats nipping at our heels. No skeletons to rob. No locks to pick or explosions to set. It occurred to me that the next few years could get pretty dull. Despite their many flaws, life is always more interesting when your archenemies aren't locked up in jail.

"Iiiirrrriiiisss!" A voice that could grate cheese filled

the quiet street. A large woman in a housedress was screaming at us from the stoop of Iris's house.

"Oh, no," Iris groaned with embarrassment. "She's going to wake up the whole neighborhood."

"Iris McLeod! What have you done to that dress!" shrieked the nanny. "You get your butt over here this instant! Your parents are on the phone!"

"I'm coming!" Iris shouted, then her voice turned sad. "I guess I've got to go. Thanks for letting me tag along. Stop by and say hi sometime."

"I don't think that will be necessary," said Kiki Strike, crossing her arms and trying to look stern.

"Oh." Iris took a deep breath and began to walk down the stairs.

"We expect to see you tomorrow night at eight," I told her.

Iris's face twisted in confusion. "For what?"

Kiki let loose an exaggerated sigh.

"Don't tell me you've already forgotten. It's the Irregulars' weekly meeting. Attendance is mandatory. No disguises, recording equipment, or toxic substances allowed."

"You mean . . . ?"

"Welcome to the Irregulars," I said.

"Anyone who saves our lives is automatically a member," said Kiki, inventing a new rule on the spot.

"I hope that dress can be saved," said Oona. "I can think of a million schemes involving a little girl in a pink ruffled dress."

"Shut up, Wong," laughed Iris.

"Iiiirrrriiiisss!" screeched the fat woman. "Get over here now!"

"Hey lady, shut up! I'm trying to get some sleep!" yelled a half-naked man from the window of the building across the street.

Iris winced. "She'll never let me go to the meeting."

"Don't worry. We'll take care of her," said Kiki. "But first we have a job for you."

"Really?" asked Iris.

Kiki handed Livia's Louis Vuitton suitcase to Iris. "You're in charge of the money for now. Just tell your nanny we were playing dress-up, and don't let her look inside the bag. Bring the cash and the gold we hid in your basement to the next meeting. Do you think you can do that?"

"It would be an honor," said Iris in a serious voice that made Oona crack up.

"Great, Iris. Then we'll see you tomorrow," said Kiki with a grin.

Iris clutched the suitcase to her chest and ran down the stairs and over to the nanny. She waved to us from the stoop and disappeared inside. We set off to meet up with Luz and DeeDee.

✳ ✳ ✳

Two blocks away, we found our friends sitting in the window of the coffee shop, keeping themselves awake with jumbo cups of espresso. Luz spied us coming down the street, and started to laugh, spraying coffee all over the plate glass window. I wondered what she found so amusing until I caught sight of our reflection. The three of us looked as if we had been dropped out of the sky by a tornado.

"Where have you been?" Luz asked once we had taken a seat at the table by the window. "I've got to get home before my mother finds out I'm missing. I can't take another summer locked up indoors."

"We've been finishing some business," said Kiki. "Have you seen Betty?"

"We just came from the hospital," said Luz. "They say she's fine. Just taking a nice, long nap."

"So everything went according to plan?"

"Yep. We set off the alarms in the Chinatown Savings and Loan, and the police were there in two minutes flat. DeeDee and I barely had enough time to hide across the street. They found Betty and Penelope, and an ambulance picked them up. In a way, it was a good thing Betty was unconscious. I can't imagine anything worse than being trapped in an ambulance with Penelope Young. That girl can't shut up."

"She is a bit annoying," DeeDee agreed.

"We tried to tell you that the plan had worked, and when we couldn't get through to you on the cell phone, we got worried."

"So we called the police and left an anonymous tip," said DeeDee.

"They were at the warehouse in no time," said Luz. "And then things *really* got interesting."

"We didn't see much of the fight, but you could hear gunshots going off like firecrackers. And then, in the middle of it all, a sweet little old man walked out of the building and down the street. He was carrying the bronze dragon. Nobody tried to stop him. It was like they didn't even see him."

Oona looked startled. "An old man? Was he Chinese?"

"I think so." DeeDee nodded.

"And was he dressed in a gray suit and carrying a black cane?"

"How did you know?" asked Luz.

"That's Lester Liu. The head of the Fu-Tsang."

"I thought he was supposed to be in China," I said.

"So did I." Oona's voice had turned thick with hatred. "If I had known he was back in town, I would have tried to look him up." She leaned back in her chair and stared at the ceiling.

"What happened after you saw the man leave the building?" asked Kiki, gracefully changing the subject.

"I don't think anyone else got away," said Luz. "They started dragging guys out by the dozen. They loaded two paddy wagons with Fu-Tsang members. Then they brought out Naomi and her friends. Naomi looked a little woozy and a couple of her friends were completely out of it."

"What about the Princess?" I asked.

Luz froze mid-sip and lowered her coffee cup. "What do you mean, what about the Princess? I thought you guys rescued her."

Oona sat bolt upright, and Kiki was as still as a statue.

"The Princess was the mastermind behind the kidnappings," I said.

"She tried to kill us," said Oona.

"We drugged her with wart remover and left her for the police," I added.

"You're joking, right?" asked DeeDee with a forced smile.

"No," I told her, my heart sinking like a cannonball in quicksand.

"She wasn't there. We didn't see her coming out of the warehouse," said Luz.

Kiki jumped up from the table and ran for the door.

"What's going on?" DeeDee cried out in surprise.

A terrible thought hit me. "Verushka," I whispered. "The Princess said she would kill her."

The rest of us hurried after Kiki, who was already halfway down the street.

We sprinted all the way across town, charged past the doorman, who folded into a low bow when he saw Kiki Strike, and climbed the fire escape to the rooftop house. There, tending to her vegetable garden high in the sky, was Verushka. I collapsed onto the grass. As I sucked in as much air as I could, I heard Luz throwing up in the bushes. Only Kiki was unfazed. She ran up to her guardian and threw her arms around her. Verushka dropped a summer squash on the ground and hugged her back.

"You're alive!" cried Kiki.

"I am so old that you expected a corpse?" Verushka laughed.

"No, you don't understand. It was Sidonia. She was behind the whole thing. She kidnapped the other girls to get to me. We rescued Penelope and Betty, but Sidonia and Livia escaped. I thought they would come to kill you," said Kiki, her voice cracking.

Verushka hugged her again. "It is my job to worry about you, Kiki. It is not your job to worry about me. If you rescued the girls, that is all that matters. Let Livia and her daughter go. We will find them again. And someday we will recover your mother's jewels. Until then, we have enough money left to survive."

"The jewels are gone. But we found the ring."

Kiki reached into her pocket and pulled out the pink diamond ring.

"It is true?" asked Verushka, taking it from Kiki's hand and reading the inscription engraved on the band.

"It was the only thing left. They sold all of the other jewels. That's why they robbed the Chinatown Savings and Loan. They needed more money."

"Your mother would be very proud." Verushka beamed.

"You know what this means, Verushka? We won't have to hide anymore. We'll have Livia thrown in jail. And we'll clear your name and live like normal people."

Verushka shook her head sadly.

"No, my darling. It is not so simple. The proof we need is still in Pokrovia. We cannot return to get it now."

"But Livia and Sidonia may have the bottom layer of the NYCMap. And Sidonia stole the map of the Shadow City from our house on Bank Street. We have to get out of New York."

"We are going nowhere. We cannot leave while this city is still in danger. You are worried that a spoiled little girl and her mother are going to hurt us?"

"It's not them I'm worried about. I'm worried about Sergei and the other bodyguards. The ones who shot you."

"Stop and think," said Verushka. "Bodyguards do not shoot other people for free. Now that their money is gone, how will Livia pay these men to shoot us?"

The words had a magical effect on Kiki. Her brow unfurled and a wide grin stretched across her face. DeeDee crawled over to where I lay, her body too exhausted to stand.

"Would you mind telling me what's going on," she panted. That's when I realized that she and Luz had missed most of the show.

*   *   *

Once we were able to walk, Verushka ushered us into the house. We sat around the kitchen table as she prepared breakfast.

"You have all been very brave," Verushka told us as she drew a large knife from a kitchen drawer and skillfully attacked a potato. "Now it is time for us to trust you with our story.

"For twenty years, I was a member of the Pokrovian royal guard. It was my duty to protect Kiki's mother, Princess Sophia. It should not have been a difficult job. The people of Pokrovia loved Sophia. When it was time for her to become queen, the country celebrated. The only person who was not happy was Livia, Sophia's younger sister.

"Livia believed she had been born to be queen. She hated Sophia, and I knew that Livia could not be trusted. One day, I saw Livia's maid in the palace kitchen, stirring a pot of soup that was intended for Sophia. Only the cook was allowed to touch the food of the royal family, so when the maid had gone, I fed the soup to the kitchen cats. The first cat to lick the pot died within minutes.

"Of course I told Sophia what I had seen, but she would not arrest her only sister. Like her daughter, Sophia could be very stubborn. She wanted to make peace with Livia, but I knew it would never work. I convinced Sophia to write a letter in her own hand describing her sister's attempt on her life. She hid the note in a secret place in the palace. If something happened to her, she told me, I would find directions to the letter. They were inscribed inside the band of her favorite ring—a ring that she swore would never leave her finger until the day she was dead.

"On the night that Sophia was murdered, I was on duty with a young guard named Sergei Molotov. It was the evening before Sophia's coronation, and she was dining with her husband and young daughter. The baby was sleeping when the food was brought in, so the adults ate first. Sophia had started to feed Kiki when she became ill. Sophia and her husband died quickly—and with great pain. When I knew I could not save them, I grabbed the ring and the baby. Sergei tried to stop me. He claimed he had seen *me* poison the food. He took the ring and arrested me. I escaped with Kiki and ran to the royal doctor, but he told me that Kiki would not live. She had eaten too much of the poison. And if she did survive, she would never be a normal child. He said it was better to let her die.

"I refused to believe him. I took Kiki and left Pokrovia. It was good thing. The doctor was an informant. He told Livia that Kiki was still alive. When the revolution forced Livia to flee, we followed her from country to country. I hoped that someday we could make her pay for what she had done. So I taught Kiki everything I knew—languages, the martial arts, weaponry. I tried to keep the terrible secret from Kiki until she was older, but she found a journal I had kept for her. After that, it was impossible to stop her."

Verushka handed each of us a plate filled with grilled sausages and potato pancakes. In front of Kiki, she set only a bowl filled with a pale, lumpy substance.

"What is *that*?" Oona asked, her face wrinkling with disgust.

"Gruel and vitamins," said Kiki. "It's the only thing I can eat."

"Livia should pay just for making you eat that crud," Oona said.

"She will," said Luz, as if there wasn't a doubt in her mind.

"So wait a second," I said to Kiki. "All this time, you were just trying to prove that Verushka was innocent?"

Kiki swallowed a spoonful of gruel.

"When I read Verushka's journal, I knew that I had to find the letter that could prove that Livia killed my parents. When I heard that she'd given the ring with the directions to Sidonia, I knew I had my chance."

"That's why you came to the Atalanta School?'

"Verushka thought I needed some friends, so she convinced me to join the Girl Scouts. That's where I first saw Oona selling counterfeit badges. I paid her to forge the documents I would need to get into the Atalanta School. I thought if I were close enough to Sidonia, I could sneak a peek at the inscription inside the ring.

"I almost did it, too. I found out that Sidonia left the ring in her locker during her swimming class. If I wanted to see it, all I had to do was get past the combination lock. But another girl beat me to it. I was there when Naomi stole the ring. But Sidonia thought *you* had taken it, and I had to set her straight. After I wrote the note, I couldn't go back to the Atalanta School. I knew Sidonia might have identified me. I had to find another way to get my hands on the ring. And I had to do it fast. Once Livia suspected Verushka and I were in New York, it was only a matter of time until she found out we were living just a few blocks away.

"Fortunately, I had another plan. When I found *Glimpses of Gotham,* I learned there was an entrance into Livia's house through the Shadow City. I asked Oona to forge a birth certificate so that I could get access to the tunnel in the Marble Cemetery. I wanted to sneak into Livia's house at night and take the ring. But Verushka wouldn't let me do it alone. So I recruited you guys to help me.

"My plan might have worked if I hadn't been so impatient. Livia was close to discovering our hiding place, and I made the Irregulars move too fast. After the explosion, I knew she would figure out who was responsible. I ran back that night to check on Verushka. But Sergei Molotov saw me on the street and followed me to the hidden house. He shot Verushka and we barely escaped. We hid in Chinatown for two years, and I had to make the kung-fu movie to pay our bills."

"Why didn't you call us?" asked Luz. "We could have helped. We made a killing on the Reverse Pied Piper."

"I wanted to tell you what had happened, but Livia

would have killed you. So I had to let you all believe I had disappeared. In fact, if it hadn't been for the robberies and kidnappings, I would have stayed in hiding. Sidonia's scheme *was* brilliant. She made me come to her. I'm just sorry for dragging you along with me."

"That is enough," said Verushka, who had taken a seat at the table. "I am tired of these old stories. When can I hear about last night's adventure?"

The five of us told Verushka everything—starting with the Bannerman Ball and finishing with Livia's wig. She was a perfect audience, clapping with excitement in all the right places and gasping at the proper moments. When we were done, she sat back and stroked her chin.

"There is one thing I do not understand. If you made her drink the Devil's Apple, how did Sidonia escape?"

"We don't know," I admitted.

"The answer is important," Verushka counseled. "I think it is time for you to visit your friend Betty in the hospital. She may know something that you do not."

"That's our next stop," said Kiki as she gulped down the last of her gruel.

★ ★ ★

On the way to St. Vincent's Hospital, we stopped by Betty's house. We planned to smuggle her out of the hospital before the police could ask too many questions, and we needed a disguise. We picked the lock on her apartment and grabbed a blond wig and a fake nose. DeeDee left a note on the kitchen counter for Betty's parents, who, thanks to a false order for Matador costumes placed earlier by Luz, were still not back from work. Betty was spending the night at a friend's house, DeeDee wrote. She'd be home in the evening. That gave us a few more hours for Betty to wake up. But once we were standing over her hospital bed, we wondered if our expectations might have been unrealistic.

Betty's white dress had been exchanged for a hospital gown, and the makeup and grime that had covered her face had been carefully wiped away. She was still in a deep sleep, and her head tossed from side to side as if she were having a vivid dream.

"They'll know," she mumbled into the pillow. "You can't trick them."

"Betty," whispered DeeDee, gently patting her arm. "You're just dreaming."

Betty forced her eyes open, straining as if her eyelids were made of lead.

"DeeDee!" she whispered hoarsely. "It's the Princess. She kidnapped herself. She knew Kiki would have a spy at the party. You've got to warn her!"

"I'm right here," said Kiki. "We're all okay. How are *you* feeling?"

"Where am I?" asked Betty, her eyes darting around the room.

"St. Vincent's Hospital," I told her. "You hit your head. But you're going to be fine."

"What time is it? I've got to get out of here," said Betty, sitting upright in bed. "My parents are going to kill me."

"Relax. We left them a note," Kiki said. Betty fell back on the pillows.

"I watched you at the party," I told her. "You were very brave."

"Believe it or not, it wasn't that bad," said Betty. "I was almost enjoying myself. Maybe I'll go to more parties. Wait! Did you catch the Princess?"

"No," admitted Kiki. "She got away."

"What happened?" asked Betty.

"We drugged her, but somehow she managed to escape."

"Oh, no," Betty moaned. "If I had been awake, I could have told you. She found the Morlock's Miracle Mixture in my bag, and figured out why the Devil's Apple wasn't affecting me. She drank the rest of it herself."

I looked at Kiki. The news was not good. "The Princess was only pretending to be asleep when we left," I said.

"We'll worry about that later. Let's take Betty home," was all Kiki said.

We borrowed a wheelchair and rolled a disguised Betty out of the hospital room. Doctors and nurses passed us without so much as a second look. We were almost out of the building when a woman's voice called out, "Kiki Strike!"

"Get Betty outside and grab a cab," I whispered to the other girls.

Luz, Oona, and DeeDee rolled Betty out of the hospital. Kiki and I turned to greet Penelope Young's mother, who sprang on us like an affectionate puppy.

"Thank you so much! Penelope told me you rescued her. The doctors say she's okay, thank goodness, just a little messy. Can you believe that a bunch of kids were behind it all? The police caught them, but I'm sure you know that, don't you."

"Yes, we know," said Kiki.

"So you'll be collecting the reward, right?"

"Reward?" I asked.

"We offered a ten-thousand-dollar reward for Penelope's return. Of course, there's not enough money in the world to give you what you really deserve."

"I don't need any money," said Kiki. "Penelope's safety is reward enough. She's a wonderful girl." I saw the sides of her mouth twitch as if she were forcing back a smile.

"What?" scoffed Penelope's mother, as if the notion of a good deed were too ridiculous to contemplate. "But you rescued our daughter. You're a hero. I can't let people think that you weren't rewarded for all you've done."

"If you don't mind, Mrs. Young, I'd prefer it if nobody knew."

"But you could be famous!"

"I'd rather not," said Kiki. "If you insist on rewarding me, you can reward me with your silence."

"But . . ." Penelope's mother started to say until she realized she was getting a fantastic deal. "Well, if that's what you want, I'll be happy to oblige."

"I'd appreciate it, Mrs. Young. Now if you'll excuse me, I really have to go."

We quickly walked out of the hospital and found a cab waiting for us on the corner.

"Jump in," said Oona. We crammed our bodies into the backseat and made our escape with the rest of the Irregulars.

★ ★ ★

By the time I got home, the story of the foiled kidnapping had broken. I switched on the evening news and came face-to-face with the same overeager reporter who had covered the robbery at the Chinatown Savings and Loan.

"Good afternoon, Janice! I'm standing in front of a warehouse in Chinatown where last night, police foiled a kidnapping. I'm afraid stories don't get any stranger than this, Janice. At four o'clock in the morning, police responded to an alarm at the Chinatown Savings and Loan, the site of a recent robbery. There they found two girls. One was Penelope Young, the schoolgirl who was kidnapped eight days ago. The other girl has not been identified and has since vanished.

"According to police, an anonymous tip led them to the warehouse behind me, where Penelope Young says she was held without access to clean clothes or running water. After a fierce battle with a Chinatown gang, police found the kidnappers unconscious in a secret room beneath the warehouse's basement. According to police, the leader appears to have been Jacob Harcott, son of real estate magnate Oliver Harcott, and his teenage girlfriend, Naomi Throgmorton. In an even more surprising turn of events, the warehouse, which is owned by Mr. Harcott's father, was found filled with counterfeit goods. Police are now seeking Oliver Harcott for questioning.

"But the million-dollar question, Janice, is who set Penelope Young free and directed the police to her kidnappers? So far, Miss Young has refused to discuss her mysterious benefactor. We can only hope

that the person responsible receives the credit he de-
serves. Reporting live from Chinatown, this is Adam
Gunderson for News Channel Three."

"The credit *he* deserves?" I yelled at the television
set. I considered setting them straight, then thought better of it.

The next morning, New York's newspapers picked up
the story, and headlines across the city screamed *Super-*
hero on the Loose! and *Who's Our Hero?* Wherever you
looked, there were profiles of Jacob Harcott and his father, yearbook pictures of The Five, and elaborate maps
showing the warehouse and the location of the hidden
room. But the only paper that had managed to get a real
scoop was the *Daily News,* which published a small item
in its gossip column.

Spotted: Princess Sidonia of Pokrovia and her
mother, Queen Livia, at JFK Airport, boarding a
flight to Moscow and rudely insulting an airline
employee when they were refused an upgrade to
first class.

I ripped the item out of the paper and set it aside for
that night's meeting of the Irregulars.

At 7:45, Iris knocked at my door. She was dressed in
black and struggling with a Louis Vuitton suitcase and a
dirty black backpack. The mysterious delivery of a case
of Angus McSwegan's Finest Scotch Whisky had gotten
the nanny off her back for the night.

"Moving in?" I asked her when I opened the door.

"Sorry I'm early," said Iris, smiling eagerly.

I had a feeling she had been dressed and ready to go for hours.

"Not at all," I said. "It's a good sign."

"I brought everything." She dropped the two bags near the door.

"So I see. Go ahead, take a seat. Do you want some coffee?"

"Do you have any juice?" she asked, looking a little embarrassed.

Betty was the next to arrive. Her face was free of makeup and her clothes were surprisingly normal. Even her trademark sunglasses were missing.

"What—no glasses?" I asked.

"I'm tired of all the disguises," Betty said. "Unless there's a good reason to be someone else, I'm going to try being me for a while."

"And to think that all you needed was a knock on the head to bring you to your senses," I told her.

"If that was all she needed, I'd have been happy to give it to her a long time ago." Oona walked up behind Betty and put her arm around Betty's shoulders. "You look fabulous," she said. "Where did you get that shirt?"

Luz and DeeDee arrived together, comparing methods of stain removal.

"I didn't know if you'd be able to make it to the meeting," I told Luz. "Doesn't your mom know you snuck out of the house last night?"

"No, Attila saved me. I'm telling you, I'm dating a criminal genius. When I told him I had to sneak out, he came over to my workshop and pretended to be me. You know, he can really sound like a girl when he wants to. It's a little weird sometimes. He told my mother I was busy and wouldn't let her inside the shop . . ." Luz's voice trailed off the moment she spotted the black backpack that Iris had left in the hallway. "You took the gold?" she asked. From the sound of her voice, she didn't approve.

"We found out whose it was," I said. "Actually, Iris did. It belonged to Pearcy Leake. We thought he would want us to have it."

"That skeleton was Pearcy Leake?" DeeDee asked. "The guy who wrote *Glimpses of Gotham*?"

"The one and only," I said.

"What are we going to do with his gold?" Luz wanted to know.

"Split it up, I guess. Think of all the new equipment you'll be able to buy. The coins are old. They're probably worth a fortune."

Luz stared down at the backpack and nudged it with her toe.

"I don't want it. Give my share to someone else."

"What do you mean you don't want it?" I asked in amazement.

"It's bad luck," she said, not bothering to elaborate.

"If she doesn't want it, I don't want it, either," said DeeDee. "You can give my share to someone else, too."

"Okay, who's the lucky person?" I asked.

"Why don't we just give it back?" said DeeDee.

"What's a skeleton going to do with a fortune?" Iris asked.

"That's not what I'm talking about," DeeDee explained. "Pearcy Leake must have died from a plague, right? I heard my dad saying that there's a team of scientists at Columbia University who are trying to find a cure for the bubonic plague. Believe it or not, it's still killing people. So why don't we give the money to them?"

"Sounds good to me," said Luz.

"Well, if you don't mind, I think I'll hold on to my share," I told them. "Somebody's going to need some money when the Princess comes back to town."

"As long as you promise not to blow it all on shoes," warned Luz.

By eight o'clock, everyone had arrived—except for Kiki Strike. By eight fifteen, we were starting to worry. Had she vanished? Would we see her again? At half past the hour, I heard a window open in my bedroom. I grabbed a poker from the fireplace and walked to the back of the apartment. Climbing through the window was Kiki Strike. I made a mental note to get better window locks.

"Do you have a problem with using the front door?" I asked.

"They're after me," Kiki said, thoroughly annoyed.

"They can't be," I told her. "The Princess and her mother were on a plane to Moscow last night."

"Not *them*," said Kiki. "Reporters. Penelope Young squealed on me. I nearly had my photo taken *three times* on the way here."

"Penelope Young squealed?"

"Haven't you been watching the news? She sold her story. She even had a piece of proof—that stupid business card I gave her mother. I don't know what I was thinking. Now everybody's looking for a short girl with white hair."

I laughed. "You're about the only person on Earth who doesn't want to be famous."

"It's not funny. How am I supposed to get anything done when there are people watching me all the time?"

"I get your point," I said. "Betty should be able to come up with a disguise for you. What would you like to be? An Eastern European princess?"

"I'm telling you, it's not funny, Ananka," said Kiki, but I could tell she was starting to lighten up.

The next morning, a blurry photo graced the front page of the *New York Post,* along with the headline: *Is This Kiki Strike, Girl Detective?* Wherever Kiki was, I knew she was cursing Penelope Young.

"Doesn't this look like that friend of yours, Ananka?" asked my mother, holding up the newspaper as I ate my breakfast.

"What friend?" I asked, chewing on a piece of toast.

"Don't be cute," my mother warned. "And don't talk with your mouth full. You know the one I'm talking about. The girl with white hair. You said you spent the night with her a couple of days ago. And she was at our house yesterday. I saw her coming out of the bathroom. She's the same girl who asked me about poisons a while back."

"I guess it does look a little like her," I said. "But the picture's not very good. It could be anybody."

"Isn't your friend named Kiki?" she asked, pointing at the headline.

"Yeah," I admitted with a shrug of my shoulders.

After being questioned by the FBI, it's hard to be scared of your own mother.

"So is there anything you'd care to tell me?" she asked.

Where my mother was concerned, it was always best to stick with the truth. She never believed it anyway.

"Are you suggesting that I've been spending my nights fighting crime with my friends? Is that what you think?"

"I don't know what to think," she admitted, sitting down across from me at the kitchen table. "You're not the same girl anymore."

"No, but maybe that's a good thing. You never found me all that interesting before."

"That's not true, Ananka," my mother insisted. "You may be more mysterious now, but you've *always* been interesting. Just promise me that you'll be careful. It's hard to be interesting when you're dead."

"I promise to be careful," I told her. "So do you really think I'm interesting?"

My mother sighed and shook her head. "You're the most *interesting* person I know," she said.

✶ ✶ ✶

Apparently, my mother wasn't the only person who bought the paper that day. By evening, New York was in a frenzy. Sidewalk vendors sold T-shirts emblazoned with the words: *I Am Kiki Strike, Girl Detective*. Within a week, entire grade schools were forming Kiki Strike hunting parties. Much to the disappointment of their parents, hundreds of girls (and a few boys) dyed their hair white and took up kung-fu.

For a while, the bizarre events that regularly take

place in New York received new attention. A cat burglar nabbed in a Fifth Avenue apartment? It must be the work of Kiki Strike. A flock of South American parrots set loose in Queens? Kiki Strike again. (Actually, Luz was responsible for that one.) When Kiki saved a woman's poodle from an electrified manhole cover, the ungrateful wretch used her cell phone to place a call to the *New York Times* before Kiki could even leave the scene.

It was funny at first, but eventually, we had to put a stop to the madness. All it took was one phone call to the intrepid reporter at News Channel Three.

"Good morning, Janice! I'm reporting live from Murray Hill on a stunning development in the case of Kiki Strike, Girl Detective. I'm here with Svetlana Jones, owner and operator of Samizdat Stationery and Printing. Now, Ms. Jones, you say that you personally printed the business card that's become so famous. Could you tell us a little about the person who placed the order?"

"Certainly, Adam Gunderson," said Svetlana Jones, a child-sized woman with a cane and a thick Russian accent. She pushed her unfashionably large glasses back and patted her hair, which was the color and texture of an enormous dust bunny. *"She was sixteen years old. She had red hair like borscht. And her words flowed as fast as the Volga."*

"I'm going to show you a picture, Ms. Jones. Is this the girl who ordered the business cards from your shop?" Adam Gunderson held up a photo of Penelope Young to the camera.

> *"Yes, that is the girl. I remember her. She said she was going to sell a story to the newspapers and become very rich. Then she laughed like crazy person."*
>
> *"Ms. Jones has just identified a photo of Penelope Young. I'm sad to report that Kiki Strike, Girl Detective was just a hoax concocted by another greedy schoolgirl. Reporting live from Murray Hill, this is Adam Gunderson for News Channel Three."*

Following Adam Gunderson's groundbreaking report, the newspapers and television stations turned their attention to actual news. But try as we might, the legend of Kiki Strike couldn't be stopped. In a few short weeks, she had attained the level of fame that it took Bigfoot decades of sightings to achieve. But with New York's intrepid reporters no longer roaming the streets in search of a tiny girl with white hair, the Irregulars were finally able to get back to business.

❈   ❈   ❈

As soon as Kiki Strike was able to leave her house unnoticed, we secretly returned the money the Princess had stolen from the Chinatown Savings and Loan and destroyed the entrance to the Shadow City beneath Oliver Harcott's warehouse. After that, we relaxed and watched as justice was served.

Naomi and The Five traded their designer clothes for the less tasteful uniforms of a juvenile justice detention facility, where they reportedly had a little trouble making new friends. Thomas Vandervoort and Jacob Harcott graduated from juvie to jail and were soon joined in the big house by Jacob's father. Oliver Harcott had been captured as he tried to smuggle himself across the Canadian border while hidden in a barrel of pickled herring. All three men could be seen riding the daily ferry to Hart Island, where they spent the long, hot summer digging graves for the city's dead. Even Penelope Young received the punishment she deserved. Fleeing from the reporters who hounded them day and night, Penelope and her parents moved to a small fishing village in the coldest, dreariest county in Maine. Though Penelope was too far away to cause the Irregulars much trouble, we'd heard that she quickly made a nuisance of herself by trying to convince any fisherman who would listen that Kiki Strike was not a hoax.

As for the Princess and her mother, they were last spotted in St. Petersburg, sunbathing at the palatial summer home of a well-known Russian gangster. A few days later, they boarded a train bound for Noril'sk and disappeared into the Siberian wasteland. We all suspected they'd be back someday, but for the moment, New York and its Shadow City were safe.

Don't miss **Kiki Strike** and the **Irregulars** in their second adventure, **THE EMPRESS'S TOMB**

THE EMPRESS'S TOMB

"Kiki Strike is our hero."
—*Girls' Life*

Kiki Strike

Kirsten Miller
New York Times bestselling author of *The Eternal Ones*

BLOOMSBURY

A mysterious runaway, a long-lost father, a haunted mansion, and a two-thousand-year-old Chinese empress . . . It's up to the Irregulars to protect the city— and save themselves.

Who's Been Sleeping in My Bed?

think it's safe to say that most fourteen-year-old girls with criminal histories would have steered clear of Fat Frankie's diner. Every morning, dozens of police officers crammed the small coffee shop to scarf down breakfast before their morning shifts. But over the summer, Fat Frankie's had become Oona Wong's favorite hangout. However illicit her business might be, she preferred to conduct it in public. She knew she had nothing to fear. Few of her fellow customers could have imagined that the elegant girl with the doll's face had once been one of the most notorious forgers in Chinatown. Oona claimed she enjoyed living on the edge—but I've always suspected she had a fondness for policemen.

As I pushed my way through the crowded coffee shop, I wondered what Oona's latest scheme might be. One year earlier she had opened the Golden Lotus, an upscale nail salon where wealthy women flocked to freshen their pedicures and swap gossip with their friends. Arrogant

and ignorant, they assumed the young Chinese women who worked in the salon could speak no English. But as they silently clipped cuticles and trimmed toenails, Oona's employees carefully recorded their clients' conversations. Oona had made a small fortune trading on socialites' secrets and stock tips, but that never stopped her from searching for new ways to pump up her bank account.

What Oona *did* with her money was a mystery the rest of us had never been able to solve. Painfully blunt, she never hesitated to point out that your lip gloss didn't suit your complexion or a giant pimple was about to emerge on your forehead. But as a matter of principle, she refused to discuss her own personal life. Though we'd known her for years, we had no idea where Oona lived or who cooked her waffles every morning. My single attempt to satisfy my curiosity had ended in a showdown on a Chinatown street when Oona caught me following her home, disguised as an unusually youthful bag lady. In the end, I promised to leave her alone. I knew one day the truth would be revealed, and having a sneak preview wasn't worth losing a friend.

I found the Irregulars clustered around a table at the far end of Fat Frankie's, a few feet from the bathroom. Dressed in a gray mechanic's jumpsuit, Luz Lopez sat with her work boots propped up on the back of a chair. Her head was bent in concentration, and her lips formed silent curses as her fingers fiddled with her latest invention. DeeDee Morlock, the Irregulars' chemistry expert, was chatting with a bald Hare Krishna who could only be Betty Bent, our master of disguise. While the other girls paid little attention to their surroundings, Oona sat with her back to the wall, her fierce black eyes skipping from person to person. I had the sense she'd been counting the seconds until the meeting could begin. When she spotted me making my way to the table, she cocked her head and crossed her arms, silently demanding an explanation for my tardiness. Oona Wong did not like to be kept waiting.

"Thrilled you could finally make it, Fishbein. Were you abducted by aliens on the way here? Or did you stop off to bore another tourist with that lecture you give on the secret history of Washington Square Park?" Oona loved a confrontation, and on most mornings I might have indulged her. Instead I kept quiet as I pushed Luz's boots off the chair and sat down across from DeeDee.

"Where's Strike?" Oona demanded.

"I don't think Kiki's coming," I said.

Betty bit her lip and Luz's fingers froze as we all prepared for what would come next.

"What are you talking about?" Oona's pretty face wrinkled with rage. "She's *got* to be here. When one of us calls a meeting, everybody has to show up. That's the *rule*."

"Lower your voice. It's too early for shouting." Of all of us, DeeDee had the least patience for Oona's outbursts. "Let Ananka finish for once, would you?"

Oona's mouth clamped shut with enough force to bite a fork in half.

"Kiki's missing," I told them. "She was supposed to

meet me last night to finish the map. She never showed up at the Marble Cemetery."

"She was probably breaking into another pet store," said Luz, returning to her tinkering. "Any of you check the papers this morning? I'll bet somebody saw an albino leprechaun releasing more monkeys into the streets last night."

"Kiki didn't set those animals loose. She'd never be that irresponsible. It's a miracle none of them got squashed by a bus." Sweet natured and gullible, Betty never believed Kiki capable of anything objectionable. The rest of us knew better.

"Sometimes I wonder if we know the same person," I told her. "But this time you're right. Kiki didn't have anything to do with the pet store. Have you guys seen the giant squirrels?"

"I saw one on the way here," said DeeDee.

"What about them?" Luz shrugged.

"I'm pretty sure the same person who's been painting the squirrels set the pet store animals free. I think I saw him last night. He left a squirrel not far from Kiki's house."

"So you went to Kiki's house?" asked DeeDee. "What did Verushka say? Does she know where Kiki is?"

"Verushka's missing, too. And she didn't take her wheelchair."

For a moment, the Irregulars sat in silence as the information thumped around in our brains like a bowling ball in a washing machine. Oona sighed and rolled her eyes.

"There goes *my* meeting," she muttered.

"I'm sorry your latest get-rich-quick scheme has been temporarily put on hold." The volume of DeeDee's voice rose with each word. "Don't you think this is a *little* more important?"

"It's too early for shouting," Oona mocked her. "Kiki disappears all the time. That's what she *does*. I don't know why everyone's so worried. None of you would even notice if *I* didn't show up for a meeting."

"Your family isn't trying to kill you," Betty tried to explain.

"What would you know, baldy?" Oona said. "Maybe they are."

"So where is the homicidal royal family of Pokrovia these days?" Luz asked, dragging the conversation back on track. "Still hiding out in Russia?"

"We don't know," I admitted. "Livia and Sidonia vanished two months ago. Verushka's sources claimed they'd left St. Petersburg, but the other day I got wind of a rumor that made me wonder if the Princess and her mother might still be there."

"Could they have made it back to New York by now?" Betty wondered. "Have you heard anything at the salon, Oona?"

For a moment, it seemed as if Oona's lips wouldn't budge. Her anger had vanished, and she'd started to sulk. "I haven't been spending much time there lately," she finally said. "But Livia and Sidonia are top-priority topics. Someone would have called me if there had been any news."

"Should we check Kiki's house?" asked DeeDee. "If you give us a couple of hours, Luz and I can disable the booby traps."

"And destroy all that work?" moaned Luz. "Come on, guys. Oona's got a point. This isn't the first time Kiki's disappeared. It isn't even the *fourth* time. Shouldn't we wait a day or two before we start ripping everything apart?"

"Maybe Luz is right," said Betty. "Our weekly meeting is tomorrow. If Kiki doesn't show up for that one, we can break into her house and search for clues."

"Okay," I said, standing up from the table. "If you all want to wait, we'll wait. I just hope we're doing the right thing."

"Where are you going?" Betty asked.

"I have research to do. If Livia and Sidonia are back in New York, there might be an item in the gossip columns."

"But Oona called the meeting, and we haven't even let her talk," Betty protested. Oona said nothing. She just concentrated on the table in front of her as if she were willing it to fly through the window.

"Sorry, Oona," I said. "What did you want to discuss?"

"Never mind," Oona mumbled.

"Pleeeeeease," Betty begged, trying to lure Oona out of her funk.

"I'll wait. It's not that important," said Oona, and I suddenly suspected it was.

☆ ☆ ☆

That night, the weather worsened. Even with the windows open, my bedroom was hot enough to roast a goat. I lay on my bed in my nightgown, using the *Daily News* as a fan. Since returning home from the meeting, I'd combed through every New York newspaper. There was no mention of Livia or Sidonia Galatzina. The giant squirrels were the day's big story.

As if to prove to the city that they couldn't be ignored, the squirrels had invaded the Central Park Zoo in the early hours of the morning and freed hundreds of animals from their cages. At 6:00 a.m., a jogger reported a pack of penguins feasting on fish in the Harlem Meer. An anaconda was seen sunning itself on the steps of a Fifth Avenue mansion, a poodle-shaped bulge in its belly. Jewel-colored tree frogs clung to pine branches like Christmas tree ornaments. Among the only animals left behind at the zoo were several enormous squirrels. The one that made the front cover of the *New York Times* had been painted on a plastic iceberg in the polar bear's habitat. It was a thuggish-looking beast with a sign that said bluntly WHAT ARE YOU LOOKING AT?

According to the papers, security tapes at the zoo had captured a shadowy figure skipping past several sleeping guards, pausing from time to time to moon the cameras. Since the vigilante's face had been cunningly disguised, and his butt lacked distinguishing features, the police were without solid leads. They had begun staking out pet stores and interrogating art students, but the culprit remained at large. Everyone in New York was anxious to see what he'd do next.

A gust of wind blew through the room, rustling the newspapers I'd tossed to the floor. I turned my sweat-speckled forehead to catch the breeze and caught sight of an unnaturally pale face framed by wild, white hair peering at me from the fire escape. When I shrieked in

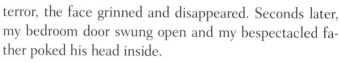

terror, the face grinned and disappeared. Seconds later, my bedroom door swung open and my bespectacled father poked his head inside.

"Still alive?" he asked, checking the room.

"Barely." I was feeling a little faint from the shock.

"Boogeyman?" he asked.

"Spider."

Having earned a degree in entomology, my father's sympathies lay with the insects of the world, and he never missed an opportunity to bad-mouth an arachnid. "Repulsive little creatures," he said, shivering with disgust. "Did you know they dissolve their prey's innards and then suck them out like a Slurpee? They're the eight-legged serial killers of the arthropod phylum. But just remember: You're bigger than they are."

"Thanks for the advice," I said.

"That's my job," he replied as he shut the door with a smile.

Once I heard his footsteps fade, I ducked through the window and onto the fire escape. Kiki Strike was leaning against the wall, waiting for me, her chic black clothes blending into the night. She wasn't exactly the picture of a princess—at times it was hard to believe she was human. Though the poison she'd consumed as an infant hadn't killed her, it had drained her skin and hair of color. And because the attempt on her life had left her allergic to most forms of food, she was unlikely to grow more than five feet tall. At fourteen, she was like a creature from a sci-fi movie, shockingly beautiful and strange.

"Sorry I'm late," she whispered. Even in the dark, I could tell there was something wrong. Her ice-blue eyes were bloodshot, her cheeks had sunk to new depths, and she hadn't brushed her hair in days.

"Twenty-four hours. I think you've set a new record for tardiness. Where have you been? I was sure you'd been kidnapped. I've spent all day trying to locate Livia."

"Verushka was sick. I had to take her to the hospital."

"Verushka's in the hospital? What's wrong with her? Is she going to be okay? Can I see her?" The questions shot from my mouth like badly aimed bullets, and my vision blurred as tears flooded my eyes. Not only was Verushka the kind of guardian I always wished I had—funny, understanding, and handy with a bazooka—I knew it was she who'd convinced Kiki to invite me to join the Irregulars. Without her intervention, I might have died of boredom long before I reached high school.

"Verushka's back at home. She's doing fine. There was something wrong with her leg—the one that Sergei Molotov shot. It started turning blue a few days ago. But the problem's under control now. In fact, she'd be mad if she knew I told you. She wouldn't want to you to worry about her. She's a tough old lady. I once watched her stitch up her own head wound with a sewing needle and some fishing wire. She'll probably outlive us all."

"I wouldn't be surprised," I said. "But how are *you* feeling? You look like you've been dipped in Wite-Out. Are you sure you didn't catch something at the hospital?"

"Nothing a little danger can't cure. What do you say we finish the map tonight?"

"I can't. Some of us have to go to school in the morning. My teachers have been complaining that I keep passing out during class."

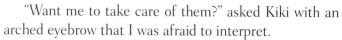

"Want me to take care of them?" asked Kiki with an arched eyebrow that I was afraid to interpret.

"I think I can handle them on my own," I assured her. "But I really do need to get some rest. My mother threatened to have me deported to the middle of nowhere if my grades don't improve."

"Come with me tonight, and I promise you'll get a nap tomorrow afternoon."

"Oh yeah? How are you going to do that?"

"It's a surprise. It won't get you into any trouble."

"But I don't want to go to the Marble Cemetery tonight," I moaned. "It's too much work."

"See," Kiki countered with a cocky grin. "I thought of that, too. If you get dressed fast, we can use the entrance in Iris's basement. Her parents are at a cocktail party."

"And her nanny?"

"The nanny locked herself in the bathroom an hour ago. She polished off a bottle of cooking sherry, and now she's singing show tunes to herself."

"I don't know, Kiki."

Kiki's smile faded as she chipped a piece of paint off the rail of the fire escape. Beneath all the bravado, something was still troubling her.

"You win," I huffed. "Stay here while I slip into something a little more practical. But you better think of a foolproof plan to get me out of school tomorrow." Back in my room, I reached out the window and handed her the front page of the *New York Times*. "Here's a little something to read while you wait."

"Yeah, I've seen the squirrels," Kiki said. "As long as they're on the loose, they should keep *me* out of the papers. Thanks to the zoo footage, nobody's looked twice at me all day. That butt on the surveillance tapes was undeniably male."

I poked my head out the window. "Worried your fifteen minutes of fame are finally up?"

"Relieved," Kiki corrected. "Another fifteen could get me killed."

In June, the Irregulars had rewarded eleven-year-old Iris McLeod with an honorary membership. Not only had she saved Kiki's life, she had also discovered a foul-smelling perfume that kept the man-eating rats of the Shadow City at bay. Without Iris's help, we could never have continued our explorations once our Reverse Pied Pipers stopped working. The kazoolike devises had been designed to produce a noise that rodent ears couldn't bear. For a while, the Reverse Pied Pipers had worked wonders, leaving only a few deaf rats to roam the tunnels. But over time, that handful of beasts had multiplied into a million-rat army. The large, fierce, hearing-impaired rodents were again on the hunt for trespassers, and anyone without the protection of Iris's perfume quickly took his place beside the hundreds of rat-picked skeletons that littered the passages and chambers of the Shadow City.

I squeezed my eyes shut and held on to Kiki's black leather jacket as she steered her Vespa motor scooter onto Bethune Street without bothering to slow for the curve. When we skidded to a halt in front of Iris's brownstone, the first thing I saw was the Irregulars' logo stamped on the sidewalk. An *i* in the shape of a girl

in motion, it marked all known entrances to the underground tunnels. Beneath an old trunk in Iris's basement lay an ingeniously disguised trapdoor. A long, rusty ladder led to a hidden room seventy feet below street level that had once belonged to a bootlegger named Angus McSwegan. According to *Glimpses of Gotham*, a nineteenth-century guide to the *dark side* of New York, each bottle of Angus's whiskey was spiked with a dash of formaldehyde, which gave it a nasty kick. It had been the beverage of choice in the Shadow City, which lay just outside Angus's door.

I saw Iris watching at the window as Kiki and I climbed the steps of her stoop. Before we had a chance to ring the bell, the door flew open, revealing a tiny blond girl in an oversized white coat.

"Greetings, Irregulars," said Iris. Like Kiki, Iris was unusually small for her age. Unlike Kiki, she possessed a set of cherubic cheeks that were often pinched by strangers who mistook her for an eight-year-old.

We brushed through the door and into a front hall lined with the hideous masks and shrunken heads that Iris's parents collected on anthropological expeditions.

"What's with the lab coat?" Kiki asked Iris. "Don't tell me you've been experimenting on the nanny again. There are laws against that sort of thing, you know."

Iris giggled. "I forgot I had it on. I was getting ready for tomorrow."

"What's tomorrow?" I asked. "Are you in a play?"

"I've been practicing for the meeting tomorrow, remember?" Iris looked offended when I shook my head.

"DeeDee and I are presenting our big discovery. The one we've been working on all summer? Remember now?"

I didn't, but I figured it was best to play along. "Oh right, *that* presentation. Yeah, we're all really excited."

"You *should* be. My discovery's going to make the rat-repelling perfume look like toilet water."

"Speaking of rat-repellent," said Kiki, "we'll need a new bottle for tonight. I ran out last time, and I had two hundred rats chasing me like I was made out of marzipan. By the way, want to come?" It was her way of apologizing for forgetting Iris's presentation.

"I'd love to," Iris said. "But my parents will be home any minute. Plus, I want to make sure everything's perfect for tomorrow. If you need perfume, there's an extra bottle in the trunk downstairs. Just make sure you're superquiet on the way out. My mom thought there was a burglar the last time you guys were here."

"Sorry about that," said Kiki. "Oona slipped on her way up the stairs."

Iris's nose twitched at the sound of Oona's name. "That was *Oona* making all the noise? Little Miss Criminal Mastermind?"

"Can't you two get along?" Kiki sighed. "All this arguing is beginning to bore me."

"I get along with *her* just fine," Iris complained. "It's not *my* fault she doesn't like me. On Monday she said that if I didn't get any taller you guys were going to sell me to the circus."

"She did?" Kiki sounded both appalled and amused.

"Just because she teases you doesn't mean she doesn't

like you," I tried to assure Iris. "Oona teases all of us. She doesn't know any better. It's like she's socially retarded."

"Retarded or not, she'd better watch out," Iris fumed, "or one day somebody's going to teach her some manners."

We heard a door open upstairs, and a tone-deaf rendition of "Hey, Big Spender" rang through the house.

"Time to go," whispered Kiki, pulling me toward the basement. "See you tomorrow, Iris. And whenever you feel the urge to put Oona in her place, be my guest."

"Thanks," said Iris with a mischievous giggle. "Maybe I will."

K i r s t e n   M i l l e r lives in
New York City with her family, where she
spends her time writing, drinking coffee,
and exploring. She is the author of the Kiki
Strike series, as well as The Eternal Ones
series.

www.kikistrike.com
kirstenmillerbooks.blogspot.com

The world of the **Irregulars** comes to life at

KikiStrike.com

- Discover Kiki's **underworld maps** of secret spaces in New York and around the world

- Read **Ananka's blog** of her travels and discoveries

- Take a **quiz** to find out if you have what it takes to be an **Irregular**

They've saved New York City twice, but now
the **Irregulars** are jumping feetfirst into
a fast-paced **international pursuit**.

Don't miss the Irregulars take on
underground Paris in . . .

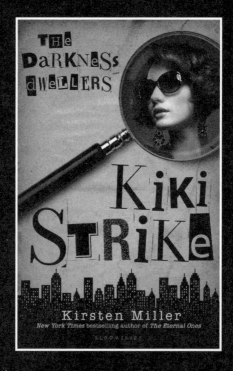

BLOOMSBURY
www.bloomsbury.com
www.facebook.com/BloomsburyTeens